C. J. CHERRYH

FORTRESS

OF

EAGLES

By C. J. Cherryh

C. J. CHERRYH

FORTRESS

OF

EAGLES

HarperPrism

HarperPrism

A Division of HarperCollins*Publishers*
10 East 53rd Street, New York, N.Y. 10022-5299

This is a work of fiction. The characters, incidents, and dialogues are products of the author's imagination and are not to be construed as real. Any resemblance to actual events or persons, living or dead, is entirely coincidental.

HarperCollins®, ® , and HarperPrism® are trademarks of HarperCollins*Publishers* Inc.

Printed in the United States of America

First printing: January 1998

ISBN 0-06-105261-2

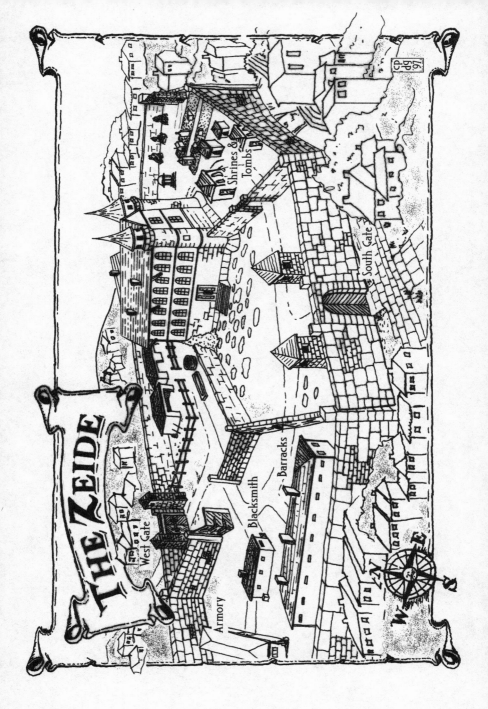

PRELUDE

Ages ago, before the time of Men, a place named Galasien grew to rule as far and wide as any records tell. Mauryl Gestaurien came from that time and that place. So did Hasufin Heltain, who may have been a prince of Galasien. Assuredly he was a wizard, as was Mauryl. Hasufin attempted a kind of magic that defied law and time and death, and would have ruled with absolute power, if not for Mauryl, who opposed him, and who at last visited the lands far to the north, whence he brought back five strangers to aid him. These were the Sihhë-lords, who wielded not wizardry but magic. In the struggle that followed, Hasufin fell, and with him fell Galasien, the citadel of which became the fortress known to the next age as Ynefel.

The five lords and their halfling offspring comprised a dynasty whose fortress was Ynefel and whose peaceful unwalled capital was Althalen. They conquered the lands of Men, had Men living freely among them, and for a golden age lasting centuries they built and learned and brought comforts and prosperity to the land.

But as Sihhë blood was running thin and a halfling, Elfwyn, sat the throne in Althalen, a prince was born, and died, and lived again, a circumstance which alarmed the wizards, the more so when other princes died one by one. By that means Hasufin crept back into influence among the living, bidding fair to succeed gentle Elfwyn and reestablish the dynasty of lost Galasien.

Mauryl led a conspiracy of wizards to prevent that succession, and had for an ally a lord of Men, namely Elfwyn's chief general, Selwyn Marhanen, who seized power, burned the capital and killed every last bearer of royal Sihhë blood he could find.

But some of the bloodline survived in the peasantry of Amefel, and in a few of the lineage who dwelt across the river Lenúalim in the district of

Elwynor. Elwynor refused to join the rebellion, and loyal Men there established the Regency, believing some claimant to the throne would arise to defeat the Marhanen lord.

It was not an unwarrantable hope in those days, for indeed every duke in the realm of Men on the other side of the river attempted to seize power. Only Selwyn proved more ruthless than any of his rivals, and established the Marhanen dynasty in Guelessar. From that time on the name of the kingdom was Ylesuin, and it ruled from Amefel eastward and north and south. Selwyn's son Ináreddrin succeeded him; Uleman Syrillas continually reigned as Regent in Elwynor, and the old capital of Althalen became a place of ruins within Ylesuin's backward province of Amefel, a province despised for its unorthodoxy, given to know far more of witchery and wizardry than the dominant sect of Ylesuin, the godly Quinalt, liked.

Mauryl, however, had no part in the wars of Men. Kingmaker, they called him; but he would not settle the quarrels of Men, ally himself to either side of the dispute, or set aside either Uleman's claims or Selwyn's to a united kingdom. Elwynor chose Ilefínian as its capital; Ylesuin chose Guelemara, heart of Guelessar, as the seat of the Marhanen kings, and Mauryl retreated to the shattered citadel of Ynefel to brood or study or do whatever a wizard did who had survived age after age of the world. Selwyn had appointed him Warden of Ynefel, and no one knew what Mauryl did, but one supposed that the world of Men was safer because ungodly Mauryl sat in his tower and kept away whatever ill might come from that place.

But Mauryl was not immortal, despite the rumors. The years sat heavily on him. His studies took their toll. And his enemy, Hasufin Heltain, was not quite banished. On a certain night in a certain spring in the reign of Ináreddrin Marhanen, beset by Hasufin's threat and working with the last of his strength, Mauryl Gestaurien worked what he knew would be his last great spell, a Summoning, to be precise, and a Shaping.

Perhaps he flinched, perhaps he doubted his intention. He had expected something rather more formidable than what he found before him. The result was a gray-eyed youth: Tristen, who arrived without the least understanding even how to protect himself . . . a young man far from any understanding of wizardry.

The youth's understanding of Mauryl, however, grew apace, and by late spring Tristen clambered about the old fortress at Ynefel with a childish curiosity about all the world, taming the pigeons of the loft, even exploring the walled-off end where Owl held sway. Ynefel was a curious place, and faces appeared in its walls, faces that on certain nights and in certain light seemed to take on life and move. But Tristen seldom saw *them at it. Every night he took the potion Mauryl gave, every night slept soundly . . . every night except one. And on that night Tristen began to understand there was danger in the world. On that night, perhaps, only perhaps, Hasufin found a chink in the wall that otherwise was warded.*

On a day not too long after, Hasufin advantaged himself of that opening. Mauryl fell at last . . . himself immured in the dreadful walls. And on that day Tristen found himself bereft of everything, left alone to face a world he had never seen or imagined.

He set out on the Road through Marna Wood, guided by Owl, in possession of a silver mirror and a book he could not read, not knowing where he was going, but that Mauryl had said someday he would walk that Road.

He came to the town of Henas'amef, principal city of Amefel, and into the hands of Prince Cefwyn, viceroy of that uneasy province. Cefwyn was heir to the Marhanen throne, and through Cefwyn Tristen came to the tutelage of Emuin, once Mauryl's student himself.

But in short order Tristen so frightened Emuin that the old man fled the court, seeking sanctuary elsewhere—for Emuin realized what Mauryl had done and set into his hands. "Win his love," was Emuin's parting advice to Cefwyn, and Cefwyn, bored, isolate amid Amefel's rustic lords, now realized he had a somewhat dangerous guest . . . and attempted to entertain the strange young man.

Therein a prince who had no friends discovered one . . . and saved his own life. For Hasufin Heltain, the ancient spirit that had destroyed Ynefel and Mauryl, had failed to overcome Tristen, and had come whispering to any ally he might find to bring him back to power . . . the enemies of the lord of the Elwynim, and also the lord of Amefel, Cefwyn's host, Lord Heryn Aswydd, who himself had Sihhë blood.

Cefwyn might have died in ambush. But Tristen, finding a horse under him and a sword in his hand, discovered gifts he did not know he possessed . . . and Cefwyn began to be sure that what Mauryl had Summoned was, in his captain's parlance, no lad from lost Elfwyn's scullery, no halfling, even, but one of the vanished Sihhë-lords, perhaps Barrakkêth himself, the first, and the most feared.

Meanwhile the plot Hasufin engendered reached to the king . . . who fell to ambush. Cefwyn, crowned, challenged the traitor, Lord Heryn. But not only the Marhanen king had perished. As Uleman of Elwynor was old and weak, disputations regarding that succession had arisen, and Uleman was hounded to his death by rebels pursuing him even into Cefwyn's kingdom.

At the Regent's death, Cefwyn met Ninévrisë, the new Lady Regent, face-to-face . . . and knew he had met his bride.

But Orien, Lord Heryn's sister, was not disposed to forgive her brother's death or to cede Cefwyn to a foreigner; and Hasufin had now a sorcerous and angry woman to do his work. Cefwyn's brother also opposed a foreign bride. And the Elwynim Lord who had hoped to claim Uleman's daughter and the kingdom was open to persuasion . . . and to sorcery.

Orien's attempt on Cefwyn's life failed. And to set Ninévrisë on her father's throne and to marry his way to a unified Ylesuin, Cefwyn summoned all the lords of the south to war, to prevent the intrusion of Elwynim rebels into Amefel . . . and win his bride her throne. But he faced more than the rebel leader: he faced a shadow building and building along that frontier, one Tristen understood, and knew for a greater threat than Cefwyn could possibly understand. Cefwyn was moving exactly where that shadow wished him to move, and Tristen had no choice but to take up arms as the army of the south of Ylesuin marched to Lewenbrook. Wizardry had allied itself with those rebels, wizardry which had brought down one Marhanen king, Cefwyn's father, and now bid fair to set its own pawn on the throne of a new kingdom.

Tristen, however, found within the book the mastery of magic, his own heritage, which had eluded him. He rode to war as lord of Althalen and Ynefel, under a banner counted anathema by the holy Quinalt, but cheered by the Amefin commons. At the last he and his man Uwen Lewen's-son rode against the Shadow that had loomed over Marna Wood in an hour when men were falling left and right to a power no sword could fight.

But Tristen rode with a sword graven with magical words of Truth and Illusion, cleaving one from the other, and wielded that weapon against the Shadow of shadows. He found himself at Ynefel, then hurled into shadow, lost to Men forever . . .

Except that fearing that his power might grow too great and overwhelm him, and draw him out of the world of Men, he had given his shieldman, Uwen Lewen's-son, power over him. He made a common soldier his judge, whether to call him back or to let him vanish from the world as too great and too dark a danger.

And Uwen called him.

C. J. CHERRYH

FORTRESS
OF
EAGLES

BOOK
ONE

CHAPTER 1

The path, slanting up through young forest to gray rock and old trees, became a hollow, leaf-filled track at its end. When Tristen reined in and stepped down from the saddle, ankle-deep in autumn, the silence on that hill was so great he could hear the individual fall of leaves as soft, distinct impacts . . . until Petelly tugged at the rein, impatient of good behavior, and leaves cracked and rustled under his massive feet.

Guelessar's forested hilltops had shown bright red and sunny gold above the fields not a fortnight ago. They had cast off much of that color in the wild winds of recent days, the result of which had piled up in ditches and against fences all along the roads. The trees on this height stood all but bare, more exposed to the winds than those lower down the trail, and Tristen scuffed through ridges of brown and gold as he led Petelly along.

He had ridden out for pleasure on this late-autumn day in this first year of his life and this first year of king Cefwyn's reign. He had come into the world as a wizard's Summoning in the soft, whispering green of spring, and he had discovered the world of Men in a summer of full-voiced leaves. He had come to his present maturity by his first autumn, with his duty to the wizard Mauryl all done, and with Mauryl immured in the ruins of Ynefel. He was, amid dreadful battles, sworn to a king who called him his dearest friend and declared him Lord Warden of Ynefel and Lord Marshal of Althalen to honor him—but the lands the king had granted him held no inhabitants, only shadows more or less quiescent and benign. He was lord of mice and owls, as His Majesty's captain was wont to say.

And what did king Cefwyn intend him to be, or do, now that he had finished Mauryl's purposes? He knew that least of all.

The leaves that had fallen earliest in the season were wet from old rains. The newest leaves, fallen atop them, left a fine, pale dust on Tristen's boots, and the brown, wet depths of the drifts streaked that dust as his walking disturbed unguessed colors: a dazzling yellow, a vivid, jewel red. Spying a particularly large dry oak leaf, he picked it up for a particular treasure and carried it with him as he walked to his usual vantage at the edge of this hilltop woods, the sheer, wooded cliff from which he could reliably look down and see his guards watering their horses at the forest spring just below.

But unexpected sunlight shone through the trees to his right as he approached the edge; and a glance showed him a distant grassy meadow and a succession of forest-crowned hills marching in endless order in the east.

He had never noticed that view before. He was amazed as he moved branches aside to reach a new vantage—even while it Unfolded to him, as strange new things would do, that this new barrenness of the woods, these revelations of unseen hills, were but one more sign of the season. The grayness of the trees in that moment of magic evoked memories (and he had so few memories) of a place all but forgotten, and then known again, yes, not here, but *there*. The deepest woods of Marna, where he had begun his life, had been gray like this in springtime. For a moment he could deceive his own heart with the sight and think he was there and then, where Marna's trees had stood so thick and dark they shut out the sun.

But here . . . here and now, the bright Guelen sunlight very easily reached him through the branches and cast all the other hills, all the low-lying meadows and hazy forested crests, in glorious gray and gold as far as he could see.

In the joy of the sight he released the captive leaf, letting it enjoy a second, unlooked-for life before it wafted down, down, to settle lower on the hill next a lichen-mottled outcrop of rock. There another gust caught it and the leaf, not yet defeated, explored the changed world on the very winds that had once robbed it of safety. Thoughtless of the act a moment before, he suddenly longed for the leaf to live, fly back to spring and become green again. He longed for all the woods to be green and the wind to sigh with the mysterious voices of his first days.

He longed to know this province of Guelessar as he had known the surrounds of Ynefel.

He longed for a thousand things, all of them dangerous.

Petelly meanwhile had trailed off at his own direction, doubtless crushing a score of remarkable leaves underfoot as he wandered nose down, sniffing under the autumn piles for whatever might prove edible underneath. He was a practical horse. Long hairs abounded in Petelly's bay coat, making him appear stockier than he was, a disgrace among the highbred horses of the guard, and Petelly's jaw, never fine, was thick and massive with beard that riffled in the wind. All the horses and the cattle in the fields had been growing shaggier by the day. The guards said the coats on the cattle, the vast chevrons of birds skeining across the skies, all were signs that foretold a bitter winter, with snow likely before the full moon. The servants in the king's household were unpacking quilts and woolen clothes and airing them where they could, foreseeing the same, and Tristen looked forward to that event with mingled curiosity and trepidation. Once the snow began in earnest, so he had heard, it would lie deep and white all winter, killing the fields, putting the trees to sleep.

Winter when it came was a last season before the full circle of a year . . . the very last season.

New to the land, he had once thought summer the mature and natural state of the world, and seen every hill as Unfolding new secrets to him forever. Then autumn had shown him nothing was forever. It brought him the bitter, dusty smell of fallen leaves, the moldy pungency of willow leaves strung in ropes, slender and yellow along the edge of the spring at the bottom of this hill. Lastly it showed him this view of hills, the secrets of all the hills of Guelessar unveiled.

But what would winter bring him? Snow and ice, yes. But now that he saw the year not as extending forever forward but as turning back upon itself, he saw life coming a circle, like a horse running, discovering itself not free, but pent in and bound to repeat its course again and again and again. What he thought he had left behind might come again. What he had thought done might come undone. And spring, when all things should come new . . . spring, in which most men looked for new life . . . he had cause to fear.

He came back to his edge, his reliable little cliff. He looked down on the four men the king had lent him, and on Uwen Lewen's-son, a gray-haired soldier whom the king had appointed to be his friend, his constant companion, his adviser in the world. He knew he should go down now and not put them to the trouble of riding up this narrow trail to find him.

But he continued to be disturbed, having found things on the hill-top not what he had expected, having thought thoughts he had never planned, and he knew Uwen and the other men rarely objected to time to sit and talk amongst themselves, which they were doing quite happily at the moment.

So he left Petelly to his search for bits of green, sure he would not stray far, or that if he did, Uwen would intercept him below. He waded through brush and ducked through thickets to the south and west of the hill . . . snagged his hair doing it, hair as black and thick and long as Petelly's mane, and by now, like Petelly's mane, stuck through with twigs and leaves. He was not willfully inconvenient to those who watched over him. But he was chasing the vision of Amefin hills, a sight and a knowledge that mattered to him in ways he could not explain. If he could but achieve that vantage before his guards lost patience, if he could come just a little to the side and past a rocky shoulder of the hill—if he could know he was not that far from his beginnings and fix the territory of his memories as a place, not a state of mind . . .

Then perhaps he could dream forward and not constantly back toward the lost things he remembered. Making peace with that, he could perhaps begin to see things as vividly ahead of him, instead of the gray space that seemed to occupy all his future . . .

Oh, indeed, he saw more hills westward, gray and brown with barren trees that he imagined might be the very edge of Amefel. And from this hill, on this day of leaf fall at the end of autumn, he imagined that he looked back all along the course he had come.

Foolish pursuit, perhaps. It was, after all, nothing but hills and gray trees like the other views from this place. It was his heart that saw the rolling hills, the land of his summer and his innocence, the land where he had met Cefwyn, the land which had taught him so much and which had nothing to do with this autumn, these trees, this hill in Guelessar. He hung a moment with his arms on a thick, low branch, the wind cold on his face, the sights of summer in his eyes, and with a sigh and a thought, he saw all the way to spring, to Ynefel. He heard the kiss of the river Lenúalim on the tower's foundations. He looked down from the high tower of Ynefel over the tops of storm-tossed trees, and out over the Road from the half-ruined roof of the loft where Owl had lived.

The narrow, rickety steps to his room came to him, too, exactly so. The study and the fireside flitted through his thoughts, warm and cozy. Ynefel was so much *smaller* a place than the high-walled Guelesfort, or even Amefel's Zeide, which hove up above Henas'amef and housed hundreds of people.

Mauryl's forest-girt tower had been so very much smaller, so much plainer in all respects, he knew that now, yet it had been so full of memorable things . . . as for instance he could recall in sharp detail every twist of grain in the weathered wood of the sill in his bedroom; he could conjure every detail and imperfection of the horn-paned window of his room, whereupon the rains and the lightning had written mysterious patterns in the night. Ynefel seemed far larger in his memory than such a small place should reasonably be, as if by some enchantment it held more life, or had been more substantial than ordinary buildings.

He remembered the loft, oh, the loft, the silky, gray-brown dust, and the pigeons on the rafters there, each and every nameless one, and he remembered the day he had discovered Owl.

Ynefel was in ruins now. Mauryl was gone. He had seen Owl last at Lewenbrook, before the banners fell, before so many died. On that day, too, the world had had a terrible wealth of detail, and every rock and every tree had found edges. Every shadow had been alive and rolling down like midnight on embattled armies.

He remembered the cold and the dark of that hour, and a shadow become substance. He felt the bitter chill of sorcery and felt—was it only memory?—a perilous slippage in place and time.

Then he knew he had gone not forward but back into memories he wished only to escape. He began hastily to retrace his steps in all senses, retreating from the sight, fleeing from the unwardened west, back toward Petelly.

The urgency grew less immediately as he left that side of the hill. It was only a hillside. Only a hillside in Guelessar, so great a relief he might have laughed at his own foolish fears. It was autumn, again, among the leaves, the opposite end of autumn, at that, from the battle at Lewenbrook, and as he reached Petelly he saw that Petelly had no concern whatsoever . . . had not even interrupted his browsing. So he had been completely foolish, he thought, to have feared anything. Shaken, he patted a winter-coated shoulder and caught Petelly's reins, leading Petelly along toward the trail and a meek and dutiful return to his guards.

Petelly was in no hurry to go, however, and with a great,

unbalancing jerk on the reins stopped and lowered his head among the leaves, sure he had smelled some tidbit he favored. It was just as easy to let him finish his search as quarrel with him.

There, close by, was the most curious log, shelved with velvet fungus.

Now here was a wonder of the woods, marvelous in its smoothness: Tristen abandoned the discipline of his horse, knelt to touch and found the velvety shelves unexpectedly tough, resisting his inquisitive, ungloved fingers.

The wood, peeling in patches, was gray and weathered beneath, long dead. This growth, on the other hand, was alive, out of that death. Was it not a miracle?

Or did spring hide in apparent death, and was spring lying hidden in winter, as signs of winter had hidden these last few days in autumn?

Were the seeds of next things always there, in the circle of the year, and was that how the world worked its miracles? The well-spring out of which things Unfolded to him said yes, *yes*, the life did not wholly die. Even in utter ruin and winter to come, there was hope. Even in a dead log were miracles waiting.

And had this particular, velvety, curious growth any virtue in wizard-craft, he wondered in a practical vein, hunkering down for a very much closer look and tucking his cloak about his knees to protect it from the damp? Would Emuin like it? He had no wish to spoil what was curious and wonderful if Emuin had no use for it, but it did look like something a wizard would admire . . . and something that might be useful, a point of change and regrowth that might have potency. He brought Emuin birds' eggs fallen in the wind—like the dry one he had in his purse just now, along with a curious oak gall from a grove near a sheep fence at Dury.

Had he feared the sight of distant woods, a mere moment ago? There was no fear in him now. At times he was well aware how he skipped from serious thoughts to thoughts other folk saw as quite frivolous, and he suspected on his own that this might be one of those moments, but the thought he had fled was past and the sight that had led him to that thought was hidden now by the hill. His guards had not yet grown annoyed with him, and he knew he was safe on this hilltop. He had also spent his short life with wizards, who as a type observed a different sense of priorities and set a different importance on strange objects than ordinary folk.

Had the fungus been there in the summer? Or did it appear when a tree died? Or did it appear only seasonally as another sign of winter?

The latter was the kind of question he would have asked Mauryl more than Emuin, Mauryl being far more inclined to far-ranging questions.

But Mauryl was gone with Ynefel, and all such questions of the natural world went unanswered these days. Emuin was far more likely to tell him the use of a fungus than the behavior of it—when he could gain Emuin's attention at all.

No, there was probably no use in bringing it with him. He could by no means bring all of it, and bringing less than that would spoil it. He meanwhile had the bird's egg, which was pretty, speckled finely brown on white, and he knew Emuin would admire it. He stood up, tugged at Petelly's reins, seeking the trail through a maze of leafless branches on what should have been a shorter route. But it proved choked with thorns. He stopped, stood, looked for a way through the maze.

In truth, the world in general had become much more familiar to him, less a-jumble with new things and unguessed words, so that in the close confines of the Guelesfort an entire fortnight might pass without his finding something new. But outside its walls, he gathered wonders and set himself in predicaments his guards indulged with kind patience . . . this might be one. He came to this hilltop for the silence and the sound of the trees, only to think without the sounds of five men and horses about him, and for a moment, so engaged, and perplexed about his path, he might almost hear Mauryl's voice saying, "Boy? Boy, where *are* you now? What have you gotten into, lad?"

A rising wind whispered through dry branches. It almost seemed he did hear that voice, that he was in some secret hiding place where it was not Mauryl who was lost, but himself, and only for a moment. He would turn around, and he would see Mauryl standing there, his plain brown robes blending with this gray autumn woods, his hand about that staff of his, his white hair and beard alike flying in the gentle whim of the breezes.

"So what have you found?" Mauryl would say, if he was in a patient humor, and Mauryl would come have a look at his log and tell him the name of the fungus and whether he should bring it in pieces back to the hall to join the vast collection of strange and curious things Mauryl treasured. Mauryl's robes, never reputable or fine, and always smudged with the dust of the old fortress, would surely acquire tags of leaf mold and dirt just as his cloak had, Mauryl's hair would have just such unseemly detritus of leaves, and his face would take on that look of concentration that was Mauryl at his kindest.

Petelly's nose met his shoulders and shoved. Tristen drew in a breath rough-edged with the smell of oak and earth and autumn, and knew that Mauryl would not be there, not at distant Ynefel, certainly not on this hilltop in Guelessar, and that he had well and truly overstayed his time, since he heard the jingling of men and horses coming up the road. His guards had grown concerned, or curiosity had moved them, and leading Petelly toward the trail to meet them, he saw to his chagrin that they had all come.

Uwen was in the lead as they came up the turn, then Lusin, Syllan, Aran, and Tawwys, armed and armored, the lot of them—as of course he was, or more or less so. He had let Petelly carry his sword, which he had stowed behind the saddle, but he conscientiously carried a dagger on his person as Uwen advised him he should, and beneath his brown ordinary cloak and leather coat, he wore the mail the king and the king's captain commanded he wear, even though he considered it very little likely that enemies would cross the Lenúalim and tramp across a good deal of Guelessar to invade this hunting preserve and climb this very hilltop. In all truth, most Men had rather not face him with or without that sword, and he suspected that the guards the king assigned him generally served him better in deterring the approach of the unwary than in fending off hazards.

He pulled and scraped his way past berry bushes as his guards arrived, jingling and breathing and thumping and creaking, four men in the red of the King's Dragon Guard, with his sworn man Uwen in plain brown. Uwen wore only the smallest black badge of Althalen over his heart, the same as he wore himself. The others, being king's men, wore the gold Marhanen Dragon and red coats.

"So what ha' ye found?" Uwen asked him amiably from horseback, with no reproach at all, while four riders fanned out among the trees to turn around, the trail being just wide enough for one horse. The hindmost of his guards was very steeply on the slope, even so. "And should we be riding back soon, m'lord?" Uwen asked. "This'd be our turning, here below, to go back by way of Cressitbrook, if ye'd rather a different road going home. As we should now."

"We should," he agreed shamefacedly. He saw his guards looking warily about for curiosities, for chills and shadows and other such events of his company, but without a word he climbed up on Petelly and eased him past the other horse's nose. Uwen turned next. The king's men turned about in the woods and followed.

The wind, an entirely natural wind, blew dust up and sent leaves across the path as they left the hilltop. Petelly danced and skipped through the insubstantial obstacle. The men rode after him in haste, and for a moment they went pell-mell down the chancy turn, over ground buried in leaves. Tristen knew the footing, and so did they all. There were no roots, stones, or holes; but he knew that there was no threat above to give any reason for haste, either, so he pulled Petelly down to a reasonable pace past the spring. They all came safely to the lower road again, sheltered from chill breezes and wayward memories by the looming, forested hills on either hand.

"No shadows," Uwen said, having overtaken him.

"No shadows," he assured Uwen. "Not a one. I was listening to the wind up there. Looking at the hills." For some reason, perhaps because it was a matter for wizards and not for soldiers, he was reticent about confessing his looking out toward Amefel. "There was a fungus I had never seen."

"A fungus, ye say."

"On a dead trunk."

"Oh, them things." Uwen seemed both relieved and amused, and it was as he expected. Uwen ventured not a ghost of a guess what the growths were named, or what their virtue was. "Ye don't eat 'em, least I for certain wouldn't. Mushrooms is done for the year."

"To come back in spring?" So many things were promised to return in the spring. And some things would Unfold to him the moment he asked a question, but some things would not. "Or in the fall?"

"A lot in spring, or in rainy spells. I don't rightly know about that up there, that kind. But cooks dry the wholesome ones in the kitchen for the off-season, so ye never fear, m'lord: there'll be mushroom soup aplenty all winter. I heard Cook say yesterday there's a special attention to mushroom soup for harvesttide on account of Your Grace."

Harvesttide was only two days off. He did indeed like mushroom soup, and he would be as happy as most in the approaching celebration if he were happy in other points, and if he knew he were welcome among the other lords, but neither was the case.

Still, it was too fine a day for melancholy on that account. Uwen rode beside him, knee to knee on Liss, a mare Uwen greatly coveted, and they were comfortable a while in silence. It was still a wooded road after they had taken the Cressitbrook way, winding deep among the base of hills where only the king's woodsmen cut wood, and where only the king and the king's friends hunted. It needed no quick pace at all, as Uwen had said, for them to reach Guelemara before dark. The road they took now showed no track of horses or men since the rains, and therefore held less likelihood of meeting anyone. The men rode more easily, far from any critical eye, talking of whatever took their fancy, and anticipating the harvesttide festival, for which the town had been preparing for days, building a bonfire of truly prodigious proportions.

Friendly voices, friendly company surrounded him, past the spring and down along the little brook that flowed down from it. Tristen listened idly and watched the leaf-paved road above the twitch of Petelly's black-tipped ears—busy ears, they were, alert to every burst of laughter and every whisper of the freshening wind out of the west.

CHAPTER 2

T here were pearls, an abundance of pearls. Cefwyn trod on one and winced, hoping it was only one of the sleeve-pearls, not some stray and costly one from the wedding crown, which lay in partial glory and strips of ribbon on the table. A mound of pale blue velvet and gold- and pearl-colored satin stood like a mountain range against the high, clear windows of the former scriptorium. The center panes of amber glass cast a bar of golden light across the room, from the embroidering maids to the far, scrap-strewn tables in this, the domain of the Regent and her ladies-in-waiting.

He endured his own wedding fittings in a hall similarly devoted to the groom's garments, a hall piled with red and gold . . . Marhanen colors, more modest heaps, however, although he was the king. He was astounded by this volume of fabric, grown by half again, he swore, since his visit two days ago. Could so much cloth possibly be involved in a few gowns for one slender woman? He had thought he was expert in ladies' accoutrements . . . but find his bride on their wedding night, in such an array?

Even finding his bride in this room proved no straightforward task, amid heaps and bales of velvet, destined for, one hoped, various other ladies of the court as well as his bride.

Amid all the ladies and maids and their stitching frames set in the advantageous light from the windows, one maid, with a deep curtsy, retrieved the damaged pearl, and another, with a deeper curtsy, snatched an imperiled length of satin fabric from his path. In what became a rapid sweep of curtsies among the women discovering his presence, he passed like a gale through a flower garden . . . and by sheerest chance the diminishing of ladies standing upright directed his eye to the group under the farthest of the three tall windows.

His bride, the Lady Regent of Elwynor, stood on a bench, curiously draped in lengths of blue cloth, with a knot of ladies about her.

Intriguing, he thought as he approached in that breaking wave of ladies rising and curtsying. It proved difficult to hold folds in unsewn velvet and curtsy at once, and the ladies' efforts all went for naught as Lady Ninévrisë shed the velvet and descended into the sea of ladies' wide, fashionable skirts.

Among so many witnesses she kissed him chastely on the side of the mouth.

"I murdered a pearl," he said between two formal kisses. "Surrogate for my Lord Chancellor." This last in a low voice as he led her off by the blue velvet mountains next the windows. "This man." The precise cause of his anger, the inane and constant repetition of the phrase *your late father found it good policy* . . . followed by what had been done for the last twelve years, a recitation undaunted by the firm statement of his own will to change that policy . . . all of that was impossible to articulate in this listening hall of daughters and sisters of great lords—northern lords at that, all of whom were involved in this contest of wills between the king and his late father's court. "This man." He was not yet up to coherent exposition.

"What has he done?" Ninévrisë asked.

"I asked for the tally of village levies. It was *not my father's policy* to deal with such matters himself. Lord Brysaulin accordingly sent the tally to the lord of Murandys and *not* to my Master of Accounts, as I instructed. But *my lord father* always had it go to Murandys. Accordingly the lords, now possessed of the information I had wished to present, are delaying me, fearing all this presages a new tax, and are already resolved, Murandys to the fore, to oppose any such collection. This is beyond incompetency. It verges on treason!"

"I should hardly think that there was any ill intent."

"Oh, I have no doubt the river simply flowed as it was accustomed to flow, in all its old channels. But more than that—" He lifted a forefinger. "More than that—I asked for the accounts also to list the notable men in the villages by name and lineage. I wished the wagons listed, the houses, the weapons. *No!* The cattle, gods forbid, the cattle and the sheep, and the granaries were all Lord Brysaulin's passion. There are no *names* in his report, let alone tally of weapons. It was *not my father's policy* to gather the names in the fall, nor the account of weapons. After two months of searching, sending scribes hither and yon, and the waiting, my Lord Chancellor has gathered for me a complete account of fields, of grain and granaries down to the half measure, and of the cattle of whatever age, oh, far more complete than my father was wont, but omitted the weapons, as something done two years ago, which he deemed accurate enough, and it was *not my father's policy* to gather the names and the strength of the muster until spring. So the recording of all beasts of whatever age, with houses *and* granaries has every semblance of a tax assessment! The lords are uneasy with the king's apparent interest in their revenues, how not? and how am I to know these men's resources if I have no names or tallies? Is it Uta Uta's-son still over Magan village in Panys, or has the old man died this summer and is his foolishly indolent and dastard *son* in charge, who will be devil a use when Lord Maudyn musters troops next spring? My father never inquired into such matters for reasons I leave to my father; but I do as my grandfather did, and with a war to fight, *I* think it reasonable to know the men of account in the villages as I know their lords, because *I* think it reasonable in me as king to know what sort of men my barons look to for their resources! I think it *is* of concern to the Crown whether a village be well led or indifferently led or led by an utter fool! I rely on such information when I rely on Panys to advance or to hold his entire contingent; and I will not do in my reign as the Lord Chancellor finds *convenient,* or face a set of barons inflamed by suspicions my Lord Chancellor has stirred up with his only half-following my orders! —And I want an entire tally of wagons, their kind as well as their number!"

He was not speaking to some child . . . but to the Lady Regent of Elwynor across the river, a sovereign in her own right. And against a wall of obstinate, self-interested Guelen opposition to his will, the Lady Regent of Elwynor was a calm, sweet, sure, and unassailable voice on his side. "He will simply have to obtain the names and weapons and the rest of it, my lord, and that will correct the impression he might have given."

"The snow will fall and we'll be holding muster in blizzards! Pray, is that a man, sir, or a snowdrift?"

"There is still time, adequate at least to amend the list."

"And with a list I wanted done with *no* extraordinary fuss! Secrecy was my aim. Quiet proceedings. —Come with me. We'll flee to Marisal, break a bowl together and set ourselves up as simple farmers."

The Lady Regent must not, by treaty, attempt to advise him in the monarchy of Ylesuin: the marriage contract had stipulated likewise that he would not intervene in Elwynor.

It was a noble notion of dual reigns over two allied realms, give or take the inconvenient fact that her capital across the river was threatened by rebels. But besides all other reasons, they loved each other . . . at least . . . they were hoping to love one another: at this early date they were merely, hopelessly, smitten.

To all of this the maids and ladies-in-waiting demurely listened, so solemn, so seemingly occupied with their stitching; and if their being within earshot served him and her at all well, the ladies would gossip back to their brothers and fathers that the king had *no* intention of a tax, that Lord Brysaulin had bungled the accounts, that it was indeed wagons and village musters at issue.

And if they were uncommonly efficient at their tale-bearing, why, the king and his intended might even enjoy their harvesttide ale without conspiracy, or at least with the buzzing of some entirely new false and utterly inane rumor, of a muster and general war by snowfall, for instance.

Meanwhile the gray eyes that looked back at him danced with complete comprehension, thank the gods, a support that propped up his sanity and stayed the true Marhanen temper—not the best trait he had from his sire and grandsire. The mouth he longed to kiss was touched with astringent humor she would by no means launch here, either, in the hearing of the selfsame barons' daughters: oh, they were both on their best behavior. And let the barons' daughters report the Regent had been discreet and seemly. Let them report Her Grace had but meekly counseled the king to be reasonable with his barons and watch her grow in their esteem—a proper, seemly woman seeking no authority over Guelen women and their secret hierarchies, oh, aye, let them all, each and individually think so. But believe, too, in their bitter jealousy. He caught the look of Ryssand's daughter Artisane above her stitching frame, and saw the fox-faced chit color and duck her chin.

"We should wait till spring to become farmers," Ninévrisë said in all sobriety, and in a voice just low enough to make the eavesdropping maids strain for possible bits and pieces of Lord Brysaulin's fate. "Beginning a farm in the winter, I fear we would starve."

"There is that," he conceded.

"Fifteen days," she reminded him, which was the number of the days they had to endure until their wedding—the consummation of a treaty as well as a bridal bed, and on both, a stamp of priestly approval. The blessing of the priests would set the king's consort beyond petty gossip and let the two of them, who ached to touch, do more than let fingertips meet in front of jealous (and spurned) young women.

Meanwhile fault-finding, book-wielding, legalistic *priests*, worst of all his inconveniences, were sniffing everywhere about the Guelesfort, also allied to various houses by blood and gold. And now the war, which had been advancing, foundered on an old man's habit.

"Gods send we reach the fifteenth day with my chancellor yet unslaughtered."

"He is an old man. A fine old man. He was kind to me."

"A faithful man." The royal temper fell with that reminder of a small, dutiful kindness when the court had been cold and uncertain in its welcome to his bride and ally. He was left with the ashes of his anger. And the accounts still in the wrong, hostile hands. "He served my father well as Lord Chamberlain. He served *me* well until I came home to Guelessar—good gods, he kept the entire realm in order in a difficult time, with wit and goodwill, and for that I owe him gratitude, but good and beneficent *gods,* why will he not simply read the order I send him? I wrote it fair. —But, oh, I know, I know exactly his ways. Through all my father's reign, when he dealt chiefly with Guelessar, we have done the harvest tally in Guelessar approaching harvesttide. So this must extend the selfsame inquiry to all Ylesuin and it must be granaries we wish to inspect, not wagons and bow-strings. I would trust Brysaulin to be honest, and to have all virtues of a good man, but, gods, even so, if I do not strangle me that man before Midwinter—"

"Hush, hush." She laid a finger on his chin, and, thus close to him, whispered, "You must go to Brysaulin, instruct him again. Be patient. You are always patient."

"I am Marhanen! I am never patient. Plague on Brysaulin. I faint for wit and converse about other than store of pikes and oats. Will you dine with me tonight in chambers—a gathering of old friends? I shall call Tristen, too. He's out riding. I'll have him in by sundown if I need send troops to find him."

Ninévrisë's eyes had changed from solemn listening to laughter, that quickly; and the gray eyes that sometimes had hints of violets (it was the first image he had seen, painted on ivory, and always what he remembered) sparkled and went thoughtful. Her voice sank very low, to escape the listeners. "Am I the prey tonight or is it Tristen? Policy must attend this festive mood. You are stalking someone."

"Good lady!" He laid a hand on his breast, above the Marhanen Dragon, worked in gold. "I am suspect?"

"Today since dawn you have held close converse with the captain of your guard, the Patriarch of the Quinalt." One finger and the next marked the tally. "Your brother the duke of Guelessar, and your brother's priest, besides a converse again with Idrys, with Captain Gwywyn, and with Captain Kerdin—I discount your tailor—"

"Your spies are everywhere!"

"You ensconce me in this nest of women all with ambitions, all wishing to persuade me to confide in them, and wonder that I know *exactly* the object of your inquiry, who was riding to Drysham today—"

"Cressitbrook. You don't know everything."

"—with his guard. It is he, is it not? Has Tristen done something amiss?"

"Tonight," he said, with a glance at the women in the distance, and with his voice lowered.

"I hear it all, you know. The Warden of Ynefel is out spying on the land. He converses with the horses, quite dire and lengthy discourses, and likely with the sheep. His birds fly over the land and bring him news from every quarter . . ."

"His damned pigeons congregate on the ledge and on the porch of the Quinaltine just opposite, where they refine their aim on the Quinaltine steps, therein is the magical offense. Winter's coming. He feeds them. Why should they fly farther afield?" He had heard enough, today, of the Quinaltine steps. And of his bride's unorthodoxy . . . and her scandalous single petticoat, especially in the wedding gown. "Join me tonight. A small supper, a pleasant, quiet evening, no one but ourselves and Tristen. And Emuin. We shall invite Emuin."

"Oh, *that* will set tongues a-wagging."

Doubtless it would—a Teranthine father, the king's old tutor, was entirely acceptable; a wizard was not; but Emuin was both.

And, damn the gossip, he missed their quiet suppers, and their days in Amefel. He missed them so much that those Amefin days, which he had once considered exile, now appeared to him in a golden glow of memory, a time when he had had few but faithful confidants every night at supper, when his table had been solely for food and intimate talk, not tiresome sessions with priests and clerks and lords who wished his brother were king. Even the banquets of state in the great hall in Henas'amef had been intimate, by comparison to the echoing hall of the Dragon Throne, where he now held court. The region before the throne was a gilt-and-ivory battlefield of policy wherein every move and every strategic alliance had been laid down by his father and now must be fought and refought and reforged by an unpopular successor. His digestion suffered in consequence, and while he had as yet found no gray hairs among the gold of his carefully clipped beard, nor a lasting crease on his young brow, he looked for them daily—even longed for them as a means to impress authority on the barons. He could no longer ride abroad, not with the press of royal business. He had grooms to exercise his horses. He could not find time for his father's hounds, who were growing paunches. He could not so much as sit in the royal bathtub on most days without papers to sign, arguments to hear, justice to do, or some petition of the Quinalt about Tristen's damned pigeons.

"Let them clatter about it," he said to his bride-to-be. "Let them have a merry round of it. There's Llymarish cheese and Panan apples stewed up with spices. There's Guelen ham and Amefin sausages and the red wine from Imor as well as Guelen ale. I had it all carted in and set by for harvesttide. I shall serve it up tonight, just the few of us."

"Seducer," said his bride. Fingers touched fingers. Oh, very gladly would he have touched more.

It was an intrigue. Everything must be, in these days of his new accession and the making of an Elwynim alliance-by-marriage.

And she saw very clearly that it was Tristen he wished to speak to, involving neither pigeons nor the census nor the desperation that, indeed, sent him here for refuge. He saw the wolves closing on him in this latest folly and he had interests to defend.

But it was, besides a necessity arrived upon him, also an opportunity grown all too rare, that he gather around him the truest hearts in the court. In the press and clatter of his father's courtiers attempting to assure their influence and those who had been in less favor with his father attempting to gain from him what his father never would have given them, he had lost the peace that he had not valued when he had had it. Yes, the king would have a live wizard and a reputedly dead Sihhë-lord at his table tonight.

The king should have things entirely to *his* liking at least now and again.

A fox traversed the hillside, a quick whisk of red and buff: Lusin noticed it first, and called Tristen's attention to it, with the remark that all such creatures were uncommonly fine-furred this year. But that was a moment's distraction. Uwen and the men, Lusin and the rest, had fallen to discussing Liss, the chestnut mare Uwen rode for the day. The stables had her up for sale, at a high price—and Uwen could not, would not. He refused such an extravagance on principle.

"You should buy her," Tristen said for the hundredth time, and Uwen, who slipped Liss apples right along with those he brought for his regular mount Gia and his heavy horse Cass, said, for the hundredth time, "It's too high, m'lord. Too high by far, —not for the mare, but for me to be spending . . ."

"I say you should," Tristen objected.

"It's very good in ye, m'lord, but 'at's household money, which I ain't for spendin'."

"You need another horse."

"If I need another horse, it's a good stout-legged gelding I'd be usin' next spring an' not bring Gia across the river. An' I can wait for a foal of hers when things settle. 'T is pure folly to be buying any forty-silver mare, m'lord, the likes of me—"

"A captain."

"As ye say, m'lord, but a poor 'un."

"You like her," Tristen said, and true, Uwen's hand had stolen to Liss's neck, and his hands said yes while his look argued glum refusal.

"Ain't practical," was Uwen's word on it. "Ain't in the least practical."

The argument always came to that.

"She moves well," Lusin said.

"Aye," Uwen said, sighing, "but too fine for me."

And so it usually went. Uwen fell to discussing a foal from his bay mare, and her fine points, and the mileposts came. Tristen, distracted, let the conversation slip past him.

It was not that the world in general had taken on that hollow grayness of wizardry at work. He felt no insistence of ghosts, and his perceptions stayed anchored easily and solidly to the road while the men talked of horses. All signs assured him that the world was in good order. Yet since his flight on the hilltop, his furtive peek from moment to moment into Amefel, he kept slipping just slightly toward that grayness both he and wizards could reach.

He had begun to look for something, he knew not what, searching with an awareness dulled by doubts and distracted by colors and movement and the occasionally puzzling discussion of foal-getting around him. That gray place was wizardry, or something like it, and he was reluctant to use it. Emuin strongly warned him against it. He ought to take interest in the business of mares and foals and all the disturbing questions of life beginning—but *this summer*, Uwen said, and *this summer* remained gray to him, without detail or shape or substance. He felt afraid when he thought of it—he felt guilty at treading into that gray space that waited there—guilty at any use of the Sight he did have. Emuin had forbidden it.

True, Ylesuin would surely have gone down to defeat by sorcery if he had not been on Lewen field at Cefwyn's side, and if the other lords of Ylesuin preferred not to acknowledge that fact as yet, he knew in his heart that the danger to the realm was not done. Sorcery might not rear up again into the threat they had faced at the end of summer, when shadows had gathered thick and threatening under the leaves of Marna Wood. The enemies they faced in Elwynor now were only Men, not shadows, but they were still fierce enemies who might at any moment resort to wizardry to prevent a Guelen incursion into Elwynor, and the uneasiness that had assailed him on the hilltop nagged at him like a stealthy movement at the edge of his sight.

Such ventures, free of Emuin's witness, were rare and brief. He worried at the gray space with some furtive sense of need, for if he was distracted by the men around him now, the town toward which he was riding all but blinded him. With its noise and its strangeness, its textures, its smells, its clatter and its truths and its pretenses, it posed a barrier surer than Emuin's prohibitions.

He had been afraid on the hilltop. He asked himself now was there a reason for the fear, or was it only the realization of so many questions, so many, many questions about the world which would never find an answer if this year was all he was to have, and if all of the days he did have left were to be spent either sitting in his room or taking brief rides in the company of these men, on permitted roads?

He longed for a wider freedom. In his earliest days in the world he could lose himself in the contemplation of the textures of common dust, and in such uncommon sights as Petelly's mane, in which a yellow leaf had just now lodged. But nowadays he had questions not so much of what he saw before him as of what he did not see, or seeing, failed to comprehend. This festival to celebrate the death of the year was one. The constant company of guards against threats he knew dared not assail him was another: while what he most feared they could not so much as imagine—not the king's men, not even Uwen, whose honesty he never doubted and who had ridden with him into the heart of shadows. Uwen's *this summer* was part of it. But not all.

Still, in this province of Guelessar he did what pleased the king and did his best to comfort his detractors. He emulated the other lords at court in speech and manners. He feigned boredom when he was near them, but he knew he never did it well . . . Cefwyn had told him from the beginning that he was very bad at lying. From his side, he found their malice tiresome and tedious, while he still found wonders to stare at in the sparkle of glass or the color of a lady's skirt—and dared not.

Ask questions of them? He dared not that, either . . . as, today, he would, if he dared, ask any man the same questions that he had asked Emuin, and still worried at, still unanswered: how long will this autumn last? How long will winter be? How long until the spring? And could Uwen imagine tomorrow . . . or next year . . . so easily? A man who was not a Man in the ordinary sense was by no means sure of such matters when wizards talked about the wanderings of the sun. There was so much else, so very much else that Men took for granted and seemed to foresee with such clear assurance, while that gray space Men could not reach was always waiting to draw him in, more real and more truthful than he found comfortable.

The year, the true Year, by which Men reckoned time, would begin on Midwinter Night. But when spring came, then his year began all over again, or at least *he* would have reached his own beginning point.

When spring came, king Cefwyn and all the men said, the kingdom of Ylesuin would go to war across the river to win Lady Ninévrisë her kingdom. *Next spring* this and *next spring* that ran through all court conversations as if winter, this dead, dying, most ominous season, were a negligible affair that they would all endure and think nothing of.

And perhaps winter and change were negligible, for ordinary men. But in his darkest hours, in everyone's blithe talk of seasons and this constant repetition of *in the spring,* he knew that Uwen most surely had a confidence and a vision of things to come that he simply did not have and had never had. Ordinary men, too, took for granted they would fare better in the next year than the last. And he did not have that confidence. He had never seen a year but this one . . . and the glance homeward this afternoon had struck a strange and persistent uneasiness into his heart, as if he had looked beyond a boundary of more than rock and stone . . . as if long-stable forces had lurched into movement today, a small slippage in what had been fixed, and he had done it. He had begun it.

Perhaps when he came full circle of a year it would complete something. Mauryl had Called him into being for Mauryl's reasons, but now that winter was coming and the wedding was near, Cefwyn found no use for him. Emuin had no time. Uwen was at *his* direction, not the other way around. That left him waiting, at loose ends, unable to imagine what that new year would bring him, or what he would do in it, or what he had ever been meant to do, beyond Mauryl's purpose for him, which had been to defeat the enemy at Lewen field.

He had survived the field at Lewenbrook. He had defeated Mauryl's enemy Hasufin and not ceased to exist afterward, unnatural creation that he was. So that was one great barrier he had passed. Should he not survive the next? He had no least idea now just why the anniversary of his beginning should loom in his thoughts as some mystic demarcation, but he found it did so with increasing force. Perhaps once he passed that day, that anniversary hour of his birth, then he would began to live years as other Men lived, with anticipation of season following season for many, many years.

And then perhaps he would see something besides gray in his future as other Men did. Or perhaps he would not.

Or was it possible then that all his gathering of knowledge, none of which precisely answered Mauryl's purpose for him, was in vain? Was it possible that Mauryl's spell would only last until it met some boundary of nature, and was it possible the year was that barrier? Might that identical night next spring send him hurtling again into the dark, all that he treasured forgotten, all that he had gathered dispersed with the elements that had made him?

Next spring would tell him.

And how long was a winter? How long, again, would autumn last? Did the autumn last the same number of days in every year?

He had asked master Emuin that a fortnight ago, trying to approach that greater, more confusing subject with the old man, but Emuin had turned yea and nay on the matter of seasons just when he had thought he understood, and Emuin had said, well, mostly autumn lasted a certain time, and added in the next breath that winter might come late this year, and, no, it was not just when the leaves decided to turn color, it was when the air grew cold.

And why did that happen? he had asked.

Because the sun goes early to bed, Emuin had said.

And why was that, sir?

Probably it grows weary of questions, Emuin had said with sudden asperity, meaning he, a wizard, and the wisest man Tristen knew, had reached the end of his patience, and the world, again, was more complex than a glance discovered.

Then Emuin, repenting, had pulled out charts and, all one glorious evening in Emuin's tower room in Guelemara (and with the jewel-breasted pigeons wandering in and out the window) had showed him the travels of the sun through the stars. Emuin said that a year was fixed, but seasons varied, and showed him the chart of a year as the sun traveled and told him autumn varied.

So what men knew about the seasons was mostly true and sometimes not; it was guessable but not knowable, discernible by its signs but obscure in its presence and in its moment of ending. It was like so many other things men accepted without wonder. Yet in that uncertainty lay the pivot point of his existence—would he continue on, or cease to exist?

Meanwhile the men talked of mares and bonfires, ale and women, and the road turned and came out of the woods for a while, overlooking first sheep pastures gone all brown and dry, then the plowed fields that foretold a village. On most of the early days in fall when they had ridden this same road, plumes of smoke had marked the horizon once they reached this point, farmers burning off the stubble, adding the stinging smell of burning barley-straw to the smoke that always hung about the valleys.

But the unsteady wind today, changing from west to south, had made burning off fields and pastures quite foolhardy, so Tristen guessed, or perhaps the farmers were done with burning. The air remained unusually clear and clean as they crossed the edge of the king's woods near Cressitbrook. A sport of wind, scampering beside the road, whipped up a skirl of leaves out of the wood's edge uphill of them, and Petelly and Liss danced side by side along a golden path, a last forest enchantment of fire colors, earth colors. Golden fine leaves of alder and birch paved the road under them as they drew a little ahead. The guards jogged to keep up, alongside the substantial stream that came babbling and flowing on their right. It was a walk through a treasure-house, the last thin arch of branches. The snow might come before they rode this way again. All the colors would vanish from the land, buried in white and gray and cold.

They rounded the hill where the road forked. They took the right-hand choice, and that led them to the wooden bridge where a marker stone stood, a pillar beside the bridgehead with the king's mark on it. Another such post, this one of wood, stood just the other side. They rode across the planks and startled a flight of blackbirds from their brigandage in the stubble of the barleyfield beyond.

The stone marker defined the point the road left the king's preserve. The fields just the other side of the bridge—indeed, the plowed land visible before this—belonged to the village of Wys-on-Cressit, not to be confounded with Wys-on-Wyettan or Wys in Palys-under-Grostan . . . there were very many Wyses, very much alike, all Guelen, even the one in Palys province, so he had heard from Uwen, who himself was Guelen (as opposed to Ryssandish, the other, dark-haired folk common in northern Ylesuin) and who had lived in such a village before he became a soldier.

Wys-on-Cressit was a place of grainfields and apple orchards and small gardens. They passed the walls of Wys necessarily as they rode down among the fields, he and his guards, and were the day's sole sensation, a band of king's men and a lord . . . *the Sihhë-lord*, the people called him, not always out of earshot, as they made signs against wizardry not quite hidden from his sight.

It happened in all the villages. At first, in his folly, he had thought himself less remarkable than Uwen. Uwen's hair had grown longer now that he was a captain, almost long enough that it stayed in its short tail, and by that dark-shot silver hair Uwen looked more the lord, at least to an eye impressed by a look of experience and a fine horse such as Liss was. So Tristen thought. But the villagers had known the stranger from the first, a dark-haired young man, young, common soldier's coat or no. Guelenfolk were commonly fair and he was not; and his reputation having gone before him, townsmen and villagers alike shut their doors when he rode by.

But lately Wys-on-Cressit had begun to take liberties . . . that was what Uwen called it. They took liberties, and seemed to expect him on certain days. Today, a new height of confidence from their beginning weeks ago of shy, curious faces peeping from doorways, the oldest and most brash of the children burst out of cover near a pigpen and ran along beside the horses as they skirted the house walls, dogs barking and chasing at the horses' heels.

"Get along there," Uwen called to the boys, and waved his arm. "Gods bless, ye fools, 'ware the horses! Ye'll find yoursel's kicked to Sassury and gone!"

The children lagged behind. Petelly was a forgiving, good-natured—even lazy—horse. Liss was steady but not as forgiving, while the guards' unmatched mounts were drawn from the general cavalry string and were both fierce and unpredictable.

But no one had suffered. They had ridden beyond the village, disturbing nothing, and one wondered what impertinence the children would venture next time. The village had lightened his spirits—as indeed his time in Guelemara had begun to have such little anticipations, such little visions that made inroads in the gray. Might he yet gain a word of welcome from the elders? It might be. If the children grew bolder, he might yet coax Wys village not to fear him. It would be one village less out of two score villages and a score of other provinces that feared his very shadow on their streets; but, alas, there was no mending fear except by patience and habit, or by the chance of some great service he could do them.

Still he had won a bit more, and not had it spoiled by having Petelly kick someone. He wondered would it be possible to ride here in winter. He hoped so, and hoped the children would still venture out—but it was one of those foolish questions, he feared, and he was reluctant to spoil the peace with a question that led to will-be and may-be and men's enviable imagining.

Two hills more and the turning of the road, at the second pasture beyond Wys village, was where they had come to expect their first sight of the town of Guelemara in the far, far distance. But today, with the last leaves on the trees along that fence row fallen, they gained their first sight of the town far in advance of that, almost by the time they had cleared the second hill beyond Wys . . . saw it as a distant walled town that spilled down off its hill onto the flatland, if one counted as part of Guelemara the outlying establishments of stables, craft sheds, orchards, and drying sheds, alike the lease-land, where the Crown allowed the settlement of some less permanent buildings.

All that sprawl the king granted to relieve the press inside the defensive walls, structures none of which must be allowed to stand if their Elwynim enemies came onto Guelen soil next spring—he could not but ride through that sprawl and imagine how the people would suffer if the war went amiss.

It would not, however, go amiss, he insisted to himself . . . it was a disorganized enemy, a small effort, if war came early and moved quickly. All their estimates counted on carrying the attack into Elwynor and not receiving any attack in return; and those estimates would hold true. He would not permit it, *he* would not, by the skills he had. The king would call on him at his need, and he waited for that one grim event that he did understand, in a season full of doubts. *There* was his purpose. *There* was a reason he might live through spring and into another year: war . . . at which he was very skilled.

They reached their turn and met the Guelemara road, then, approaching the town across a generally flat extent of pastures, apple orchards, and last year's barleyfields, the town appearing to drift in the sky on a sea of gray apple branches.

It had three walls, all pale stone. The hill's crown of walls and its centermost buildings were limestone brought up from the south, white by day, but gilded now with a late sun above the orchards; and the Guelesfort, the citadel, stood as the town's highest orna-ment, mere planes of light and shadow at this distance, next to a second, smaller height, a second rise of planes and angles of shadow—and that sight brought no cheer.

That second height was the other power in Guelemara, the Quinaltine, where the His Holiness the Patriarch sat, immune to the threat of war and disapproving of any act of wizardry.

There was, all at a blink, both the sunlight and the shadow in Ylesuin: the king's citadel of the Guelesfort, where the sun rested; and the Quinaltine, where true shadows moved. The palace was his home, as his home must be wherever king Cefwyn decreed; the sun loved the Guelesfort precinct, and for all Cefwyn's tales of Sihhë ghosts and haunts and cold spots on the great central stairs of the main hall, he had himself seen nothing of the sort, not a shadow, not a hint of one that had ever been. It was the shrine, the great shrine of the Quinalt, that was the truly haunted precinct, and he detested it.

He had that far view before him for a long way. Uwen talked about barley harvest. He was content to have the comfort of Uwen's voice, although farming did not Unfold to him as knowledge

27

Mauryl had bespelled him to have—or it simply was not knowledge a long-dead Sihhë-lord had ever needed, if what Men believed of him was true. He listened to Uwen, and learned about barley, how it grew, what conditions were good for it, how the harvest had come in tidily before the rains, and how at harvesttide and with the wedding in a fortnight and a day, they were going to have ale to swear by.

CHAPTER 3

Petitions, writs, and a proposed decree lay in the pile on the desk in the royal study this late evening, not a one of them without a tangle to the tale. The stack contained every argument and counterclaim the king had heard, and heard, and heard a third time for good measure since he had returned to Guelemara, none of them as serious as the matter of the census tallies, thank the gods, but among them, and as potentially damaging to his plans, lurked the discontent of the Holy Father . . . whose distemper was not all on account of the pigeons.

Supper was in the offing. Someone had come in, two pages had gone out, and Annas his household steward, now a king's chamberlain, passed his desk moving as fast as his ancient legs would carry him. Cefwyn became unavoidably aware of gesticulations by the door, then of confused pages shooed off in conflicting directions, and more sober doings between Annas, a small man of modest pale browns and great dignity, and the commander of the King's Guard, Idrys, a tall, mustached man of black armor and numerous weapons. Those two generally debated matters and questions that the king was very glad to leave to the pair of them, and he pursued his letters, not expecting to intervene unless disaster was at the gates.

The point under discussion now, however, seemed to regard rousing master Emuin from his tower, which meant waking him from the diurnal sleep natural in a man who spent his nights peering at the stars, omen-taking, and scrying gods-knew-what in candleflame

29

and water. The king did not want to know what master Emuin did in his tower. He refused steadfastly to countenance complaints regarding master Emuin, his tutor, a Teranthine, having a place in the honors read in the Quinaltine at harvesttide, as he refused to hear the complaints about his bride, his friends, his consorting with Elwynim lords or southern barons, or his uncommon (for a Marhanen) association with Amefel, a heretic province, mostly Bryaltine in faith and, gods knew, many of its people of tainted *Sihhë* blood.

Nor, latest controversy in the reports Idrys had brought him, did he regard the to-do in the Guelesfort over his choice of plainer fare for the harvesttide feast, a scandal for the cooks and for the lords who fancied their stomachs too delicate for Amefin barley soup instead of the traditional leek. He consented to both on the table, but by the great gods' indifference, he would have the barley soup, himself, providing the Guelen cooks could produce it unscorched.

A new king inevitably met such complaints and such resistance to change. Traditions opposed him, even in soup bowls. He could *not* please the fisher- and farmerfolk of Murandys to the north of Guelessar if he pleased the apple-growing province of Panys to the east of Guelessar: his choice of harvesttide fare had political and economic symbolism, and his father had done thus, and promised this, and so on, and so on. As with soup, so with religion: he could not maintain his ties to his old tutor Emuin and at the same time please the Patriarch of the Quinalt, the sect which had risen and prospered under his father. He had already drafted a reply to His Holiness . . . *we shall consider measures which may suffice, regarding the good appearance of the steps* . . . And meanwhile his longed-for informal supper with his bride was all but on the tables and word arrived on the lips of a page that they had indeed located Tristen within the town, late, unseemly, but advised. In a calmer state of mind he began a reasoned missive to Lord Brysaulin . . . *we command you send this day to all the villages specifically to ask* . . .

Then, another commotion of the pages, alas and alack, his own intended russet velvet was discovered in better light to have a stain on it. The senior page, with him since Amefel, and now Master of the Wardrobe, was devastated: Annas went off to settle the matter and there was peace as far as . . . *tally of carts.* . . .

"The bats and the owls are out of sorts this evening," Idrys remarked dryly, quietly shadowing the light above his desk, "and master Emuin will attend. Annas has provided him clothes. We have waked him."

"Provided clothes?" He was mildly dismayed, and looked up at his captain, quill stopped. He had not seen his old teacher in . . . it must be a fortnight, perhaps a little more. Well, perhaps since the oath-taking and festivities of the court last month—or was it more than a month now? But the old man had looked quite well. Emuin seemed admirably content, having reclaimed his former choice of residences, the Old West Tower, and since he was a Teranthine father, he had been served, quite handsomely served, by respectable, soft-spoken Teranthine monks. He had naturally assumed his old master was well, if nocturnal in his pursuits.

"Wherefore is *Annas* now providing his clothes, pray tell? Where are his own servants?"

"He discharged the grayfrock brothers," Idrys said. "Some time ago."

"All of them?"

"Both of them. There were two, my lord king. He faulted their clumsiness with inkpots."

He had not known. He was appalled. "Does no one attend him?"

"The Lord Warden has seen him at least twice in a sennight, and sent to him daily."

"Tristen has seen him." Tristen would never neglect the old man, so, there, he had not neglected his old friend and tutor: *Tristen* had been seeing to him.

"The Lord Warden's servants have seen to his linens and his meals," Idrys said. "But master grayrobe is less among us mortals than among the stars lately, so it seems. I do think he might do with more blankets in that tower."

That *Idrys* evinced concern was troubling. Idrys, the darker eminence of his household, had been his father's man, then his, a man who would stick at very little, and who was not restrained by any pity or scruples from the deeds a prince had to do. He supposed that in some sense even Emuin had been his father's man, but that was so long ago it scarcely signified. Master Emuin had been *his* tutor and his brother's: Emuin was his most trusted councillor of the last few years, a man all in grays: gray of purposes, of arguments, grays of the Teranthine order, which cloaked Emuin's confessed unorthodoxy. There was never a question in which Emuin could not deliver a perhaps or an if, never an issue in which Idrys could not find a counterinterest and a suspect motive.

Master grayrobe and master crow, Teranthine cleric and Guard captain, the guides of his misspent youth. Each, Annas making the third leg of a stable tripod, had presided in his separate authority over a young, notoriously wastrel prince: but now that he had been crowned king, and especially since he was facing a war in Elwynor, taking census of his resources and arranging the movement of men, why, he supposed he had been far more in Idrys' company than in Emuin's the last month. He had not known his old teacher was living in need of blankets.

The man counseled the king of Ylesuin, for the gods' sake. How could he not find two more servants? Or browbeat the palace staff into service? Or at least complain. Why had Annas not told him?

His pen had dried out, and he discovered he had spotted his fingers with ink. The staff had by now found his second-favorite doublet immaculate and acceptable . . . he had surprised the pages by his choice of the shabby favorite, when so much lately had been the court finery. But tonight he wanted his comfortable clothing, not even the lightest hint of martial defense—no leather coat, no bezaint shirt, none of the weight that habitually bore on his shoulders, his ribs, his stomach, and his disposition. The few souls he had called to his table were, among all their other virtues, the friends of his heart, the friends on whom he relied.

He had included his brother Efanor in that number, after anguished thought, after wavering yea and nay for an hour, and finally deciding that, yes, he must. He simply must. Efanor had little in common with his friends and companions. Efanor, duke of Guelessar now, since Efanor had become next in line for the throne, had not shared in those difficult and dangerous days in Amefel, except the very last, and Efanor's piety was a discouragement to any levity, even in a lady's company. But Efanor's feelings would be extremely hurt if he left him out. He most earnestly did not want to hurt his brother, and he had invited him, but he dearly, fondly, foolishly hoped Efanor would not pray over supper.

In the welter of attempts to sway his judgment, he needed the assurance that he could still reach his true friends. A new king in Guelemara, attempting to maintain his own will against the entrenched powers of the northern baronies, had very many concerns in the establishment of his household, the management of which was Annas' job; and had vital interests in finding out things some barons might have hoped to hide from a less active successor—that was Idrys' purview. And in searching the stars, his faithful counselor Emuin was seeking out the fortunes of his reign: he saw that as needful, considering what they had faced at Lewenbrook, a practice in which he feared that the Holy Father—and his own extravagantly pious brother—would find some dangerously righteous objection.

But he knew how to defend Annas and Idrys and Emuin, who had long records of service. Since the barons could not prevail there, it was Ninévrisë about whom the objections circled. Ninévrisë, and, gods help him, Tristen, Warden of Ynefel. The last Lord Warden had not left his tower. Tristen had. That there was reason he should have done so, that Ynefel stood in ruins, none of these considerations sufficed to deter religious objection. The Quinaltine had no wish to hear of wizardry on the battlefield, no wish to know that sorcery had confronted the army and that wizardry, not piety, had turned the attack—and neither had the northern barons, notably absent from the field, any wish to hear about Lewenbrook.

He had most urgently to marry, remove any potential leverage priests might have on him, and then to hell with the religious quibbles: he would do as he pleased then and be damned to the barons. He had to produce a victory, make heroes, create precedents that would settle all this tangle, bribe a few key barons with grants that would make them betray their brother lords, and most of all he had to do the deed quickly, trample over custom, shorten the mourning for his royal father no matter how Efanor frowned and cast him anguished looks. He had to marry soon and very suddenly to dash the hopes of Ylesuin's assorted nobles and eligible daughters: his marriage would place all hope of a daughter crowned out of reach of any of the baronies . . . most notably out of the reach of the duke of Murandys, Prichwarrin, who had been counting heavily on snaring him into a familial bond that would make Prichwarrin ultimately kinsman to kings.

But hot-tempered, self-assured Luriel, Prichwarrin's lovely niece, had abandoned her prince when he was governing Amefel, a province rife with assassins and on the edge of rebellion. She had gone to Henas'amef when her prince was made viceroy in Amefel quite clearly expecting to reign like a queen consort and had been so certain of him that she had set herself in his bed to win his undying love. But she had grown bored with the lack of festivities in that rustic province, and because there were no more suitable, more beautiful, more favored ducal daughters in all Ylesuin, why, she had no fear of his looking elsewhere and she had flounced out of Amefel.

Her uncle Prichwarrin, after all, was the most important baron, the most necessary ally to a king-to-be, and her position seemed secure.

She had not considered *outside* the bounds of Ylesuin, however, since no Guelen lady had ever had to consider outside the bounds of Ylesuin for a rival—and now Luriel languished in Aslaney, with no marriage, no husband, and no prospects. Luriel, greedy Luriel, so sure she was clever, had certainly suffered the most pitifully in his plans, and was certainly a grievous disappointment to her uncle . . . who doubtless clung to hope and prayed for an outbreak of sorcery, treachery, even a breath of scandal or a trip on the stairs that might at the last moment prevent the king marrying the foreign Regent.

Lately Cefwyn felt sorry for Luriel, truth be told, and took her plight as something he would have to deal with in some honorable way . . . a title, a handsome husband. He had one in mind. Meanwhile marry he would, and marry Ninévrisë he would, and in fifteen days he would have made clear to all of Elwynor that the Regent of Elwynor was not his prisoner, but the ally of a Marhanen king with a potent army, a king *with* the Quinalt's blessing, a king able to fight the rebels (all this a powerful blow to rebel claims) before the situation across the river grew more dire, and able to set Ninévrisë on her throne and march away without claiming Elwynor as his own.

Let one of the Elwynim rebels claim to sit as *King* and not Regent, and then the Quinalt might well see another resurgence of wizardry on their very doorstep. A prophecy current in Elwynor foretold the end of the Elwynim Regency in a King to Come, and it was only to be expected that they did not expect the Marhanen to fulfill it. Sooner or later a bold rebel would find some wizard or worse to attest his legitimacy and assuredly claim Sihhë blood in his ancestry (common enough in Elwynor, and in Amefel). He had argued *that* possibility to the Holy Father and seen real fear dawn on the man's face. The Quinalt, that other power in the kingdom of Ylesuin, had never demanded piety of the Marhanen kings; and gods knew his grandfather and his father Ináreddrin had been willing to accommodate unorthodoxy—for the very calculated purpose that they might one day gain Elwynor back into a union of kingdoms, as it had been one realm under the Sihhë kings. His father and grandfather had very carefully maintained a blind eye toward Sihhë symbols and remnants of the Bryaltine faith in Amefel, precisely to keep that heretic province attached to Ylesuin. And they had continually declared the Elwynim to be more or less Bryalt in hopes of fitting Elwynor into their crown: all that, they had done, and the Quinalt Patriarch had blessed their actions no matter how questionable in doctrine.

But accepting a bride of Elwynim blood for the grandson without quite reclaiming that lost territory was pressing matters to the limit. The compact between the Marhanen kings and the Quinaltine was stretched thinner than at any time in Ylesuin's brief history.

And pigeons now shat upon the Quinalt's porch, by petty sorcery, gods save the day.

He had for a little while avoided being in public with his old friends. See, he would say to the Guelenfolk, who were the heart of Ylesuin, nothing has changed. The gods favor the king and the Quinalt, and there will be peace with Elwynor . . .

After a small war.

There will be piety and fear of the gods . . .

But remembering the enemy's wizardry, why, we do have wizards. Be assured they are quiet ones. Pray excuse the pigeons.

Ignore the slight grayness of master Emuin. Ignore the very conspicuous darkness of the banner of the Lord Marshal of Althalen, alike the new Warden of Ynefel, resurrected from anathema and death itself . . . I had never planned to love him like a brother.

Worst of all—there *was* a claimant for the throne of Elwynor that he both believed and feared *was* the fulfillment of the prophecy—he knew, and Emuin and Idrys knew, and Ninévrisë herself knew, but he was far from sure Tristen knew.

And he could think of few things that would make Tristen more miserable.

It was almost time. He walked the long corridor from his private office toward the state halls, a vast, well-lighted corridor of fine tall windows with the royal Dragon blazing gold on red, Marhanen heraldry all but dimmed now as sunset shone like fire in the two clear panes to either side.

He saw commotion at the doors ahead. Arrivals had begun. Efanor, he discovered, had come in early, but not too early, and Cefwyn met his brother with a warm embrace, a genuine embrace—though the ornate and overlarge Quinalt medallion Efanor affected turned between them as they met and stabbed painfully through the velvet. Efanor flattened it to him and renewed the embrace, laughing.

"Did the books come, the two from the south?" Efanor asked.

"Have they come? I've not seen them, gods, when shall I have the leisure for books again? Annas!" he hailed his chamberlain, who passed down the hall at a fair clip, shepherding servants and pages who should not be in the receiving hall, gods alone knew why the young fools had chosen that traverse precisely as guests arrived. "Annas, where are these books my brother sent?"

"In the library, my lord king." This on the retreat, pages scattering.

"In the *library*. Why the library, for the gods' sake?" He was promised a first text of the natural philosopher Manystys Aldun, observations of the ocean he had never seen. Efanor had recovered his summer baggage out of now-disgraced Llymaryn, and with it, his forgotten birthday gift, arriving in a pack train which must finally have reached the capital. Cefwyn had waited for it for months . . . was eager to read the text . . . when he might find the time. Being king, he had not his books in his room—but in some damned great room full of books where he could find nothing.

But then Emuin arrived, far from the dire condition Idrys' report had led him to believe . . . looking a little like an owl roused by daylight, true, and a little windblown, but properly scrubbed and tidy. His beard, whiter this fall than its previous streaked gray, was well combed. He wore gray, always gray, and bore the Teranthine sigil conspicuous on his chest. It was a war of medallions tonight. "Well, well, and welcome," Cefwyn said, feeling thin arms beneath the robes as they embraced. "They led me to think you had dismissed your servants, master grayrobe."

"I have! Pottering about, moving my stacks, oversetting my inkpot . . . if I want ink spilled on my charts, I can do it myself."

"I can find you other servants."

"And spying. Spying!" This with a knit-browed glance at Idrys, who stood to the side, loquacious as statuary.

"Idrys means you nothing but well, old master," Cefwyn said.

"And gives you his report of my reports. If you wish the state of the stars, ask *me*."

"I shall," Cefwyn said, suppressing a smile. *Your Majesty* was almost unheard out of Emuin's mouth. In the old man's mind, he suspected, he was still the towheaded royal urchin, leaning inconsiderate inky elbows on precious books.

But for Efanor, also Emuin's pupil in former days, there had been nothing from master Emuin but a polite nod of his head, a solemn, formal, and entirely correct: "Your Highness." Did that sting, oh, far more than any omission of royal honors? Cefwyn did not guess. He worried about it.

But meanwhile Cevulirn of Ivanor had arrived hard on Emuin's heels and slipped in silently, leaving his guard outside, men of the White Horse. Cevulirn was tall, thin, all gray and white in his colors, a man who might fade into mist and fog. He was not that imposing until one looked him in the eyes or saw him with horses or on the battlefield, and Cefwyn had seen all three. Cevulirn was the one of all the southern barons he was most supremely glad to have linger in the court—speaking of spies, which Cevulirn assuredly was, ready to bring the southern barons immediately back to court if the northern ones beset the king with undue demands for favors for their personal causes.

And that well suited the king, who did not want to meet those northern demands and who looked to the south, the alliance he had once forged desperately against Elwynor, to support him most strongly in his determination to gain his Elwynim bride.

"My friend," Cefwyn hailed him, and for two entire breaths had time to ask Cevulirn the state of his affairs, but not to hear the answer, before Ninévrisë herself arrived.

He had not taken account that he had neglected to invite any other woman. The court, which remarked every nuance of what the king did and did not, would surely remark that particular indiscretion, plucking it out of the overheated air in the kitchens if they lacked spies among his servants.

But he and his companions of this hall had made a warlike council in Amefel both before and after Lewenbrook. The politicking around the ladies' court in Guelemara might be thick as bees around a hive, and the bees might buzz about Ninévrisë's future status, and the proprieties of a good Guelen lady, and, gods witness, whether her simple bodice and single-petticoated skirt was a fashion to be copied or a scandal to be deplored. But the ladies of the bower never quite acknowledged the one truth most entirely unwelcome to their imaginations: that Her Grace was a head of state, not some ducal daughter to be judged by them; and that Her Grace would have been attended to this hour, not by ladies, but by four good men, lords of Elwynor, had they not fallen in her defense in an act of memorable courage. Her Grace the Regent of Elwynor had led men of twice her years under arms and been obeyed in the field and in the council chamber; but alas, alas for the gossip, on this side of the river she did not entrain family influences which might define her status with the women of this court or their ambitious priests of the Quinalt . . . how else could they know her worth? And, gods! her petticoats were insufficient.

Her Grace the heretic arrived with only the four of the king's guards assigned to her, to sit in the intimate, doubtless drunken company of half a score men at their leisure, including a king ill reputed as a prince . . . oh, depend on it: the gossip would fly by morning. Here they were, if a wizard-priest, the captain of the King's Guard, the king's pious brother, and the silent lord of Ivanor could possibly be counted raffish and daring . . . why, Cevulirn was a southerner, after all, and not a good Quinaltine, but Teranthine like master Emuin, if Cevulirn ever chose to make any philosophy evident.

Clatter, clatter, clatter of women's gossip, and be damned to them and their suppositions. The king did as he pleased tonight and needed those he gathered close to him. His heart needed them.

It wanted only the Lord Warden of Ynefel's haunted precinct to complete the evening, and Tristen was, not uncommonly, late.

CHAPTER 4

Cefwyn had said there was no need of formality. *As we did in the first days,* the message had said, but they had gotten in from their ride just at sunset, and had to wash, and dress in clothes fit for the king's supper table.

Tristen wore dark brown and Uwen wore green, no badges at all of Ynefel's dark repute (which he escaped whenever he could) and this time no weight of mail or defense of weapons. The guards—there were always at least four at the king's private chambers, besides the score up and down the hall outside—knew them and let them in without their having to say a word.

"The lord of Ynefel and Althalen," the guard informed a hurrying page, and the page bowed and led them quickly down the reception hall to the smaller banquet hall—past Annas, hurrying about as usual, then past Idrys, who was never far from the king. Idrys had a seemingly lazy attention for them, as sharp-edged as ever—Idrys missed nothing at all, and seemed uncommonly amused.

The page showed them into the hall. Gratefully, it was not to be one of those state affairs, with tables reaching from the front of the hall to the back, in double rows, a din of voices and lute players in which no one could hear what happened a table away: those affairs could never be arranged in a single day. The invitation tonight had been a surprise, and set in the Blue Hall, which was actually mostly gilt, with only touches of blue in the ceiling. Tristen had been here once before, just after the oath-taking, in what Cefwyn called the coziest hall in the king's apartments.

There was Emuin looking scrubbed and like his old self; and Ninévrisë was talking freely with Efanor, who was smiling, tonight, and without the doleful priest who often came with him. Even the pages were those who had attended Cefwyn in Amefel and whom he had kept in service, though other lords had besieged the throne with offers of eligible sons and nephews.

Best of all, Cefwyn came and clapped him on the shoulder, bidding him welcome; and for a few distracted moments Cefwyn talked to him about the weather and the wedding and the harvest.

"I hear the barley is exceptional," Tristen said, and Cefwyn gave him a wondering look.

"Uwen told me today," he confessed, and Cefwyn laughed.

"It *is* a fine harvest," Cefwyn said. "Come, come, are you too warm with that cloak? Boy! —Gods, they've heated the hall like a forge."

Tristen surrendered his cloak. Uwen had deserted him for the outer hall and would have his supper there, Tristen was sure, where Uwen would be far more comfortable with the Ivanim guard, and with Idrys' lieutenant, than among lords.

Meanwhile it was impossible to follow anything Cefwyn said; Tristen's thoughts flew entirely asunder. He had come in from riding all unsuspecting. He had taken to eavesdropping on his own guards for the sheer comfort of voices and here he was, snatched into a gathering of all his own old friends. He felt his heart more than fill; he felt it loosen from its habitually guarded state, and he looked about him in sheer dangerous delight . . . aware of Ninévrisë as he was of Emuin.

He saw Emuin's frown from across the room.

He ducked his head then and made his presence in this world and in the gray space instantly smaller and quieter.

But damp the happiness, no, it could not, and Ninévrisë crossed the room to meet him and take his hands.

"Tristen," she said with great warmth.

"My lady Regent."

"You look very well," she said. He tried not to reach into the gray space. They could speak with no word spoken—alone of everyone but Emuin she could reach there, as her father had been able to do; but only scarcely, a wisp of a presence at the strongest: she was no wizard. She only had the heritage, and had consciously abandoned it.

"Here we all are," Cefwyn was saying just then, summoning all of them to table. "Come, come, everyone, no standing on ceremony tonight. By royal decree among the lot of us, I make today a start on harvesttide, no great echoing halls and long speeches, no worries, not a care. So be at your ease, all my good friends, my dear soon-to-be-bride—sit by me. Emuin is a priest—he will keep the proprieties."

"No priest," Emuin said. "I am most carefully not a priest."

"Close enough for propriety in this company: a cleric, a man of years and dignity. My lady to my left, Efanor to my right hand—Cevulirn, next Efanor, Tristen, opposite, then my good master crow. Gods, what joy to see you."

They talked a moment. Efanor delivered a very long supper prayer, and after serving and conversations began again, Cefwyn talking of horses, of the weather, the prospects for the winter . . . and the spring, Idrys reminded them.

"No," Cefwyn said, then, "no, not a word on that matter. I did not bring you here for any council of war, only for the pleasure of seeing you. Friends, look you, a gathering of friends. That is all my pleasure tonight."

"My lord king," said Cevulirn, and Emuin lifted his cup.

"Friends," Cefwyn said again, "with whom I can say with particular significance that this has been both a bitter year and a good year."

"Aye to that," Idrys said.

"A year of ending and beginning, a year of loss and finding . . . and all of you were with me through the storm. I drink your health, your wealth, your fortune for long years to come, and I hope for many more days in which we can gather like this."

Cefwyn drank. Then Efanor got up from his chair. "Gods rest our father," Efanor said then, lifting his cup, "and gods rest them all who died, and gods save the king and the Holy Father."

Everyone drank to that, too, though Cefwyn did not seem entirely pleased. It was like Efanor to bring the gods and the dead into everything, and he was not quite sure Efanor should in all propriety have paired the Patriarch with the king.

"Gods save the Lady Regent," Cevulirn said, in his turn, "and all her faithful men."

That meant Elwynim and heretics. Everyone drank, and that did please Cefwyn, but not quite so well Efanor. Tristen began to fear he might have to say something himself, and all wit immediately escaped him. He decided if he had to say something he must bless the king and all present, which was no great difficulty; but fortunately it seemed the gods-saving was done, and the rest of them were spared having to invent something.

Instead they began to talk and eat until they had done for the soup and bread. Annas supervised the pages bringing in another course, and they sat and ate, not overmuch, and drank, not heavily. Tristen found himself thinking of the noisy lords of the south—thinking with a lightening of spirits how Sovrag would take to the autumn ale. The lord of Olmern would be very drunk and very loud by now, and inevitably talk of matters no one would approach head-on with the king—but Sovrag would always go straight to necessary matters, and most of the time people would laugh, or pretend to laugh, even if they were offended. In fact he liked the man as he liked Cevulirn; and he found only the dimmest joy in Efanor's pious prayers, for which he was very sorry.

But it was a warm, good gathering. They talked about the harvest, and the festival, and whether the scarcity of cloth was a matter of merchants downriver getting rumors of war from Imor and holding back goods: Cevulirn thought not. His dukedom of Ivanor was more southerly than Imor, though entirely lacking a riverport. Cevulirn, who usually spoke very little, succinctly told what he knew regarding the downriver merchants and their quarrels, and why he thought they were not shipping cloth—which lay rather in a quarrel between two lords. Then the talk wended to the grain harvest, and almost inevitably to horses, and finally to the duke of Murandys, Lord Prichwarrin, who wished to breed the northern Spestinan horse (it was almost a Word, a sturdy sort of horse Tristen did not think he had ever seen, but he imagined such horses as stocky and winter-bearded like Petelly) crossing them to the southern Byssandin breed, the native horse of the Ivor plains, not to the Crysin breed that the Ivanim rode, a type which they had bred up from the Byssandin. It was horses, hounds, and hunting where Guelenfolk gathered in numbers, and Tristen listened to his second discourse on horse-breeding for the day.

Cevulirn, with Cefwyn, opined that Murandys was likely to lose the strength of the Spestinan and add all the faults of the Byssandin shoulder, which produced a notoriously unpleasant gait. That led them to a mare Ninévrisë had brought from Elwynor, that Cefwyn much recommended and that Cevulirn greatly approved; and thus back to the spring campaign, and the ill-made tallies, which Ninévrisë declared they should not discuss tonight, no, firmly, no.

So back to the breeding of horses and the plenitude of hay this fall, a good last cutting. The conversation all was light and pleasant, until at last Emuin enjoyed too much ale himself, fell asleep, and two pages had to see him off to his tower. Ninévrisë made her departure at the same time. So did Cevulirn and then Efanor; and Tristen thought it clearly time to go.

But when Cevulirn and Efanor were out the door of the Blue Hall, Cefwyn stayed him for a moment with a hand on his arm, and offered him, of all things, a purse heavy with coin.

"Sir?" he asked, perplexed.

"Penny day, we call it. A custom. The day after this, folk high and low repair to the Quinalt, either at high services or any hour of the day after noon, if they will, and drop the harvest penny into the collection box. Supposing that you have no great abundance of pennies, I give you these, for yourself, for Uwen, for your household, to give to the Quinalt."

"Yes, sir," he said. He was unaccustomed to handling money. He wondered what a sack of pennies might buy, and he was already planning to go later rather than early and to do the deed quickly. He did not like the thought of the Quinaltine roof over his head. He wondered if he might send Uwen to do it for him, and whether there might be coins left over.

"For each of your servants and Uwen and yourself. It is important," Cefwyn added, "that each man make his gift with his own hand. The harvest penny repairs the Quinalt roof."

"Does it leak?" It seemed an odd way to deal with an urgent situation; and he made Cefwyn laugh and clap him on the shoulder.

"Not for at least fifty years, but a benefice once accorded never goes away, not where the priests are involved. Supposedly now the money goes for the widows of the town, which is a good work, but most of all, understand, it requires even the king to make pilgrimage up the Quinalt steps, and there to drop in the harvest penny to show his piety. You are not frequent in your observances . . . truth, you have not been, on my advice. This time, you must do this with your own hand sometime during the day. As I shall at the high ceremony."

"Yes, Your Majesty." The warmth of the wine had deserted him in the chill of imagining that place of groined arches and pillars that stood like forbidding watchers. But Cefwyn clearly had some compelling reason for sending him there, a reason he was sure had nothing to do with the Quinalt roof, and Cefwyn's hand on his shoulder drew him close as they walked the outside hall toward the doors.

"Efanor has warned me before this," Cefwyn said. "You know the priests are discontent with Her Grace, and entirely distrust the southern barons, who are not Quinalt, excepting the lord of Imor Lenúalim. And that they are also very discontent with master Emuin, who is far, far closer to me than the Quinalt has ever found comfortable. They will wish to find fault."

If they disapproved Emuin, it was very clear by extension that they disapproved him—which was no news at all, but troubling.

"For my sake, do this," Cefwyn said. "Bring the penny. Scrupulously, on the day. Uwen will guide you. There will be a state procession, all due formality. You need not suffer that. You may go later. You may do me and my lady a great service, if only you can carry this off with no untoward events. Above all else, we mustn't have an untoward event. Dare you? Can you? Will you?"

Uwen being a Guelenman, and Quinalt whenever he was asked, Tristen knew he could rely on Uwen to know at least about the general behavior expected with shrines and gods. He had never delved deeply into the question of gods, fearing that powers and magics which ordinary Men claimed to exist, and which he thus far could not find, might lead even their strong friendship into uncomfortable places. He had felt Uwen's discomfort with the subject at any time they skirted near it. But it seemed circumstances now and at last called for him to deal with gods—and with priests, who said the gods naturally detested him.

Still, Cefwyn would never wish him harm, and if Cefwyn asked him, for his sake, to drop a penny in a box, that was after all a small thing, however foolish-seeming.

"I will," he said.

"I have all confidence in you," Cefwyn said, still with that sober look, the two of them walking slowly. "Understand, my enemies will try to catch you. The closer we come to the wedding, those who oppose me see themselves and their influence sitting farther and farther from the court, and themselves with no further means either to bend me or to change the treaty. The southern barons see the advantage to themselves of our treaty with Elwynor. But the northern barons have old grudges with Her Grace's land. They wish nothing so much as to diminish Her Grace to a subject, her kingdom to a province. They have had two short months first to find the nuptial agreement will not permit that, then to wish me to break that agreement, marry Her Grace, then invade her kingdom and loose them so they can plunder it."

"You would never."

"I would never. That took them a few days of the two months to learn. Then they proposed forms for the ceremony that would accomplish the same thing: they wanted to insert clauses in our vows that would make my lady far less a sovereign than her husband, and then they would demand their king take advantage of them. But, another few days of scheming and composing, and they simply cannot find a chink in the betrothal documents we crafted in Amefel, do you see? So now they wish to insert other clauses to let them claim Elwynor for our heirs; but we have them there, too. The northern barons went to the priests, absolute in their belief that *they* might find weakness in the documents. But that failed. Now with fifteen days left before the wedding, the only hope, their only hope, is to find some wickedness to charge against Her Grace. Their time is running out, and the harvesttide, when there is so much license and so much drunken behavior, and the public ceremonies, with the king and his friends on view, is their best chance to arrange some inconvenience."

Had this something to do with pennies? He was not entirely enlightened.

"I asked Cevulirn to remain here in winter court," Cefwyn said, "which is a great hardship for him; but with him here in Guelemara the northern barons know they cannot get personal agreements unwatched by the southern lords during the winter, and *that* also limits the mischief I have to deal with. They can put nothing past him in the way of agreements or decrees that would favor them and not the south—and they fear to propose anything too extravagantly against the treaty because they know the south favors it. But now, fifteen days left, recall it, they have discovered a new hare to chase. Under the agreements we have crafted most carefully, you understand, Ninévrisë will never be queen of Ylesuin, but a reigning Regent in Elwynor, a head of state equal to us, with—with! mind you, *no state clergy except herself*. Once the marriage is sealed, the barons may not alter that, nor insert men *or priests* into her councils, nor demand she become Quinalt. Murandys, Corswyndam, Sulriggan . . . all oppose this clause."

"Sulriggan is banished! How can he oppose it?"

"Not truly banished. In disfavor. Mark there is a difference. His nephew attends on my brother. Or attempts to attend. Here is my point: since we have the marriage agreement protecting Her Grace, they may try another way. They may attempt my friends. And of my friends, *you* are as likely an object of their plotting as my lady is. An accusation of sorcery, of any sort of impropriety, would create an immense storm, possibly a delay. Anything you do amiss. Or fail to do—or that she fails to do. It's their last chance."

"I understand." He did. He knew the other lords disapproved of him, all except Cevulirn. "What must I do, then?"

"Be wise. Be wary."

"I am, sir." All the events of Lewenbrook were in that declaration—all that thunderous, terrible realization in which he had known a book without reading it; in which he had understood all that was in it. That was what lay between him and the fecklessness some, even Cefwyn, continually expected in him. Even Cefwyn had not known the moment he had changed, or in what odd ways. He had no idea how winter behaved. But he knew how to defend himself, and he knew spite when he saw it. He knew the workings of the court. Thus far, he evaded them.

Cefwyn's hand rested on his shoulder as they walked. "I never take you for a fool. But be aware, most of all, that His Holiness is not a pious sort of priest. And I must explain one other thing to you. The Regent of Elwynor, Her Grace's late father, always did the office of chief priest as well as king; and this is a matter of great concern to the Quinalt. They want to assign a priest to Her Grace and will not accept her acting in priestly ways."

She is a wizard, he almost said. He was not sure how much of that truth Cefwyn knew, although he was sure Cefwyn had some notion. And was it for that reason the Quinalt objected? Should he, in trust of Cefwyn, in good faith, tell all he knew and discuss the question? Saying could never be unsaid, and absent Emuin's agreement, he dared not, when two people were happy and almost wedded, whatever that entailed.

"They want to assign a priest to Her Grace," Cefwyn said. "They disapprove of women."

"There are no women at all in the Quinaltine?" He remembered robed women, women in white, carrying candles.

"Not as priests. Not, therefore, as reigning kings, who have the function of priests, or to be lord of a province—"

"Lady Orien was."

"—Lady Orien is a sorceress, good lack! They hardly approved of her in any respect! And I never consulted the Quinalt in the marriage agreement. Nor needed do so, in Amefel. The point is, they disapprove women in high places. But the marriage treaty, made and sworn to in Amefel, under Quinalt, Teranthine and Bryalt auspices, says Her Grace shall keep all her prerogatives. *All* her prerogatives, without exception, it's written in the treaty, and, lo! a meddling clerk in the Quinaltine discovered this aspect of the Elwynim Regency ten days ago—which I have not told Her Grace. Murandys and Ryssand came fawning up to me saying she cannot act as a priest, demanding she declare a faith, and for a certain number of days, messages have outnumbered the autumn leaves."

So men and women being wed *could* have secrets one from the other. It relieved him somewhat of guilt. It was not wrong for Ninévrisë to have held secrets, nor for him to leave them be.

"Then," Cefwyn said, "then, a few days ago, the Quinalt came with a new thought. If she has not accepted a priest, she cannot be sanctified, and if she is not sanctified, she cannot accept a creed. Without a creed the Quinalt recognizes as godly she cannot swear a godly oath or receive one, and without swearing there cannot have been a treaty *or* a betrothal."

That would be disaster. "The Quinalt in Amefel said it was an oath and they certainly knew she was Elwynim."

"The Quinalt here is higher and *they* know she is Elwynim, but if *it* says there is no treaty, then we have no treaty. Or we have a dispute that will take two realms to war and bring down the king. I have sworn *that* to His Holiness, who has no wish to see the Marhanen kings fall, though gods know Murandys and Ryssand would step into the breach in an instant. —The plain solution is, settled five days ago, Her Grace will declare she has always had a faith, her father was her priest, and therefore His Holiness will accept the treaty."

"How does one declare a faith?" A troubling thought came to him. "I have sworn to you, and I have never—"

"Hush, hush, *hush!* never say so. The short of it is that the barons have demanded of *her* to declare a faith, thinking she cannot satisfy the demand . . . and then they would be rid of the treaty and the marriage except on *their* terms, which Her Grace would never accept. But the Bryalt faith such as they practice it in Amefel is *very* near the Elwynim practice. So I understand. So a Bryalt priest has now sworn my lady has had him for a priest since she came to Amefel and from *before* the treaty. It is, of course, a lie, but necessary to protect the treaty. You must never say so."

He understood that much very clearly. "Then you *have* told Her Grace about the barons."

Cefwyn drew a breath. "Some days ago. And she agreed far more reasonably than I would have thought. She is so good a soul, Tristen. So brave."

"I do admire her, sir. Very much."

"She will accept the Bryalt priest to sign his name as her priest on the marriage documents. He will swear to continue to be her priest, that is, to stand at my lady's elbow while she reigns in Elwynor, which he will, and meekly so, on his life. When he is there he is under her authority, and how much authority she accords him is by her will, not mine, and not the affair of His Holiness. His name is Benwyn, a man of little ambition, a scholar, a man who likes his table, a harmless sort. You have not met him. But you may."

"The Quinalt accepts the Bryaltines as priests? I thought they refused to do that."

"The Quinalt detests them as half heretics. But it *is* a recognized faith and it makes her no heretic, which is what *His Holiness* wants, now, because *he* knows I will press this to the uttermost, *including* breaking from the Quinalt myself if he denies me in this. My grandfather made the Quinalt what it is, my *father* preferred them over the Teranthines, and by the gods I can do the same for the Teranthines over *them* if they cross me. —Which is neither here not there with us—I see your frown. Say only that my lady has declared herself Bryalt, she has a priest who will disappear from significance once she stands on Elwynim soil, and she will, in that tangled understanding, pass under the Quinalt roof on penny day with no statement whether she is a priestly or unpriestly sovereign—damnable nonsense, all. But such words entail power in *this* world. The Holy Father must perform the marriage. This is the sticking point. This is the difficulty. I need the Quinalt's goodwill, Tristen, or I must break the Quinaltine's power, and I will, *if* I must. But I have a war to fight. And I had far rather the Holy Father's goodwill. We are *almost* to an understanding that will make the Holy Father *my* ally for benefits I can accord him, and if you could, by will or wish or whatever small, very small wizardry you or Emuin together might manage, . . . keep the pigeons away from the Quinalt porch."

"The *pigeons,* sir?"

"I know, I know 't is such a small matter. But I need the Holy Father in a giving mood, and they have fouled his porch, they have continually fouled his porch, and they make him think of wizardry, and of you, in a most unfavorable light. His dignity is threatened. Can you prevent them?"

He was utterly confused. "I can try. I shall try, sir."

"I knew you would. I know you have a good heart." Cefwyn after all seemed to have something more on his mind, and Tristen waited, silent, until Cefwyn plunged ahead. "Never let them *see* you work magic. Not with the pigeons. Not with anything. Ever."

"It's not a thing one could see, sir, will I or will I not. I will try."

"If you could only observe the *forms* of orthodoxy, Tristen." It was not at all about the pigeons, now, but all in a rush, the desire of Cefwyn's heart, he thought. "If you could banish the pigeons, and come under the Quinalt roof, and make that offering, thus acknowledging the authority of the Quinalt . . ."

"Like Her Grace, do you mean? To tell a lie?"

Cefwyn looked confounded. And finally said, "Yes. A small, an accommodating lie. For appearances. To let an important old man feel that his *dignity* has been respected and will be respected in future before witnesses he wishes to impress. Do I offend you?"

"No, sir. You can never offend me."

"I have given you the pennies. And best you send yours by some other hand if you cannot come under that roof without some . . . without some manifestation. But I have seen you go into the shrine. I know that you can do it. Can you do it safely? Or will the . . . will the candles go out, or mice and bats break out, or any such thing?"

"I don't think so, sir. About the mice and bats, at least. And the candles. I can go in."

"Can you give the penny? Can you walk in, the place deserted, and drop a penny in the box? I do not ask you go in with the ceremony and the priests and all, in the morning, only to go alone in the afternoon, with your guard. And witnesses. Well that there be witnesses. I shall have to arrange someone to go in with you."

"Witnesses."

"In case they lie. The court goes in the morning, in a great ceremony, singing and trumpets, all of that . . ."

"As it did when the barons swore."

"You were there."

"I was there, sir. I watched from the door. I could attend with the court, if 't would serve."

"*Could* you do that?"

"I will." He had attended in the shrine but he had not lingered. At summer's end, Cefwyn had crowned *himself,* on the field, and that meant Cefwyn had not taken the Crown of Ylesuin from the hands of His Holiness. The Quinaltine Patriarch had wanted Cefwyn to come into the Quinaltine shrine and have the Patriarch set the crown on him all over again. But Cefwyn had not been willing to be crowned twice; so he had only taken the northern barons' oaths of fealty in a Quinaltine ceremony, those who had not sworn already in the south. "Will it make the Patriarch happier?"

"If you could do that, if you could simply stand with the court, if we could quiet the general fears that the king and his house as well as his bride will go off to be Bryaltines or worse, that all the south will break out in magic like a pox, why, then, gods, yes, it would make him happier. If we win the Holy Father, then Murandys and Nelefreíssan, and finally even Ryssand must fall in line. The lords break every law of the Quinalt themselves almost every day and twice on holidays, but they fear heresy. They do honestly fear it . . . as if the gods being waked up by another man's sins should then notice all that *they* do amiss. The Holy Father has his own methods, the Quinalt being the holder of all treaties, and if he approves, then he will bring the rest of them into order." Cefwyn drew a great breath and gave him a long, solemn stare. "You are the most unskilled liar ever I knew. But if you could take only a little instruction, learn what will be done, stand quietly, *do* nothing wizardous . . ."

"I am no wizard, my lord. I am not."

"No wizard as Emuin is no cleric. If someone were to show you what to do, and when to stand and when to appear to pray . . . make the gesture . . . make the people sure you are *not* of wizardous substance, that you will not burst into flame or break out in warts. You don't have to convince the Holy Father. The Holy Father well understands political religiosity. He respects it—he frankly prefers it to devout faith in those he supports. What will win him is your making the offering, showing respect for his authority—publicly bowing to him."

"Ought I?"

"For me. For Her Grace."

"Then easily. I might go to the Quinaltine and meet the Patriarch and swear to him if you wished."

"No. No. No. Know this. His Holiness is Sulriggan's cousin. He will never be your friend. Never expect that. Say *nothing* but good day to His Holiness or any priest, on any occasion."

Sulriggan again. He was a very troublesome man, the lord of Llymaryn, not attending court this winter, in Cefwyn's extreme displeasure, after he had left the court of Amefel in disfavor. He was never guilty of treason. When Cefwyn had had great need of every man he could muster, Sulriggan had not been there, had suffered no wounds at Lewenbrook, where the southern barons had proven their courage; and in shame, Sulriggan had sat all autumn in Llymaryn, with even Efanor angry at him. That much was no inconvenience to anyone.

But that His Holiness the Patriarch of the Quinalt was Sulriggan's cousin, and the king must court *him*, that was terrible news. No one had told him that. It made matters very much more difficult.

"I would become Bryalt like Her Grace. I could do that. I could say I was Quinalt. If I am to lie, had I not as well swear to the Quinalt?"

Cefwyn looked as if he had swallowed something startling and uncomfortable. Idrys had lingered at the doors, throughout, and looked askance when he said that.

"As well slip a raven in amongst the doves," Idrys said. "*That* would be a sight."

"That, from master crow," Cefwyn said, in the way he and Idrys were accustomed to trade barbs. "I slip *your* black presence in amongst the pious priests and they bear it."

"I am no wizard," Idrys said, "nor reputed to be dead."

"Mind your tongue!" Cefwyn's order was not humorous, now.

"Reputed, I say, my lord king. *Reputed* is the simple truth, which the lord of Althalen would by no means deny."

"Dead, sir, I am not sure of."

"Gods." Cefwyn's hand rested on Tristen's back. "My good friend. My friend most innocent. And yet grown far more clever. Gods, if for fifteen days, a *gloss* of piety . . . an instruction. Merely an instruction in the ceremonies. It would tantalize the barons with doubts . . . distract all gossip from Ninévrisë . . ."

"My lord king," Idrys objected.

"No, now, a *gloss,* is all. Efanor will always discuss religion . . . would deliver him sermons for hours if Tristen were willing, at least to make him aware of the forms and the rites. If 't would raise no apparitions, no blackening of the offerings, no souring of the wine, . . ."

"No, my lord king," Idrys said firmly. "No, no, and no."

"The Patriarch is a practical man, a shrewd man. He knows what there is to gain and lose. A little gesture, no deception at all . . . simply a due respect . . ."

"Much to lose," Idrys said. "Do not trust His Holiness."

"Oh, never. Never. He never deludes me. But he quite confessedly finds my brother's honest devotion far more dangerous to him than a host of Emuins and the entire Teranthine brotherhood. Or the Bryaltine. Did you know my father tried to have me declared a bastard? And His Holiness would not. His Holiness does not want a truly religious man. He does not want my brother, and if he would understand that Tristen is doing this only to please the Quinalt, gods, *flatter* the old fox . . ."

"Yet he must have appearances. By every tenet of the Quinaltine, he cannot countenance a Sihhë-lord beneath his roof!"

"Appearances indeed. His Holiness dares not disillusion Efanor, but no more dares he see Efanor on the throne; and he knows now he cannot cozen me, threaten my friends, and still maintain his income. He damned well *will* find a niche in his piety for the Sihhë, such a fine niche it will cover and explain the Quinalt's murder of them at Althalen and its approval of my grandfather while it explains its acceptance of Tristen of Ynefel whom—*whom* we have never proven is Sihhë. It may take Quinalt scholars a month and a wagonload of parchment, but when the Quinalt covers its own sins, it covers them in ink, in seas and oceans of ink, deep enough for fishes. So, *yes*, yes, Tristen, my dear friend, yes, if you could find it in you to listen to my brother's pious instruction, learn the forms enough to go through them, gods! if you could publicly wear some trinket of a relic to prove it will not blast you, if you could attend in chapel and not provoke omens . . . a convert—gods, a Sihhë convert. What would the Holy Father do?"

"One cannot imagine," Idrys said dryly, and in no greater approval, so that Tristen himself had doubts.

But Cefwyn showed none at all. "A Sihhë convert, a donation, a royal abbey . . . that would salve the wound of the coronation I wouldn't let the old fox do over. Gods, more than justify the Sihhë in the Quinaltine. If they make a way in for *Tristen*, the heresy of the whole of Elwynor becomes a trifle. We could see Ylesuin and Elwynor together accommodated in a doctrine that could admit *you*, my friend. A month or two, a few donations, is all you would have to endure, attending ceremonies with the court, being punctilious in your observances—"

"Hazardous," Idrys said.

"But filing in with the court, out with the court, bowing when the court bows, attached to my brother's well-known, prickly piety . . . *Efanor's* convert. And my brother is Marhanen. Efanor will know exactly the stakes. Religious that he is, I shall have him simply to understand this is political—he will still try to secure Tristen's soul, none could daunt him, but Efanor will see this act as exactly what it is, will know why it is, will defend Tristen as a point of honor. In my brother's keeping, close by his elbow, there's no way for Murandys to come at him, not a bit! And in the spring, once we launch our forces into Elwynor, then Tristen will ride with me far from the Quinaltine, for the summer long. By next fall, good gods, he'll simply do what most converts do, attend only on holy days and at funerals. Blessed once is blessed, so far as the commons know and so far as serves His Holiness's purposes. It's the door by which we admit the whole oxcart. It's the *gesture* His Holiness wants. And to get it, we make his Holiness accommodate the halfling Sihhë . . . *never* suggest that Tristen is more than that. *Halfling* is ambiguous enough for any negotiation; and after they admit the halfling Sihhë then they take the whole damned court of Elwynor."

Next fall. Next *summer* had daunted him and he had seen *no* prospect yet that far ahead of him. Tangled and dubious as it all might be, it did serve Cefwyn, and protected Ninévrisë, and brought him to the spring and through the unimagined summer, even to the fall to come with a *use,* a purpose, a duty to do. Gray space gave way to imagining a time yet to come, days and months ahead.

"Your Majesty," Idrys said. "We should consider this at some length."

"Do *you* have objections?" Cefwyn asked, looking at Tristen. It was clearly a request not to hear any. But Idrys' doubts were not to disregard.

"There are shadows in that place," Tristen said. "So you should know, sir."

"I don't doubt there are," Cefwyn said, and gave a short laugh. "Gods know my grandfather's crypt is likely the bait for them—he feared the dark excessively. Chandlers have never been so prosperous as in his reign, good faith." He patted Tristen on the arm. "But do you understand what we are about? My brave friend, my very brave friend, if you can do this—if you can do this . . . and not affright this priest . . . gods forbid the Patriarch should ever meet the like we met on Lewen field . . . then we can accommodate Her Grace and her whole realm in the exception we craft for you, who *are* the Warden of Ynefel, which *is* and has always been the legitimate title of a lord of Ylesuin. They have to regard the current Lord Warden, and to treat *you* as lawful and entitled, and exempt from requirements that bind other lords: we have a precedent, good gods, we have a precedent in Mauryl Gestaurien, what *was* done *can be* done, and our penny offering, if we can do this, will create this niggling little exception through which we can settle the whole question of Quinalt doctrine *and* the status of halflings, hedge-wizards, Bryaltines, sprites, spirits, shadows, ghosts, and gods know what! Good great gods, *we have a precedent!*"

"Consult Emuin," Idrys said. "My lord king, I beg you ask him before you undertake anything with His Holiness."

"Ask Emuin to your satisfaction, but if he finds no urgent reason against it, and if Tristen can endure my grandfather's ghost, —dear blessed *gods,* I would find it convenient if you could walk in with the royal procession."

"I will, sir," Tristen said, and Cefwyn proposed they go aside for a last cup of wine, a seal on their agreement. "Sit with me a moment," Cefwyn said, and, Idrys being absent about business with his lieutenant, and still less than pleased, the two of them sat beneath the tall windows in the hall, in this set of rooms so very vast the servants always arrived out of breath. Night had long since filled the high window above the little table, and candlelight danced on the imperfections of the glass as on the embossings of gold cups that were the ordinary of Cefwyn's household in these days.

"You have been very patient in my neglect of you," Cefwyn said, "and I know how difficult it has been for you in Guelessar—difficult for Her Grace, too, with no assured rank or title, gods know what her people believe is her condition among us. Yet I have had to leave my friends to fend for themselves for a while. It is so important, what we do, simply to assure I have the power to launch this war, this one chance to catch the moment. We have the rebels across the river, building forces by the day. If Tasmôrden moves to take either the bridges or the capital before the winter closes in, he will have all winter to consolidate his hold. He will gain followers and Her Grace will lose them, murdered the day Tasmôrden sets foot in Ilefínian. But I have never needed explain war to you."

Uwen and the guards had told him Ylesuin would not wage war in winter. But Tristen himself wished the contrary . . . nor at all the hesitant, difficult sort of warfare he kept hearing proposed as winter raids. He knew who and where Tasmôrden was: the strongest of the rebel claimants to the Regency of Elwynor camped on the road that led equally to Guelessar or to the Elwynim capital of Ilefínian. Tasmôrden was thus able to go either direction, and to go quickly.

Cefwyn hoped Lord Elfharyn in the capital, loyal to Nineᵛrisë's
father Uleman, could hold the capital in her name through the winter . . . and divide Tasmôrden's attention. But if Tasmôrden ceased
to believe their feints at the bridges, and if Ileſínian fell to
Tasmôrden quickly, and he was then able to secure himself behind
Ileſínian's walls before the snows, then . . . then it was a far grimmer
situation, with many of Nineᵛrisë's people in a way to suffer for it,
and many to pay with their lives.

"We should have camps across the river," Tristen said to Cefwyn.
"We should cross the bridges now. We should make the threat so
strong he will have to regard it, and not dare move on Ileſínian."

"*If* Lord Brysaulin can find me wagons. I have had some moved
in. But how many others might I rely on? Gods know. My chancellor counted haystacks, not wagons."

Wagons. Always there was the consideration of moving in
force, never striking with the light cavalry, which Tristen would
have wished, against this quick-footed enemy. He had believed
from the first day in Guelessar that they should move at once
and not delay for marriages and swearings and musters and the
objections of all the northern barons. He had thought the first
time he had heard of Tasmôrden rising against Nineᵛrisë's claim
to the Regency that they should be straightway across the river on
the southern bridges out of Amefel, march to the capital with
light horse, receive it from Elfharyn, who would almost certainly
yield it to Nineᵛrisë as soon as she appeared at the gates, and only
afterward hold the land by drawing heavy forces across from
Guelessar . . . but, no, Cefwyn had to receive the oaths first. Then
it was deep autumn. Then they dared not launch a campaign,
because it was bound to be laborious and slow in rainy autumn.
Tristen frowned at what he heard now, which only confirmed
what he had already thought; and now he saw the map as if it
were before him, the bridges that led from Amefel to Elwynor
repaired this summer; likewise those that had once led from
Murandys to Elwynor in the north repaired this fall. "We might
still move. Open an attack from Amefel, now. Cevulirn can carry
it. You have the oaths. The north may be unready, but the south
could march and the north could move as soon as they can. In the
meanwhile Tasmôrden will not have Ileſínian."

"We have to move as planned. The eastern and northern barons
must come in . . ."

"No."

"No?" Cefwyn looked wryly astonished, not angry; but only then did Tristen recall that no one said no to Cefwyn these days.

"No, sir," he said doggedly, compounding the offense, such as it was, out of his friendship and the fact that for a month he had had no chance to give his views. "Move Ivanor in from the south, out of Amefel. That would save Ilefínian. It lies far closer to that border. Tasmôrden would *know* a force out of Amefel could come at his back at the river, and he would race to reach the capital to prevent us taking it. We could move faster, with only the light horse, out of his east. If he besieged the town, that would put him between two and even three forces if you brought in the heavy cavalry from the north and the Lanfarnessemen came in from the southwest."

He thought that Cefwyn would agree. The resolution seemed there for an instant, the fierce enthusiasm of the summer. But worry and doubt worked there, too, and he saw Cefwyn's deep unhappiness and disbelief in his own answer.

"We cannot."

"But if we had the Guelen cavalry and the Ivanim, moving quickly—before the snow—would the north object to winning the war, sir?"

"The south must not be the source for a move across the river."

"It only makes sense—"

"The south is tainted with sorcery, do you see?"

"Not since Lewen field—"

"In Guelen minds it is tainted with sorcery. Amefel is full of heretics—in Guelen minds. Her Grace must win based in the *east*. In the *east* of Elwynor are folk strongly kin to Guelessar and Murandys, Guelen in all but name, and even some Ryssandim. I know, I know you see the way clear, you do have a strong argument, and if it were all a soldier's reasoning, Tristen, I would entirely agree with you. It would save lives, and very precious ones, particularly of Her Grace's best advisers. But it is not a soldier's reckoning; it never was. It is a king's reckoning, and a new king's at that. I must come at this war from the north and east for the same reason I ask Efanor to make a staunch Quinaltine out of the least likely man in my kingdom. It is *appearances,* Tristen, all appearances. For very good reasons the *north* must win significant victories in this war. Then it will be their victory, not the south's, and because it is their victory, and their *northern* glory, they will support the agreements we make and help me forge a peace out of this long war. No. It is not all a soldierly reckoning. But it is the one that will have a peace at the end of it."

Not if Ilefínian falls first, Tristen thought to himself, seeing a walled city, a towered city as vividly as he saw it in his dreams. And for this instant he dreamed of it in hostile hands, and saw the war dragging on in what might *not* be easy victories for the Guelenfolk. He saw blood flowing, and knew that the satisfaction of the northern barons would wait into summer, and into greater and greater hazard.

"Does Her Grace agree with the plan?" he asked Cefwyn pointedly; and Cefwyn frowned darkly.

"No," Cefwyn said. "She does not agree. But the plain fact is, we simply must not seem to encourage the tainted south. The entire question regards Elwynor's fate, Elwynor's freedom, and the treaty. It's not a great war, it's a little war, and we must run the risk to give the north its importance."

He was entirely appalled. *The tainted south*, as of Cevulirn, and Sovrag, and Pelumer, even proper and rigidly Quinalt Umanon, who had stood with them at Lewenbrook? *The tainted south?* Cefwyn spoke in disparagement of others' opinions of it, he was sure of that. And, a little war? Men would die, and the longer they drew this out, the more men would die."

"The same as the penny," Cefwyn said, "the same as our agreement with the Quinalt. It *is* appearances. And, forgive me, I have to command and lead the northern barons in the field. Because of appearances, since the Aswydds, I have appointed no lord in Amefel and left the province vacant. I will elevate *none* of the Amefin earls to power on that southern border, because I will not have the entire south, with an Amefin duke, playing ducks and drakes with policy by urging their views, meddling with those bridges—or leading armies and forcing a fight. I have a viceroy there, and I keep it so. I will *not* have help from the south, above all else."

"Yet you had Cevulirn stay at court. Is he the tainted south?"

"Never! Never in my heart. I trust him. I do trust him. He knows the game. He knows what I have to contend with. As Idrys knows. As you are most surely learning. We cannot always do what is most soldierly. We have to do what is politic. And what is politic is a northern victory, and an advance through these specific villages that will settle *appearances* for the Guelenmen I lead; gods help me."

He was not done with questions. Too much was cast in doubt. "You trust Lanfarnesse. And Olmern."

"Lanfarnesse commits to nothing. Olmern . . . *far* too unsubtle."

Sovrag was only recently a lord, and indeed, would not be at home in the Guelen court. Sovrag had nearly caused a duel in his few days here, except the king had forbidden it. Lanfarnesse, old Duke Pelumer, would protect his own folk first, but even so, Pelumer would have been a strong support to Cefwyn, stronger by far than Murandys.

"No," Cefwyn said further. "Believe me in this. Hard enough that I swore all the south to me before I took the northern oaths, hard enough that I came back with a wedding sworn, sealed, and sure before the north ever had wind of it. And this last I say to you in secret, a thing that only Idrys knows . . . only Idrys. Once the wedding is done, once we have the Quinalt seal on that document, we shall indeed advance to the river and set up martial camps, not only on this side, following *exactly* the path you suggest, and threaten Tasmôrden before the snow lies deep."

"And shall we move in Amefel as well?"

"Not in Amefel. We'll have men under canvas in the snow, come what may, making sure of those eastern bridges, distracting Tasmôrden and his conspirators from Ilefínian."

Driving him inevitably toward Ilefínian, Tristen thought unhappily. Pushing him toward the south. Denying him the bridges made it sure he would go against Ilefínian. And if *only* someone were there to face him—

"—bitter work," Cefwyn said, "hardship for the men; but if we could bring the eastern provinces of Elwynor to welcome Her Grace next spring and rise against Tasmôrden, she might sweep unchecked across the east like a triumphal procession. *Then* we might cross from the south shore of the river, too, and come from two directions, up and down, to Ilefínian. It would fall in a moment."

"I might go to the Amefin shore when the army goes to the river," Tristen said. The prospect of winter in tents did not seem so impossible or so unpleasant to him as a winter idle in Guelemara, taking lessons from the Patriarch. He had longed for employment, for some reason for his existence, and still the notion of *next fall* wafted in front of him, the thinnest of promises. There were so many mistaken decisions in the wind, any one of which could rise up to bring disaster to Cefwyn's fortunes. Cefwyn said he must be here, and learn religion, and appear to be Quinalt—but if the army was, in fact, to move, he should be ready to move as soon as the wedding was done. The northern barons' vanity, their quarrels with each other thus far had not fielded an army, but rather kept the one they did have home until a wider bloodshed of Elwynim and Guelenfolk alike was all but inevitable. On his life he tried not to wish for things, and he distrusted his own desires, but he wished Cevulirn to the fore and Murandys in obscurity. "Far more gladly would I sit in a tent than in the Quinaltine, sir. If it were possible, this I would ask to do, myself, more than anything."

"No," Cefwyn said, though gently. "No. My good friend. There you may not, not now, not yet. We need no wizard-work on the river shore, I assure you, not at this stage of affairs. We *need* your agreement with the Quinaltine. Your peace with the Holy Father."

"Then when I have peace with the Quinaltine—*then* I could go down to Amefel. From the south I might cross the river with a small force this winter, a very small, a quiet band, and reach Ilefínian. The Patriarch will wish me gone. So let me go. Give me a single troop and I shall be no trouble to you." The plans, the very detailed plans, were clear to him. The gray space was gone, in favor of a vision so clear to him his heart beat high with thinking of it.

"No, no, and no." Cefwyn's hand descended on Tristen's wrist where it rested on the table. "You must have nothing to do with the taking of the capital, not a thing, do you see? It must not be by wizardry that Ninévrisë wins her throne. And that is what everyone would say if you did that on your own."

"I am not a wizard."

"No," Cefwyn said, and pressed his hand hard. "No, my brave, my good friend. No. But you are not the lord of Murandys, either, and the Guelen duke of Murandys and the Ryssandim must give Ninévrisë her throne. Then they will support her rights and make peace with her kingdom."

He perceived to his discontent that the reason of Cefwyn's fear was still the Quinalt, always the Quinalt, a fear which he had discovered prevailed over all better sense in Guelessar; the Quinalt, and the like of Sulriggan, whose work he had seen in Amefel. The Holy Father, Sulriggan, Prichwarrin of Murandys, Corswyndam of Ryssand, none of them were friends of his nor ever would be friends of the king. That was the worst harm the Quinalt did, maintaining Sulriggan and his kind in influence because it needed to have a threat in order to bargain with Cefwyn, whom otherwise it could not frighten. For two months it had had the wedding to threaten. Now Cefwyn asked him to defend Ninévrisë by turning its attention on himself, just long enough for the marriage to become a fact. In a soldierly way he understood such a diversion.

But would the Quinalt improve its actions once the wedding was over? Would it become Cefwyn's friend simply because Cefwyn flattered it? He thought not.

His situation and Cefwyn's had grown very tangled, but dearest to his heart, at least tonight he was again in the king's close counsel, and therefore and for the first time in weeks he saw hope, hope of the same sort that Cefwyn himself saw: only let there be a wedding, only let them have the agreement of the Quinalt, Cefwyn said; and now he thought the same. Let there be a wedding, and then he would have men and weapons and then he would make Cefwyn's kingdom safe.

And *then* there would be peace and safety and all Cefwyn's friends would be together for a thousand thousand such evenings. Dared he hope so? He had grown wiser, and dared trust less in the world.

"I shall send Efanor to you," Cefwyn said. "Tomorrow."

"I shall expect him," he said to Cefwyn.

"Was it a fine evening?" Uwen asked him as they walked back, Uwen with a moderate glow of ale about him. "Was it all to expectation?"

"Very fine," he said. "Very fine, thank you. Efanor will come tomorrow, to teach me the Quinalt's manners."

Uwen coughed, which he did not take for a cough at all.

"For Cefwyn's good," Tristen said. "Like Wys. Very like Wys. To please the northern lords and the Quinaltine." He thought that told Uwen enough.

"Well, mostly, aye, ye puts your head down at the right times and does as others do, and there ain't that much to it."

"Cefwyn gave me a purse of pennies to give. For the roof."

"Ah."

"I have two days. The court will go there, and I will go, all together. And you must tell me what to do."

"Oh, well, as to that understandin', don't ye fret, lad." Uwen alone could call him that, generally not until they walked clear of Lusin and the others, as they did now. And Uwen had seemed much reassured about his visiting the Quinalt when he heard it was the penny offering. "Say what the lords say an' do just what they do. 'At's the straight and simple of it." Then a frown. "—There ain't any small shadows like to come out, is there? No untoward appearances."

"No," Tristen said fervently. It was what Cefwyn had asked. "No." He was worried about the visit to the Quinaltine, but Cefwyn had directed him smoothly through the confusion and movements of the court before this, and he was the more reassured to know he was also under Emuin's advisement. If Idrys talked to master Emuin and neither of them found strong objection, he feared nothing in meeting with Efanor, at least. Efanor was tedious, but genuinely learned, and intelligent, and well-disposed, and he was indeed puzzled about the gods and the other manifestations the Quinalt here claimed to see, far more than in Amefel, along with miracles and some sort of magic. The priests never wanted to call it magic, and perhaps it was not: if spirits so potent as regularly came and went in the Quinaltine, he would have expected to notice them in the gray space. Above all if there were common appearances of gods within the Quinalt, not an arrow-cast from the walls wherein he lived, he thought Emuin would have warned him not to stray there.

Yet Emuin *had* forbidden him the gray space, so long as he was in Guelemara.

Emuin, however, had affected to take the priests all lightly . . . and Emuin *was* a priest, though not Quinalt, but Teranthine. He never saw Emuin pray and he never heard Emuin blessing this or that as Efanor did. He found it all very curious, and the prospect of gods both intrigued him and posed him questions. Dared he ask Efanor to show him a god, or to teach him how to find one?

But perhaps gods were furtive spirits and refused to visit where there were crowds. Some shadows were like that. Perhaps priests met gods only when they were alone and the lights were dim.

Perhaps gods were a special kind of shadow. If that was the case, then that might be the reason he always felt uneasy when he looked at the Quinaltine. He was curious about the priests, too, and wished to learn why they both tolerated shadows, which was dangerous, and feared wizards in general, who were not.

Idrys came back. Idrys had not gone far. "So?" Cefwyn said, when Idrys and he were without servants, in the private, the guarded, hall. "Out with it, crow."

"I?"

He flung a glance at a face that had no expressions, but two, the arched eyebrow and the rarer play of mirth. There was the one, but not the other, tonight, and had not been from the time he had spoken to Tristen. He had brought his wine with him. He drained the cup.

"You, crow, you *know*, you think, you *guess,* and you suppose. Wherewith? On what account? And do you dispute me?"

"Not I, m'lord, oh, no, not I."

"Out on it! You reek of disagreement. You breathe disagreement."

"I fear no manifestation of mice and demons in the shrine when he appears. I do look for opposition. To set the lord of Ynefel as the focus of the barons' discontent denies that they have weapons. And that he does."

He set the cup down hard and picked up the pitcher. He set down another cup beside it, he, the king, servant to them both. He filled both, and gave one to Idrys. "Stand down from your watch, crow, and unburden yourself. I saw you frowning through supper. Plague on you! Can you not be festive?"

"About the safety of my king? Rarely these days."

"And wherein am I threatened?"

"The mooncalf *is* the prophecy, my lord king. You cannot deny it. We all know it and Her Grace knows it. The Elwynim look for a King to Come. And you pretend there is no danger."

"Tristen is exactly right in his advice, you know. Plague on the northern barons. These dithering fools will cost us lives, they will cost my lady's men lives, and by the Five if an incursion out of Elwynor lands boats on Murandys' shore, I'll send troops to Prichwarrin's relief by way of Ivanor. Lord Maudyn sends me anguished letters. Damnation! Men will *die* because Lord Prichwarrin insists on delays and Lord Brysaulin mistakes my reports."

"If it was a mistake."

"Do you say it isn't?"

"I would never accuse the Lord Chancellor as to the reason he sent that report to Prichwarrin. It would hardly be politic. And I have become a politic man. I must be, else I will surely offend you."

"Politic." He drank a mouthful and found it flavorless, the result of too many cups before. He set the cup down, gently, this time. "Damn him."

"Damn Prichwarrin? Or the Lord Chancellor? Or Mauryl Gestaurien?"

"Leave Tristen out of this damning. He is not a political man."

"He is Sihhë," Idrys said, "he is Mauryl's heir, he is most indubitably Mauryl's parting gift to the house of the Marhanen and the house of Syrillas . . ."

"All these things we admit."

"And dare I say you have had my advice, but you follow master grayrobe's by preference. Now what will Your Majesty do?"

Win his love, Emuin had said, regarding the danger Tristen posed. Win his love.

"Now are we afraid?" Idrys asked. "Now do we wish we had done otherwise?"

"No, we do not!" He cast Idrys a scowling look. "Mauryl prevented harm to us once. And twice. Tristen is my friend. They are rare in this climate. Exceeding rare."

"Mauryl Gestaurien, Mauryl of Ynefel, Mauryl Kingsbane, Mauryl King*maker* . . ."

"Crow, what point are you making?"

"I wonder what point my king is making. You will win Her Grace her throne back. And then what? Twice on a week, boats will ply the Lenúalim to bring the king his bride, his bride the king . . ."

Idrys came very near the mark. Dangerously near. Cefwyn looked elsewhere, into the shadows, of a mind to forbid the topic, but wondering how much the man closest to him had assembled out of bits and pieces.

"Go on."

"Because she will not sit the throne?" Idrys ventured. "Because you *have* the Elwynim King to Come sworn and sealed to you in fealty?"

Things had such a dull sheen in Idrys' hands, sheen of gray iron, sheen of well-oiled metal, knives, and swords, and sharp-edged daggers. He could turn even friendship to base, cutting metal.

"The oath between us is fealty, not homage. I left him free. Ignorant that he was at the time, I left him free!"

"How ignorant is he now, more to the point, Majesty? How much does he fail to guess? And while we discuss the intricacies of Her Grace's oaths and pledges, promises and prayers . . . by what is Lord Tristen sworn, and how is he bound?"

"By friendship if nothing else!" He answered in haste, because he was stung; but it echoed of Emuin's advice. *Win his love. Win his love,* because nothing a king wielded would ever constrain him.

That which a wizard wielded . . . perhaps. Perhaps it could. But Emuin could not.

Idrys lifted his cup with a quizzical expression, a tilt of his head. "Forgive the northern barons a certain bewilderment: you are the king of Ylesuin, and do not agree that the throne of Elwynor is a Regency? And if a Regency, for what king? And if not for a Guelen king, for *which* king, pray? Has Your Majesty explained that point to Her Grace?"

"You tread now where you have no welcome."

"But he is your friend," Idrys said, "and so all things can be resolved."

"Yes, they can. They *can* and they will be."

"The barons of Ylesuin will not accept him as a leader on the field. It will create dissension. And the commons of Elwynor rally to Lady Ninévrisë? Some may. Some may not. How will you restrain Guelen soldiery from provocations? There will be bloody battle, my lord king, far bloodier than you wish to contemplate. There will be slaughter. You rely on the northern barons as you are determined to do, and look to it: there will be slaughter when Guelenmen march across those bridges. Do not delude yourself. There is no gentle war. Aye, yes, Tristen is right: come from the south, come from the south because you will have such allies, you will make such bargains, and you will do better to parade your allies in front of southern troops, not northern."

It was not the first time for that argument. Cefwyn still held to the other side, the one that sought to reconcile Murandys and Ryssand to the war, and not to split the kingdom in bitter division . . . as perhaps he could not avoid; but he tried to prevent it. Looking to the day of an allied Elwynor, he tried to avoid it.

"And if we have the north opposed, that slaughter will go on. There will be other provocations. There will be other chances for war. We can both foresee them. We must have war stopped, crow. We must fight a little war *across* the river to avoid a more grievous war here, among our own barons. We must have no more, no more fighting to give wizards a foothold in our lands. No more, crow."

"Then remember you sent your royal father advisement regarding the lord of Ynefel. Did you not, my lord, advise your father regarding him and the Elwynim prophecy? And if to your father, *then* to your father's intimates, *and* to Lord Brysaulin?"

Dire thought. Chilling thought. "Brysaulin is an honorable man."

"For the welfare of the realm . . . to what other guides would an honorable man resort with his king dead and the Prince consorting with wizards? My lord king will have to inform me. As we all know, I am from time to time uninformed on points of honor."

To the Quinalt, to Murandys, to Llymaryn, to *Efanor,* if Lord Brysaulin had ever relied on anyone. And Efanor had been choleric and convinced of perfidy in the days after their father's death.

"Remember that Lord Heryn Aswydd was the purveyor of truths to your royal father," Idrys said, "and I would not begin to imagine the fervid imagination of Heryn Aswydd."

"Or the scope of his lying tongue."

"Nor all imaginings. He had substance on which to practice, my lord king. And you yourself sent that message, which your father's natural suspicion would have taken for ten times less than Heryn's *loyal* truth."

"And thus my father relied on Heryn, and thus died. Add to it the work of wizards, the work of priests, which I count little different . . ."

"Oh, never say *that* in council."

"There are many truths I don't say in council, crow."

"And to me?"

He gave a bitter laugh. "Perhaps I have a secret. Perhaps not. If I answered that you'd know, would you not?"

"If I answered *that,* my lord king, I would serve my lord king less well than I do. Tristen of Ynefel is far too potent a wizard to loose in this war of petticoats and pennies. He cannot become Quinalt."

"Yet he must appear, *must appear* in public. The more he stays hidden the more rumors fly about him, and better him now than Her Grace. That . . . that, I cannot allow."

"It is a risk."

"All things are a risk, master crow. Let my brother practice persuasion on him. Let the Quinalt do its best. Efanor is not a fool . . . he if anyone knows what was said that provoked my father to ride to Amefel, into Heryn's trap, and all he will say to me is that Father distrusted me and Heryn fed the fire. Efanor himself *burns* to atone for believing it and for not dissuading our father; that compels him. He *is* faithful to me. Say that he's faithful, master crow."

"To my observation, he is."

Cefwyn let go a heavy breath. "There is no great love, now, in our brotherhood; but guilt, that we have, each of us, each for not loving the other, I suspect. He loves the notion of loving me. But Tristen *is* my brother. And that galls him. Is he jealous?"

"Jealousy is a sin, Your Majesty. And His Highness hates his sins, every time he does them."

"Someday I must make peace with him. Inform him. Inform him he will inform Tristen on the Quinalt, make a godly man of him . . ."

"A Man, you say."

"Close as he *may* do, damn your wit. Mine's fled." He set the cup down emptied, resisting the impulse to fling it at the wall. "Hates his sins, does he? So do I. So do I, crow. And my father's sins, how do I number them?"

"I left your father's service," Idrys said. "He no longer liked my reports regarding you. So I ceased to make them. It seemed a fair arrangement."

Uwen went off to his small nook to sleep and Tristen let his servants put him to bed, his very comfortable bed in an apartment far finer than he had had in Amefel, rooms on the highest level of the Guelesfort. The bedchamber had evening stars painted on the ceiling, and white clouds against a dark sky. The glow from the newly banked fire in the fireplace showed him just a little of that paintwork, a shadowy view sparked with the silver inlay of a star catching the firelight.

A sword stood sheathed beside the fireplace. He had had master Peygan forge him a blade after Lewenbrook. *Truth* was the symbol on one side of it; *Illusion* was written on the other. But it had gone unused in Guelessar. Now he asked himself where he might write *Appearances,* which had been Cefwyn's word tonight. He would become friendly to the Quinalt, for Appearances. He would join the barons, for Appearances. He would avoid magic, for Appearances.

The sword stood in the corner, in disuse. Other men practiced. Uwen practiced. He did not, hating the feeling that came on him when he took up the thing. It was another kind of Unfolding, a terrible one, sure of its power and uncaring.

To secure peace with Elwynor, to end the war that had existed through the reigns of Cefwyn's grandfather and father . . . dared he hope now that Mauryl's purpose for him extended that far? He would, in the spring, cross the river into Elwynor for Ninévrisë's sake, and there deal death with that sword, but he would not win, because it would offend the barons.

There was so much temptation to know, to reach back, and to bend his life backward, backward, backward, until it met itself on the Road.

And he knew the way back to that Road. He had found it today, on the hilltop. But it was a terrible way, fraught with dangers. He perceived that if he truly used it he risked his own existence. A young man sitting against a tree in Marna Wood perceived a terrible presence, like a shadow in the woods ... and he had been both young man and shadow. Dared he be a third presence? Dared he reach toward Ynefel again by that Road, to see whether it was still safe? The young man had seen nothing. The shadow had fought shadows, and Hasufin had ruled that Road.

He dared not venture that way again. His heart beat hard at the very thought.

Lying on his back, his hands on the fine, thick, comfortable bed-clothes, he reached out, instead, all forbidden, for Emuin, and found the two presences he knew well in the Guelesfort, one on the floor just below him: Ninévrisë was unaware of him, was thinking instead of Cefwyn, all warm and full of love. He skimmed away, and above him, aloft, up in the dark, found Emuin in his tower, Emuin, whom he trusted would answer him, call him a fool, tell him when he was right and wrong and whether he dared even contemplate gods.

—*Master Emuin.*

The old man was not quite startled, but disapproved his intrusion, a chill wind in the gray space that wavered and then paid attention.

—*Idrys will come tomorrow to ask you,* Tristen said. *Cefwyn says Efanor will tell me about the Quinalt if you approve, sir. I know you disapprove my venturing here, but Cefwyn says I must visit the Quinalt with the court in two days. He believes it's a question of appearances, and it will please the Patriarch. Dare I?*

—*It seems you have already agreed and I have little to do with it. The old man was still shadowy and faint to him, tattering in the pearl-gray winds of the place. Why? Why have you agreed to this?*

He could not lie in the world of Men with any great skill at all. Here, it was far more difficult. And he knew in his heart he had agreed. Because I want to be free, master Emuin. And because I think Cefwyn is in danger of these barons as much as of the rebels across the river.

—*Free. Free. What does that mean, free ... do you at all know? Free of what? Free from what? And what more could you do for Cefwyn than you have done?*

Hard questions. Fearsome questions. Free to help my friends. Free to defend Cefwyn. Free to ride through Wys village and have the children not take alarm. And what I might do stands in the

*corner yonder. By my own will I would never touch it. But I will,
for Cefwyn's sake, when I must. These men that press Cefwyn with
their wants, they are not his friends. Never were they mine, nor will
ever be. I could win Cevulirn, even Lord Pelumer. Never these men.*

*The gray space shadowed, showed clouds, rare detail, in this
place that teased the eye with no shapes at all.*

*—Beware of anger, Emuin said, and the clouds grew lighter.
Anger and folly walk arm in arm, young lord. Enough that Cefwyn
dallies with them, do not you join him.*

*—I shall meet with Efanor, by your leave, sir. Idrys is on his way
to ask you. He counseled caution. But Cefwyn said . . . Cefwyn
said if the Quinalt could shape a way for me to enter, it would
shape a place where all Elwynor could fit.*

*—Revising their doctrine to accommodate Mauryl's heir, is it?
And so master crow will consult me. A wonder in itself. Master
crow will consult. Most often things are already settled and have
grandchildren, before master crow consults. Gods save the king, I
say.*

*—Can they? Save the king, that is? What are the gods, sir? Are
they shadows?*

*—I'm sure I don't know. I leave that knotty matter to His
Highness. I leave him heaven and hell and all blessedness. I made
that choice for good and all when I took up wizardry again. And
what I gave up, the gods know that, too.*

—Is Efanor wise, sir?

—Ah, now you ask me.

—Shall I rely on him for truth, sir? He perceived master Emuin
retreating from him, growing more distant, and more distant again,
and he erased a little of that distance, enough to make himself heard
without shouting . . . erased a little of that distance, because he
could do such things here. He could do more than master Emuin in
this place, truth be told; but he knew his own ignorance, too. *I ask
your advice, master Emuin. I ask you plainly, are there gods, master Emuin? And are they as Efanor will tell me?*

—There is a greedy, conniving man in Murandys, the answer
came back to him, troubling, at the edge of sleep. *There is the love
of comforts in Llymaryn. There is a frightened man in the
Quinaltine. Those three things and those three men move half the
court. Ryssand's malice would be powerless without Murandys'
greed. As for gods, there may be. Go to sleep. Do what I cannot prevent you from doing.*

—Ought I not, sir? Ought I to do what Cefwyn wishes, and lie, as he wishes—or not?

—Ah, now the second true question. Now that it's far too late, the question none of us can answer. Go, do as you can do. If Idrys comes tomorrow to consult me, probably I shall agree. Cefwyn held you out of all questions and now he places you in the heart of them. That will have consequences, young lord, and predicting these things might change them. You will do as you will. Efanor seeks gods. Let Efanor beware lest he find one he does not expect.

Emuin was fading, and slid away from him. Perhaps, Tristen thought with a chill, priests or gods could hear them. But he had seen no one else in the gray space. That Ninévrisë was so close and he had not heard or seen her during his converse with Emuin meant they had been more subtle than her near and sleeping presence could detect. She was in a way their sentry, and never knew.

He lay in his bed, beneath the painted sky. A staff faithful to him was sleeping all around. Uwen was there, his day guards, too, asleep, while the night guards stood their posts. He felt the presence of a full score lives, knew their solid, mortal faithfulness to him, a precious attendance, and frail, and protecting all he was. He could fight battles and lead armies. But the simplest of his servants was wiser in the world than he, and understood, perhaps, the questions he would never answer.

In bestowing Ynefel on him and not on Emuin, who would have been the more reasoned choice, Cefwyn had cast far too much on his understanding, and it still was so scant. Emuin would say, always, *Judge for yourself, young sir.*

Or, *Gods know.*

Did they, indeed?

CHAPTER 5

Dry leaves wandered, amazingly so, and flew even over the walls of the Guelesfort, stark, stone precinct that it was, lodging in such unlikely places as against the little ledge of the study window where the disapproved pigeons gathered. Through the open side pane, Tristen plucked a leaf from its resting place, and fed breakfast crumbs to the birds that crowded up at the little window, careful to see they each had their share. They fluttered and they flapped. They were greedy birds, and could be unintentionally cruel to the weakest.

They had no respect of the Quinalt porch, or the Five Gods, and he tried to think what to do about it. The pigeons had no respect of him, either, not a bit. That was why he courted their presence, because for all their sudden fears and frights, they had no respect for him. They or their cousins had been at Ynefel and at Henas'amef, doing no worse than here. But the Quinalt's dignity was too frail for them, so now he must send them away, if he could find the means. He wished he knew how to tell them he was sorry. He would wish them home, if any had come from Ynefel. He would wish them a safe flight over Marna, and safe lodgings in the loft.

But would a boy bring them the stale bread, and sit in the loft and try to read?

Perhaps he still would. Or did. Or they would find their way to that place and those days. He was far from certain. He only wished them safety, and if he might draw a little of the light of the gray place out to touch them, and protect them—

"His Highness Prince Efanor," a servant darted near to say, and startled the pigeons into a cloud of cold, sunlight-silvered wings. Magic unraveled.

He had not expected Efanor so early in the day. Uwen had waked red-eyed and looking miserable this morning and at his behest had gone back to bed . . . rather too much of autumn ale last night, Uwen had said, greatly begging his pardon. Uwen would be chagrined when he knew their visitor had come and his guard still abed.

He had forewarned Tassand, his chief of household, that Efanor might come . . . he had not, however, imagined that Efanor would arrive on the clearing of breakfast from the table. He had not yet heard from Idrys . . . though Emuin had said he would say yes when Idrys asked. And had Cefwyn made a special point of telling Efanor *before* Idrys had roused master Emuin? Efanor was a great deal easier to set in motion than was master Emuin.

It was unkind to think so. But Cefwyn did have such ways. It went with being king, he supposed, and with being sometimes too clever for his own good.

So here was Efanor, early, and after a late evening when any man might be excused a certain sluggishness, Efanor's face shone with a daunting cheerfulness.

"Good morning to Your Highness," Tristen said.

"Good morning to you, Your Grace." Efanor had brought with him, Tristen saw, a small book, the contents of which he suspected. Efanor had given such a gift to Ninévrisë.

"If it please Your Highness," he said. Everyone observed formality, with Efanor, as if he were somehow fragile. "I'm sure there's tea, easily, and I think there might be cakes. The fireside is the most comfortable place. The red chair is the best one."

"I have a gift for you," Efanor said just before they settled, and presented him the tiny book, an exquisitely bound and jeweled little book with the Quinalt sigil worked in gold.

"This is beautiful," Tristen said with sincerity. He was very fond of books of all sorts, and it was one of the prettiest he had ever seen. The writing inside was that intricate sort priests favored, but which he had learned to read. "Thank you very much, Your Highness."

"A book of devotions," Efanor said. They sat down next the moderate warmth of the fire, Efanor in the red chair. "I hope Your Grace will consider them as more than a convenience of state. I know my royal brother's notions. He bids me show you the forms and he cautions me against confusing you, intending of course that I teach you nothing. But I will give you honest, earnest answers, Your Grace, if you wish the honest truth. I would be pleased to give you honest answers."

"I would be interested in the truth, sir, thank you." He felt awkward in the extreme, though he was relieved to know Cefwyn had been honest with Efanor. "What do the priests know about gods? That seems a place to begin."

"May I ask, . . . Your Grace." A clearing of the throat. "Tell me. To begin. —What do you yourself hold about the gods?"

"I wish to see one."

"One would hardly expect to see one, Your Grace. That is, ordinary men would hardly see them."

"Perhaps, however, I might." He had already resolved not to tell His Highness about the gray place. Emuin had always held that secret. So had everyone who could go there . . . unless praying sent one to some special place he failed to go.

Efanor's troubled countenance, however, said that he might have misspoken even this early in their dealing. "That you are Sihhë would be no advantage at all in seeing them, I fear."

"I may be Sihhë," he corrected Efanor gently. "I am almost certain and everyone says so, but there are other possibilities."

"As—"

"Galasieni, perhaps." He named Mauryl's lost people. "It's possible. Though I think Sihhë is more likely."

"Neither would make it easy for you to approach the gods. Nor the chance that you may be Barrakkêth, and an enchanted soul, a despiser of the gods."

"Perhaps," he said. It might be true. It was more likely than other origins. He himself concluded nothing, accepted no past name, and perhaps by that refusal made his own essence chancier in the world, more difficult to seize on. "But I am Tristen. Mauryl named me when he Called me, and I should not say differently, Your Highness. Knowing less than Mauryl knew, I should never change my name."

Efanor seemed more and more distressed. "Tristen, then. But magic is not your way to the gods. Believe me that it opposes your salvation."

Was there indeed a way to leap over his origins and seize on a life such as other men had? And were gods the way to live past the spring? Emuin had complained he had lost his salvation, taking up wizardry again. But he would not discuss Emuin's affairs, told to him in confidence, with Efanor. "And what would favor it?" he asked Efanor.

"Faith. Good deeds. Prayer. The gods' good grace and mercy."

None of that seemed difficult, or even daunting. "It hardly seems difficult. Except finding the gods."

"You cannot do it by wizardry."

"I understand so."

"Nor by magic."

"How, then?"

"Pray and listen. Pray and listen. One hears them in one's heart."

There at last was a hint. Magic needed the heart and the will and the inborn gift. "So one need not be *born* hearing them."

Efanor hesitated. "Men can learn. Whether their power could extend to a Sihhë, no one knows. I asked my priest what I should say to you, and he was entirely at a loss. A very learned man. A very fine scholar. But he knows nothing, nothing that he finds of help. There is a chance, a chance that His Holiness may receive a word, and find a blessing especially for the Warden of Ynefel, considering Your Grace's office and goodwill to the kingdom. There is no question of your being malevolent, none, sir. Even His Holiness admits your services to the realm, as indicating a type of divine calling."

"It was Mauryl who Called me."

Efanor seemed to think the matter over for some few moments.

"But the gods will all that's good," Efanor said finally. "Harm never comes from them. Magic can harm."

"Against the gods' will? Is magic more powerful?"

"For a time. Only for a time. The gods set all things right."

"Then the gods would have defeated Mauryl's enemy without Mauryl?"

"Perhaps not in a time convenient for us," Efanor said.

"But if they can prevent harm and will not to do that, then is that justice?"

Efanor stopped a second time, and now he was frowning. "The Brisin Heresy holds so. A wrong view. The gods cannot be unjust."

"But if so many died and the gods might prevent it—"

"Perhaps we should go to the book," Efanor said, in that way Emuin had with him, too, when he had persisted too long in a question. "Read the first devotion. Aloud. Let us begin on firmer ground."

He was slightly dubious, unsatisfied in his suspicion that, if the gods were greater than magic, then they might have prevented

Hasufin altogether, saved very many lives and set the kingdoms in the very peace they were seeking through war with Tasmôrden. But perhaps it was deeper than that. And on any account he was not willing to offend Efanor, who was here for his good, and for Cefwyn's. He was anxious about reading the book, as Efanor wished him to do: he feared Words far more than he feared knives on any ordinary day, but he opened the little book to its first page, and read: *"Blessed are the Five Gods by whom all the earth is blessed. Blessed is the man who hears their voice . . ."* So it *was* a voice, he thought. That was what he should be hearing. *"Blessed is the man who does their will . . ."* That made Blessed clearer. He read, and heard no god's voice, nor even Emuin's or Ninévrisë's, only the crackle of the fire. The text went on some little time regarding Blessedness, which seemed to bear on the gods and their approval, and probably on having the gods for allies. It seemed desirable, if the gods wanted safety for his friends, and if they could be trusted.

"Are the Teranthine gods the same?" he asked, interrupting his reading.

"Mostly," Efanor said. "Except the Teranthines believe in indulgence for sins. And allow"—Efanor hesitated and seemed to choose a word carefully—"master Emuin's curiosities. You might be Teranthine, easier. It has a much wider gate—Yet it seems you refuse it."

"Not refuse. Master Emuin has never offered to teach me."

"Read the devotionals. Practice the things I will show you, merely the forms, merely the show of respect. Read that each day. If you fail the Quinalt, there may be hope in the Teranthines. You could do worse than that for your soul. And pray the gods send you understanding."

"Read until the Words Unfold to me? Like that?"

"Gods forfend." Efanor knew about the Unfolding, if not the gray place. Whether a godly man ever experienced that Unfolding or not was a question. "It's not magic. Remember that. Use no conjury—I charge you, no conjury."

"But the Words will Unfold, all the same?" A wizard's book held dangers and knowledge. He had lost Mauryl, who had used to explain things to him, and since in large part lately he had lost Emuin, Unfolding had replaced those guides, an understanding that had arrived continually, sometimes with a chill and a fear and sometimes with delight, all paths down which he sometimes began to suspect Emuin himself could not follow. "Your Highness, with all my heart, I thank you for coming here."

"Love the gods," Efanor said. "Love those who made the earth and everything in it."

"Do they make the seasons and the forests?"

"The mountains and the sky, the rivers and the sunsets and all."

It had never occurred to him to wonder how the mountains and the forests came to be. He thought rather that the forests grew from acorns and such, and that mountains simply were. Nothing greater Unfolded, nothing in fact Unfolded at all, so perhaps he had found no key to it yet. It caught his curiosity but offered no answers.

But where *had* the world and the mountains come from?

Darkness gaped around that wondering. He saw looming ahead of his inquiry that Edge the gray place could make, the place toward which he had no wish at all to go. He all but dropped the book, and came back to himself with a skip of his heart, sweating, finding himself all too close to wizardry.

But Efanor had never stopped talking. Efanor rattled on about the gods' making of the world, and how the Five Gods had shaped the hills and made the rain come at their whim, pouring water down from the fountains of heaven.

Fountains of heaven, Tristen said to himself distressedly. Were there discrete sources of water aloft? None of that agreed with the gathering in the air that he felt as the rain and the clouds, on which he was sure Emuin could call at need: which he supposed that he could call on, too, though he had never tried. Everything Efanor said should have excited his heart; but none of what Efanor said now about making all the world perfect explained the weather or a forest in all its changes.

"If the world is perfect, why should there be seasons?" he asked before he thought.

"Because the gods will that there should be seasons," Efanor said.

"But if they made it perfect," he began, venturing just a step further, Efanor seeming so sure on that point; and Efanor interrupted him:

"Perfect in its changes."

That was indeed like Mauryl when he asked too much, not to hear the question.

Why should there be seasons? he still asked himself. What good were they? But nothing leapt into his imagination. Nothing even came to him with the unsettling surety that Mauryl's enemy had had for him. Nothing at all Unfolded to him except the sole, troubling idea that the world had had a beginning.

Of course it might reasonably have had a beginning. *He* had had a beginning, at some time. He had had *two* beginnings, if he counted a birth he believed lay somewhere between Mauryl's own origin and a second wakening at Mauryl's fireside.

He wished he dared ask Efanor whether shadows had been part of the world when the gods made it, or whether they had come later; or whether the gods themselves were a form of shadow. Sometimes the dead were.

But Efanor urged him to go on to the second devotion in the book. He trusted Efanor, and with none of his questions answered he began to read.

"The works of Men are evil in their inception. The works of the gods are blessed. Lean not to the counsel of Men but to the word of the gods . . ."

Some men maintained he was not a Man, so leaning elsewhere might be to his good. He had never truly considered Men to be Evil, however. He had generally avoided considering Evil at all, even the shadows. They were not evil. Some were even kind. One was a little girl who played skip in the grass near Althalen. Could that be evil?

Then all at once the word Evil tried to Unfold, spread itself in such darkness he flung away, stood on his feet and faced the slanting pale sunlight of the window some distance removed from them, trembling. The fireside flung warmth at his back in a chill otherwise all-encompassing.

"Your Grace?" Efanor's voice came faintly from behind him. "Lord Warden? Gods bless, evil avert. The good gods bless and preserve us from evil and all its works . . . are you having a taking, Your Grace? Should I call your servants? —Should I send for Emuin?"

He had frightened Efanor. He was sorry. As for him, he was able to see the floor now, and mark a place beneath the chairs, in the stark sunlight, where the servants had not been attentive in their dusting. He was able to see the minute imperfections that clouded the window glass, and made ridges on the surface that caught the light differently; he could see the bubbles within that the glass, that, if one looked at them very, very closely, seemed to reflect everything around them . . . but he had never been sure that there was not something living inside, as harm or hope could lurk in imperfections of a wizard's construction.

All these things. The carved back of a chair, with each imprecision of a carver's art, the small ripples against the grain where the intent had clearly been a smooth line, but the natural wood had thwarted it: he had watched carvers at work, how the sweet, pungent curls of wood flew so thick and fast it was a wonder, and the smell was heady as wine. An oak grew in the forest, keeping its inner heart secret, for very many years; and a man thought of a horse as he carved and that horse in a man's mind added itself to the secrets of the oak's heart and made something that was neither horse nor oak. In such a way the world of Men grew. His fingers traced the carver's work, and his own skin was a miracle of subtle color, the working of bone and sinew was a miracle as his hand found the imperfections in the representation . . . itself a sort of spell.

"Lord Warden?"

Dared a man force an oak into such a pattern?

Dared a wizard force a soul into a new shape? Or, direr question, *could* one do it?

And was it a horse in essence, shaped by man, or was it an oak? Was it a Man's thought of a horse, potent with freedom, rendered substantial, or was it in its true, its wizardous essence, still a tree, responsive to all that a tree was, aged and steady and deep? When one enchanted such a thing, to which did the wizard appeal?

He trembled, in that thought. What had Mauryl wrought, in him . . . what had Mauryl changed, and not changed? Yes, men said he was Barrakkêth, first of the Sihhë-lords, who had warred against Men and had no mercy. So Hasufin had said, too, and even Mauryl had called him flawed. But, following Mauryl's example, *he* said that he was Tristen, and that the sum of him was changed, whatever the grain of the wood from which Mauryl had wrought.

"Lord Warden." Efanor had risen and stood beside him, and pressed some small object into his hand.

He lifted it, saw his own flesh and the Quinaltine emblem alike pale with the morning sunlight or with the burning intensity of his seeing. The medallion was a disk about the size of a large coin and wrought into it was a lump of glass with something curious and dark inside.

"It doesn't burn you, thank the gods. Keep that with you." Efanor made his fingers close on it. "Put it about your neck, in the gods' good name, and let all men see it. Gods forfend you fall in such a fit in the Quinaltine. You have had none of your falling fits for months. Gods save us from the hour."

"I had a Teranthine medal," he said faintly, for it was true. "I still have it, forged to my sword, now, when master Peygan remade it. Cefwyn gave it to me. I value it extremely."

"Keep it. Add this to its blessing and wear it day and night. Gods save us, put it over your head, so—if one protection serves, two may be stronger, in the gods' name . . ."

Efanor's speech had grown distracted, fervid, and frightening to him as he slipped the chain over his head, settled it beneath his hair and outside the small folded ruff of his shirt which rose above the doublet. The medallion rested on his chest, doing him no harm, but no good either, as far as he could tell.

He realized then that it was made of silver, and doubtless precious in some eyes; but silver had magical meaning as well. In Efanor's goodwill, he was given two gifts now, a book and a piece of silver, and it struck him that such gifts were exactly such as Mauryl had once given him. Was it like the horse, and the oak, and did the semblance of Mauryl's gifts to him create a bond of another kind, himself magically allied with Efanor? Yet he already had the silver near his heart before that thought had come to him.

"You must wear this in full view," Efanor said, "when you go into the Quinaltine. Show everyone you can wear it. But *dare* you go into the Quinaltine when the candles are lit and the gods are invoked? You were at the oath-taking. Were you there throughout?"

"Yes, sir. I was." He had found the place oppressive and had slipped back to the door, behind the columns, that day. But in the intent of Efanor's question he had been there.

Efanor looked at him closely as if he were estimating his strength, or his character, or both, and with fear in his eyes. "I value that medal greatly," Efanor said in the hush of their small area near the window. "And you would not mistreat it, nor use *it* in any magic, would you? I pray you not, whatever you wrought with the sword."

"No, sir. I would never, if you ask it. Or I will give it back if you had rather." He made to take it off and almost succeeded in returning the gift; but Efanor's hand closed on his urgently.

"You have far more need of it. Wear it. Read the book daily. Think on the gods morning and evening. Pray for their help. There may be hope for you. I know there is good in you." Efanor found it necessary then to amend it: "I *believe* there is good in you, lord of Ynefel; I wish with all my heart to believe it."

"That is a kindness I shall remember." Efanor, fearful, anxious, muttering entreaties to the gods he revered, had pressed on with a courage far surpassing the people of Wys, with great goodwill, even concern for his welfare and Cefwyn's. And for that he wished the greatest good to Efanor, and counted him at least among those he loved, or wished to love, if so much fear did not stand between them. For Cefwyn's sake he would put up the appearance Cefwyn asked for, he would do what Men did and attend the Quinalt, as resolutely and with as little joy as he would brave a battle line. But for Efanor's sake he would venture the little book that claimed Men were evil, and he would see if there were answers in it, or if there was a hope of his making peace with the Quinalt once and for all.

"Please, sit down. Take a cup of tea, sir. If you would. Explain the manners I have to use."

With evident relief Efanor began to expound the gods' authority. They were deep into the question of the moon and the stars when Uwen came out of his room, distressed.

"So what *are* the stars?" he had just asked, and Efanor had seemed not to know the answer. But Efanor leapt up, seeming to take the interruption for a rescue from what he feared was too difficult a question.

"Uwen Lewen's-son," Efanor said. "You'll be near His Grace in services, —at least nearby."

"Aye, Your Highness."

"Good," Efanor said. "Very good. Pray Your Grace keep the amulet close, and think on it, and read and study, and if Your Grace does have more questions I very earnestly urge, no, I *command* Your Grace come to me, and not ask others." This, with a look toward Uwen. "Of the gods' mercy ask no one else. I cannot guess the damage."

"I thank you," Tristen said. "I thank Your Highness, very much."

"Accept the gods' guidance," Efanor said, half under his breath, seeking to leave. "The gods' will. The gods' will, in all things. Gods attend."

Perhaps it was his asking about the stars. Perhaps Efanor had business he had to attend. But in that state of glum anxiousness Efanor left, Tassand and the servants standing by in respect of their royal visitor. Tassand still looked worried as he fussed the empty tea service away.

Uwen, too, was distressed. "I wisht I'd known His Highness had come in. I wouldn't have slept for the world."

"Emuin approved it."

"Did he, m'lord?"

"He knew, at least. I don't think he entirely approved. But he saw no harm in it."

"All the same, m'lord, ye should take a great care what ye say wi' His Highness, who trusts priests an' talks to his, every night. Ye might scare a man wi' your questions. Ye truly might, not intending it. And I think ye may ha' done it."

"I know," Tristen said in a low voice, and showed him the little book, scarcely the size of his hand, and the medallion. "He said this would keep me safe and I must read the book. Do you think so? Dare I?"

"M'lord, I don't know what ye dare."

"Is it wrong for me to have?"

"I don't know any harm to Your Grace's having it," Uwen said slowly. "But that's a relic he give ye. That's a holy thing. The Quinalt fathers is a flighty lot."

"They fear me."

"That they do."

"*You* pray to the gods. Do they hear you?"

"I pray to the gods, on holidays. On a battlefield. Truth be known, that's the way of most men."

He knew that answer. He wanted more. "And do the gods talk to you, Uwen?"

Uwen laughed, of gentle startlement, Tristen thought. And shrugged. "No, m'lord, nor does I look to hear 'em."

"Do you think priests hear?"

"I leave priests entirely to their business. And rightly you should, m'lord. The gods speakin', m'lord, it's just a way of sayin' folk get notions in their heads and it seems like they come from somewheres beyond 'em."

"Wizards cause that. The notion to leave a latch undone, a moment of forgetfulness . . . that is wizardry."

"So ye warned me, m'lord. And so I take great care, and keep strongly to my habits. But that's what folk say is the gods speakin', too. And for the gods' sake don't ask a priest, m'lord. Never ask a priest."

"I thought all along praying might be like going to the gray place."

"Gods save us, lad, ye didn't tell about that."

"No. I didn't. Not to anyone but you, who can't go there. I thought priests might have a place, too. I've never met a priest there, except Emuin, who's not to count—yet they seem to try very hard to go there. Efanor tries. I felt it once and twice, and yet I never saw him there, not truly, so I thought there might be some other place. But I dared not ask him. And Emuin never will answer me. He simply will not say."

Uwen made that sign again. He knew he baffled Uwen, and worried him, and sometimes made him go off and think for a while without saying a word.

"Well, you was right to keep quiet about it wi' His Highness," Uwen said. "And I'd go on keeping quiet about it wi' His Majesty, though I don't think ye'd daunt *him* at all. I just think His Majesty's happier sayin' he don't rightly know what ye do when ye just stand here starin'. If His Holiness asks, so to say."

"Or what *do* they think?"

Uwen thought about that. "They ain't never mentioned it that I ever heard, nor could I ask a priest, so I wouldn't know. Master Emuin might know, but I don't. *Is* there harm in the gray place?"

"Yes. But I would never let harm come out of that place, Uwen. I would never let it near you, or Cefwyn, nor even Lord Prichwarrin, who has never done me good at all. The harm isn't always there. It isn't there now, but it might come, and it might come seeking me, my friends and all that help me. But believe I will not allow it. I shall never allow it, Uwen. And there is no harm that I do by any magic there, except against the harm that comes at me, and that I fight with all my strength. There is all the truth about the gray place."

"M'lord, I have no doubt. An' if I could go to that wizard-place there and stand by ye, I would."

"You do. You do, Uwen, simply by being by me, and with me. You lend me strength. As Cefwyn does. As Emuin does—Most of all you make me wise."

"Oh, I hope wiser 'n that, m'lord! But what I think, it's a good thing there's you and master Emuin to see what they're up to in that magic place, since it don't seem a lot of the things there is ever up to good to us common folk. —But for gods' sake don't ever be hinting about that place to His Highness. Not ever. Ye was very wise not to say so. And I'd think twice and three times afore I said a careless word to him on deep matters no matter he's a good man. There's that priest o' his giving His Highness advice."

"I shall be very careful," he promised Uwen, hoping that he had been as careful as he thought. "On penny day I shall be particularly careful. Though it doesn't seem difficult, what they wish me to do."

"Babes do it," Uwen said. "Ye get blessed, ye walks by the altar, ye drops the penny, ye bows to His Holiness, ye get blessed again . . . ye walks down the middle aisle to the doors and out again. The king goes first, and ye stands near him and then the whole lot walks back to the Guelesfort, that's all ye do. Ye're supposed to be prayin' the day long, but the most don't. Mostly folk drinks too much and eats too much and they dance at the harvest fire till it's down to ashes and the drums and the pipers is too tired to go on."

"The children in Wys fear me less now. Though after all this long they still run."

"Youngsters always run. They're a silly, giddy lot, like sheep. Same wi' townsfolk. They ain't no wiser 'n Wys. But best ye stay indoors. There's too much ale flowing at the feast. There's some as might be fools, and then ye'd have to turn 'em to toads and that'd do fair for it all."

Uwen was joking with him. He was glad Uwen would. He treasured it above any silver or gold. "I think you're right," he said.

CHAPTER 6

T he doors of houses and shops
had been hung with wreaths of barley-straw for days. Now straw
wreaths bedecked the ironbound oak of the Guelesfort gates, and
straw covered the cobbles ahead of the court procession. The whole
court walked this pathway, the king and the Regent foremost, and
then Prince Efanor, Duke of Guelessar. After him came Lord
Brysaulin, the Lord Chancellor, all the lords in their precedence, and
attending each, their ladies and their families and their sworn men.
The King's Guard formed an aisle on either hand along the short
distance from the gate to the Quinaltine precinct, and beyond them
common people stood to watch.

But other common folk beyond the barrier of guardsmen bore
unlikely burdens toward the square. A man had a basket of sticks on
his shoulder, another a broken wheel—for the bonfire, Tristen
guessed, townsfolk bringing wood, straw, all manner of fuel for the
great fire that was laid and ready for the public celebration across
the open square from the Quinaltine steps. The pile of wood must
be very high by now—and indeed, when the line wended within
sight of the square, in their view past the line of the Guard, the pile
had doubled its size from yesterday. It towered in front of the
Quinalt, a bonfire to burn up all the year's scrap and chaff and prepare for Wintertide, besides taking away sins and bad memories.

So Uwen had said last night at supper . . . that the common folk
wished for luck by building it. They wished to burn up all the bad
memories and keep only the good. He meditated on that as they

walked in the procession, himself in his black-and-silver holiday finery and Uwen in his finest black velvet, a lord's man, and entitled to walk and stand among the highest in the land.

But within the courtly precedences, the fortresshold of Ynefel and the ruins of the old capital ranked—so they argued—last in the procession of the lords, behind the position that Amefel, least of the provinces of Ylesuin, would have held, had it had a lord to walk in the ceremony at all. But the order of their proceedings did not admit him as a king's officer, though he suspected that best described the office of Lord Warden of Ynefel, a defender of the marches, a power without a province.

They could not rank him, as Ynefel, *before* the duke of Murandys; they could not rank him before any of the northern barons without ruffling their feathers; and certainly they could not admit any importance to a wizard's tower.

But as it happened, once the column formed, Tristen found himself not utterly hindmost. Behind him came the banner-bearers of the notables of the town, the great silken billow of the red banner of the town of Guelemara, with its golden Castle. In front of him and Uwen, his banner, flew the silver Star and Tower of Althalen, and the Sihhë Star of Ynefel, remade.

The two who bore his colors now were veteran soldiers, not Lusin or his ordinary lent guards, as he had expected, but two men Lord Cevulirn had sent, Ivanim who were eager to please their duke, and, Tristen suspected, who were also glad to bear a banner for the pride of the south (scarce here) and pointedly for the honor of the field at Lewenbrook, where *northerners* had been very scarce.

Sulriggan's banner was here, however, the green banner of Llymaryn preceding his nephew Edwyn, farther forward in the honors . . . Tristen was not so wise in the affairs of the north or the delicate points of their protocols, but he did notice that precedence, and knew that it did not please Cevulirn, nor Cefwyn, and probably did not please the middle provinces, the apple regions, as the soldiers called them.

He had learned the banners: Guelessar, quartered, the Marhanen Dragon on a red field, alternate with the bright gold Quinalt sigil on black; Elwynor: a Tower, black-and-white Checker with gold and blue; Murandys, blue field, bend or, with white below and the Quinalt sigil, or; Llymaryn, green, the Red Rose of that house: it had been a red rose crowned if Llymaryn's grandfather had found early followers in greater number than the Marhanen—and there had actually been a crown above the Rose, a crown which had discreetly disappeared as Lanfarnesse and Murandys and other troops had all sworn to Selwyn Marhanen of Guelessar.

There was the gold Sheaf with bend and crescent of Marisal, and the blue field and blazing Sun of Marisyn; there was the blood red of Ryssand with the Fist and Sword; the pale azure of Nelefreíssan with its White Circle . . . besides Isin and Ursamin, Teymeryn, Carys, Panys, Sumas, and Osenan, a bright forest of banners. And after obscure Osenan, Cevulirn's banner, the White Horse of Ivanor, the only southern banner except the two black banners of Ynefel and Althalen, Althalen no longer royal, but merely a district in Amefel.

Trumpets blared as they ascended the steps toward the Quinaltine. There was a general, astonished pointing toward the black Sihhë banner; onlookers along the way made signs against harm such as the villagers had once fervently made in Wys-on-Cressit.

The bells rang as Cefwyn and Ninévrisë mounted the steps and entered the shrine, Cefwyn in slight precedence. The lords with their banner-bearers trooped up between the opposing lines of the King's Guard and the Prince's Guard, standing on the steps, soldiers in bright Marhanen red against the upright barley sheaves and other gold and brown signs of autumn and harvest. The banners, too, following the lords, filed inside. The banner-bearers set themselves about the columned sides of the central shrine as Tristen followed the other lords through the solemn, oaken doors.

The way for the lords and their captains to walk was straight ahead, and he followed behind Cevulirn, down the main aisle of the high shrine, with the banners sweeping as a bright wall on either side. A clerestory was above, and sunlight shafted down into this smoky region of incense-burners, lamps and candles.

Uwen took his place, standing among the benches of the captains. Tristen walked on as he was obliged to do, still behind Lord Cevulirn, in a stifling cloud of incense; and as Cevulirn went aside into a row of the assembly, he followed, last on the row, nearest the aisle. Everyone remained standing. There were only two rows in front of him; and past Panys and Nelefreíssan he could see the front of the shrine. The table centermost at the head of the aisle had candles on tiers among gold plates and vessels. Altar was the Word. And on either hand and around the rim, it was decorated with oak boughs. Plates stood heaped with acorns and apples, with nuts and grain scattered about the table covering, singly and in piles.

The Patriarch arrived from the side of the place with a light sound of bells, and flung water at either point of the altar, using a silver spoon and a small vessel. The actions in a single stroke assumed a kind of sense, that all the doings here involved less the gods than the Lines on the earth.

Uwen had said there would be no magic. But the sprinkling of water was magical. The establishment of the line was magical. The altar was a *focus* of this effort. The Patriarch walked back and forth in his occupation, laying down a Line, quite clearly walking the principal Line in the area, if one looked at it.

But the Patriarch was not walking them as one did who meant those lines to hold fast against shadows. There were four, five, six previous established Lines, all askew from what the Patriarch was building; he could see them clearly now that the Patriarch had brought the principal one to life. They all showed in different degrees, and Tristen stood beside Cevulirn, his hands clenched on each other and his lips firmly shut against the wish to protest this folly. Immediately in front of him was the lord of Panys, and in the first row Cefwyn stood, all the court, and the captains and officers of the court, silent, respectful of this place, this very strange action.

The priests carried in a smoking brazier, and they cast in incense that rose up in stinging clouds. Tristen fought a sneeze into abeyance; some lord did sneeze, ahead of him, a shocking disturbance of a silence that rang in discord off the columns and the roof.

The Patriarch was still walking back and forth, laying down his new line athwart the old, and not in the least regarding the domain of shadows beneath the place, whether intentionally or accidentally. Immediately beside the altar the discontinuity was worst: a gateway for shadows, if one cared to make sense of the jagged overlay of lines, and Tristen averted his eyes and his perceptions, resolved not to look in this world or the other at the moment. Shadows were there, jostling one another . . . perhaps Selwyn Marhanen, for all he knew; he was one who might press to the fore; but Tristen made no inquiry of them. Whether all shadows had been alive at one time, he had never known nor wished to wonder at this moment. He refused to look, but he refused to shut his eyes, either, although they stung with incense. He listened to the Patriarch recounting the year's doings, how Ynefel had fallen, and wickedness had broken out in Elwynor—the Patriarch could hardly fault Ninévrisë for that, since the wickedness named meant the rebels; but one could easily mistake it. His Holiness spoke on about the great shadow, about

Lewenbrook and the struggle against darkness, and heard him explain to all the lords how there were great events afoot. They were stirring words about bravery and righteousness and doing the gods' will.

But do you not see the shadows? Tristen wondered distractedly. Do none of you see?

The Patriarch talked about prosperity, and good harvests, and how it was clear that Ylesuin was favored by the gods above all other lands, and how the gods had only revealed their truths to the people of Ylesuin, who bore their special blessing and therefore had a special responsibility to continue those blessings by showing a giving and humble spirit. His Holiness said that as long as gifts flowed freely and abundantly to the Quinalt and as long as the people celebrated the harvest in godly ways, shunning drunkenness and licentiousness—that was a Word that stirred disturbing images—and shunned the offer of power which did not come from the gods, they would prosper.

And what of Ninévrisë? What of Elwynor's prosperity? Tristen asked himself.

And do offers of power come from the gods? he wondered. He certainly knew one offer which had not, when Hasufin Heltain had come out of the dark and led Lord Aséyneddin of Elwynor astray. Hasufin had tried to lead Mauryl himself astray, but had failed at that. Was this a god? Or a shadow?

That was a disturbing question.

Shun reckless behavior, His Holiness said. Seek godliness. Be prudent and sober.

It was enlightening, meanwhile, to hear the Holy Father talk about prosperity and victory in war . . . but everything the man said would have been far more convincing, Tristen thought, if he had had the least confidence the man knew that the other great Lines under the gods' abode even existed. His Holiness talked about seeking wisdom. But meanwhile he kept walking on that single line, one that was quite unnervingly askew with the Line on the earth that a long-ago Mason had laid down true to the earth. But His Holiness went on declaring that new line sacred by his actions, his incense, and his pure water, his intentions and his assertion of presence, and most of all by its single, blue-shining disharmony with the land and the hill.

The shadows grew increasingly uneasy in this venture of Men above them, uneasy and restless, and Tristen restrained his anxiousness as the gray place increasingly, urgently cried for his attention. The air seethed with motion just at the corners of his eyes whenever he would dart a glance at the other lords or at Cefwyn and Ninévrisë. He was less and less sure it was safe for him in particular and in this place to be making wishes he did not understand, even wishes for the king's welfare and the safety of Ylesuin, and even at the Patriarch's behest, all the while he could not make sense of what the Patriarch was doing with his incantations. All the actions on this mistaken line, if mistaken it was, seemed to weaken, not strengthen the Lines that held back the shadows, which had begun to seep out along the glowing reds and roses and faded blues of the lesser lines, to seek along them and grow confused and baffled.

It seemed to him suddenly then that he understood what he was seeing: that Masons had laid out the lines of the Quinaltine and walked the Great Line where the walls would stand, and protected the places where doors and windows should be, and if those had been the only Lines that had ever existed here, all would have been well and safe and the shadows would have flowed along them and obeyed those doors and windows. But those latter-day Masons had for some reason laid their Lines over something that had used to stand there, some prior work of a master Mason that could not be removed, or at least had never been properly removed or reshaped. And those second Masons had done it not merely once, but many times, or falteringly. In his small experience of places on the earth he had met nothing like it; but to his understanding, it was almost certainly the source of the difficulty he had always felt with this building. The Lines on the earth were confused by the builders of the place, further confused by His Holiness, who had not the least idea what he was doing. The Guelesfort was always what it had been, so far as had ever impressed him; but the Quinaltine had had another, older beginning, and no one, no one, since its other beginning, had ever set it right.

More, years of priests kept attempting to establish yet another set of Lines by their observances, across a division in the building that had been a door, on one level, and yet had been a wall another time, and then yet a third time a wall, with doors and windows in that earliest age. Openings overlay walls all about this great hall. What should have let shadows flow entrapped them, and immured them, and created pockets of distressed souls that seethed and struggled behind the banners, behind the acorn-baskets of the table, especially where two of the previous efforts had made an unintended doorway.

He no longer saw the candlelit stone or the incense; he saw streaks of blue light, and shadows milling there in increasing violence, a darkness in motion, wailing, attempting to flow along the new, misaimed line the priest established, a line that failed to meet the ward of the vanished door on one side and that had only the slightest of barriers established there.

Foolish, he thought. So foolish. There was power here, although nothing acute, and it was no help at all to be walking back and forth, back and forth as the Patriarch was doing, with a very weak force, luring the shadows to one side and the other like hounds following a tidbit, leading them to desire their freedom and then, with a turn, frustrating them.

Perhaps the torment of the shadows had to do with the gods, who were supposed to be five in number, and somehow bright, as shadows were not—the very antithesis of shadows, as he understood from Efanor's earnest but vague instruction; and he wished he had had the chance to ask Emuin, who had evaded him by having his door latched, which might have meant he was asleep, or might not. Emuin disapproved in general and yet refused him the excuse that might have prevented his instruction; Emuin disapproved the penny, too, he feared, or so he gathered out of that surly silence. Go ahead, Emuin seemed to be saying by this odd behavior: I disapprove in the extreme, but neither will I counterpose my will to your curiosity or Cefwyn's insistence.

Emuin must have known about the Lines. Emuin spoke about gods, and salvation, and Emuin must have known about the Lines. Could both things be true, this blind show, and could the gods still exist?

Back and forth, back and forth paced the Holy Father in what Tristen knew now was folly. But he judged the temper of the Lines and their jagged traps and knew that, frustrated as they were, and angry, the shadows were far from breaking loose. Most of them were weak, and had no power to do real harm even if they did break free . . . certainly none could do so by daylight, when they had less power. It was the sheer mass of their accumulated anger that was daunting, and it vexed him that Cefwyn stood unseeing in front of this thing. Whether Ninévrisë, who was able to enter the gray place, might be aware or not . . . he doubted it. But his mere thought leapt suddenly to her thoughts: he felt her confusion and the oppression of the shadows around them, and was *aware* of her presence as a point of light amid the demishadows of others.

He felt another presence, too.

It was behind him. He felt three or four, enlivened points of light. Not shadows, but wizard-fire, the sort that ordinary men never saw, and fear leapt up in him so high that he clutched the rail in front of him. He was almost aware of Cevulirn . . . he had never known there was wizard-talent in Cevulirn. Not even Lewenbrook had provoked it. And in being aware of that very dimmest fire, he saw Ninévrisë like a blue-white star—and Efanor with ever so faint a spark. He was aware of Emuin, high aloft and some distance removed; and of six or seven very dim presences out among the guards, or the people, and one among the banner-bearers along the sides, also in the shrine.

What was it? he asked himself. Could he have failed to see what glowed softly in Cevulirn, or had the danger at Lewenbrook, so strong, so thunderously dark, blinded him? Or had the Patriarch's folly encouraged the faintest sparks in two in particular he knew were not the Patriarch's followers? Was it a defense their hearts raised? And if that was so, how must *he* seem, to anyone with eyes to see him in the gray space?

You *burn,* Emuin had told him once.

He was trembling as the Patriarch finished and took up the box that he hoped would hold the pennies and give them their escape. The Patriarch lifted it on high, then held it before him. The singing of women rose high and full, echoing around the hall. The sunlight speared through a heavy pall of incense, and oh, at last! the ceremony was ending. First Cefwyn, then Efanor, then Ninévrisë filed past and dropped a coin into the box as the lines of the assembled nobility began the recessional. Lord Brysaulin passed and dropped in his penny as the row emptied and Cefwyn led the procession out to the fanfare of trumpets. The Dragon banner of Ylesuin swept in from the side, the Prince's personal standard, the black-and-white Checker and Tower of the Regency in Elwynor and the standard of Guelessar moved close upon them, the various king's officers yet to come, and then the barons. The second rank of nobles joined the file past the Holy Father and now the column went out the door.

Then the next row was moving, last but his. How should he find Uwen? It seemed in this arrangement that the lords' captains had to follow as best they could; and he feared making a mistake and calling attention to himself, or breaking one of those weak patterns. He was far from sure the Holy Father would know it if he nudged something magical by mischance, but certainly if it had been intentional wizard-work, a misstep would draw attention.

Cevulirn was moving now, so it was time for him. He drew a deep, anxious breath, wished nothing ill to happen . . . but Emuin had warned him to wish very little. He thought very hard of being as harmless as he could be and of burning very, very dimly in the gray space as he followed Cevulirn: he wished to show no more fire than Cevulirn himself, and wished to do no more harm than Cevulirn did. He had the penny, the metal warm in his hand. He followed Cevulirn's example and dropped his gift into the slot, not looking into the Patriarch's face as he let it fall. It hit others inside with a metallic sound, and he turned away, seeing the bright sunlight of the high arched doors as refuge toward which he walked.

He followed Cevulirn's gray cloak out toward what had become dimmed sunlight, with the smoke overhead a haze above the door, a stinging haze stirred by the passage of the great banners. The White Horse of Ivanor swept in from the side. His own banners flowed in before him, a black transparent veil against the daylight in the doors, and preceded him as he walked out and down the steps. He was glad to breathe the clear, cold wind, glad to be away from the shadows seething at his back.

The smell clung to him. He walked still behind Cevulirn, saw Idrys shadowing Cefwyn, now, ahead of him. There was Gwywyn, captain of the Prince's Guard, with Efanor. Then the captain of the Guelesfort, and then Lord Maudyn, commander of the forces on the riverside, and all the captains, and then the barons and their captains, and then the minor nobility of the town of Guelemara itself, all spreading out on the steps and below them. The guard captains overtook their lords, and the groups formed again, separate in colors, but not in so much sunlight as when they had gone in: clouds had swept in above the square, rendering them all shadowless, breaking down those ordinary barriers of daylight. People in the square had surged forward as the first banners came out, and for a moment the people made signs against harm, and held far back from him. The very sky seemed made of pewter, and ominous, and no one saw it.

Uwen silently joined him, a relief and a comfort as the Patriarch came out and stood on the steps above them. The old man lifted the box left and right, toward the frowning, ominous heaven.

No! Tristen wished to say, as all of them, commons and nobles alike, looked up. He saw harm. He could not say from what. But harm . . . indeed.

The Patriarch lowered the box, and from behind him filed two rows of priests, each carrying a bundle of sticks, out and down the steps, curious sight to behold. The priests reached the bottom of the steps and proceeded on across the square. Had not Uwen said the priests did not approve the bonfire? Yet they brought their bundles of sticks, and flung them on. Cheers attended the act.

"What are those bundles?" he asked Uwen, beneath the noise and the cheering.

"The sins of the lords," Uwen said. "And the bad old things. All goin' into the fire, m'lord."

"Mine, too?" he asked Uwen, having a sudden, irrational hope of mending what he could in nowise reach, things his skills had done, things he had not done, fears he had brought to the land and hopes of others that he had not met. He knew he was flawed. Mauryl had said so from the start; and Emuin generally refused to teach him. Between Efanor's gods and the burning of sins, dared he hope?

But in that moment a cruel cold wind had begun to blow, a chill gust that snapped banners and tugged at cloaks.

Uwen was not instant to answer his foolish question, either. "Such sins as ye have, m'lord, which by me ain't much. Certainly not compared to some I could speak of." Uwen was wrong in that: If he was the Sihhë-lord some thought, if he was Barrakkêth, then had he not sins? And if he was not the Sihhë-lord Mauryl had Called, was he not flawed? And did not the little book Efanor had lent him speak of flaws and sins as one and the same?

But Uwen took a lighter tone, as talk and merriment broke out on every hand for no reason that he could see except the tossing of the bundles on the pile. "Truth is, m'lord, I don't know about the burnin', but the ale flowin' free, and the dancin' and all, that do cure the heart. If rain don't drown all tonight, folk'll dance their feet bare tonight, and the ale will flow, and all. Gods bless, the sins they'll burn tonight ain't even committed yet."

The trumpets sounded, and the lords all turned behind the royal company, and they all trooped toward the Guelesfort, away from the square.

Tristen felt greater relief with every step away from the Quinaltine and its tormented shadows. The ale was flowing already, as he saw along the sides of the square, where huge barrels were set up and where no few of the common folk had gathered even during the royal procession. In the distance, now that the trumpets were silent, a street drummer and a flute player struck up a lively tune. That lilting sound of the flute lifted his spirits; and if he simply looked straight ahead, he could ignore the warding signs people made against him, and that muddle of lines and trapped shadows he had seen. Could Emuin fail to see it?

Yet Emuin was, after all, a Man. All but him . . . were Men.

He had the Quinalt medallion about his neck. He had never even remembered it during the ceremony. He had never seemed affected, or to affect anything at all. That was good, perhaps, but he was increasingly disappointed.

He had met no gods, after all, only poor unhappy shadows. He imagined that the shadows would stir about madly over the next few days, lent substance by the offerings and the reinforcement of the skewed line, and perhaps they would attempt escape briefly when the sun was hidden and no light penetrated that darkness.

But nothing the highest of all priests was doing could free them. Trapped spirits were indeed the unhappiness that had troubled him about the place. They were the power in the earth there, too many dead, too much forgotten and disregarded. He could not imagine the Mason who had done the last construction, ignoring all that was done before.

But somehow the walls had not fallen down nor had the place broken out in irruptions of spirits. He supposed that the last Masons had been the very likeness of the Patriarch and the priests, blind to what they were doing, or even deliberately transgressing something they had knocked down and wished to obliterate—as the Quinalt truly tolerated no opinion but its own and evidently deluded itself that its will had more potency. In that sense the Lines might have been jumbled by choice, and the sight he had seen might be truly the Quinaltine as Efanor refused to see it, as even the Holy Father refused to see it—a site at war with shadows, a trap to the dead it professed to safeguard in holiness.

Yet, he thought, did master Emuin look on such things unmoved? Or wherein was the difference between Emuin the priest and wizard, and Efanor the devout and princely man, except one wished to *know* and the other wished to believe, and the former wished to keep all his secrets and the latter wished to spread his opinions about to acquaintances?

But dared he think . . . both were Men, and all he had for guides, and this was the quality of his advice now that Mauryl was gone? The enormity of ignorance directing him was beyond all his fears.

They passed through the gates of the Guelesfort, crossed the courtyard, where the servants had gathered in some number, and where lords' men who had not been in the processional sought their particular station through a waving forest of banners. Lords sought Cefwyn's ear, braving the cold rain that began to mist down from the pewter sky.

Tristen did not attempt the press about Cefwyn, himself, and the cold dissuaded him from lingering. Lusin and the others had found his banner in the confusion, and he had two of them at least with him as he and Uwen went toward the steps that led into the keep. The courtyard had grown crowded with the wives and daughters of the lords, women in finery who had come out into the chill and damp, a lighter set of voices momentarily surrounding them. A gust brought drops of rain and squeals and orders to go inside.

He should have felt elated, he thought, to have pleased everyone and to have gotten through the ceremony; but before they were quite inside the rain began to pelt down. Lightning whitened the yard, and the brightly clad ladies and the courtiers alike cried in alarm and pushed and shoved to be indoors.

Cefwyn and Ninévrisë, however, and their guards, had first claim on the steps and the doorway, leaving the barons in the rain arguing about precedence. An argument broke out after Cefwyn had gone in, everyone at the steps disputing their rights, standing in a downpour to do it.

Tristen chose not to contest with the barons and their entourages, and stood there, his cloak wrapped about him, he and Uwen and Lusin and the rest, with the rain coming harder and harder, dripping off his hair and wetting the stone cobbles until dirty water flowed from the roof.

"Sins won't burn in this," Uwen said. It was a joke, Tristen was sure, but it rang with unusual force in the bitter wind, above the squabbling of the barons.

CHAPTER 7

I t were a fine occasion, all the same," Uwen said when they reached his apartments. Tassand met them to take their dripping cloaks, eager for news and hoping, perhaps, that their lord, rare in his outings, had had a success. "Not a trouble at all. M'lord did right well."

Other servants brought towels warm from the fire. There was a fine, even an extravagant late breakfast set out for him and for Uwen, Tristen was delighted to discover, on a festive table decorated with oak leaves and apples. After that, comfortably fed, he gave the staff their pennies, so that they might at whatever drier and more convenient time go make their offerings themselves.

But then the holiday became like all other days, and Tristen took himself to his reading—curious, cautiously searching Efanor's little book of devotions for hints of purposeful entrapment of the dead as an activity of the priests, or any persuasive reasons for the mismatch of lines in the Quinaltine, but he found nothing that led him to any hint of understanding.

Meanwhile Uwen had gone somewhere, perhaps down to the stables in spite of the rain, where he spent a great deal of his free time—currying his horses, braiding and combing and talking to them when he thought no one was listening—courting Liss, and asking himself for the dozenth time could he afford another horse?

Uwen talked to horses: his lord read. By afternoon the sun had come out, brightening the roof slates. A bar of light from the window glass crept across the little codex, making his study easier: the hand that had copied it had spared no ornament. It was fine, and beautiful, but difficult in dim light. He meditated the nature of gods and the servants came and went, keeping the fire in order, arranging things in his bedchamber, all those myriad mysterious things they did that meant the household was far less dusty than Ynefel had been, and the candles miraculously renewed themselves when half-burned.

He wearied of the gods' little book and sought the Quinalt in the *Red Chronicle*—a history Cefwyn had lent him, a tale of betrayals of the Sihhë, of murder and fire, and the raising of the Marhanen standard for the first time with royal honors.

Toward sundown the clouds came back and stole the bar of light from the far wall. Rain spattered the glass again. He chased memories that eluded him, and Tassand came in as thunder thumped and boomed above the town.

"M'lord. It is certain you will not attend in hall tonight."

That was a question. "No, I shall not," he agreed, and turned his thoughts for a moment to the staff, flexed shoulders weary of leaning forward. "Tassand, the staff should go down to the square, to dance or drink as they please, tonight. I should wish they did, except for the rain. How does the sky look?"

"Dark to the west, m'lord. The staff is thinking of the staff quarters on account of the weather, to open a keg there, by Your Grace's goodwill."

"Please do."

"M'lord."

Tassand went off pleased—Tristen never refused his servants, and Tassand had had no doubts of being granted the indulgence, Tristen was certain. He went back again to his reading of Efanor's little book, now by candlelight, having found nothing all day long of deliberate entrapments, except an exhortation to the gods to *preserve our souls from harm.*

Might the priests believe the souls of the Quinalt dead were safer in that jumble, that endless maze, offering doors and taking them away with the next mismatched line of Masons? They were mistaken.

The little codex talked of a hell of punishment, too, for the wicked. Was that, instead, what the lines supplied?

Uwen came in at last, rain-damp, as a murky sunset stained the sky beyond the windows.

And from some small commotion in the servant's quarters, flush-faced servants under Tassand's command brought in an especially fine supper for him and for Uwen, food Tassand said was from the king's feast downstairs, especially the ham, which Tassand highly recommended, showing him into the little hall with a flourish.

"Have we leave to take these things?" he wondered. His staff was zealous for his sake. But he well knew how his servants were concerned, indignant, even, for his sake, that *their* lord was not welcome in the king's hall, and Tristen had at least a niggling suspicion that Tassand might have done something desperate and daring and treading on the edge of the king's good grace—certainly that of the king's kitchen.

Somehow Tassand failed to answer his question, and several of the servants were a little the worse for ale, but they all seemed very happy. They spread the little table at twice its ordinary length, set more oak leaves about the dishes (perhaps some captured from the window ledges or searched out of the yard: no oaks grew on the height of the Guelesfort), and brought in a fair supply of festive braided bread thickly topped with poppy seed, intricate constructions which he found almost too delightful to eat.

Uwen, however, showed him how when he was a boy (strange to think!) they had used to unbraid the bread as they ate it, and how one braiding meant prosperity and how another meant long life, and how one was for a good harvest and why they baked a whole apple into one kind of bread.

"So's there's plenty all year long," Uwen said.

"And does it make it sure?" was his question. It seemed to him it was a good start, at least. And Uwen unbraided a bit of poppy bread and wrapped it about a bit of ham as a new muttering of thunder foretold rain on the celebration outside.

"Sure's anything in this world," Uwen said, as from the servants' quarters there was an occasional burst of undecorous merriment and a hissing of hush, hush, hush, as Tassand and the staff brought out the next course.

It was not the dancing he regretted, which might not now take place in the square, if the rain that spattered the glass fell much harder. It was not the feast in the great hall he regretted, where Cefwyn and Ninévrisë would be; thanks to his servants their food was as fine. But he could easily grow melancholy this evening, remembering with fondness his days in Amefel. He knew he had no business feeling sorry for himself. He had a fine supper, the regard of his staff, the favor of the king . . . but on thinking of the ladies, the bright-gowned ladies, who glittered and flashed so beautifully in the candlelight as they danced, he began thinking of the festivities downstairs and imagining the music he could not hear—remembering how on such a remarkable evening in Amefel a lady had come to him, the darkly reputed duchess of Amefel herself.

He knew now how very foolish he had been, and how dangerously foolish Lady Orien had been, for that matter; and he could sigh now (with some understanding of the company of women, about which the guards had a great deal to say), for the chance he had had to court a lady.

And though Ninévrisë was his model of all true ladies, he recalled the music of that night, Lady Orien's beautiful face and white shoulders . . . her beautiful hair. Red, it was, a most remarkable red that accorded well with the dark green of the Aswydd colors. Her skin was pale, and the gown had shown him very much of the wonders of the lady's form.

And that night, if he had walked into Orien Aswydd's snare and only just gotten out unscathed in his innocence . . . as it had been in those days . . . why, there were just as certainly traps set for him downstairs in the gathering this evening, traps that he would disappoint by his absence. So he might be satisfied—indeed, *should* be satisfied with his own table. He was sure he did not regret Lord Prichwarrin of Murandys, for example, who was testy and difficult, nor Lord Corswyndam of Ryssand, who greatly disapproved of him and made no secret of it.

Ninévrisë would be there, among the ladies, a sight he wished he could see . . . but he could not be seen near her; he could not be near Cefwyn, either, of course. And in the way his servants, having had too much ale, laughed and became cheerfully foolish . . . Cefwyn's guests might imbibe enough of the ale to become far too blunt, and that, among Men, would require he defend himself, which meant he would have to kill the offender.

And that would certainly put a sad cap on the festive evening. So it was folly even to regret the feast downstairs.

He looked toward windows now dark with night. Fire glow shone on the stonework. "It does seem they managed to light the fire after all," he remarked to Uwen.

"Right about sundown they did," Uwen reported. "So Tassand was sayin'. They put canvas on 't all the day, and now she'll burn even through the rain, if she gets a good blaze up and if they're lucky."

"So the sins will burn after all." When he went to the window, fine clear glass with not many bubbles at all, he found that the bubbles acquired the glow from the square. He could just make out the fire itself, and a bobbing mass of dancers. "They have indeed. The light touches all the walls."

"It do that," Uwen said, coming up beside him.

He thought if he opened the small side pane, he might hear the music, but the rain would come in and Tassand and the staff would have to clean it. "Go down to the square if you like."

"I, m'lord? Not I."

"Do. Tell me how it was. Take Lusin and the men and go down." He thought of the other element of his life, the old man whose days were topsy-turvy and who waked generally by night, to look at stars which would hardly shine on this thunderous evening. "I can go up to Emuin and bring him his breakfast. I swear I'll not go elsewhere."

Uwen's eyes danced, though his face was solemn. "Not I, for my oath, m'lord; and not Lusin, for his. There'll be ale here, by your leave. 'At's enough for holiday, an' we'll all visit the old master."

Uwen meant that, being *his* sworn man, he would not let him go unguarded tonight, and that Cefwyn, who had Lusin's oath, would be sorely displeased if Lusin left his post. So the guards had to stay and go with him as they were accustomed to do . . . more so, he supposed, since sometimes he did go alone to Emuin's tower. He was not at all surprised at Uwen's insistence, however, with so many people coming and going in the Guelesfort tonight; and if he dismissed Lusin and the men on his authority, he supposed they would stand outside defying him on Cefwyn's.

But meanwhile the heavens truly would not oblige master Emuin's observations tonight. So perhaps Emuin would have time to spend.

"Tassand," he said, "the basket for master Emuin. Has it gone up yet?"

"No, m'lord," Tassand said. "Against the likelihood, m'lord."

They knew his decisions before he made them. He was pleased, annoyed and, over all, amused. He had grown fond of Tassand in the months they had served him, Tassand and all the staff that bore with his oddities and his lapses, and perhaps, yes, they took unseemly liberties (there was, even as he thought it, a peal of merriment from the hall beyond) but, yes, indeed he encouraged them.

And perhaps master Emuin would turn him away; last night Emuin had not even opened his door to take the evening offering.

But this night he would get Emuin's attention, or he would stand there till it opened. If Tassand had made a special feast, then Emuin would enjoy it.

"Bring it," he said, and when the basket came, along with it came an entire small keg of ale. So it was clearly conspiracy among all his guards and servants and now himself to bring the holiday feast to master Emuin. He said not a word about the keg, only tucked in the little treasures, too, which he had set by for master Emuin. In high spirits and great resolution he carried the basket himself as he and Uwen left the apartment, gathering up Lusin and the men on the way.

So they marched down the hall, him with the basket, Uwen carrying the keg, and Lusin and the three others clumping heavily behind, clattering with weapons, bearing a second basket of the poppy-seed cakes, which had somehow ended up part of Emuin's breakfast arrangements. He saw that several cups had also come in the substantial basket of cakes; he suspected sweets in the bottom of the basket, and his guards were extraordinarily cheerful as they opened the door that led to the drafty stairs.

Emuin maintained no guard himself, at least no visible one, only that loud bell that rang below when someone opened this door leading up to the tower where he was now solitary. It was a deafeningly loud bell, when one was standing by it, enough to wake the old man when he was sleeping. Wind swept through, damp with rain. The drafts that swept through Emuin's chambers above were constant. The servants before they had left had complained that powders Emuin was mixing ended up drifting over all his books and onto the floor. Likewise smokes of his frequent combustions had sooted the rafters far beyond reason. Books turned their own pages in the tower, and the servants had claimed haunts. But there was no magery about it, only ill-fitting shutters and a tower that drew like a chimney. One could feel the waft of cold air up there at every opening of the downstairs door that led to the tower stairs, and Tristen hoped that their opening of the door had not disturbed any of master Emuin's charts or blown rain in to soak his books: he had wished his guards to shut the door as quickly as possible and to hurry up the steps.

Thunder cracked. He stopped midway, daunted, wondering if it had been overhead.

"*That* were close," Uwen said behind him. Tristen looked down on a spiral of his men as Uwen signed against harm, he and Lusin and Syllan and the rest, ale keg and all. Close indeed, but there was no sign of damage above. Tristen ran up in haste to make up for the pause, the men clattering and panting behind him, and at the little landing outside the study, rapped at the rough wooden door, not at all expecting an answer, in master Emuin's ordinary way of hospitality, but simply because it always seemed polite to do before trying the latch.

Hearing nothing from inside, he pulled the cord and let himself in, leaving Uwen and the guards to sit at their ease on the steps, as they did habitually when they attended him here. Simply in opening the door to admit himself he loosed a gale that dislodged a half score of parchments inside, and he quickly and guiltily shut it at his back.

"Bother!" Emuin was at his worktable, having just slapped a measuring rod down to pin an array of parchments across the table surface.

"Supper, sir," Tristen said cheerfully, "a holiday supper. Breakfast, of sorts. But there's the holiday ale. There's a keg of it outside, in Uwen's keeping."

"Breakfast," Emuin said. "No ale. Ale muddles the wits and I need mine, young sir. But tea would be very welcome. Cursed rain." Emuin composed a rattling stack of selected parchments and cleared a small space on his huge chart table. Then, with some ado, he poked up the embers in the entirely inadequate fireplace, added tinder, then a few sticks, and raised a little fire. He looked into the sooted teapot, seemed to decide there was sufficient water, and swung it over the fire on its dragon-shaped hook, the tower room's one elegance.

"Well, sit down, sit down," Emuin said, and Tristen set out ham and bread on the table, settling himself as Emuin set out two chipped pottery cups and a spoon of dubious recent history.

Emuin wore nothing like the finery he had worn to the king's hall two days ago. Emuin's second-best gray robe, the Teranthine habit, had threadbare spots and the hem was out, not to mention the ink stains. Ink blackened his thumb and two fingers. His white hair hung in ringlets, looking damp, probably from a determined look at the heavens. As Men went, he was old, quite, quite old, Tristen had come to understand—older, perhaps, than most Men ever came to be, and Emuin had lost patience with things he had seen too many times. That was what he had said about the court and his servants alike.

But novel things interested him. "I thought you would enjoy these," Tristen said, laying out the oak gall and the bird's egg.

"Thrush," Emuin said of the egg, and that Word Unfolded in a delightful song, a moderate-sized brown bird, ample reward for his care in bringing it back unbroken. "Ah," Emuin said, and admired the oak gall. "Very useful." He set it by in a place of honor. They sat near the only warmth, and wisps of Emuin's hair, drying somewhat, flew about in the drafts, what of it he did not braid into an immediately unwinding pigtail.

The water boiled while they talked of autumn colors and the leaves and why evergreens did not cast their leaves at all, a conversation Tristen was sure he never could have had in the king's gathering below, for all his regret of the jeweled ladies. They poured tea as the sounds of merriment wafted up from the town square through the unshuttered windows.

"The fools," Emuin said, in the chilly drafts. "They'll be soaked. It's for the young and the foolish out there tonight, no question."

"Burning sins, Uwen said."

"Would they could get all of them. I've a few to contribute. We could toss Lord Corswyndam on the pyre."

He could discern Emuin's levity. Not so with everyone he dealt with. He could laugh at the image of someone carrying stiff old Lord Corswyndam like a log of wood and flinging him onto the fire. The lord of Ryssand was not Cefwyn's friend, nor was he Emuin's. Corswyndam and Lord Prichwarrin of Murandys, however, were very good friends, to no one's comfort that he knew of. "Do they do the same in Amefel? Do they burn sins?"

"No. Not in Amefel. They burn straw men. But they'll be dancing and drinking everywhere across the northern land tonight, in Guelessar, in every province, Panys and Murandys, Teymeryn, Isin and Marisal."

"Everyone *calls* them northern."

"They do."

"But they lie east."

"Only from Amefel."

That was a perplexing thought. There was something about Emuin's remark on sin-burning that had begun to trouble him, as if something very troubling were trying to Unfold, and he resisted it, knowing it could only upset him on a night when he had no wish to be disturbed, only comfortable in Emuin's company.

"Devils try to come in on the wind," Emuin said, "so northern folk say, so they chase them with fires. In the south they celebrate the first day of winter, and on Midwinter Day they light the fires again, to encourage the sun."

"And do they? And does it?" he asked, hovering close to the thought of bonfires as warmth, and remembering a book, not Efanor's little book. He had burned that book in a like great fire, but the words of it, words he himself might have written, kept bobbing up to the surface of very dark waters. They were words he had written . . . if he was Barrakkêth. He huddled his long limbs close, fearing with all his soul what Emuin might say next.

"There are no devils and the sun does very stubbornly as it will. But one is north and one is south. What the old people did, their descendants do, not even remembering why. Now in the northern duchies they burn up sins. I truly doubt its efficacy, but the Quinalt has never put a stop to it, only made it sins, instead of enemies."

Great fires like the fire at Henas'amef. They had burned Lord Heryn's men. Had that pyre burned their sins with him? Fear of the fire had not daunted Lady Orien or her sister Lady Tarien, but it daunted him.

Great fires, pages of a book curling and catching fire, and bodies of men blackened and twisted. The smell of it came to him, a memory, or a spell-wrought understanding. If he was Barrakkêth, he had had no mercy on his enemies, so they wrote. If he was Barrakkêth, he had overthrown lost Galasien centuries ago, and reigned over Men in fire and blood. So his books said. In fire and blood the Sihhë dynasty had risen; in fire and blood it had gone down at Althalen, when Cefwyn's grandfather had burned the last halfling king, another great fire.

Was it for his sins?

If he had burned, was he pure? And if he had come back into the world, had he come sinless? Men thought not, it was clear. Even Emuin thought not.

There had been five true Sihhë. Five who had come down out of winter, bringing their weapons, their knowledge of war, their innate magic. They had not been wizards, to *call* on magic, or sorcerers, to reach where wizards scrupled to reach. The five had been Sihhë, and the magic was *in* them, without any line of demarcation between the bright and the dark: they had lived long, very long, and the magic in their halfling progeny had run thinner and thinner and thinner, until it all ended in fire, in unwalled Althalen.

Only then had Mauryl withdrawn entirely from Men and shut

himself in the fortress of Ynefel. Only then had the realm split in two: Ylesuin had had the Marhanen kings; and Elwynor had declared the Regency under Uleman, then a young man, and settled down to wait . . . for a true king, a Sihhë king, the King to Come, so long as Uleman lived.

Now Elwynor had grown weary of waiting. Now every hedge in Elwynor produced a claimant, a rebel, a man who wished to deny the Regency could pass to Uleman's daughter Ninévrisë . . . certainly many Elwynim were ready to deny Ninévrisë if she married a Marhanen king. So Elwynor burned villages for their sins. He saw the bright, bright fire, and the black shadows that had been Men in his dreams of Althalen. They hoped to stop the burning, he and Cefwyn, and put an end to fire and sword.

"Why do they say north?" He had been chasing that thought, among worse ones, through the mazy paths of the oak grain on the tabletop, and he was suddenly moved to ask a question, to escape the chance of something more Unfolding. North was a potent question. It was the question of the Sihhë. But the sudden query confused Emuin: he saw that. "North of what mark do they reckon, sir, to call Amefel the south?"

"Ah," said Emuin, then, and appeared to consider the question. "That is to say, north of the Amynys before it flows into the Lenúalim. That was the old boundary, the Guelen boundary, if you would know."

"And where is that river? Well south and east?"

"East and bending north, if you would know. Between Marisyn and Marisal."

"Yet Amefel is north of that, too. And Amefel they always reckon south."

"So they do. And slant their maps out of true to make their own lands seem more level, gods forbid that Ylesuin should tilt."

"So why should all the land this side of Assurnbrook be called north when it clearly lies due east?"

"Because in the old days, when the Sihhë ruled, one dared not say *Men*."

That was a curious notion. It was also more talk on that score than he had had of Emuin since the day Emuin had shown him the travels of the sun. He had a sip of tea and rested his elbow on the scarred table. "And how would that be?"

"Because the Sihhë ruled, and by *north*, one quietly meant the lands above the Amynys, and *that* meant all that was the freehold of

Men. All the provinces the Marhanen held . . . so when one spoke of
the north doing a thing, it generally and far more quietly meant *the
Marhanen dukes* did a thing. This was before they became reigning
kings, of course. And rather than ever say, the provinces where Men
ruled, as opposed to Sihhë, it was the fashion to say, the northern
provinces. They were a restless lot, fomenting rebellions. *The north
did this. The north did that.* You're quite right, of course. But there
were the lands loyal to the Sihhë, at Althalen; and there were the
lands to the south. All the lands. The Sihhë ruled to the *sea*, young
lord."

Blue water. An endless water, sometimes blue, sometimes gray or
green.

White headlands and low marsh.

He caught himself, bumped the teacup with his elbow—was dizzy
for a moment. A Word had come to him. He knew the sea. In this
world, the sky thundered and flashed with light, and in the other the
waves thundered, and crashed against a shore.

"Guelenfolk came out of Nelefreíssan, a long time ago," Emuin
said, and helped himself to the ham that had come up in the basket,
twice over for good measure. "And probably so did the Elwynim,
part and parcel with the Guelenmen and even the other sorts of
Men, the Chomaggari and the Casmyndanim on the coast, truth be
told, but never whisper *that* suspicion in the Quinalt's hearing, good
gods, no, the Chomaggari are twice-damnéd heathen dogs and the
folk of Nelefreíssan are of course distinct even from Guelenmen,
who have the gods-given right to have the capital in Guelemara. So
Guelessar is ever so much more Guelen than the Nelefreimen . . . if
you ask a man from Guelessar. Ask a Nelefreiman, and he'll tell you
the opposite. But to both the whole coastland is damned."

"Do the Teranthines think so?"

"Oh, aye, that the Chomaggari are damned, so any man that raids
a Teranthine shrine as the hillmen are wont to do is clearly damned,
quite heartily and justly so in my opinion, too. But the Teranthines
are rather sure—and I agree with them—that in the very long ago
most of Men in the whole world were living up in Nelefreíssan and
Isin. Now, this becomes important for you to know, now that you
ask. This was at the same time when the Galasieni were lording it in
the south and up and down the Lenúalim. Then Mauryl comes into
the tale."

"Was it long ago?"

"Very. Nine hundred years at least. And Mauryl's magic brought down Galasien, conjuring the Sihhë to do it for him . . . or he brought the five Sihhë-lords down from the north, as you please, which I think is the truer telling . . ." Emuin cast him a sidelong glance, head ducked, under a fringe of wind-stirred, grizzled hair, a close, questioning look. "Would *you* know how that was, lad?"

"No, sir," Tristen said uncomfortably, hoping that he never did know. He heard tales of nine hundred years and of centuries of Sihhë rule and hoped that the ancient wars never fully Unfolded to him. "I truly do not."

"Well, well, but be that as it may, the Galasieni vanished, or whatever befell, Ynefel became as strange as it is, so strange even the Sihhë left it and built Althalen instead. The Guelenfolk and their Ryssandish kin came pouring down from the north like bandits— hence the real root of their identifying themselves all as northern now, if you take my guess, long after they have ceased to be northerly at all; hence the more northerly, the purer Quinaltine. We southerners, we of Amefel—"

"Are *you* of Amefel?" He was not sure he had ever heard Emuin admit it.

"As near as I am of any place. Aye, say I am of Amefel. And in the Guelen thinking, the pure Guelen thinking, we who are both Men and out of Amefel or anywhere to the south of there are fallen from Guelenish purity. If you want the deepest secret, the one for which the Guelenfolk despise the south, we mingled with the Sihhë and, gods save us all, the lowly Chomaggari."

"But are not the Elwynim northerly and more north than anyone?"

"But mingled their blood most of all. Yes. Hence may they be damned, *in* the Quinalt's thinking—or that is the house the Quinalt scholars have built themselves into, a house without a door in it, if you ask me. A highly inconvenient house, since you came: they have said very many things they have now to unsay or damn their own king. And *that* would not be good."

"Damn Cefwyn?" He was appalled.

"Some did wish Efanor to be king. —Is it only your men outside, men you know? Are you sure of them?"

"Yes," Tristen said, wondering what Emuin might intend to say on this chancy night. Harm seemed to tremble in the air. He found himself afraid for no reason, or perhaps for every reason. "Uwen is there. And Lusin and his men."

"Good. Good. What are they about out there?" This as a voice outside became a little louder and fell off sharply.

"Ale," Tristen said, and reminded him: "They have the keg."

"I'd not have strangers' ears to the door while I ask you: how did the business this morning go? Are you still damned, or perhaps sanctified and blessed now, perchance? I see that Quinalt trinket of yours. I *burn* with curiosity."

Would Emuin now say nothing more of the Quinalt damning Cefwyn? Cefwyn had threatened the Quinalt. Were they equally matched? Was there potency to a Quinalt curse? But he had quite forgotten the relic Efanor had given him. He put a hand on his chest, where it rested. It was chill, but very little more chill than his hands, in the gusts from the open window. He hoped it meant no harm, and that it brought none with it.

"Things went well this morning, sir, at least that there was no trouble. Efanor had given me this, if you will."

"No manifestations. *Good* "—lightning lit the window and thunder cracked—"*gods!*" master Emuin finished, holding his own hand to his heart. "*That* was a crack, was it not?"

"It sounded as if it hit the roof." It had shaken the thoughts loose from his head. The rain was blowing, spattering drops clear to the table, and onto parchments where much of the ink was poor and ran. Tristen got up quickly and shut the window the old man insisted on keeping open and dropped the window latch—chilled, when he came back, his clothes wet, the autumn wind having blasted them to his body. "I wonder you keep the window open, sir."

"I prefer it."

"If you wish—" He offered with his hand toward the window.

"No, no, one soaking's enough."

"Mauryl feared an open window, very much so. He warded every window. I shut mine tight. I open them to nothing after dark. In all respect, sir—"

"At Ynefel I should ward everything in sight. But we have the Quinalt to protect us."

"You jest, sir."

"Extremely."

"Why do you?"

"What?"

"Keep the window open?"

"I invite evil. *If* it should be abroad, I wish to know about it. I'll not have it slipping about, prying here and there. Let it come here. Let it try me. I'm old, and ill-tempered."

It was a reckless idea. But the great shadow, the darkest one,

Hasufin, was gone. And it made a sort of sense, that if there was any other weaker shadow prying about, or sending out inquiries into Guelemara, then it might be drawn here, to wizardry and an open window, rather than below, to ordinary folk, where it might work far more mischief in an unwary populace before anyone noticed. Wizardry working ill likely would come in small ways, at first, at the most unguarded hearts. At least Hasufin's malice had started that way . . . the prompting of ill thoughts, ill deeds, fear, suspicion. It had grown stronger. Ultimately it had killed a king.

And if some threat came full-fledged, stronger, noisier, larger, rolling in like sunset, it would come from far away, so that Emuin might well have clear sight of it in a tower lifted up above the clatter and smoke of the town. The disturbance he had seen in the Quinalt this morning had no immediacy here, aloft. All he could touch of the Quinalt's troubles from here was an agglomeration of souls, not an orderly disturbance, and it mustered no threat: it could not get out of its confinement . . . that was precisely the problem. Even the lightning, a hammerblow from the heavens, had not released them, striking nearby, as it had. Release the Masons' wards entirely and the souls would scatter like mice when the door was opened.

Came a timid knock. A crack of the door, that made the storm howl through the seams of the shutter. Uwen looked in, ever so carefully.

"Was you all right, m'lord? We got to thinkin' . . . we should ask, beggin' your pardon . . ."

"Yes, quite safe here, Uwen. We've shut the window."

"M'lord," Uwen said, and gently closed the door.

"So how *was* the Quinalt?" Emuin asked in the settling of a disturbed parchment to the floor. "And did you remark anything odd about the place?"

"You've seen the Lines."

"Oh, aye. A mare's nest, a thorough mare's nest. But one cannot say that to the Quinalt. No such things exist."

"They don't see them at all?"

"Blind as bats."

"Shadows are trapped there. Many of them." But he was sure now that was no news at all to Emuin. "What do you know about the shadows there?" he asked, while he had the old man's attention and while Emuin was inclined to talk. "Do you *know* what used to stand there?"

"King Selwyn feared Sihhë ghosts extremely in life. Ironic, his resting place."

"There are Sihhë there?"

"At least there some that are not wholly—or holy—Men."

The water boiled, for a second infusion. Emuin got up, measured tea into the cups and poured the hot water. Tristen took his and stared at the floating bits of leaf. He took the spoon in his turn, sank the flotsam in the cup before he sipped the hot liquid. The steam flew away in banners on the persistent drafts. Rain spatted against the shutters.

Here in the Guelesfort itself were shadows, a few in this tower, which crept in the crevices of set stone and along the joins of wooden floor and stone walls. They ran beneath the table and among the shelves of pots and herb bundles and scrolls and codices which somehow the two brothers had never dusted.

"Not Men," Tristen echoed master Emuin. Often when Emuin had left a subject he would not then go back to it, not for a very long time, and sometimes never. But this was too intriguing a thread to let go. "Was Hasufin—was Mauryl—were they Men?" He had asked that in a hundred ways and never been satisfied. "Am I? Or what *is* the difference? Guelen and Galasieni, you say. But what is the difference?"

"Oh, many."

His shoulders fell. Master Emuin was going to evade the question again.

But then master Emuin said, pensively, "The earth is old. And regarding the shadow at Ynefel, the older a shadow, perhaps, the stranger it grows. There were folk the Galasieni ruled, and there was a shrine of sorts where the Quinalt stands today, so I suspect. One feels it especially in storms. One hesitates—" Emuin looked to the window, as the sounds of thunder rolled above the roof and ale-driven merriment thumped from behind the door. "One hesitates to prod such things, especially when one had really as lief not have the answer, or have to deal with it at the moment. Some things are easier to call than to settle back again, mark me. I do not think these in the Quinaltine are apt to break forth. I have rarely seen them and they are few."

"They were thick, sir. There were hundreds . . . behind the Patriarch . . . every time he walked the line."

"Are you quite sure?" Emuin was paying full attention now, and the easy feeling had left the room. "I felt nothing of the sort this morning. And I was attentive."

"I felt you in your tower," Tristen said. He had assured himself there was no threat. Now he was not so sure. "But you say you saw nothing this morning."

"No, not I. But I'm not—" Emuin hesitated. "I am not precisely of your heritage. Perhaps some answered you who would not seek me."

A small chill had come into the tower, perhaps a breeze; and there was quiet for a moment between them.

"Perhaps I shouldn't have gone there," Tristen said. "I *asked,* sir. I did ask . . ."

"I will not prevent you from the things you do," Emuin said. "Only *your* will can do that."

"Advice, sir. Advice, if I ask it—"

"Only *one* will should guide what you do . . . *Mauryl's* will, in all that he laid down, is sufficient. I have known it longer than you, young sir, who still deny it, but perhaps not."

"I have done all Mauryl's will."

"Nothing that regards living men is ever finished—Living *men*, in whatever sense. And gods know, nothing that regards wizards is ever settled, and Mauryl Gestaurien, twice so. No, I cannot advise you, *especially* if you will take instruction from Efanor."

"But you knew I was meaning to speak to Efanor, sir. If you even in the least feared I shouldn't go this morning, could you not at least have advised me of those fears? Could you not have advised me at least of your will? Can you not say . . . as Mauryl would say, young fool, here is a thing you should not do?"

"Did harm come today, all the same?"

"None that I *saw,* sir."

"And did anything break forth?"

"Nothing. Nothing did that I *saw*, sir." He had never yet admitted his glance into the west and his misgivings.

"Would you have permitted harm to break forth in the sanctuary?"

"No, sir. Not if I saw it."

"And are not your eyes and ears sharper than mine?" Emuin did not wait for his answer. "Then *I* should by no means have stood in your path, should I? Oh, aye, to the contrary, you would have done whatever Cefwyn asked, come fire, come pestilence, you would do all *he* asked."

"Did I not swear to do all Cefwyn asked? He is the king. I swore to him."

"A folly, but one that had to be. One that will have your fate bend you *or* him until it has what it wills, will I, nill I. I advise you, but you will not hear me."

"Then what is this fate? What is my fate? A word, a word. You say it, sir, and I hear it, but it will not Unfold to me, it never will Unfold. Tell me! If I *can* do as you say I can do, then *this* I will, and, will I, nill I, my wishing does no good at all. You never answer me."

"Fate? A chance word, a folly, an empty word like Efanor's gods. I shall never advise you beyond what I do. Abandon hope of that. Inform you, perhaps I may, if 't will serve Mauryl's will, as may be, or may not. Shall I listen to you, when you become willing to inform me of your will? —or his? Aye, that will I, also. But I would be a fool to say to you, desist. To the wind out there, perhaps, but not to Mauryl's Working. You must govern *yourself*, young lord. Do you understand what I am saying? That no wizard made *can* govern your lightest whim. And did I tell you the *wrong* thing, and divert you from Mauryl's Working, gods know where we should be. Swear no more oaths to anyone, if you are wise. If you wish my advice, I give it you in this one thing. Do not bind yourself. Fealty you had to swear. Every man must have a master and every *Man* must have a lord. But as you love Cefwyn, be careful of your oaths and, as you are not a *Man,* beware of making promises. Mauryl's will is a burning fire. And it lives, young lord, oh, it lives."

"Mauryl is dead! I have done all that Mauryl willed me to do. Have I *not*, sir? Answer me! If I have power over anything, *answer me*!"

That silence resumed. There was only the crackling of the fire, Emuin meeting him stare for stare.

"And I still can defy you, young lord, and do, by whatever effort."

"Why? Why do you not go down that stairs and stand in the hall tonight and advise Cefwyn, if not me? What do you hear up here in the wind and the weather that you will not tell anyone?"

"It is not cowardice that keeps me at this post," Emuin said, and gestured toward the window. "What might come by that route, I will face. Not your thwarted will, sir, that I will not. And yet I *will* say no to you when you harry me for answers."

I would not touch what Mauryl wrought, Emuin had said to him once and again tonight. And that was in its way a damning stroke of terrible, lasting loneliness. If not Emuin . . . if not Emuin, to touch him and comfort him and advise him . . . then who? Who would there ever be?

There was Cefwyn, that friendship, that faith. But even that grew thin.

"Do you fear me, sir?"

"Not you," Emuin said somberly. "Not your heart. Not your intentions toward Cefwyn or Uwen or myself. And what *did* you see in the Quinaltine? And what was your sense of the place, you of the far sharper sight?"

"Nothing I felt I should fear, sir, in so many words. I had thought I would fear it. I looked for gods."

"For gods." It was almost a laugh. Or a sob for breath. "And did you find them?"

"No, sir. —Not Efanor's gods. I saw no sign of them. But you say there are wizards' gods. There are the Nineteen. —Are there not? Do you *not* speak to them?"

Emuin shrugged and evaded his eyes.

"*Are* there, sir?"

"You are a most uncomfortable young man."

"And everywhere I go I am uncomfortable and uncomforting. Everyone says so. So do you."

"You have your lessons in discourse from Idrys, none other, gods save us."

"You say, *Gods,* sir. Do you say it for no reason?"

"Oh, always for reason. In my frequent amazements. *If* I were not a Man, I would be amazed less often, perhaps, and perhaps I would know your answers as surely and smugly as the Patriarch. But I am a Man, and therefore say I, *gods!* this and *gods!* that and *good merciful gods!* at least several times daily. The sad truth is that I *don't* know your answer, young sir. If I were all a Man, I would have faith in the gods. But a wizard's soul is outside the pale. That is the price one pays." Emuin drew a heavy breath. "I have hope. I still have hope of the gods, that is the true answer."

"But not hope of the Quinalt?"

"Have *you* hope of the Patriarch? I have not. Tell me what you did see, what you did feel when you were there?"

"Discord."

"Like hearing trumpets all out of tune. That kind of feeling."

"Yes, sir."

"You have given your penny tithe and you wear *that*." Emuin indicated the medallion, with the dark substance at the center.

"I have the other one, too, that Cefwyn gave me, the one bound to my sword. The Teranthine one, that he said was yours. I would not part with it. Efanor says two is surer than one. But ought I to wear his at all? Is there harm in it?"

"Now you ask."

"You would not answer me before!"

"Blood of the martyrs, indeed," Emuin scoffed. "There's no harm in it, except to the sheep that bled for it, I'll warrant that with no difficulty."

The slaughter of sheep disturbed him. The thought of blood inside something he was wearing even more disquieted his stomach. "I shall take it off if you—"

"No, no," Emuin said with a wave of his hand. "His Highness gave it. Therein is its virtue, young lord, no other. A gift in love is impervious to ill wishes. Even if it harmed the sheep. Children doubtless enjoyed the mutton for their suppers. And Efanor does love you, in his way. Such is the way of the world."

"He gave me a book of devotions. I left it downstairs. I might bring it—"

"Harmless, too. I can judge from here. The Quinalt has no power."

"The Quinalt say the gods made the world."

"Perhaps. Lacking witnesses, I would not say whether it was made or found. The Quinalt credit the gods for all good, their enemies for all harm. It keeps things tidy."

"So was the world always here?" He felt himself still on precarious ground, but he warmed to the exchange, cautiously. The tower chamber felt warmer since he had shut the window, at least by comparison to the earlier, wind-blasted chill, and the rain, after its initial violence, made a pleasant spatter against the shutters. He found his limbs relaxing out of their hunched and shivering knot.

"And where is *here*, pray?" Emuin cheerfully answered question with questions. "Is it where you and I are? Or might it be where two other men sit, and if it is, where is the center of it and when did it begin?"

"I have no idea, sir. *I* was found. Or made. Or Called." He could use such levity. He had learned it in Cefwyn's company, and he had the satisfaction of seeing Emuin look askance at it.

"Yet have eyes, and ears, and senses all. Is Efanor so certain and can the king always be so dubious?"

"Cefwyn himself never seems to regard the gods."

"Nor did his grandfather."

"But Efanor said one could *hear* the gods. The Quinaltines think so. Is it true?"

"So say the Quinalt priests. I've never quite heard them. Nor expect you to."

"Because of what we are?"

"Because I doubt the Quinalt priests ever do."

"Then should I read what Efanor gave me, this little book? Should I go to the shrine on special days as Cefwyn wishes? Or not?"

"I dare not," Emuin said then, and losing all good humor, sketched some figure in the spillage of water on the table.

"What do you not say to me?" Tristen asked him, and received the quick, bright, and utterly intent look of Emuin's eyes.

"You looked west, did you not?"

How had Emuin known?

"Why?" he asked Emuin. "Why? Ought I not?"

"You looked west, I say. What did you see?"

"I saw . . . nothing that alarmed me."

"Is that so?"

He was uneasy now—he recalled with shame his rapid retreat from that place. His subsequent preoccupation with a fallen log, a curious fungus. He had stopped thinking about the west. He had simply stopped thinking about it, unwillingly preoccupied with a curious log . . . as he had learned to use a preoccupation to wall off untidy thoughts. Was it wrong to remember Ynefel? Was it wrong, sometimes, to think of being there, where he had been happy, —even when he knew it was dangerous?

"I thought," he confessed, "I thought of Mauryl. Of last spring."

"And was there a shadow in this thought?"

He tried to remember, troubled by Emuin's delving into what he had woven into a day of distractions. He was unwilling to remember. His wits refused him. And he knew that was dangerous. He drew a deep breath and tried to seize the threads of it. "I saw the shadow of a shadow. I remembered days and nights at Ynefel. The window of my room. Later—I remembered seeing weather on the horizon. Or thinking it might rain."

"It never rained that day."

"You didn't ask me when we met at supper."

"I forgot it," Emuin said, and that was itself a disturbing statement . . . natural though that was in the confusion of guests and a festive evening.

"So did I forget to tell you. And you were asleep. And I had forgotten it."

"It never rained that day," Emuin's voice was flat as if it was no surprise "Yet you saw *weather.* So you say. And did it see *you?*"

"I think not, sir. I took care not." Now he could not remember the sky that day. The chill seemed deep for a moment, and it was very difficult to confess. "Yet I confess I took care that you failed to see me, too."

"Was it the first time?"

"No. The first time in a while, sir, but not the first time. You never—" He began to say *you never advise me,* but that was no excuse. There were no excuses in wizardry or, though only he knew the laws of it, in magic. He strongly suspected that magic was even less forgiving and he knew his folly, that he had thought back, and back, and it had felt so safe . . . at first.

"I still can catch you out," Emuin said, not unkindly.

"It was not a long moment that I stood there. I offer no excuse, sir. I can't even promise not to do it again. It seemed—safe at that moment." He struggled to remember all the sequence of things, but that was one of the mazes on which wizardry could lead: that they would not assume an order, or a right sense of importance against what seemed far more urgent. Around the tower things seemed to change by the moment, both things that had been and things that might be. "I felt afraid and I ran."

"*Did* you?"

"I was afraid. Afraid I might *be* there in the next moment."

Emuin drew a long slow breath and leaned back. "Is it so, now?"

He had no words to say what had happened to him. The words Men used hardly compassed it. "It felt—" Still there were no words. He *had* words. But they were not in the common tongue and they stuck in his throat. And he had never, strictly speaking, told Emuin all that had happened at Lewenbrook. "I felt in danger. I felt myself in danger. If I thought it came near anyone else, I would have said so at supper that night."

"Your goodwill is our shield, my young lord; it was Cefwyn's shield in battle and it stands so, now, with all of us. I trust your looking west and I trust your going to the Quinaltine, little I can do about it." Emuin had shut away all mention of that disturbing hour as firmly as he had shut the window. No, he wished to say. No, I have more to say.

Yet he could find none of it to say. And despaired, then, that he never would. Emuin had ceased to listen.

"—Would a game of draughts suit you on this noisy, rattly, windy night?" Emuin asked him lightly. "I fear the Quinalt and their bon-fire are drowned by now, half-burned sins and all. Quinalt sins, to boot. Gods send they make no omen of it."

"There. You said it again."

"Said what?"

"Gods send."

"Plague and pest. A manner of speaking. Men do have them."

"Gods, sir?"

"Manners of speaking!"

"Yes, sir," he said. Emuin had closed off the subject. Emuin tried to joke with him, he tried to joke with Emuin and now he had got-ten a rise of Emuin's eyebrow. And a spark of humor in his eye. He fanned it. "Dare I have them, too, then?"

Emuin rose from the table, sighed, walked toward the shuttered window. And stood there. "The winter stars are rising and the rain and the foolish fire blinds all my observations. —But all they do down there changes nothing." Emuin looked at him, and that spark was back, defiant, when a moment before he had seen a weary old man. "You and I are here. And chance is abroad tonight. So are a paltry few shadows. They gathered by the fire down there, too. They danced. Poor fools. For a few hours they were not enemies."

"Who, sir? The shadows are not our enemies?"

"Nor are we our own, for a few hours at least." Emuin came back, filled the teakettle. "Best we two sit together, drink tea, and play draughts till dawn. Bid kiss my hand to the Quinalt, and their gods. I don't advise you, understand! I inform you the course that *I* would take; that I have taken, gods know, simply to live in Guelessar. Do all that Cefwyn recommends regarding the Quinalt— since you don't consult me in such things I gladly provide no advice. I do not object to your wearing the silly medal, nor talking to His Highness, but finish going to the shrine as soon as you can. *That* is not advice, either, young lord, only good sense."

"Yes, sir." He accepted the chastisement, and the advice.

"Plague and pest, I say. Deliberately you did not ask me." Emuin found his cheerfulness unexpectedly. Mauryl had used to swear at him, sometimes in despair, sometimes in laughter. And Emuin was very like him, in important ways. "Bother the tea," the old man said. "Steal us two cups of the ale from the guards out there. To be sure of its safety, understand."

CHAPTER 8

Wine flowed, along with the traditional ale and beer. The drums and the harps and pipes played through the rumble and crack of thunder, and the lords of Ylesuin and their ladies, their sons and their daughters, all moved in their sprightly, graceful patterns through the dance, safe and dry, immune to the storm that reports said had drowned the bonfire and dispersed the wilder celebration in the square for good and all this time.

The king had been wont to be down in the square at harvesttide, dancing the bawdy peasant dances in his misspent youth, oh, two long years ago, committing new sins while burning old ones. If one were lucky, one could burn them all by morning, new and old, and wake with a light conscience, an empty purse, and a well-earned headache.

This year, crowned, having spent last winter in Amefel, Cefwyn sat a thinly cushioned chair of state on a stone workmen had brought in at great effort, to raise that chair of state a handbreadth above the chair of the woman he could not make queen of Ylesuin, a handbreadth of difference which the king had to remember every time he and his bride-to-be stepped down to dance, a handbreadth of a separation and a symbol of his good fortune not to be in Ninévrisë's position, a beggar at a foreign, a hostile court. He would not, by his own will, have accepted the damned stone; but he had accepted it all the same, marking down the lord of Ryssand, Corswyndam, in his personal disfavor—for some future time.

The Quinalt had begun to yield until, today, with Ninévrisë casting in her own penny with her own hand, acknowledging Quinalt authority, doing as other lords did with the Quinalt countenancing it, there had been a tacit agreement on the conservative side that she was indeed a head of state and a lord among lords—Ninévrisë wore her circlet crown of office tonight, another point of debate, so he wore the heavy state crown of Ylesuin, and their respective peoples' honors were preserved by a hand-span stone block.

His grandfather had set himself on the Dragon Throne by murder, baldly put, —had turned on his sworn lord, Elfwyn, the halfling Sihhë, and burned the palace at Althalen, enriching those who followed him. His father, too, had been notoriously jealous of his power, bewilderingly blind to lords fattening their purses by any means they could devise. His courtiers were sure the new-crowned king meant to do something clever, and betray his word to Elwynor, and enrich his faithful barons with new lands beyond any dream of acquisition they had had under his father.

On the other hand—could the new king be a fool? Perhaps he might be weak, and allow his barons to demand far more of him than a stone step. And they still might conquer Elwynor.

Thirteen days were left before the wedding, and then he would have the woman beside him irrefutably, immutably, and *legally* his ally, his wife, *and* the love of his heart, a giddy, frivolous, undutiful pleasure he had never looked for. He bought the priests with that block of stone—as well as with the arrangement that kept the lord of Althalen in his rooms and his old tutor Emuin tucked away in his tower. He congratulated himself that they had carried off the ceremony this morning without a disaster, and in truth the court was abuzz with the presence of the Lord Warden in the shrine, wearing a holy relic of the Quinalt, no less. There was hot and heavy converse at this very moment around Efanor and his priest, who swore to all inquirers as to the authenticity of that medal, dashing hope that it might be a lie. True, some skeptics looked askance at the foul and, in their claims, *ominous* weather tonight, but it was autumn, good lack! when rains were ordinary. What did they expect?

The whole court did know that their new king had been engaged in very chancy business across Assurnbrook, in Amefel. There were far too many eyewitnesses to sorcery. No man who had stood on Lewen field had a precise recollection of all the events there, but every man who had stood there knew that he had seen *something* terrible, and that Elwynim and the king's odd friend the Lord Warden of Ynefel all had something essential to do with the victory there. In some versions it was the gods themselves who had rescued the Dragon Banner and carried it blazing against the enemy. In others the light that had dawned across that field was spectral and sorcerous, and the Lord Warden of Ynefel had carried the lightning in his hand. Tristen could not, gossip said, even stand in the presence of a priest. He would perish as a lump of cinder if he laid a hand on a Quinalt emblem. He would fail to put in the harvest penny. He would melt at the threshold, and the holy images would avert their faces.

Clack, clack, clack of gossip, all done to death today as Tristen paid his penny like a good Quinalt man, wearing a medal of holy martyr's blood—attested by the most incorruptible, tiresome priest alive, one so holy even His Holiness avoided his company, *Efanor's* priest, Jormys, him in the rope belt and rough-spun yonder.

Now perhaps they were saying, over there in that knot of gossipers, the wonder of it! the holy Jormys had converted a Sihhë-lord . . . when he knew damned well Jormys had been afraid to go into that room and only Efanor had gone.

He owed his brother a great favor for that act of courage.

"Cevulirn dances very well," Ninévrisë said, plucking at his sleeve. "Do you see? And with Murandys' niece."

He did see. He had just caught sight of the couple. The thought of the gray, grim lord of Ivanor in the midst of an intricate paselle was astonishing in itself, but the duke of Ivanor had unexpected graces, back-to-back and then face-to-face with the duke of Murandys' fair-haired younger niece in the quick-moving courtly patterns on the floor.

Now *there* was a match. The lords did not favor one another.

The niece—Cleisynde was the name—was a stiffly Quinalt little piece. And looked far less graceful than did Cevulirn, as if she had never danced before. But her eyes, ah, her eyes worshiped. Cevulirn was a distinguished—and wifeless—lord.

"Cleisynde," he said. "One of your ladies, is it not?"

"One of the more agreeable," Ninévrisë said. Some were not. He knew, for instance, that Ryssand's daughter Artisane was a particular thorn in Ninévrisë's side, a bearer of tales straight from Ninévrisë's small circle to her father. And Artisane, also in view, cast a predictable frown at Cevulirn every time the dance turned her from her own partner, Isin's son.

"Ryssand's daughter has eaten sour fruit," he remarked. "Do you see? Is it Cevulirn's partner she disapproves so publicly?"

"Artisane's brother is dancing with Odrinian," Ninévrisë said.

Oho. Sour grapes and bitter leaves for supper. He saw the couple in question: a pretty pair: Odrinian of Murandys, a child, youngest sister to his discarded mistress Luriel—a far kinder and less wise heart, Odrinian; and a merry bit of hell's best work there was in that young whelp, the heir of Ryssand. Brugan was his name, vain ox.

"Don't frown so," Ninévrisë said.

"My former mistress. That is her sister."

"Ah." Ninévrisë's hand, fine and strong, was locked on his between their thrones. "And now you repent?"

"In ashes," he said, and at that instant a peal of thunder racketed through the hall, making both of them jump.

"I have kept no secrets," he said, looking not at her, but straight ahead, at Odrinian and Brugan. Then he did glance aside. "And have given up all of them, I swear. Hence Murandys is not pleased, any more than Ryssand. I shall bring Luriel to court only by your leave."

"I give it," Ninévrisë said, and her chin tilted in that way she had, the pretty girl of the miniature, the entrancing woman who had his heart. "I trust if I needed fear comparisons my lord would *never* have proposed she come."

"Gracious lady. None. It would be a rescue for the lady. A kindness."

"The lady is in distress?"

"Her father blames her, now. She languishes; in immodest, imprudent letters, protests she loved me, were not Amefel's heretic ways so oppressive she could not stay with me there . . ."

"Oh?" A sidelong look. "And do you answer these letters?"

"I forgive them. They have accumulated to the number of three, in two months. I don't think Lord Prichwarrin knows about the letters. I know they come through Odrinian. Luriel is despondent. Hates her father. Misses the festivities. Has no hope. And so on."

"She would not be—" Ninévrisë left a delicate silence, beneath the sparkling music.

"I do think she would plead it; or manage it, if she dared. She wishes a recall to court, over her father's wishes, declares she will drink poison else . . ."

"Good gods."

"She will make someone an unfaithful wife. I have in mind Ursamin's nephew."

"He is notorious!"

"A matched set, I assure you."

Ninévrisë looked at him. "And how many such? Orien Aswydd. Tarien, her sister . . ."

"Both safe in a Teranthine nunnery. And beyond that, women of ambitions more easily satisfied. I have confessed them all, already, every one."

There was silence. A hand listless in his. His heart told him a conversation had skewed wide of its target, broached matters indelicate to have brought to light in this hall, before witnesses.

"If you wish to fling something," he said quietly, "pray wait."

"Oh, no, no, no," Ninévrisë said, and fingers twitched to life and pressed his. "I only mark them down with the rest."

Disturbing. "What 'rest'?"

"Oh, the rest." Ninévrisë's eyes sparkled, just a little.

"The rest of *what,* pray? I have no faults!"

"So far their names are Luriel, Orien, Tarien . . ."

"Fisylle, Cressen, Trallynde, and Alwy."

"Fisylle, Cressen, Trallynde, and Alwy. —Alwy? My maid?"

"I said that there were minor indiscretions."

"Good gods."

"And you said you would forgive me."

"I had no notion they outnumbered the royal Guard. Should we march *them* across the river? Or dare we give them arms?"

"Nevris, sweet love . . ."

"Dare I say *I* had suitors in Elwynor?"

Now his heart beat faster. "Less numerous than mine, I hope."

"Oh . . ." The silence went on, beneath the music. Then cheerfully: "A list."

"My lady Regent, . . ."

"No more 'sweet love'?"

They were in front of tenscore witnesses. He dared not leap up, stare at her from a slightly superior height, in his own hall. There was only that damnable, undignified block of stone, and only her hand within reach.

"To the last breath," he swore. "Dance with me. You have me bothered. You have done it, fair."

"The lady may come to court," she adjudged quietly, and pressed his hand as he rose and drew her to her feet, careful of the damned step. The music and the dancers drifted to a stop.

"A country round," he said to the musicians.

There was a murmur in the hall.

"I trust Your Grace can follow me," he said, as the musicians wandered erratically into the sort of jouncing tune they played in the square. The thunder rumbled above the roof, and the drum rattled out a rhythm to the pipes. The lutenist confessed a peasant knowledge of the tune, "The Merry Lass from Eldermay."

No simple touching of hands, a linking of arms, a whirl, a sweep, a series of chaining steps, and he partnered a lightly moving wisp, a sprite, a whisper of satins and velvet, alone on the floor until Cevulirn partnered Cleisynde out. Then the young men persuaded young ladies, one after another, some quick to learn, some not, and some already knowing the measures. Old Lord Drusallyn brought his lady out, and then Mordam of Osenan and his portly wife dared the measure.

There were sour faces on some, laughter among the rest, most of whom watched in safety. "This is far more like Elwynor," Ninévrisë said, on two breaths, back-to-back for a moment, then facing him, palms touching. Her eyes were gray, not violet: the miniature-painter of a year ago had tricked the eye with violets in her hair. They were gray as the rumored sea, gray as a cloudy day . . .

Gray as Tristen's. Her dark hair and gray eyes were alike conspicuous in a land where the rule was fair hair and blue as his own. Her blue-and-white gown, the colors of Elwynor, swirled across the red and gold of his own kingdom, heraldry bright as battle flags. All eyes might watch as the old blood of Elwynor and the new of Ylesuin trod an autumn dance that might be old, itself. The Quinalt countenanced it, but deplored its license, slowed the music, discouraged the torch race around the bonfire and did not at all approve the offering of straw men; so the countryfolk threw in mere straw bundles, but it meant the same. Everyone knew.

Round and round they went, one dance and another, until the music ran down, quite, until the dancers were out of breath, and he and his bride were in the center of the floor, all eyes toward them.

He had stolen an acorn from an oak bough, in the festoons and boughs about the columns as they passed. He gave it to his bride, with a bow, the finish of the dance, a Guelen peasant's gift to his lass in autumn, a wish for prosperity and children. The onlookers, those that could see, hung upon the gesture; and Ninévrisë, knowing or not (though he thought she knew) tucked it in her bosom to the applause of those around.

Applause spread, and whispers. The gesture was unexpected, it was common, daring, and native to their land. The dreaded

Elwynim cherished the seed of a Guelen oak, the hope of children, and the old wives and the lords of Marisyn and Marisal and Isin nodded together, smiling, whatever glum thoughts Murandys and Ryssand might hold. The talk among certain lords of the middle provinces would denounce the act, and their ladies would say, Oh, but did you see how they love one another . . .

Then the lords would be more glum. Nor could he convince himself that he would bend the like of Nelefreíssan, Ryssand, Murandys. The ladies of those provinces might laugh and applaud with their sisters of the middle provinces, but they were Guelen, and more skilled than their menfolk at dissembling.

They would have to say to themselves, with barbed jealousy, How beautiful she is!

But later they would say among themselves—his eye caught the unanticipated presence—Did you mark the Patriarch's stare?

Gods, when had the *Patriarch* decided to attend? And for that exhibition . . .

Did you see the look on the Patriarch's face? The word would run the whole town by morning, along with: *The king's brother was not smiling.*

Efanor was worried, that was certain.

And when Cefwyn drew Ninévrisë back up the two steps to sit and take a sip of wine, he stared at his younger, his pious Quinalt brother in glaring disapproval of the stiff-backed Quinalt priest who dogged him everywhere; at the Patriarch he dared not glare.

Efanor stared back, but not so fiercely; worried indeed, and seeking to signal him with that glance.

Something was wrong. Cefwyn gave a lift of the chin, a look. Efanor came up the step and bent close. "The Patriarch is here," Efanor said in a quiet voice. "The Quinaltine. A lightning bolt has struck the roof. And a *Sihhë* coin has turned up in the offering."

His wits were still reeling from the dance, from the touch of Ninévrisë's hand, still resting in his, his so-ready distrust of his brother, his repentance of that failing. The significance of the lightning strike was appalling . . . expensive. A donative for roof repair indeed, at a time approaching winter.

A Sihhë coin. Omen, on penny day. The other words had reached him late.

"What damage to the roof?"

"The roof? The sheeting is burned clean through. But the *coin* . . ."

"It was not Tristen's. However it came there, it was not Tristen's!"

"However it came there, the lightning struck, brother, and the penny offering is *tainted*. His Holiness has come here . . ."

"Someone has done this against *me* and against *him*." Temper had not served their father well. Efanor visibly flinched back, the hapless servants stood appalled; voices stayed scarcely in whispers, as the musicians played a stately madannel.

"They could not manage the lightning!" Efanor said.

"They had already done the other! This is treason. This is *treason*, and His Holiness damned well knows the likely hands that put that coin there."

"Brother," Efanor said, urgently, pleadingly . . . like looking into a mirror, Efanor's close presence, the two of them bearded, blond, blue-eyed and royal; but there was only a princely circlet on Efanor's brow, not the weighty, galling crown, which at this instant was pressing on a throbbing vein. Efanor's face was going red. So, likely, was his. "In nowise could a cheat manage the *lightning*! That is somewhat beyond a mortal man, you must admit it. And do not say *damned* with His Holiness!"

"Tristen did not do this," Cefwyn said through gritted teeth. "If it is wizardry, would he damn *himself* and leave a coin to prove his guilt?"

"I admit I would not think it."

"*No* sane man would think it!"

"But what enemy of his in Guelessar would *touch* such a thing? The Quinalt? *And there is the lightning*. They had turned out the offering. And the lightning struck, just then."

"Not every enemy of the Marhanen is a Quinalt painted *saint*, brother, and I would not exclude Sulriggan from this act."

"He would not! *And there is the lightning!*"

"Sulriggan would sell his mother's bones as relics, never mistake it." He saw, behind Efanor's shoulder, His Holiness, Sulriggan's cousin, ready to approach him, in public. "What have we? A damned *procession*? Fly the banners, shall we?" The musicians still played, but the conference on the dais had drawn all attention, and conversation and dancing flagged throughout the hall. The king's dancing was over if he attended this importunate storm of priestly anguish now.

And if he withdrew prematurely to face some controversy over ill omens and sorcerous miracles, he knew exactly the kind of flutter ready to break forth, the gossip of servants and minor priests who

126

were always in the fringes with ears aprick, and who had stood just near enough, in the way of things. Even his Guard, his faithful Guard, was not immune.

More, he would leave a roomful of the very lords and ladies no other event of the season would assemble until the wedding, lords and ladies who would talk, of course, about the only thing worth their speculation: what the Patriarch had wanted that was so urgent. And about his bride. And about the country dance. And about Tristen . . . and the coin. And the weather. Give them the space of a single dance to have the news out of some servant and give them two dances more to have the tale embroidered into sorcerous manifestations over in the Quinaltine, with the smell of Althalen's haunted fire and his grandfather's ghost.

He beckoned with a crooked finger, a finger that bore his father's ring, now his, as the whole burden of Ylesuin was his, and only his. Efanor supported him, yes, had come to him in this, but Efanor had not used his wits to keep the Holy Father from bringing the matter *here,* oh, gods, no, Efanor's ordinarily keen wits scattered to the several winds when His Holiness willed this or wanted that . . . *yes, Your Holiness,* gods preserve Your Holiness . . . kiss your *robe,* Your Holiness. A year younger than he, Efanor was in his period of youthful credulity, of piety, of devout belief riding hard for a fall: he had spent his own time of easy belief, thank the gods, chasing women and believing himself all-wise, to far greater profit to the realm.

"Your Majesty," the Patriarch said, trembling: well he might tremble.

"Your Holiness." He kept his voice low. Even yet, despite the hush, only the servants might hear; and Efanor, leaning close; and Ninévrisë, whose hand he must abandon, sitting beside him, she could hear it all.

"There was . . ." A monk had attended His Holiness as far as the dais, unbidden, and the Patriarch summoned him—which was no one's damned *right,* to summon someone else into the king's presence; but His Holiness, being overwrought, had the gods to excuse his lèse-majesté. His face remained white and thin-lipped as the monk came near and unfolded a small white cloth which, indeed, contained not the king's bronze penny, but a silver coin of some age and, indeed, Sihhë origin. The Star and Tower were quite clear to see, age-worn and bright on tarnished metal.

"Distressing," Cefwyn agreed, "but in nowise attributable to the lightning."

"The coin appears as what it truly *is*, Your Majesty. It could not maintain a sorcerous guise in the offering box. The gods—"

"The gods have raised a seasonal storm over our heads, and the banner-tower has been hit at least six times in *my* recollection, so why *not* the Quinalt roof? That it coincides with a sly act of treason—which is what this is, Holy Father—is happenstance. It was a terrible crack—we heard it here, and more than one; but you are not a man to jump at a stroke of thunder. I've known you far steadier. Bear up."

"Someone has worked *sorcery*, Your Majesty. The penny is the offering for the *roof* and the lightning blasted a great hole in it!"

"And whom do you accuse? Make an accusation, Holy Father. Or are we to assume what the dastard that did this *wished* us to assume? I am defender of the faith. Before you invoke *me*, be sure, I charge you be sure, or say you do not know."

The Holy Father knew exactly what was meant on every hand. And there was deep silence.

Cefwyn waved his hand, dismissing monk and coin. "It is not his. I don't know whose it is, but it is not Tristen's."

"Your Majesty—"

"We *gave* the Warden of Ynefel a penny, a good *Guelen* penny."

"The coin then—"

"*Dare* you say it? Again, *be sure*."

The Patriarch took in his breath. "The meaning of it I can name, Your Highness. It's a *curse*, a working against the Quinaltine, a strike at the very sanctity of the holy precinct."

"The *meaning* is someone who would gain by it, someone wishing to harm me, harm the Lord Warden, *and* mislead Your Holiness, if it were possible, which I trust it is not, Your Holiness being no gullible or common man." He spoke sharply, harshly, his tone exactly his father's when he was crossed: he had that gift, he had the stare, he had been informed of its use since his boyhood, and he used it now like a weapon, knowing with a sinking heart that whatever he did in this hall, gossip was already flying between the Quinalt precinct to the Guelesfort kitchens and it was a short step to every noble house in every province—by fast riders, if they believed the whole of it. The music stopped. The dancers stood waiting, listening, all but leaning forward, awaiting some definition of the moment, some characterization of the news from him and from the Patriarch, the temporal and the spiritual pillars of their lives.

Where in *hell* was Idrys? His captain had stepped out of the hall, as he was in the habit of coming and going in his duties. And damned ill timed, this absence.

"I will tell you," he said to the Patriarch in deadly calm, and the utter stillness as the nobles as one body, on one breath, attempted to overhear their voices. "Some enemy has done this, and if he has employed sorcery—" He gathered all his wits, seeing a hole in the Quinalt roof as not subject to denial, only interpretation. He reaimed the lightning bolt, in a word. "—it came from across the river, *as has the hand that did this,* no friend of Her Grace, but her bitter enemy. Considering there is Sihhë coinage scattered in hoards all over whatever lands the Sihhë-lords once ruled, why, no great difficulty obtaining such things. But who would do such a thing?" Quiet as his voice was, he let it rise just a little, to give some well-judged reward to the eavesdroppers. "Who would practice sorcery against us? Who stands to gain?" Oh, he had his own notions on that score, pious Ryssand not excluded, but he named the ones that served his purpose. "All that might gain by preventing us are *across* the river, fomenting rebellion against Her Grace and harm against our people, which I will not countenance. The Lord Warden gave the penny *I* gave him to give, nor has any store of coin at all. I am sure of him. I am sure of my lady. We need look further, to someone both cunning and with something to gain."

Murmuring broke out, the hindmost of the eavesdroppers wanting to know what was said, drowning all voices. *Idrys* had come back, thank the gods, using that small door beside the throne by which the king and his intimates might come and go in other than formal entrances; and that look and slight lift of Idrys' head told him that Idrys had news he should hear immediately, and aside, in that room.

Damn. *Damn* the timing. There was danger here, grave danger: and the heart of Guelessar was *not* the simple court of Amefel, where the king could do very much as he pleased and know himself upheld by the five barons of the south and the lord viceroy of Amefel, if not by the Amefin peasantry.

But the barons of the north had been his father's men and would far more gladly have been pious Efanor's. Here, in extremity, he had to call, not on Cevulirn, who would stand by him with a clear loyalty, but on such pillars of the Quinalt faith as the duke of Murandys, Lord Prichwarrin, accustomed to having his father's ear for every triviality and resenting him bitterly for refusing to grant him all the favors his father had granted. His grandfather had known how uneasy the crown rested on a usurper; his father had held it more legitimately, but had placated the lords of the north in his reign. Now they were accustomed to being cajoled, led by their desires and their purses, their pride coddled, their ambitions satisfied, often by the one power that *could* rule Guelenfolk and Ryssandim alike, the one unifying element in all the provinces.

And that one unifying element was *not* the Marhanen kings. It was, and ever had been, the Quinalt, and the Patriarch.

And *damned* if all the Patriarch's disposition had not hied him here on the genuine fright of a levin bolt and the mountebank slip of a coin. His Holiness had *Efanor* unnerved. He could see his brother's face—insanely gullible where it came to the Quinalt and religion. Where, oh, where, was the brother he had plotted with as a child?

But the lightning stroke, Efanor had said again and again. *But the lightning stroke—*

He had to answer the matter. "Your Holiness," he said, "I shall see you in the privy chamber directly. —Your Grace," he said to Ninévrisë, reaching his hand to hers, where it rested on the arm of her chair. "I shall have the roof patched and someone *hanged*, if I find the culprit. We have guards to set, and messengers to send to the bridges and the riverward villages in case your enemies have any remote gain in this circumstance. We will not require any long conference to do that. —Ivanor." He had all attention, and had used it, summoning Cevulirn forward. "At the king's pleasure, you pipers. Play, play." He rose, drew Ninévrisë by the hand as Efanor and the priest cleared a seemly path. "Dance. Sip wine. Trust Cevulirn." He passed Ninévrisë's hand into Cevulirn's, a gesture not wasted on the jealous northern barons; and by that transit all the display of finery and all the scores of days of women's work was saved, in his *not* curtailing the evening. Certainly it was a breach of custom for the festivities to continue without the king, and certainly he dared not set Ninévrisë in any authority over the hall . . . but the confidence that the matter the Patriarch brought was being answered without an inconvenience to the court brought a relief and if not a mood of outright celebration in the wiser lords present, at least a willingness in the company to maintain themselves assembled and within reach of information. The young, whose whole consideration was very much the dancing, might take the floor with Her Grace and Ivanor.

The musicians limped into unison and the drums struck up a

modest paselle. The duke of the Ivanim bowed, Ninévrisë bowed, and every head in the hall inclined, furnishing his moment of escape as Idrys held the door beside the dais, and his personal guard fell in, quickly.

CHAPTER 9

Where *were* you?" he asked
Idrys in displeasure as they walked in the shadows of the passage,
His Holiness, with Efanor, being obliged to a more circuitous route
to the privy chamber. "More to the point, where is Tristen? Gods
give us witnesses. *Tell* me he is with witnesses the last hour."

"Tristen is closeted with *Emuin*," Idrys hissed back. "Lusin and
Syllan are with him. And Uwen."

Cefwyn stopped so quickly that the guards behind them brought
up desperately short. Idrys was a shadow against the few candles in
the privy chamber beyond the tapestried passage, a dark and ominous shadow. It had always been Idrys' business to know all that
went on. And Idrys knew, within the Guelesfort, where Tristen was,
and what was happening. But the Quinaltine and its doings were all
but impenetrable territory to Idrys' men.

"Tristen left his apartment," Cefwyn reiterated.

"With a train of Your Majesty's guards and his own man all the
while. The guards are sitting outside Emuin's door in his tower.
Tristen is inside."

"Emuin himself is not pure in their eyes. We dare not have this
break out. *Damn!* Where were you? Why did you permit this?"

"I heard the commotion with the Quinalt. The damage to the
place is extensive. And I regret the Lord Warden went to the tower
this evening. But that is not the worst. We have a courier from the
river. Tasmôrden has moved his army south at dawn today."

Devastating news. He caught a deliberate, a difficult breath.

"Is *that* what you were about?"

"I was down in the guardroom, I beg Your Majesty's pardon." Idrys rarely had to. "The shore-fire was lit, one fire, after dawn this morning, and since that hour, a courier has come from the shore to us. We assume the direction of movement is toward Ilefínian, if the observers saw it clearly, if he was not hindered in lighting a second beacon."

A partisan of Her Grace of Elwynor, on the far shore of the Lenúalim, had risked his life to bring them that much, lighting one of a combination of fires that their posts on this side could see. One fire, southerly, meant alarm and movement toward the south. Gods send mud, was his thought, thick mud with this downpour, on the roads between Tasmôrden and the capital of Elwynor. Gods send sleet and snow and ice to shield Her Grace's capital. Her partisans would be slaughtered to a man once Tasmôrden breached the gates and got into the town: few of her supporters could maintain their secrecy, though the wiser ones would hie them out the gates and southward as fast as they could. And if the Elwynim rebels *had* moved and (considering Efanor's damned levin bolt) if *sorcery* had risen in very fact, and ridden this storm—then gods save them.

Gods, *could* it *be* wizardry? If some wizard joined Tasmôrden, there would be the devil of a war.

The candleflames in the sconces swayed: a door closed in the privy chamber. His Holiness had come in.

Damn, again. The Quinalt roof was far from his concern, balanced against this news; and yet it was the point of attack—and correctly so. Everything depended on a few scorched roof slates. Tristen's safety was at issue because of it. *Ninévrisë's* safety was. A charge of sorcery attached to his dearest, his most loyal, his most intimate friends . . . might be sorcery indeed. But *not* Tristen's. And it was at least possible it was no more than ill-timed chance.

"Set a watch on Tristen," he said, very quietly, and walked from behind the sheltering tapestry into the dim chamber. He settled himself on the cushionless, cold chair, and the guard brought in two candles, in a room tapestried in the deeds of the Marhanen, the murder of the Sihhë, the raising of the Quinalt shrine, the battle against the Elwynim. The predominant color was red, Marhanen red, the red of blood, red of fire, red of royal power.

For two pennies and a breath of breeze tonight he would order the walls stripped and the tapestries added to the year-fire, His Holiness, his roof, and Tasmôrden across the river be damned together.

Perhaps he should *be* such a king as his grandfather had been. A judicious murder or two, friends protected, and his enemies, even clergy, not allowed to leave this room alive—no tales whispered by servants either. He looked sullenly at the Patriarch's pale presence in the dim light, with Efanor, like him, in Marhanen red, just behind, and wondered how the Patriarch had dealt with his grandfather and survived . . . for this had been his grandfather's priest, raised, with his entire sect, to primacy in his father's reign.

"This fatal penny," he said, before the Patriarch could open his mouth. "This *attack* on the harvest festival, and on the welfare of the realm, and on *me*, Holy Father, I find disturbing; I agree that it may be sorcerous, but not from my hand, not from the Lord Warden's hand, not from any *friendly* hand. I call on Your Holiness to uphold me in this matter. I trust Your Holiness will adhere to me as you adhered to my father, as faithfully, as staunch in defense."

"Your late father, gods give him rest, upheld the Quinalt, and did not accept a breath of witchery in his court."

"Nor I! *Dare you say so?*"

The Patriarch, being a canny old man, was not set back, however lightning-rattled. "I say that wickedness is afoot and it will seek out the unwary, Your Majesty. It will find doors. It will insinuate itself at any opportunity. It was lately potent in Amefel."

"It was lately potent *beyond* Amefel."

"In Elwynor!"

"By news just now arrived, we may spend a winter knowing *Tasmôrden* sits in Ilefínian killing every man who favors Her Grace's cause, and if you would surmise where we might look for sorcery, let me remind Your Holiness sorcery killed my lady's father, killed her loyal men, and made her an exile in this court. If I had had a little less discourse on the height of my seat and the colors of the hangings for harvesttide, if I had had my reliable reckonings out of the villages faster, and not bungled beyond all redemption, if we had had the enthusiasm of the Quinalt behind this war, we might have done something to prevent this disaster that now confronts us. Sorcery, aye, *sorcery*—"

"The coin—"

"Did we search every purse? I think not, Holy Father. But I know that Lord Tristen's gift was pure! I gave him the coin myself, since he had none, Holy Father. I gave him a purse of good Guelen pennies, and such as he had, he gave to you. Wherein some traitor to me in

Guelemara attempted to foment disharmony at this hinge point of the year, or whether the enemy of Her Grace had a hand in it, in such dire news from across the river, I hold the action on the one hand impious and hostile sorcery, and on the other hand *treasonous,* Holy Father!"

He ran out of wind and words alike and lost the thread of his thought altogether. He had heard his father's rages at his advisers and as those went, this one had its effect; but temper passed beyond policy and overwhelmed his reason. There was utter silence, as his brother and the Patriarch alike sifted through that spate for pebbles safe to pick up. A candle spat. It was that deep a hush.

Two deep breaths forewarned the Patriarch's intent to speak. "I assure Your Majesty, we are fully in agreement on sorcery, but the Lord of Ynefel *is* not willingly Quinalt, however noble Your Highness's effort." This last with a nod to Efanor.

"He is no further from us than Bryaltine," Cefwyn said, straining at the truth, which was that Tristen knew less of any of the three faiths than he did of pig-keeping.

"But a Sihhë soul," the Patriarch said, "if he has a soul. Which is to debate . . ."

"If he had not a soul, how could a wizard have gotten him out of death? What did Mauryl bring back to this world, if not a soul?"

"He said the devotions," Efanor ventured, bending all those years of priestly study, arguing with the Holy Father on Tristen's behalf: it was a gallant effort, and Cefwyn drew a breath of gratitude.

"Yet," the Patriarch said, "sorcery gained power with that coin—"

"Bother the coin!" He gathered up the scraps of his eloquence. "Your Holiness, the Quinalt is our strength, our reliance, and to make a breach between Crown and Quinalt, who would benefit? I don't doubt that one might have ridden the other, but *it was not Tristen. Look to Elwynor!*"

"Yet . . ." The old man trembled, wobbled, and still, the adder, attacked: "Yet . . . to bring that banner, into the shrine . . . Your Majesty, *we* may see the worth in the Lord Warden, but the Lord Warden is not even a *man* in the sense that Men are Men, and to bring those symbols, charged with sorcery, into the very shrine . . . I did fear, and objected, if Your Majesty will recall. Therefore, our defenses were breached."

"Nonsense!—Forgive me, Holy Father, but *nonsense!* A good Guelen lady stitched *that banner,* as you name it. It did not come from Ynefel, not a stitch that the Lord Warden owns came from

Ynefel, no medals, medallions, coins, cantrips, nor spells that Your Holiness ever detected or complained of, which Your Holiness can as well say in public *quickly* and in that hall, if Your Holiness has any care of my goodwill."

"Yet . . ." the Patriarch said.

"Yet." He recovered breath and composure. This was *not* a religious man. This was a man of temporal power, affrighted by the manifestation of nature, a man frightened into belief in his own predecessors' creation in these hours of darkness and lightning strokes.

"The Star and Tower are not benign, lord king. There will be talk."

"Which you can quell *at will*, Your Holiness."

"The Crown and the Quinalt must stand together against sorcery, Your Majesty. But *that banner* cannot be sanctified. I feared no good would come of it. The gods themselves failed to sustain the roof."

The hell with the roof, he wanted to say, and glared, but dared not. That was the thing: he dared not. There were limits which neither he nor the Patriarch had yet searched out with each other. He only prayed for the pragmatic man to rise to reason with him, the old man he knew.

But that old man had heard the report out of Amefel, and gods forfend he believed his own sermons, to think he and the gods of his sermons could match the real, rolling darkness on Lewen field.

"This is a sign," the Patriarch said. "Very clearly a sign. Your Majesty, I stood beneath that roof. I heard the strike! My ears still ring with it! The people in the square, sheltering from the rain, they all fled in terror. What will they say around about the town?"

"What the Quinalt *bids* them say," he said angrily. Gods forfend, too, that the old man should take to faith in his own gods at this pass. "The Quinalt can mend this rumormongering."

"Not against this, Your Majesty. We cannot *lie* to the people. We cannot ignore sorcery! We cannot shelter it, or permit it in the sacred precinct. I cannot countenance it."

"Are you telling me, Holy Father, that you will *bar* the Lord Warden, in *my* court, from your door?"

"I beg Your Highness not test the gods."

"This is *treason*, Holy Father. Look out, or you will discover my grandfather in me. Do not *dare* to tell me . . ."

"Brother." There was starkest fear in Efanor's face. "I beg you. *Is* this what you wish? Dare we have this division? I was not at Lewen field. I had not that honor. But I heard the reports, Holy Father. I know that the Lord Warden helped overcome sorcery."

"With sorcery," the Patriarch said hoarsely. *"Sorcery with sorcery,* that is the point, lord king. You wish me to bless this marriage, you wish me to say grace over a union with the Lady Regent, which while unorthodox offers a hope of the gods' grace over the far shore, but in the Lord Warden you have an association I fear owes more to *Teranthine* advice than mine. —We are willing to bless this union, Your Majesty, do not mistake me!"

The last was just in time. He had drawn breath to reply.

"—And shall," the Patriarch hastened to say, all but choking on the words. "And shall, with all our good offices, Your Majesty. But *how much* of the strange and sorcerous will you ask good folk to countenance? Where shall we draw the line, —but at Assurnbrook, as we have always drawn it? You say that I can prevent the gossip. What shall we do? Fly to every house, of every common man who ran from the public square tonight as bits of the roof came down, and bid the commons not say a Sihhë presence cursed us? How shall I say, in all observances, *'bless the king and his court'* when one of that court is Sihhë? How shall I say, *'strike down the unbeliever'* when he sits in the congregation? How shall I say, *'the cursed signs and symbols be far from your houses'* when that banner stands in brazen contradiction?"

His Holiness had named the real argument when he had said, more *Teranthine* than my advice. *There* was the old fox he knew. There was the old man's concern: *Emuin's* influence with the new king. Now they were down to realities.

"Your liturgy is no older than my grandfather. Change the words."

"Your Majesty cannot ask that!"

"If Your Holiness wants his roof patched, *change the damned words!*"

"This is an unseemly discussion!"

"This is a royal order. A command of the Crown. Dare you deny me? I say Tristen is an ally, Tristen is *our friend,* and a defender of this realm. Do not attempt my patience, Holy Father. Do not dare do it. He stands where Ynefel has always stood, and I would recommend Your Holiness not tamper with that bulwark."

"I say I cannot prevent the gossip, Your Majesty! I say no one can call back the lightning bolt, undo what eyes have seen in the square tonight, *or on Lewen field.* There will be disaster. Mark me, if there is one stain, one taint, now . . . what if it taint the marriage?"

The old fox, Cefwyn said to himself, seeing the look in the old man's eyes. The malevolent old fox. The man who had damned near reigned *during* his father's reign, and the last years of his grandfather's, at least where peace in the realm was the issue. He was well capable of having dropped that coin in, himself, even after the lightning stroke. He was a dangerous man. He had always been a dangerous man, snuggling right up next Marhanen warmth, looking for advantage from the Marhanen, most chancy in allegiance, seeing he had, now, a hostage.

Ninévrisë. The wedding.

Oh, this was a *fit* adviser for his grandfather.

Dared he think . . . *dared* he suspect that this priest had always ruled the rulers, by seizing upon and increasing their fears—fears of ghosts, in his grandfather; fears of his own heir in his father, driving the wedge between father and son, brother and brother?

The thought came on him like the levin stroke next door, stopped his breath and robbed him of clear thought. He had hated Aséyneddin, who had slaughtered men of his, but that was war. He had not been fond of the assassins whose heads had graced the fortress gate in Henas'amef, but that was political, and they had been Aséyneddin's men, following a lord's orders. He had hated Sulriggan, and Heryn Aswydd. But had *this* poisonous man been the author of his father's fear of him, setting him away from him, always, always at arm's length, so that Ináreddrin had preferred Efanor to his dying breath?

He looked at his hands, resting joined across his belt, studied the sword scars on his knuckle, the lesson he *would* not learn, no matter how many times master Peygan had whacked right past his guard with exactly the same move.

He had learned. He needed no one these days to hit him three and four times. He looked up at His Holiness, —smiled his grandfather's smile, and saw his brother blanch and the Holy Father's jaw set.

Did he need the Holy Father? The Holy Father might hold his fiefdom from the gods, but he needed the blessing of the Marhanen king as much as the king needed the Quinalt's.

But later? After the wedding?

"A narrow path," he said, "a *narrow* path, Your Holiness, royal disfavor on one side, in which, who knows, I *might* find a new Patriarch and Your Holiness might suffer a fatal indigestion. Consider your path: royal disfavor on the one hand and a wakening of the Old Magic on the other. Sorcery, you fear—so say I, and I tell you, I will have myself a new *priest* before I suffer any discommodation in my marriage, in this campaign, in the installation of Her Grace as Regent of Elwynor."

The Holy Father's face had gone stark and pale as ivory. A vein throbbed in his temple. The thunder still rumbled overhead.

"Your Majesty is close to blasphemy."

"Dare I suggest, Your Holiness, that Your Holiness has seized marvelously on opportunity tonight. I daresay some priest would confess, if questioned stringently, and, oh, I would not stick at that to get that confession, never doubt me. Such a man would swear that Your Holiness bade him obtain a Sihhë coin among the small practitioners of magics that still flourish, yes, even in Guelessar, even in the heart of Quinalt piety. I know I could find such a man and his tale would be whatever I wish. The lightning was only opportune."

"Brother," Efanor said, overwhelmed, "for the good gods . . ."

"Oh, let us not couple good and gods in this priest's company. His Holiness would create a breach between himself and me only if he were an utter fool—which he is not. Being no fool, nor dealing with one, he will bless the wedding and make very certain there are no ill omens or offending liturgy in the ceremony. He has overreached himself, coming perilously close to extinction. Let us see if we can arrive at a definition of our positions, we two, tonight. *Now.*"

"I advised two kings, most gracious Majesty, I counseled your grandfather and your father. I advise you now for your good, that the Quinalt can find exception for everything you ask. Everything but one. Nor can I unsay what is being said in half the houses in Guelemara tonight. If Your Majesty wishes not to see a breach between Quinalt and Crown, let him not place the Quinaltine at odds with him! The northern barons are in doubt of this marriage. The Quinaltine, on Your Majesty's part, would stand firmly with Your Majesty, but cannot do so with the presence of that banner and such allies!"

"I shall value Your Holiness's view," Cefwyn said, coldly purposeful as the old man was purposeful in every well-prepared word. "Her Grace has a strong right to inherit of her father the Regent, and now this new Usurper is advancing on her capital . . . with wizardous assistance, Holy Father. Threatening all of us. *As witness your roof.* Tristen it was who came to us with the first warning of sorcery, Mauryl's heir, and would I had understood that warning earlier than I did, but I suggest if Your Holiness *can* muster the wherewithal to turn sorcery from the Quinalt roof, Your Holiness should consider doing so quite urgently. Even so great a wizard as Mauryl Gestaurien did not withstand what assailed us at Lewenbrook and could not safeguard his tower from destruction or his own life from extinction. Dare you take up the battle—without the Warden of Ynefel?"

"The prayers of the righteous are not to be despised."

"Excellent. Pray away and keep a supply of roof tiles. Meanwhile we stand a chance of settling the Elwynim succession in a lasting peace, gods send us common sense. As Mauryl's heir, Tristen opposed hostile sorcery by force of arms on Lewen field. And did Your Holiness wish to hear us who *were* on Lewen field, I do strongly believe that we are appointed one vital chance, *by* Mauryl's defense, and that the gods have guided us to this marriage, these unlikely allies—"

"Do not lesson us on the gods, Your Majesty!"

"Do not lesson *me* on policy! Sorcery has bent all its strength to prevent this marriage!"

"To *gain* this marriage, equally well!"

"Oh, no, no, no, you dare not say so much, Holy Father. I assure you, you dare not say so much. *I was there,* Holy Father. Sorcery threw the rebel Aseyneddin at us, at Lewenbrook. That failed. Now it advances on Ilefinian through Tasmorden's attack; and *if* that lightning bolt that descended on your roof is sorcery, then the prayers of the righteous did damned little to prevent it. Sorcery tried once to overthrow us. It tries to cast misfortune in the path of a marriage *it does not want*, Holy Father, and if there was by any remote chance some sorcerous transformation of a good Guelen penny, I suggest *sorcery* did so precisely to discredit the heir of the Warden of Ynefel, who has fought against an enemy that—by the gods!—I shall send you to face *in his stead,* if you wish to replace Ynefel in the battle line. How say you to *that,* Holy Father? Dare you?"

That hung in the air, and occasioned immediate reconsiderations and retrenchment: "Your Majesty is in our devotions constantly. We only suggest possibilities."

"We value your goodwill, Holy Father."

"And who will say, if this is sorcery, that there may not be another, fatal attempt? If it is sorcery that directed the lightning, I pray Your Majesty come to sober thought that, as you may believe, *I* did not direct it. Your Majesty wishes a wedding free of omens. I cannot again countenance the banners in *the holy sanctuary*, my lord king!"

"*You* cannot countenance!"

"*In the name of the gods,* I cannot countenance them. The gods bless and keep Your Majesty and Her Grace of Elwynor. The Tower and Checker will have our blessing. *But I cannot abandon every principle of the faith!* Even the Star and Tower we will bless at need . . . and, yes, defend as an ally, perilous though it be." Was it a shudder he saw? Had the man sensibilities and scruples after all? "But not in every service, on every holy day dare we keep that banner in the sanctuary, Your Majesty. We dare not provoke wizardry to cross the river, if wizardry it was, as I do very much fear. And alliance with the Lord Warden may cost us far more than we yet reckon. These things have a cost!"

Fear. There was the word. His Holiness was not the young priest who had stood with his grandfather, or exorcised ghosts from the Guelesfort stairs.

Cefwyn stared at him in bleak consideration, leaned forward, chin on fist, and stared longer.

And longer, while his heart beat hard with anger and his eyes refused to see except through a dark pall. Something thumped into place; it felt that way. Safety for Tristen—power to his southern lords—comeuppance for Ryssand.

"Amefel is vacant," he said at last, out of that moil of shadow, and saw his brother open his mouth.

And shut it.

"Tristen might do very well in Amefel," Cefwyn said with a deeper breath, and leaned back in the seat of judgment, regarding all before him. "What says Your Holiness?"

"To make this creature lord of a *province*?"

"He is already lord of Althalen and Ynefel, within the selfsame province. You wish no untoward doings; I wish a peaceful wedding and an end of talk about the roof. Dare we agree that we agree?"

Again, a hesitation. A quaver in the voice. A man who had danced with lightning was, whatever his other faults, grateful for simple things. "Yes, Your Majesty."

"Never mistake me," Cefwyn said, and left a long silence. "Never mistake me, Holy Father. As I shall never mistake you. We each have our domains. Never cross into mine."

Stare met stare. But the Patriarch did not state the converse. There was a measurable difference, then, in what they dared.

He had, he hoped, just made that everlastingly clear. And he would have himself wed, and Tristen—

Tristen.

"Tomorrow," he said. Wounds were best done quickly, thoroughly. He had no wish to contemplate the issue. And knew what he had done, in anger and what he had to do, for a winter's peace. And did his enemies know, as Idrys knew, what Tristen was? "Tomorrow, in the Quinaltine, he will swear. Roof or no roof you will witness his oath."

"Yes, Your Majesty."

"Good rest, Holy Father. I trust you have adequate escort. A wrap against the weather outside."

"Completely adequate," the Patriarch said, and took the cue, saying nothing regarding prophecies, Kings to Come, or the Elwynim Regency.

Efanor saw the Patriarch as far as the door, but he lingered. Idrys did not remotely think of leaving.

"My lord king." Idrys broke the silence. *"Amefel?"*

"Tristen has a chance," Efanor cried, "a mere chance, to rescue his soul. And you are damning him! You are giving him over to a sorcerous province, where he has no shield but magic, when here he had a chance at holiness!"

This last was a curious proposition, the only genuine question of faith he had heard in the last quarter hour. The first was only the surface of the question that ran, at depth, *Has my king taken leave of his wits?*

"Where *else* can I secure him a livelihood, if you please? Ynefel and Althalen are ruins. I have him where my servants and my guards can provide for him . . . but that also places him near me, near Ninévrisë, near very sensitive matters. I can call him back at need. I *shall* call him back, and meanwhile I provide him a banner they cannot fault."

"Many another man in difficulty," said Idrys, "one appoints a small pension and a village sinecure. A province does seem extravagant."

It was perhaps the measure of his mood tonight that only Idrys could set him in a better humor. And Idrys did not say the half of what he was sure was on Idrys' mind.

"He cannot fend for *himself*," Efanor said. "How can he manage a province two hundred of the king's best troops cannot keep in order?"

"And where *else* shall he be safe?" The temper rose again. "If you were less familiar with priests and more with me, brother—" No, that was not fair. "Forgive me. But this entire business is connivance."

"The lightning stroke—"

"Bother the lightning stroke! It happened and that old fox had already planned to trot out that blaspheming coin! I'll warrant he had one in the hoard he keeps, his own coffers."

"Brother, that is blasphemous."

"Mark me, mark me, that is a villainous man. You heard him. I shall have my wedding if I banish Tristen. Does that measure the true depth of his conviction? Mark the day. I shall have within a fortnight a request for his cousin Sulriggan, his reinstatement in my favor."

"You need not grant it."

"Did you not hear? Threats fell left and right. That is a *malevolent* man, who hounded our grandfather with fear of hell, our father with fear of *me*, and drove our father to his death with his suspicions, brother! Piece the account together, for the gods' love! Our father would not have trusted Heryn Aswydd if he had not trusted the Holy Father first."

"That is extravagant." Efanor's face was white as death. Efanor had *seen* the Holy Father at his political worst and heard the truth tonight.

"Words kill, brother. They need not be sorcerous."

"But the lightning stroke, I say—"

"Brother, —"

"My lord king," Idrys said in his calm, even voice, "the court, meanwhile, will be in doubt."

The hall and the dancing. He drew a breath. "Brother," he said more moderately, even pleadingly, "open your eyes. I grant you your lightning bolt if you grant me that this *coin* is political, not godly, and we are in mortal danger of this man's ambitions and his determination to keep what power he has. Your priest may be godly. But the Patriarch is no honest priest."

"I think you provoked him too far, sir."

"*I? I* provoked?"

"My lord king," Idrys said.

"We have the court to settle," Cefwyn said, shoving aside all fruitless argument. "My decision stands. Lord of Amefel, successor to the Aswyddim, him and his issue, as they may be, in fealty to the

Crown, which he will freely swear. Idrys, send a messenger to him; send to the Patriarch, officially, that tomorrow afternoon, come wrack, come ruin or a hole in the Quinalt roof, we will stand before the altar, that the banner of Amefel will stand there above those of Ynefel and Althalen, which will be all the comfort we afford His Holiness, and the court will attend in *their* goodwill on such an occasion."

He rose, then, and in Efanor's shocked silence led the way back through the short passage and into the warmth and motion and music of the royal ball.

He had resumed his perch on the stone-propped seat, alone, before the musicians saw him and tinkled to a stop, with the dancers.

He stood up. The dancers bowed. The one whose head only nodded was Ninévrisë, who came to his outstretched hand, Cevulirn attending her, and received his smile . . . on which he was conscious the whole room hung.

He handed her toward her seat: she stood beside him.

"The Quinalt roof is not as serious a matter as one might have feared," he said, and with coldest, most matter-of-fact address of policy, he let his face frown. "But it was meant by Her Grace's enemies to be far more serious than it was. *Sorcery* has done its worst, and now, *with the Patriarch's blessing,* we shall answer it. We shall ask the Lord Warden of Ynefel to march south to bring Amefel into our hand and to give these sorcery-dabbling rebels a pause for reflection the winter long. To that intent, *with the Patriarch's blessing—*" How he loved taking the Patriarch's name in vain! "—we create him duke of Amefel and grant him all titles the Aswyddim held. And, *with the Patriarch's blessing,* we bid him hold the southern marches." In the general impression, by his fondest hopes, it was now not for the Lord Warden to defend himself against charges of sorcery, but for the Lord Warden to deal with *all* such sticky questions of sorcerous attacks, as was the Lord Warden's post when Mauryl had held it. He had, at a stroke, settled Tristen in the one place he had never considered it possible to settle any friendly lord, but where it was most reasonable to settle Tristen, in a land which would welcome him, at a moment when the court, reeling from sorcery, wished protection of a sort that might be effective, but not in their witness.

And in a place where prophecies and sorcery could do their worst: *win his love, Emuin had advised him.*

There was confused approbation from the young, there were far more sober looks from the old, and perhaps even looks of relief in several faces, Murandys and Ryssand chief among them, who were glad to have the Lord Warden south of *them*, or in hell, whichever would come soonest. They had won their assault . . . the king's friend was leaving. But the king, let them realize it soon, was not pleased with them.

He sat down. Ninévrisë sat beside him.

"Are things as well as that?" she asked softly, who did not know her capital was under attack, and he held her hand and kept a pleasant face to the court, as he waved them to resume their dancing.

"Be brave. Tasmôrden has moved on the capital."

There was silence. The fingers in his clenched slowly, but he trusted she kept her serenity, as he trusted her in all things else.

"There is no other word from the river," he said. "Meanwhile the Quinalt roof has a hole in it and the Patriarch calls it sorcery. I am sending Tristen south for all our safety." He almost said, *until the wedding,* and then with full force it came to him that, while the appointment at last gave a friend an income of his own and a living land to stand on, it entailed obligations that would keep Tristen from court for far more than a season, if he saw to them in earnest. *Win his love,* Emuin had advised him. And Emuin himself would not oppose the force that Called a Sihhë-lord from the grave.

Knowing Tristen as he did, yes, Tristen would indeed take those obligations seriously. When had Tristen ever failed an obligation, once he had taken it up? It came to him, among other, more tangled considerations, that he might not so easily get his friend back once he had sent him out—and that thought afflicted him with a sudden melancholy.

Of course he had Tristen's friendship. Of course he had his loyalty. That was unquestioned. Of friends he had ever had, there was none so sudden, so close, so maddening . . . none had made such a place in his heart as Tristen had, none ever let him rest so confident as he did, that he could neglect Tristen even a little and take him up again, as bright, as faithful as in the summer—or send him into the heart of wizardry and get him back again untarnished. Of course he could rely on Tristen. Of course they would always have their friendship. Of course Tristen could come back again, when court was gathered about the king—and if Tristen did rise to rule Elwynor, why, what loss? His bride, all his, her home unharmed, but her loyalty turning entirely to him. That, with Tristen for an ally, a loyal man. It was beyond planning, now. He had advanced the first piece on the board.

But if Ilefínian fell easily to Tasmôrden's forces and left time before the snows, and if Tasmôrden had some notion of securing southern bridgeheads to outflank Ylesuin's incursion from the north—two curs chasing each other's tails, yapping and snapping—why, that lightning strike, if it was Elwynim-sent, had just put Tristen square in Tasmôrden's path. Then let wizardry do its worst; he had no more effective weapon and no stauncher friend.

It still had a cold feeling about it, to have done it all at a stroke, loosing Tristen to do what he would in the south, when he had before this had warnings from Emuin that what Tristen willed to do subtly *bent* the affairs of other men. Tristen willed very little and had his desires generally satisfied by feeding pigeons.

Dangerous, something still said to him. He should surely have asked Emuin.

And did sorcery strike the Quinaltine and Emuin not send him a warning?

It was the late hour. It was the accumulation of bad news that so set his worst premonitions to wander.

"We must stay an hour, no more," he said to Ninévrisë. She, better than he, had full cognizance of all it meant when Ilefínian should fall, all the tally of names of men who might be in peril of their lives when Tasmôrden rode in. "Whatever happens, the court must not say we were cast down by the news."

"This movement of my enemies was almost certain to come," Ninévrisë said in a faint voice. Her fingers warmed in his hand, and kept a light hold. "The beacon was lit?"

"That is all we know," he said. "Idrys is trying to learn more, but there is nothing we can do to prevent Tasmôrden's march, save hope the skies open and the road bogs."

"And that certain ones would run for safety," she said. "But they will not."

"On the other hand," he said to Ninévrisë, and closed his hand on her fingers which had become rigid, "if there is a bright spot in this, it means Tasmôrden has not lingered to fortify the east shore against our crossing. Tristen coming to the south may disturb his sleep further. I doubt he will have foreseen that. And gods know, Tristen can deal with sorcery."

"Gods, that we had another month. Or that the snows would come."

"Gossip be damned. I should get you from this hall."

"No, my lord. No. Otherwise, I shall have to endure the ladies' gossip, and their questions. Not yet. Not yet, please you. I wish to be much more settled than I am." Nails impressed his palm. "On the battlefield one knew one's enemies. I know them here, but have not a weapon against them, none."

"Name me them!"

"Oh, Artisane. Artisane, chiefest."

"Of her I cannot relieve you. Not until—"

"Not until the wedding. Nothing until the wedding. Oh, I mark them down, every one, every petty remark. Men in the field have far more manners."

"I much doubt it."

"A man knows there may be blood. These women will shed someone else's, blithe as jays. Even their fathers they hate. But hate me more. And I *endure* them. They carry on their Elwynim war with every look, every stitch they sew: ill-wish me? Oh, if they could. And cannot. Clatter, clatter, clatter, the wicked, wicked, *foreign* woman, and just *one* petticoat, la! *what* is one to think?" He heard her second indrawn breath. "If they could sew harm into my wedding gown, they would, ever so gladly. Every one of them disappointed in their hopes for you, and here am I, the stranger. I should fear the cups I drink if not for Dame Margolis."

"*She* is a good woman."

"A good and a brave woman, but her they despise as common. I can do nothing." The voice he loved, the voice that lifted his spirits, trembled. "Nothing to defend her or myself."

"After the wedding," he said in regret. "Then—then they will have affronted *me*. They should take sober note. Is there no one else you can rely on?"

"None. No one but Margolis. —Perhaps, in small ways, Cleisynde." There was still a perilous little quaver in her voice, which was a knife in his heart. They had played at ignoring their enemies. He had thought her safe, serene in her wit and her own worth in amongst such little, niggling attacks. He had thought she had ridden above it all, unassailable within the ladies' court, a battle of petticoats and pearls irrelevant to the damage men did one another in war. She had ridden and camped with soldiers, faced sorcery and ghosts. Needed she guard herself from Ryssand's sixteen-year-old daughter?

From Artisane's sallies of wit, good gods? Ninévrisë was Regent of Elwynor.

"Ilefínian," Ninévrisë said, then, the outwelling of her deepest, most painful thoughts, and her hand felt cold as ice. "Oh, gods save them, gods save them. *Ilefínian.*"

CHAPTER 10

I n a quick succession of moves, Emuin took three pieces.

Tristen looked at opportunity . . . regretted winning. It seemed somehow discourteous to the old man. The whole night, since that dreadful shock of thunder, seemed uneasy, tottering with chance and overthrow.

"So?" Emuin asked. The two of them were poised above the scarred board of white wood and red, with counters of opposing color. And the necessity became clear.

Regretfully Tristen skipped his counter from one to the other of Emuin's pieces, taking every one.

"Oh, pish!" Emuin cried.

"I think you wished me to win," Tristen said.

"No such thing," Emuin said peevishly, and drank a sip more autumn ale. "Set up, set up. Another round."

Tristen set up the counters again.

"Clever of you," Emuin said, sounding unhappy. "Vastly clever."

"If you had rather set aside—"

"No, no, no, I enjoy a challenge."

Emuin was peeved, all the same. And had not seemed entirely surprised until the fifth, sixth, and seventh captures all in one: at that finish, the old man had sat back in his chair, glaring at the board with a slight squint, as he did at times at his scrying bowl.

Tristen set up quickly, and let master Emuin take the red side this time.

"Learning quickly, we are," master Emuin muttered, making his initial moves.

"I do try, sir."

Emuin shot him one of those looks from under his brows. The noise from the square below the Guelesfort had been quite loud during the game. Now it had fallen away to a hush. Their candle had burned to the half and the fire sunk in the grate. It was a moment in which all the world seemed to be the round walls, the table, the light on Emuin's face.

"So do we all, lad," Emuin said to him. "So do we all make honest effort, but you are a clever lad in spite of us all."

"I had no wish to win, sir."

It made Emuin laugh, the crashing together of a thousand wrinkles, and then a quick settling. "It is no contest, else. I know my measure. Learn yours. You will not learn it by cheating for *my* side, young lord. Play your own."

He felt a heaviness in the air then, as if the room had swung round, as if the heavens had wheeled full about, not that a thing was true now that had not been true a moment before, but that he sat at a further remove from the world, looking on a small stone room, piled high with clutter, at a young man and an old one, with a board on the table between them, and all at once the banging of the door below, the clatter of his guards getting to their feet outside and challenging someone.

Emuin looked toward the door with a playing piece in his hand, and paused. Whoever had come had engaged Uwen and the guards quietly, after clumping up the stairs, and then the latch of the door moved.

An officer had arrived: Pryas was his name, a king's messenger.

"Your lordship," the man said, and already Tristen had begun to rise from his chair, with the sure foreboding that something had changed in his quiet existence, and that some disaster had befallen. "Your lordship, His Majesty bids you know, although he has had no time to set his seal to it as yet, your lordship is made duke of Amefel, and set over that province, your lordship to be provided troops and staff, wagons and guards, horses to a sufficient number, and all honor. Your lordship must swear to His Majesty tomorrow noon for Amefel, with public ceremony, and depart for your lordship's capital the same hour."

He heard. He felt the wood of the chair under his right hand. He was aware of Emuin getting to his feet. Of Uwen regarding him with fear. There was no hint now that Uwen might have drunk any great deal, neither he nor Lusin nor his other guards.

"How shall I answer?" he asked Emuin, not that he was unwilling to obey Cefwyn, but that the implications of the moment stretched beyond his understanding.

For two months Amefel had been under the king's viceroy, Lord Parsynan, and Cefwyn had declined to depose Lady Aswydd in her exile, refusing to change that arrangement to a permanent grant of the province, refusing to decide on any claimant.

And what of Lady Orien Aswydd? Some had said she should be beheaded. Her brother had been beheaded and burned for his crimes, and Lady Orien was far from innocent of malice against the Crown. Had Cefwyn decided, then, she should die? He would be very sorry if that were so.

"I shall not advise you," Emuin said.

At the same time there arose a great deal more clatter below. More men were coming up the winding stairs, and there was no way for more than two men to occupy any step or for more than three to stand in the doorway, even sideways.

"There's Annas come in below, m'lord," Uwen said. "An' two of His Majesty's pages."

"His Majesty's staff," Pryas said, "His Majesty's officers to arrange the wagons and all, as many as necessary, all His Majesty's household to assist your lordship in the particulars and orders tonight"

"I shall pack, then," Tristen said, envisioning taking Petelly and Gery, his two light horses, and a bundle of clothes, with Uwen—Uwen would go with him, he was sure of that. But troops and staff, wagons and guards? The enormity of the undertaking began to dawn on him. Should he have Tassand, then? Would he have to leave his servants behind? They were a presence he had come to rely on, even to enjoy for their wit and their company.

And what would he tell the viceroy in Amefel? That he was dismissed? Or what *would* become of Orien Aswydd and her sister?

"Pack, is it?" Emuin said in a faint voice. "Pack, should we?"

"Shall you go, sir?"

"Pack. Pack for the gods' love! Yes, I shall go. How should I not go? Sends us to Guelessar for two months and sends us back again in a thunderstorm . . . what in the gods' good mercy is the boy doing?"

He meant Cefwyn. Emuin was never much on protocols.

"Do you know why we're sent, sir?" Tristen asked of the king's herald, and the man answered quietly,

"On account of the Quinalt roof, your lordship, as seems likely, but I have no word from His Majesty, except that we need a count of wagons from your lordship, how many your lordship may require."

The Quinalt roof, Tristen thought, and when he asked himself what might involve both the Quinalt roof and his sudden dispatch to Amefel, as Emuin had said, in a thunderstorm, then he knew indeed that the great clap of thunder had been more than noise.

Amefel, then. But it was not as bad as could be. The king was safe. He could not feel any joy in his appointment, nor quite sorrow, either, at being sent south. But Men said winter was a season of little traveling. He contemplated the pieces on the board, thinking that the king had just moved pieces, too, in a strategy directed steadfastly at freeing Elwynor and defeating Tasmôrden. And that was well, too, and he was glad of it. He saw movement as on a battlefield. Danger came clear to him, danger in his separation from Cefwyn, and that distressed him; yet there was nothing he could do. He had deluded himself two nights ago with hope of change back to the way things had been, with hope of being invited again into closeness with Cefwyn, and with Ninévrisë, and now, unexpectedly—this.

But as on a battlefield or a gaming board, not every movement needed be straight to the mark. Many games could come of a fixed number of squares. And not all moves were down a straight line.

"I shall have your answers, sir," he said to Pryas, "at least I shall send word about the wagons when I've asked my staff."

"Your lordship," Pryas said, and took his leave, as quietly as a man could on a stairs crowded with his guard.

But Annas came up then to fill the vacancy, informing him of a thousand things that had to be done immediately. Emuin was clearly distressed, fussing about, putting charts into stacks.

So all that the two of them had done or thought of doing was upended, every plan set aside. He would not march with the king to the riverside this winter, or even in the spring. No. Far from it, he would be in Heryn Aswydd's place. He would be in charge of the province the Guelenfolk least trusted—and he knew the histories of lords, the bloody necessities, the cruel certainties. He had felt them Unfold to his comprehension as war and the use of a sword had Unfolded to his hand, and he *knew* the duty that was set on him. It rose up like dark waters, it flowed over him, a necessity, a charge from a friend, a duty to the Amefin villages, the people of the town. Cefwyn made this duty *his*. And could he do otherwise, now, than go to Amefel?

Annas talked to him of the necessity for provisions, clothing, the ordering of his servants, the staff that he should take with him, rather than relying on the Amefin, who had been restive and uncooperative with the king's viceroy. He should have his own cook, his own pages, all these people brought in from Guelessar. So Annas said.

"The cook in the Zeide was very kind to me," he said quietly and in absolute certainty. "I have no wish for any other. And if I am duke of Amefel," he said to Annas, "should not the pages all be Amefin?"

Annas fell silent then a moment, as if he were thinking and rethinking his needs. And remeasuring him. "Still," Annas said, "you will keep Tassand."

"I would wish to keep Tassand," he said, heartfelt truth. "And Uwen will go with me. I would wish Uwen to go."

"No question of that, m'lord," Uwen said, and he had had no doubt of it. But as regarded the rest, Tristen stood in the mad whirl of change and preparation, feeling by no means as lost or as desperate as he had been in the fall of Ynefel, but feeling that bits and pieces were falling about him all the same, the second home he had had, as it were, falling in ruin and broken timbers—but this time he was no lostling, bewildered by the world. This time he knew where he was going and what his resources were.

He went down to his apartment, Uwen and Lusin and Syllan with him, to find it in as great an upheaval.

"Your lordship," one of his night guards said, red-coated men of the King's Guard, whom they had left to stand duty by the doors, "there's His Majesty's servants here, sir." This last to Uwen, who was in charge, and sobered but reeking of holiday ale.

The door was by that time open. "M'lord," Tassand said, at the door, and by Tassand's tone and the presence of the king's servants going to and fro in the apartment, along with the disarrangement of clothes out of the bedroom and onto the chairs, packing was in progress. Clearly the message had reached his servants.

He sat after that in an apartment rapidly ceasing to be his, in every bundle carried out to the wagons. His tenure in the Guelesfort and his safety in Cefwyn's company was likewise ending . . . piece by piece, like the fall of the stones, the little ones, the great ones. It still felt like ruin, and everything he had planned had to be questioned.

Then Idrys came, slipped right through his defenses and into the apartment, and turned up leaning in the doorway to his bedchamber.

"Sir," Tristen said, all attention, and rose to deal with him, for Idrys was always on the king's business, whether or not Cefwyn knew about it.

"Your Grace," Idrys said. "His Majesty will not come here, must not see you, you understand. There are those who will notice, if he should."

"I understand, sir. Bear him my goodwill."

"I shall. By my orders you will have Captain Anwyll with you. Rely on him."

Tristen frowned, no disrespect of Captain Anwyll, who was an honest, good man; but for Uwen's sake. "Uwen will be enough, sir. He will be entirely enough."

"For Uwen's sake, take Anwyll to command the Guard at least through the winter. This is my advice, and no slight to your man."

Idrys asked nothing for personal reasons, and had no reason to prefer Anwyll for his own advantage. But it was still unacceptable.

"Uwen is my captain," Tristen said, "if I am to have a household. I shall take Captain Anwyll only if he respects Uwen, sir."

"Who is a sergeant come captain in a great hurry and who has done very well in all of it. I say nothing against Uwen Lewen's-son. But to keep accounts you will need men, both military and civil clerks; you will need a quartermaster; an armorer—master Peygan can recommend a man."

"I shall take master Peygan's advice," he said. He ill liked to dispute Cefwyn's word. But he had arranged in his own mind how things should be. "The rest will be Amefin, sir."

There was a small silence in which Idrys looked him up and down. Idrys had taken his measure before this, and spoke to him frankly, as he would never discourage Idrys from doing. But he did not wish Uwen countermanded by a newly appointed Guard captain who was, he was sure, Idrys' man.

"His Majesty has appointed a duke of Amefel, then," Idrys said with a look that did not disapprove him, but that was much more guarded than before. "His Majesty regards you as his friend, sir. I trust that remains true, and will remain so."

"With all my heart, sir. I should never do anything to displease him."

"His friends *must* displease him," Idrys said. "Few others will. Say rather that you will keep your oath to him, and that says all. It even explains why you must leave court and the likes of Sulriggan may return."

"He will not, sir!" He was appalled. "Has His Majesty recalled Sulriggan?"

"The final price for His Holiness's blessing tomorrow. Sulriggan will return into the sunlight of His Majesty's favor . . ." Idrys' sarcasm was rarely so evident, and Idrys' grim look rarely so transparent. "His Majesty might pack off the lot of them, ten to a bundle, and keep you by him, but that would mean war with the Quinalt, which is not to any advantage just now. I'm giving Captain Anwyll strict orders, and all honor to Uwen Lewen's-son, whom I may not order, I am giving him the benefit of my opinion relayed through a man I trust. I would have kept Emuin here, next to His Majesty. My choice was not regarded. His Majesty must not have any loud commotion arising out of Amefel, and, I entreat Your Grace, there must be no dealings across that border with Elwynor. Satisfy those two conditions and you will do His Majesty a very great service."

"Earnestly so, sir. He explained to me the reasons for proceeding next spring with an advance from Guelessar. You did overhear."

"I did. Gods know there are worse choices to set over Amefel, far worse. Beware of Aswydd influences, have none of that house near you, have your food tasted, and do not be misled by plausible villains. Spend modestly, but for the gods' good grace, attend Bryalt ceremonies faithfully and speak with all courtesy to the Quinalt patriarch in Henas'amef. Give a donation to the Quinalt shrine. The man's a sullen prig, but you'll serve His Majesty if the reports that go back from that priest to the Holy Father contain no wild speculations on sorcery. Don't let the hedge-wizards sell their charms in the market. It sets the Quinalt's teeth on edge. I ask all this for His Majesty's sake. Neither I nor His Majesty care how many charms against toothache the old women sell. Only don't have them hung openly in the market, or worn on the street, or the rumors will fly that you promote Sihhë wizardry and practice gods-know-what in private. Take master grayfrock's advice in all things. His Majesty will sorely miss it. *Someone* should use it."

"Emuin will not give it me when I ask." He understood what Idrys was telling him, and earnestly agreed with the sense of his advice; but it was a point of frustration with him that he had no advice from master Emuin, and yet the man was up in his tower sending down bundles, baskets, and crates, protesting that the night was too short and never offering to stay in Guelemara to safeguard Cefwyn. "I never asked him to go with me. Yet he will. He will not advise me. Yet insists on going."

Idrys frowned, hearing that. "Well," he said, "well, at noon tomorrow, in the Quinalt, roof or no roof, advice or no advice, you will swear for Amefel. There will be appropriate ceremony, the town turned out. His Majesty is doing this in full witness of the barons, compelling His Holiness to hold the ceremony and the barons to stand and pray over it. If you have any governance over the lightning, Your Grace, I pray you keep the roof from further damage tonight. We already have Sulriggan back among us. His Majesty pleads with you to assure no untoward events between now and the ceremony. And let us enjoy clear weather if you can manage it."

"I have no governance over the weather."

"A jest, if you please."

"Yes, sir. But you should know—you must know: the Lines in the place are set amiss." He wished to keep no secrets from Idrys, whose opinion of him had survived the direst suspicion, and he knew he could not affright the man. "And there are shadows, many of them. But I have no sense that they have broken out. The lightning bolt will have been a disturbance to them, but I have no sense that it made matters worse."

"The lines are set amiss," Idrys repeated.

"The Lines that keep shadows in their places. All that keeps a place safe."

"Is it urgent?" Idrys, of all men, was ready to listen to his estimation of threat, and he was careful, accordingly, not to give a false sense of alarm.

"I don't think so. I have no sense that they've gotten out, or that they might, easily. The walls are intact. Ynefel had many holes in the roof, and they never mattered."

"At Ynefel, you say."

"Only the windows. And the doors. When it fell . . ." He never liked to remember that, the wind and the wailing and the groaning of timbers. And the silence after, with the occasional fall of heavy beams. "But the shrine will not fall. I don't feel there's danger of that. I shall swear to Cefwyn. I shall be his friend. I shall hope—"

He had not said it aloud since he had heard the news. "I shall hope he will call me back again, in the spring."

"He will need all his friends," Idrys said soberly, "but tell me, Amefel, since Amefel you will be, and Ynefel you are, and I certainly do not forget the latter, these days—what little shall I do, against lightning bolts? How does one defend him against wizardry?"

"Latch the windows," he said, then remembered a Man could rarely see the Lines on the earth, and smiled, as Men did at foolishness. "Leave nothing unattended. It comes most by carelessness, most especially when the wizard is far away or weak."

"*Which* wizard?"

It was an entirely apt question. "I don't know, sir. I truly don't. Never forget to do what you always do. That's the important thing. It makes Lines."

"Doing what I always do . . . makes lines."

"Very faintly so, yes, sir. Most of all, it makes wards. All over this vast building, latch windows, latch doors, set a watch. Especially, sir, —especially over Emuin's tower."

"Why would you say so?"

"Master Emuin might say. But a latch *is* a ward. Windows are whole when they're latched. Doors are whole when they're shut. And Emuin's tower has not been shut, not for a long time."

Idrys regarded him gravely. And heard him, he hoped, even with a thousand other things to attend.

"Have you need of anything yourself, then?"

"Forty silver."

"Forty silver. Precisely forty?" Idrys seemed bemused. "Among all else His Majesty's accounts can manage forty silver. Why, may I inquire?"

"To buy a horse, sir. The stable wants forty silver. And I have none. And there's a mare Uwen favors. I think he should have her."

Idrys loosed the purse at his belt and solemnly gave it to him, but with a slight wry smile. "You will have a quartermaster to handle the accounts, Your Grace, for which we may all be relieved of worry, myself not least. He will manage the rather large box and the pay for the troops, who do expect funds on a regular schedule. I pray you, put the horse and its equipage to His Majesty's funds and save this rather considerable purse for yourself, for your own personal needs. There are at least sixteen gold crowns in it, which are each eighty silver, which should keep Your Grace in honest coin of the realm at least until you come into your own lands, whereafter you may levy taxes and keep a portion for your own use with whatever mercy you see fit. Count Uwen's horse among the army purchases, in His Majesty's name. If anyone along the road says you gave them Sihhë coinage, *I* am here to swear about this purse and so says His Majesty, and His Highness, who wishes you good and godly progress."

"It is very kind, sir."

"I shall miss you, lord of Ynefel, most unlikely, but I shall miss you. I shall not see you until the spring, if all goes well. But the lord of a province has couriers at his disposal. Don't fail to use them, at need. Keep me informed, and keep His Majesty informed, at whatever need."

It was not at all surprising that Idrys set himself first in that account, not surprising and not at all against Cefwyn's interest. Tristen firmly believed so, and held the heavy purse in both his hands, rich in gold, in all material things Cefwyn could give him. But the protections all of them had woven about themselves were, like Lines on the earth, stretching very thin, worrisomely thin. "I shall, sir. For his sake, I shall, most of all."

"Fare you well," Idrys said solemnly, and again, in that low, deep voice of his: "Fare you very well, Your Grace."

BOOK
TWO

CHAPTER 1

Water dripped from the rafters, falling *plop! plop!* on the benches and making sooty puddles on the paving stones all during the ceremony, but no one affected to notice.

The building was shaken. The roof had been breached. The lightning might have loosed a considerable force within the world of shadows. But, to Tristen's critical eye, that mismade Line on the earth had held fast . . . and the faltering magical barrier behind the Patriarch gave forth no troublesome shadows.

Still, when he stood to take the Holy Father's blessing and when he knelt before Cefwyn to swear as the new duke of Amefel he heard little of what the Patriarch said, in his general unease and in his sense that if anything could go wrong, it had its best chance then and there, to the peril of him and Cefwyn and the peace all at once. Kneeling in his armor and surcoat, he stared balefully at that roiling mass of shadow while he affected to keep his eyes on the pavings. He willed it not to advance, and *plop!* went the water, a puddle collecting on the altar, right beside the Patriarch.

The shadows made him giddy. He concentrated on the intricate carvings of the panels below the railing and willed *that* to be the Line.

Plop-plop! The dirty water threatened everyone's fine robes, and a big sooty drop had landed on the Patriarch's shoulder, the stain of a hundred years of candles that had sent their smoke up to the rafters now coming down, washed free, like burned sins returning.

He wished the rain outside would stop.

And just then the light began to increase, the shrine and its statues and its columns growing brighter and brighter around him as if the sun had just broken through the clouds outside.

The Patriarch's hand came near his head, failed to touch him, and the Patriarch himself looked up: Cefwyn looked up, and since all those present did, Tristen turned his head and looked for the source of that light, which was indeed the sun coming full through the canvas patch they had put on the roof.

The return of the sun had made a momentary silence in the ceremony. He thought it a hopeful thing, himself, but Murandys and Ryssand and no few of the lords made signs against harm.

"The gods smile at us," Cefwyn said sternly, standing beside the Patriarch. "And on this hour."

"A blessing on the hour," the Patriarch said in haste, "and on the realm." The soot had stained his robe, but in his anxiousness he had not seemed to notice.

"Rise," Cefwyn said, and Tristen rose. The trumpets sounded. The Patriarch stretched out his arms in dismissal, and chanted a blessing on the assembled lords of the realm. *Confusion to our enemies,* the Patriarch said. *A plague on the infidel and a blessing on His Majesty . . .*

Words echoed around and about the columns. Tristen looked up again on his way out, where the sunlit patch of canvas covered the ample hole. The rafters aloft had caught a great deal of rain, and puddles stood on the stone pavings and on the benches. The shadows among the columns seemed more absolute in that strange light from above, some put to flight, others grown more terrible.

Yet the breach had not damaged the wards, as Ynefel's loft had had a great hole in it, which Mauryl had said was negligible. Such was the nature of bindings, and wards, and magic.

The shrine let them go safely into the early-afternoon sun, the banners first: the Dragon banner of the Marhanen kings lifted, gold and red. Then, in the precedence of the hour, Amefel, red, with the black Eagle outspread, flew for the first time on a gusting wind, Amefel between the two black standards of Ynefel and of Althalen. Cefwyn stopped beneath the banners, under the clear sky, in the witness of the town, at the top of the Quinalt steps, and held out his hand, staying Tristen at his side.

The people of the town had turned out as they would for any occasion bringing out the clattering pageantry of soldiery, lords and banners. The joyous ringing of Quinalt bells startled the hapless pigeons from the roofs of the Guelesfort and they took flight in a great upward beating of wings against the sun.

I am leaving, Tristen wished the maligned birds to know. He had never yet worked any magic to forbid them the place. He remembered that now, and was concerned for their fate. I am going from this place, he wished to tell them.

And then he thought, Will any among you fly to Amefel? Are you the same birds as I knew there? Can such small, frail birds fly so far as that?

Winter is coming, snow, and ice. So they tell me. Take care, take care. Find me in Amefel if you wish, if you can, if you dare. Come there safely and soon!

Pealing of the bells, flowing cloth, black and red, stretched across the wind, and the martial tramp of soldiers ringing back from the walls of the Guelesfort: such were the impressions of the moment. Uwen, he was sure, was at his back, and Lusin and the guards waited before him, all ahorse.

"Stay," Cefwyn said to him, a hand on his arm. The bells, having rung out their chorus, left a numb silence and the last pigeons had fled. "My dear friend," Cefwyn said publicly, loudly, and it echoed off every wall and house around the square. *"My dear friend."* Cefwyn turned him and embraced him in full view of the people, as the very air grew still. "I did what I could," Cefwyn said close against his ear. "Believe in me. Believe in me, Tristen. Trust me that nothing has changed in our friendship."

"I do," he said, in all earnestness. "I shall." In such a silence it seemed even so that people might be listening, so he added as they broke apart: "Your Majesty."

"Take care, Tristen. Take great care." Cefwyn looked up, a glance at the windswept heavens. "We might have used the weather-luck last night," he said, attempting a laugh. His grip bruised. Meanwhile the people waited, as all the banners hung limp in a momentary want of breeze, then snapped and thumped with a wayward gust. "The gods send you safe on all your journey. My brother, hear me, my brother dear as blood, you will always be in my heart. Never doubt it."

Brother. He had looked for no such thing, and he held that word of all Words close to his heart, he who had had neither father nor mother nor mother's love nor ever been, himself, a child. He had just had the Holy Father's blessing, and the solemn words of his own oath of fealty and Cefwyn's pledge to him still rang in his ears. Words, Words, and Words fell like hammer strokes, pealed like bells across the sky.

But undeniable truth was in the silence of the people in the square, the anxious faces, and most of all in the parting of Cefwyn's hands from his arms. Cefwyn had no power to prevent this moment, and now as he moved from Cefwyn's embrace, it felt as if someone had moved from between him and a cold, random wind, one that now would gust and blow and chill him to the bone. He refused to look back as he walked down the steps, nor did he look around as he met Uwen, who offered him Gery's reins. They mounted up. All the rest of the column that would ride down and away with them began to move at his first start forward.

He allowed himself one glance, and saw Cefwyn standing on the steps as he imagined he would see him. Then he turned Gery's head away and led his column across the face of the assembled nobles.

He had a thousand questions for Cefwyn, oh, a thousand thousand questions . . . but there had been no time before now to ask, and now that their necessities drew them too far, too fast apart, he feared there might never be. Brother was a Word, but not a word that could bridge the moment. He saw Efanor amid the crowd of nobles, Efanor with his priest beside him, and he saw how Efanor signed a pious wish for him. He knew Efanor wished him well despite all his fears and his jealousy, and he felt a small pang of regret for Efanor, for Efanor's faith in absent gods, and most of all for Efanor's failing of Cefwyn's love . . . he knew that he was himself the thief of Cefwyn's affection; and forgiven by Efanor at oh, so great an effort. He saw Cevulirn besides, and imagined warmth in his narrow eyes, at least approval of the choice.

But he saw nothing but cold stares else, on the part of the dukes of the north. They were constrained to be there, detesting his presence the while, and he was sure they were in some remote fashion responsible for his departure: he had heard the story about the lightning, the Quinalt roof, and the coin and knew none of them could guide the lightning, but they were skilled at guiding spiteful words. He understood their rules, now, rules set forth in all the chronicles of the Marhanen reign, and how the barons had supported Selwyn Marhanen, one of their own, to be king over them not because they loved him best, but because he was the only one they all feared, the only one who could hold them from fighting each other. Was it not still the same?

He understood, too, the structure they had woven, the realm of Ylesuin, how all the barons' influence over their own people and all their rights with the king were posed alike on agreements that rested on oaths, and oaths as they saw it rested on the Quinaltine's validity; they would not keep their word unless they feared the gods' wrath on them, and therefore they believed that no one else would keep his word unless he was similarly afraid. They were not Cefwyn's friends. They were certainly not men Cefwyn would ever call brother, and yet they each desperately sought closeness to the king, each seeking any chance to outdo his neighbors. They feared Cevulirn because Cefwyn loved him; feared Emuin for many of the very same reasons. And Ninévrisë . . . oh, greatly did they fear her influence.

So how much more must they distrust Mauryl's heir . . . and how ready were they to see omens in the lightning last night . . . omens of overthrow and attack on themselves, and most of all, evidence of forbidden wizardry.

(It was no damned wizardry, master Emuin had said this morning. Why not ask those who *know*, good loving gods? No, no, no one consults a wizard. Everyone in town takes advice from His Holiness on the matter, when if His Holiness had a smidge of wizardry, he would never have a hole in his roof, now would he?)

He could all but hear Emuin's voice echoing down the stairs . . . as in the square, now, before him, the banner-bearers moved to the lead in a clatter of hooves on cobbles. He saw the half-burned bonfire . . . rain had put an end to it.

Uwen moved up beside him in a small burst of speed as he eased off Gery's reins. There were thirty men behind them, a clattering column of soldiery, as they left the square and entered the town.

Master Emuin might avow there was no wizardry in the stroke. But it had been a large and incontrovertible hole above them in the ceremony—workmen had put that canvas over it last night, a task the hazard of which Tristen could scarcely imagine, going up in the dark and the rain, and with the lightning still playing in the clouds. So much men dared, relying on the gods, and on the luck Uwen so often invoked.

But was it only blind chance that had dislodged Mauryl's Shaping and set him on another Road? He dared not guess, and he thought that Emuin protested too loudly: Emuin knew, must know, must be aware of the damage done in his leaving Cefwyn's side. And did Emuin deny there was wizardry abroad?

Now the sun speared down into the street ahead and people fell back from his path, not cheering, precisely, a few making a faint pretense of it, and the children skipping along for a better view. Red Gery danced sideways as well as forward, excited at the noise of trumpets and the flutter of banners ahead. The men behind him were a night without sleep: no few had drunk too much before they had the news and had struggled to work through the night in spite of aching heads. The king's entire household had stayed awake, cobbling together a ceremony with no advance warning: Cefwyn had done everything possible to show him honor, arranged the ceremony of his swearing as elaborately as any swearing before him—and precisely because they had done it not two months ago for the northern lords, it had come off in good order, right down to the trumpeters, who this time had not made a false start in the middle of the Patriarch's dismissal of the assembly.

So, with a document, an oath, and a blessing, he was lord of a province, and with his banners flying in full view of Guelemara he was riding away to a place he had regretted leaving in the first place. If only it had meant returning to an Amefel preserved in time, an Amefel the way it had been, with Cefwyn free and themselves in all the company they had had there, he would have been deliriously happy.

But the world had changed since summer, in far more than the fall of leaves. He had asked what winter would bring, and now with a nip in the air despite the sunshine, he saw it bringing change, change, and change, himself swept along across dirty cobbles and past doors still adorned with autumn garlands, moving toward another season of doubt, and hoping for reunion in the spring, on a battlefield.

One unanticipated, utterly foolish pleasure, however, dawned on him amid all the other assaults on his heart in this short ride down the street: this morning he no longer went in unrelieved black. He had become lord of a color, a banner, an emblem, lord of a living land, with people in it, and cattle and horses and orchards and all manner of things that were not true of Ynefel and Althalen. And, against the brown and gray dying of the trees and the threatened white of winter, he bore no quiet color, either, but red, red darker than the Marhanen scarlet: red of rubies, red of old blood, red of roses at dusk.

So many things a color might be, both good and dreadful; but above all else, as of this morning, his colors and his garments need no longer be the black of Shadows. The king's own tailor and Dame Margolis, the kindly lady who had done such duty for Cefwyn before in Amefel, had marshaled a sleepy, harried band of tailor's apprentices last night. Guelesfort servants and even the cloth-seller's wife, sister, sons, and daughters had turned out, working by lamp and candlelight. They had bled from pricked fingers, the evidence of which was on the last-done fabric of Uwen's coat; and it was thanks to them that he wore a surcoat of red cloth this morning, with the Amefin Eagle in black on it. It was thanks to them that he had that banner.

And thanks to them and by the king's grace, red Eagle patches covered the royal Dragon on the man who bore the Amefin standard and who would bear it on their journey . . . Gedd, his name was, a sergeant of the Guelen Guard, who had fought with distinction at Lewenbrook. Gedd carried the banner of Amefel, and beside him, bearing the banners of Ynefel and Althalen on either hand . . . those riders were his regular guards, Lusin and Syllan, by the king's leave and their own choice.

In unforgiving sunlight the coats and patches of all his guard were a slight mismatch: it was the king's bright Marhanen scarlet with the black Amefin Eagle in a square of ruby red, and every townsman who saw it must know whose service had lent the guards to Amefel, but he had no doubt Cefwyn intended so.

Most of the men Cefwyn lent him would return, in due time; but his own guards would not. Lusin and Syllan, patching the Amefin Eagle to their coats with their own stitches this morning, had recklessly called the Sihhë Star lucky for them and left the king's service.

"Better prospects for the likes of us wi' his lordship," he had overheard Lusin say. "Fools we ma' be, but this is a lucky badge for me."

"Ye ain't regardin' the priests, sir?" Syllan had asked, and Lusin laughed in a way that said, no, he did not regard the priests' warnings.

"The lad ain't no black wizard," Syllan said then. "An' if ye go to his service, I'm wi' ye, an' I think the lot of us is in the same mind."

Hearing that, he had stood there, not knowing whether to admit he had overheard them or not, and finally walked away, hoping his guards would go on in the good luck they believed in, and fearing he could not promise them whatever luck truly meant to them. He knew Luck for a word Men set great store by, and his guards said if a man had lost it, he was in a sad state. But it was a word that never quite Unfolded to him: a word Men used, men like Uwen, who had no power of wizardry or magic at all, and they used it in hopes that all things would chance to their benefit without a wizard arranging it. He suspected that he could wish his guards well and happy to far more effect than they could wish for themselves, and willingly did so as he was riding down with his company to the gates of Guelemara.

But it was fraught with hazard, such a spell. Their going with him set them in harm's way not only of weapons but of wizards and shadows. He very keenly remembered Lewenbrook, and the young man who had carried his banner onto that field, but not off it. What he wished well, his enemies were most apt to wish ill in any moment of his inattention . . . and in that thought he was afraid to wish them anything at all. He had all along left them and Uwen as much to their own fates as he could, fearing he knew not what . . . Hasufin was dead, which was no surety: Idrys said that *he* was dead, too, and here he rode down the middle of Gate Street, perhaps far beyond Mauryl's wishes—or perhaps not.

Now that they had begun this movement, this shifting of power within Ylesuin, the thing had acquired its own momentum, in the king's orders, Idrys' orders, Annas' orders, Emuin's orders, Uwen's, Anwyll's, and his own orders at the last, and it was no less the movement of an army than it had been preceding Lewenbrook: the wagons, as then, had gotten up to the Guelesfort before dawn to load, and the last had gotten down again by the West Gate well before the swearing so they should not impede the processional of the cavalry. The number of wagons and mules and carts, carriages, oxcarts, drivers, artisans and craftsmen, horses and grooms, had been certain almost from the moment one oxcart had been necessary. The oxcart dictated their speed; their speed dictated nights on the road, and those nights dictated all the additional wagons. Alone, with a small troop of the Guard with a change of horses, he could have ridden to Amefel in two days, if he were put to it . . .

But that was not to be. Annas would none of it, and insisted yes, they must leave in the morning, but they must arrive with all due ceremony, having given due and decent notice to His Majesty's viceroy—a fair consideration. For the viceroy to maintain his dignity was an important matter; and the viceroy should not be suddenly deposed: the province was restive, prone to rumor, and the appearance of dignity and deliberations in the transfer of authority was essential. There would be a careful exchange of documents and a proclamation read before the people.

Then the viceroy would need, so Annas had proposed, the self-same carts to carry his own household and his troop of the Guelen Guard home to Guelessar, leaving Amefel with a new duke, blessed and sworn and sealed by the Crown in Guelemara.

That they had been able to accomplish the documents, the cere-mony, the gathering-up of a ducal household, the muster of wagons and guard all in only so few hours preparation—indeed, if people wished to fling the word *magic* about regarding the lightning bolt, he thought his orderly departure and the appearance of the banners should excite even greater comment. Their only grace was that the Dragon Guard was always ready to move and the heavy carts they needed in such numbers were the carts the Guard had already gath-ered to move equipment to the riverside for the winter camps, gath-ering which was the work of days in itself.

Preceding the bawling confusion in the stable-court before dawn and the organized and thunderous turnout of cavalry in the square this morning, everyone in the company had seen a numbing, frenzied succession of hours when any single thing going amiss could have delayed everything. Any small matter had become a contention, an argument, a waving of arms and shouting among his servants, his guards, the king's servants, the king's guards. And now that every-thing was accomplished and they rode through the Old Gate into the lower town he began to draw easier breaths. He passed under the gated arch of the Crown Wall, the citadel's official limit and the old-est defenses of Guelemara, and said to himself that, lightning stroke and all, things today had gone with far, far more ease than he would expect if some hostile wizardry were still at work.

The crowds were less then, and below the limit of the citadel, in ordinary streets, the wind was chill; the cobbles of the lower town were still wet from last night's rains and the overhang of buildings shaded them from the sun. Idrys had asked him for good weather, a jest, yet he wondered in a small, guilty thought whether his own wishes had anything to do with the clearing of the sky. He had cer-tainly wished the lightning remote from doing further harm. Wishes, too, had more potency when something like the lightning stroke had already set the ordinary world askew. Difficult as it was to move things that were well set and deep in their habits, things now were prone to change: like the leaf he had dislodged and let fly a second flight on the hill, things once shaken could be budged again.

One had then to be cautious. Once gone sailing on the winds, leaves were prey to any waft of weather.

Any whisper of magic.

And he *must* be careful for days, until the world settled again.

So he thought, as urchins in their brash innocence waved or chased along beside the column of guardsmen. So they might do on any day of their rides. He smiled at them, thinking such thoughts, waved a black-gloved hand at a small cluster of better-kept children who ducked aside and hid. It might have been any morning they had ridden out for pleasure, except the scarcity of people about their work, except the banners and the number of men behind him.

At the town's outer gates, the same gates they had gone out and back again so many times for their rides, a handful of the Dragon Guard had already made sure of their way. No last-moment oxcarts barred their way out this morning, no inopportune gaggle of geese or other flapping fowl met them in the gate. The gate stood open for them as a last curious few craftsmen came out from the smithy and the chandler's shop nearby.

Then a foolish, yapping dog, escaping all precautions and evading the Guard, ran out to trouble the horses. Gery cow-kicked and threw his head, but the yellow dog was a veteran, one that had attended their morning rides a little distance from the town, and he did so today, driven to complete frenzy by the unusually long column behind them, racing up and down as they passed the thick walls of the gate.

But this time the yellow dog would wait in vain for their return.

Good-bye, he wished the creature, who was a familiar, a known hazard. Fare well and safely back to your own door and a warm fire.

Live long. There are too many dangers. Too much is uncertain in the world, and winds are blowing today you know nothing of, silly hound.

In a single stroke he became sure of it. Wizardry was working in the whole event and a yellow dog had convinced him of it by doing nothing at all out of the ordinary, a measure against which to see all the extraordinary things that had happened in a handful of days, from doubt of his welcome to surety he belonged elsewhere. He drew a deep breath and gathered up the reins of magic as warily as he held red Gery's, resolved to let nothing else slip.

"Fair day for a ride," Uwen said, as they passed under the darkness of the last gate arch, and it seemed Uwen had been as worried as he, only then daring speak. "Not a cloud left in the sky, m'lord, and us almost on our way in good order."

"Let us all hope for fair weather," Tristen said. Beyond the town main gate they faced the sprawl of the dwellers outside the walls, the untidy mud of stables and henyards and poor men's huts, and few here came out to greet them. Their road was straight as an arrow past the maze of unplanned lanes and dwellings, and at gathering speed, until they faced no more of Guelemara than apple orchards, plowed barleyfields with furrows standing in water, and a slop of mud on the roads.

Then:

"There's Captain Anwyll, m'lord, waitin' for us."

Indeed, a band of men and wagons was arrayed beside the crossing, that of the first honest road between the outlying fields and the nearest orchards. The inflowing band stretched out of sight among the apple trees, and they brought the remounts from the stables outside the town walls, a large number of horses. As the head of their column swept past, Tristen looked to the head of Anwyll's group in a moment of anticipation, immediately slowing his pace and that of the rest of the column to the amble they would generally keep on the road, a pace which allowed the riders behind to close up without being spattered by riders in front.

The influx of horses brought the grooms, too, notably Aswys, with his particular charge, black Dys, and also with Uwen's heavy horse, Cassam, and the boy that tended him. There was Petelly, a weed among the nobility of horses—and, yes, Tristen was very glad to affirm, there was Liss. He had told Uwen to go to the Guard Master of Accounts, who was getting no more sleep than they last night, and to buy the mare before they left. He was determined Uwen should have his honor, *and* that horse, in front of every man in Amefel.

"There she is," Uwen said. "*There* she is. Gods, she moves."

"She is beautiful," Tristen agreed.

"Too fine by far for me," Uwen said for the hundredth time.

"Not too fine. I have three horses. You have two. You'll be my captain in Amefel, and my right hand. Do you say not?"

"Aye, to standin' beside ye, m'lord, wi' my heart's blood. Better your shieldman than your captain."

"I say otherwise."

"M'lord, captain of Althalen's one thing. The field mice out there don't much need a captain, and they don't set great store by ciphering."

"Ciphering." This was the first mention of ciphering as an argument.

"A captain's got to have ciphering, m'lord. Myself, I need to look at a warehouse to know how many men's provisions is in it, none of this ciphering."

"But you can reckon the grain for the horses. And the clerks write it down. Is that not ciphering?"

"Oh, aye, on my fingers, but the clerks come back wi' their accounts writ down and I still need to see the warehouse in front of me. So ye can't ever make the likes of me into a captain of the Dragons, m'lord, so there, ye can't, on a fine horse or not. I ain't but a good sergeant of the Guelen Guard, what's had more luck than I was ever due, and I'm more 'n content to be at your side, m'lord. Ye should take a man like Anwyll."

He had made up his mind regarding Uwen's post in Amefel as surely as if it had simply Unfolded. It was so, that was all. On this day of magic trying to escape his will, he still chafed at Anwyll's being in charge this morning. He was resolved that the man should go back to Guelessar by spring, with compliments to Idrys, since he was sure Anwyll was intended to be Idrys' eyes and ears in Amefel. He took no offense in Idrys' having spies. That was not the issue.

The horses came in without incident. The next ring road about Guelemara, that from Dary village, showed a long line of wagons and carts from beyond the gray-brown haze of the young apple trees, all lumbering toward that crossroads, to intersect with those they had already collected. They were to come in just behind the first hundred of the mounted troop . . . or so they should, but they were arriving too soon.

"They'll sink to the axles if they slow down," Uwen judged. "Get 'em into line will they, nill they, m'lord, an' no stopping. That lane's a damn bog."

"Say so," he bade Uwen, after which Uwen rode immediately aside to talk to Captain Anwyll, and after that, back in line to shout orders to move the standards and the Guard ahead at a trot, making room for the wagons. In that way the vehicles came in with no hindrance and no slowing down.

"All the wagons are here, except master Emuin's," Captain Anwyll reported then, riding up in the line from the crossroads. "He sends word he'll join us at our lodgings tonight."

"Tonight."

"As best he can, Your Grace. He said he was served by fools."

Emuin had not come to the swearing this noon, nor remotely wished to, Tristen was sure. He had last seen master Emuin raving at the servants who carried his chests of fragile phials and his aged and brittle-edged piles of documents, his stacks of codices and venerable scroll-cases down the perilously winding stairs to the upper hall, where his baggage waited. Emuin had sworn all his borrowed help was feckless, vowed that he could move no faster by the king's whim or any other, and threatened, when last he had seen him to inquire, that if the servants or the king's officers came one more time to ask when he wanted the carts and mules assigned to him to be in the courtyard, he would invent a spell for toads. Emuin had not finished packing by daybreak, nor by midmorning, and now that Anwyll reported his carts had not made it down the hill during the lull in street traffic during the ceremony, as they had last arranged, Tristen began to be more concerned.

"I set ten guards to escort the good father at whatever time he sets out," Anwyll said, "in event that the night might overtake him on the road. They have a tent."

For that forethought he forgave the captain his presence. "Did he have the parchments down?"

"I didn't go up, Your Grace. The way was clogged with baskets. There was no moving on the stairs."

"Well you did leave men with him," Tristen said.

Six mules, an oxcart and a wagon were allotted for master Emuin's baggage alone, and if their effort were to come raveled, if there were any adverse Working, it struck him as ominous, that Emuin was late.

But on the other hand it was certainly no wonder that the old man had fallen behind in his packing when it was a miracle the rest had gotten on the road. He, who had no scrolls or codices or boxes of powders, had three mules only to carry his armor and his clothing and an ox-drawn heavy wagon for his tent and field equipage. He had thought down to the last, when they told him it had indeed gone onto the wagon, that he might leave the heavy tent and chest stored in the armory, since that equipage would only have to be transported back again to Guelessar when the army marched in the spring—but he had a sometimes restive province to defend, and now more than a remote chance that Tasmôrden might breach the long river border, or attempt his defenses this winter—and if he had to go into the field in the cold of winter, then it was better to do it under canvas.

And that meant he had to have the tent which would serve as a headquarters; and if he had that, then all the tents that belonged to a company of two hundred, with their gear, had to come: more carts, more oxen, more gear. The Dragon Guard, Anwyll informed him, did not camp in the field like the rangers of Lanfarnesse. There were horses, tents, cooking pots.

And since they had that encumbrance, then came Dysarys' and Cassam's caparison and armor in their heavy canvas weather casings, the horse-armor not being for ordinary wearing; and if those, why, then other things. The horse gear made a considerable bulk in itself, not only that belonging to Dys and Cassam, but also the spare saddles for Gery and Petelly, Uwen's Gia and now Liss: the brushes, the ointments, the warming blankets, all of that, and the personal gear belonging to the horse grooms. Then because the mounted guards had their own farrier and his equipment, and the medicines, spare tack, tools and blankets for all the four hundred horses of the troop of two hundred men—they added sacks of grain, since they had no time for the wide grazing otherwise needful for the horses and the oxen over the several days they would be on the road. They hoped for hay or easy grazing at least two of their nightly stops, else they would have carted that with them, too.

There was also the company physician and the store of bandages and physic for all the guardsmen themselves; and two hundred men's winter gear and clothing.

And far from least came the quartermaster and the precious chest that contained the guardsmen's pay and the funds for supply in the province.

Before all was done, that section of the train which supported the Guard and their light horses numbered no few ox-drawn wagons, each with its drivers and their modest amount of baggage. And last in the train of wagons and carts (he had seen it arrive) Tassand and the servants rode in a covered mule cart, the sort that ladies favored: the king's household had provided it, none of the servants being inured to days in the saddle, and it lent the last quaint touch to what had indeed as well have been the movement of an entire army toward Amefel.

Too, he had accepted Idrys' offer of an armorer to go with him, Cossun, until last night the juniormost assistant of master Peygan himself. So he had promised that man, too, a living, besides providing him a horse, a cart for baggage, and two armorer's apprentices and their personal equipment.

So many had proved unexpectedly willing to join him, of men who had known him in Amefel this summer . . . Gossan, a man who otherwise would never be a master of his craft, had surely weighed the dark repute of Amefel as well as the chance of war reaching the walls of Henas'amef this summer, and made a dangerous choice in a handful of hours. All who joined him had done so, perhaps in hopes of bettering their lots in life . . . a chance which came in war to soldiers, sometimes to craftsmen through hard work and good luck, and very, very scarcely in the case of a clerk.

He had so many hopes going with him today, even when every stride Gery made was carrying him away from Cefwyn's close friendship. Cefwyn needed loyal men . . . and by utter chance or someone's intent, he found very many of them going with him.

But Emuin, who had never doubted an instant he must come, but who would not advise him, delayed for powder pots and parchments.

CHAPTER 2

Your Majesty this, Your Majesty
that, *yes,* Your Majesty, *as you will,* Your Majesty . . . and watching
from the upper floors, out the window, His ill-tempered Majesty
had a perfect view of the Quinalt roof with its canvas patch . . . of
monks struggling with ladders, of the Quinalt square with its ordinary scatter of business. No one minded the wrath of the gods and
the dreadful omen of the lightning now that the imagined threat of
the young Warden of Ynefel was gone from them. The barons no
longer needed feel besieged or distanced from the throne. The
stranger in their midst had departed back into Amefel, where almost
any impiety might be tolerable, oh, and at long last, His Majesty's
wizard tutor was going with him, an untidy presence lingering from
Selwyn's harsh reign, lingering far past need, in certain opinions.

Tristen's going had left a certain untidiness behind, a tower emptied, pouring bundles down the stairs, a fine set of apartments
stripped of presence.

It had left another kind of emptiness behind, too, and Cefwyn's
heart ached for it. He discovered he had not taken advantage of the
time he had had. He had not said to the barons, as he ought, Damn
you all, and done as he pleased from the very beginning of his reign.
No, no, with all the wisdom he had observed in his father (and now
he questioned it) he had tried to keep alive his father's alliances. He
had come into his capital with a southern victory and a foreign
bride, and let the attacks come at Tristen because he knew Ninévrisë
had no defense.

But, gods, he had not understood the persistence of those attacks, or their cleverness, or that they would dare this much. He had made a clever move of his own, sending Tristen south—but he had not prepared himself for the look Tristen had given him when they stood apart, there on the Quinalt steps. He had not recalled the bitter lessons of his grandfather, of betrayals, and the harm that a word could do. He had not recalled the bitter lessons of his father, how absence could estrange two hearts . . . and now he worried about it.

But he would not be so set about hereafter. And he had not at all given up Tristen, or Emuin, or any of his friends. They were where they needed to be. If a king could push and prod wizardry into working for him, then he had made a necessary move, and moved wizards where fools would threaten them at their peril. Let him get the reins of power firmly in his hands, and then he would remember every favor and every score that wanted remembering. His grandfather, entombed in the Quinaltine yonder, had had the barons in fear of him when he was alive. He, like his grandfather, had faced armies. Could he not, in his turn, daunt a paltry handful of court gossips? The servants, the court, the Quinalt . . . no one would have dared tempt king Selwyn as his barons had tempted him. And they were not as clever as they hoped.

His father Ináreddrin had learned only two tactics: playing one rival against another, which his grandfather had done very skillfully, and compromising—compromising constantly to secure his own safety: he saw it very plainly from the vantage of this bitter morning, this window he had looked out since childhood. Ináreddrin had set northern Quinalt against southern Teranthines, northern barons against southern barons, son against son and devised a clever path through their objections—but, again, he had always resolved matters not by decision but by compromising what he wanted. Son against son on the other hand had been easier game—give the elder son no love. Give the younger son, Efanor, all honor, all credit with the northern barons, knowing very well he was robbing his own heir of support. What was it to him? He'd be dead and in his tomb when the account came due.

And lo! his father indeed died and here was he, standing at the same window, facing the same decisions, making choices his father should have made with an iron hand.

But not entirely recklessly. He longed to go down and at least bid Emuin safe journey as the old man was setting out. But then the very point of sending Tristen away was to still the rumors, and if the barons thought him weak and biddable, let them think it only for another dozen days. He should not go to Emuin.

Quiet the rumors, give Tristen the winter in Amefel, give the realm the feeling of real danger on the border, oh, and then the Quinalt would see magic much differently. Gods, gods, but he looked forward to sending a few lords on horseback through the mud and brambles and into the range of bowmen and see whether they did not soon view Tristen of Ynefel as their very savior.

The king being angry, the king's servants would not come near him. But the tread that crossed the floor behind him now, soft and with the whispered grate of armor, he knew: he took no alarm, and saw a grim, dark-mustached reflection in the glass.

"Well?" he asked that reflection.

"Things are as well done as may be," Idrys said, "m'lord king."

"Satisfied, are we?"

"Mauryl's heir has grown far cannier, and more adept than many think. Send him back to the nest and he will grow indeed again. But he is still the innocent, in many ways. I authorized forty silver, by the by, for Uwen a horse."

"A horse." In the depth of his melancholy, in the tottering of Marhanen rule in Guelessar, he found an act of Tristen's still to astound and amuse him.

"A mare. A surplus of the guard mounts. A fine horse, as happens. I applaud Uwen's eye."

He almost found it in him to laugh. "Good gods, I give him a province and *that* was his concern."

"Oh, I daresay he had many concerns, but this was the one he could reach, to please a man he trusts. I approve his reasoning."

Idrys' speech was sometimes barbed, sometimes indirect, rarely straight to the point. For Idrys, this was blunt. And Cefwyn was less amused.

"I take your lesson, master crow."

"You confound your enemies, Majesty. They never foresaw his appointment to Amefel, I do agree. And the fools among them imagine Ynefel will go quietly to his tower and become absent for a few decades of years, like Mauryl."

"Tristen will not," he found himself saying, and in the ghostly reflection saw Idrys' implacable visage. "Should I fear him?" he asked, perhaps because in the strangeness of the day and the stripping away of his resources, fear did occur to him, the barons' fear, the fear of Guelenfolk, of all the north . . . and his own fear, deep and little confessed. "I *don't* fear him, master crow. There is no malice in him, nor ever has been. And what I've done, *I* choose. The hell with them all."

"I should be remiss if I did not point out—"

"Damn your pointing out, Idrys!" He spun to face his Lord Commander. He had by no means meant such an outburst. It had been waiting all night and all morning.

And Idrys looked not at all surprised to receive it, saying smoothly, imperturbably, "Yes, Your Majesty."

"Neither ambition, nor self-will, nor greed for land. None of these things move him, Idrys. He is the best man ever I knew."

"He is not a man," Idrys countered him. "As m'lord king may well remember."

"A man in all points but birth."

"Oh, aye, a birth . . . *that* small matter."

"Damn you, I say."

"As Your Majesty may please," Idrys said, and for some few moments they stood side by side, overlooking the workers who assayed the Quinalt roof, like the movement of ants in the sunlight.

It might have been any ride they had ever taken in Guelessar, though at a slow and plodding pace, the banners comfortably furled and cased now that they were out of sight of other men. The banner-bearers talked together in quiet voices, alike the Guard, riding behind them, Captain Anwyll with his aides.

At their first rest Uwen changed off to Liss to ride, and gave Gia a rest.

"Two fine horses," Uwen said, in delight at the mare, fairly beaming. And then, soberly, and blushing, "M'lord, it were still very good of ye."

"If I can please no one else," Tristen said, "I would please you."

Uwen blushed, bright red. "M'lord."

He wished he had not said that. He knew not what to say to soften it.

"His Majesty's given ye a province, m'lord. And in the Quinalt's eye. The northern lords', too. We'll be back again. Ye'll see His Majesty by spring, and 'twixt me and you, the town will be cheered up by then."

"He had to take Sulriggan back."

"Oh, well, but sooner or later he'd have to, and His Majesty knew it an' Sulriggan knew it. It was sooner, is all, by about a couple of months, and ye can lay to it his lordship Sulriggan'll catch cold before any battle. He probably wishes His Majesty had stayed choleric until after the war and never would call on him at all, but there wasn't a chance of that, anyway, so all he gets is a few months to work his way back into better graces. The Holy Father has a rotten weak reed of a cousin in Sulriggan, that's the truth, and whoever relies on him, His Majesty'll chew him up bones and all."

"Perhaps he will," Tristen said. "At least I doubt Efanor will believe Sulriggan again."

"His Highness has his eyes open more than some thinks," Uwen said, and for a time they rode talking of Efanor, and then recalling Amefel and thereby the stables in Amefel, and wondering whether they could improve the drainage in the stables sitting at the bottom of the hill.

Perhaps, Tristen thought, Cefwyn had not been entirely unwise to send him south. Very near Cefwyn's apartment, amid all the gathering of the court, he dared not even wonder what Cefwyn was doing, or how he fared or whether the land was safe . . . dared not until he was far from the walls. But today, at this distance from the men around him and in command of the column as it was, he simply drew a deep breath, reached, and the world was wider by half again. He was aware of Uwen, of the horses, of all the men and all the patient oxen, even of the wheeling hawks that soared, fearless of the chill autumn winds, looking for mice or sparrows.

Poor creatures, he thought, seeing a hawk stoop beyond a leafless copse of trees. He forever pitied the hunted, and thought of Owl, and wondered where he laired, nowadays, whether he had gone back to Ynefel now that it was free of threat.

He was thinking like a boy again, and making wild and foolish conjecture, as he had done on the hilltop. But, oh, he could dare more. He could draw the gray light to the sunlit world, he could do battle with shadows if he found them—

But he had far rather simply be aware of the lives, the living, the loyal and the loved. He had proposed to sleep in the saddle, but unexpectedly found his thoughts too rapid, racing ahead of the slow wagons. He was unavoidably morose at the thought of leaving Cefwyn and Ninévrisë, but he breathed with increasing anticipation of the road and the freedom ahead.

The sun was warm enough to raise a slight sweat on his shoulders when the wind slacked, and the wind did fall and stayed still in late afternoon. They rested from time to time, changed horses, for the horses' ease; and Uwen, trading Liss for Gia again, looked well content, a man with an old friend and a new and trying to assure one of his affection without slighting the other: all at once it Unfolded what Uwen was doing, and how he loved both, but Gia more, the other being all to discover. Was not a king much the same, when he had to consider who sat next him at table?

And the world, in widening, slowly widened behind them, too, to the subtle feeling of cold water, the smell of sweat, the shapes of stones.

"Master Emuin is finally on his way," Tristen said, drawing Uwen's curious glance.

"He's leavin' the gate?"

"Oh, farther. By the little stream we crossed, the one near the rocks, with the old tree with the hole in it."

"Does he come so far on the road and ye not see?"

"He can slip about when he wishes," Tristen said, "better than I, I think. He's quite clever. I think it comes of being old."

"And what does he say?" Uwen asked, and Tristen wondered that at once. A sting of displeasure came back.

"He bids me mind my business," Tristen said, laughing.

Uwen cast him a sidelong glance. His gray hair blew in rising wind as the sunlight found it, all against a blue sky. Light touched Uwen's weathered, cold-stung face with perfect cheerfulness.

This is where I must be, Tristen thought then, absolutely certain of it, for no reason. This is where Uwen must be, with me. We belong on this road . . . and all is well.

Other men are where they *need* to be. But Uwen and I are where we *must* be . . . there is a difference.

Then came, with the cold chill of water, with that clarity of sun on stones, the uncertainty of certainties that seeped out of the gray place, but it was Emuin's troubled doubt that owned this fear. Come rain, come lightning, come spells or wizards' wishes, this muddy road was a thread stretched out strongly toward Ynefel . . . it ran *there*, Tristen thought, and thought of his window at night, the rain crawling across the horn panes. But that was but one place of all the places it led.

Ink followed the goose-quill tip, red wax dripped onto parchment under a window full of sunset. The royal seal made a scant, a listless imprint.

Cefwyn fixed the duke of Ryssand with a cold stare then and did not himself pick up the parchment, or invite the duke to do so. An anxious page fidgeted and failed to move.

The Patriarch himself slipped in and did the deed, picked up the rattling document and bowed without quite looking Cefwyn in the eye.

A disappointment.

I am coming to hate this man, Cefwyn thought of Corswyndam, Lord Ryssand. Corswyndam was a lank, hawk-nosed, wet rag of a man, the sort that smothered any enthusiasm, disapproved anything not to his advantage, used the Quinalt as sword and shield and purse of pennies, and had interest in nothing that did not serve his own interests.

He had not the luxury, now, to hate the Patriarch. The Patriarch was thus far too useful. Why, if there were no Patriarch, then that parchment might have rested on the table until the page called a servant to move it. As it was, the Patriarch clutched it in reward of services rendered and no one present mentioned exactly what those services were.

But the king met with the duke of Ryssand and the duke of Murandys, and officially settled the matter of Sulriggan's return on the very evening the king's friend was on his way to Amefel . . . and the king had the small satisfaction of seeing no triumph on any face *except* the Patriarch's.

The two lords had looked to enjoy this evening. They had looked, perhaps, to accusations of sorcery, and expected better of the Patriarch than they had gotten. But the Patriarch knew on what table his meals were served henceforth and forevermore, and knew that the two lords at his back felt betrayed, and therefore he had double reason to stand close by his king.

Sulriggan would return to court, the Patriarch's cousin; and gods send the duke of Llymaryn would be prudent, now, having coasted so close to royal anger. Ironic, that the king's two best allies in the troublesome north might turn out to be the Patriarch and his cousin Sulriggan. He never would have seen that as likely. But Emuin had left him in order to advise and restrain Tristen, a far chancier element. That left, of royal intimates, only Efanor, only the Regent, only the Lord Commander, several other officers, and Cevulirn—a gray, often silent presence.

So at present, in the court as it was now and for time foreseeable, yes, the Patriarch was his ally and Sulriggan was the Patriarch's man . . . such as he was.

He smiled on the Patriarch, a warm, a proprietary sort of smile, the sort he denied the two lords. He meditated on the rewards of piety, on his new use of the gods, from a perspective he had not had until his enemies hewed down the tall tree that was Tristen . . . or at least, until he lengthened his view of the realm not as protecting a small, threatened circle of intimates but as reaching to his good neighbor Amefel, his good neighbor Cevulirn of Ivanor, his dearest love the Regent from across the river, and hell take these two barons. He had the Patriarch, and soon he would have Sulriggan, both in the center of his hand, clever as they had thought they were, and neither would be anxious to see that hand ever become a fist.

"I add," he said to the Holy Father, "I add the welcome of the Marhanen house, and the use of the bedchamber lately in use by the duke of Amefel, for residence within the Guelesfort." He said nothing about the cook, that unholy power in Sulriggan's household. Within the Guelesfort, the lord of Llymaryn had to rely on the Guelesfort kitchens, and be damned to Sulriggan's culinary tastes. There was a second thorn in that royal rose, too, that Sulriggan would not be guesting with, say, Ryssand or Murandys.

"Your Majesty," the Patriarch said. And the dukes of Ryssand and Murandys looked out of countenance. Supper was preparing, and they all were invited, in a court composed exactly as they had wished, *purified* of wizards and their conjuring.

Barley soup tonight and so long as the harvest held out. Plain Amefin fare. The royal cook might rebel, but it would be barley soup every evening, not a Ryssand leek in evidence, Amefin venison and Llymarish beef, and not a fish, not a one, from Murandys' weirs.

A taste for plain fare gave him an excuse for sending wagons and messages to Amefel. He was writing a letter in request of sausages and the state of affairs in a province that had never concerned his father except as a source of wool, taxes, and rural discontent mediated by a lord he had trusted far too much.

He recalled an Amefin tailor, a chandler, even the mason who had repaired the stable wall. Perhaps there were walls about the Guelesfort that wanted patching, or perhaps the king needed a winter cloak of fine Amefin wool. Oh, there might be spells sewn into it: the whole province of Amefel was rife with heresy.

He should not favor Amefel alone. If there were fish, they should also come from Sovrag's people, who caught them downstream of Murandys, when they were not engaged in petty brigandage. It was a poor province, when it was not raiding; and a royal purchase of fish might give relief to Sovrag's neighbors, among whom was Cevulirn. If there was grain, the south had that. If there was timber and stone, there was sullen Imor. *Damned* if he would sit helplessly nodding to the demands of the north. They had set him at odds with them and declared their war against his friends in pettiness and shadows. He knew them, and he knew their taxes and wherein they chose to pay the Crown in bags of grain and barrels of salt fish, which they took from the hands of their peasantry.

Refuse Murandys' salt fish? Levy instead a demand for timber and labor? To glut the fisheries without warning would lower the price of fish, which the people could eat as well as sell, but it would threaten Murandys and force him to look to Ryssand for the timber. Diminish the requirement for timber the king could not: he needed it for bridges.

Best consider carefully which of his lords he wished to push at the other, and for what goods, and who would cheat whom, if he demanded, say, *gold* of Murandys, declaring a royal distaste for barrels of fish. And where would Murandys obtain gold? Selling that fish to Guelessar at, perhaps, a lower price.

Perhaps merely opening the discussion tonight of a distaste for fish would so alarm Murandys as to make him far more amenable. Or there was another possible topic of interest, which he had never mentioned, awaiting its usefulness.

"Do you know," he remarked to Murandys, "Lady *Luriel* sent me a letter. Several of them, in fact."

He saw the intake of breath, as Murandys, his mind set on the Patriarch's cousin, realized he had an overlooked piece on the board, his niece, who did not love him, who had been writing letters on the eve of the king's marriage and risking the king's perhaps unfavorable interest. Cefwyn smiled his grandfather's smile quite consciously, and rose from his chair.

"We'll discuss it," he said. "The tables are laid, I'm sure, gentlemen. We expect your company."

Nestled between two hills, a Quinalt monastery occupied that small wedge of flatland created by the road's branching to Marisal in the south and to Amefel to the west. Clusyn was its name. It was a waystop the king's party had used on its way to Guelemara; and thanks to its provision for travelers at any season Tristen found no need to make a camp under canvas, a great benefit, which obviated the necessity of unloading a significant amount of canvas in a rising damp and, worse, loading all that canvas up again in the morning, when the air was bitterly cold.

Instead a traveler met safe walls, and their company even found meals waiting. The king's messenger, on his way to Amefel by post-horse ahead of them, had advised the monks such a number of men would be following him by evening, and that news had had the honest monks baking up leavened bread, entire baskets of it coming hot from the oven right at sunset. Monks had swept out the sheds and the space along the south wall, provided hay for their horses, and managed their arrival as a marvelously efficient process, one monk directing their wagons to the end of the yard, where at another brother's direction each set of drivers might unhitch its team on the spot and lead them to the appropriate area by the stables, oxen to one side, mules to this place, horses to that. The next wagon went beside that one, and the carts in the order of march, and so on, all by the wan light of a setting sun and shadows lengthening over the modest walls . . . walls the purpose of which seemed to fence out hungry deer, not hostile men.

The men of the Guard found their accommodation in a disused drying shed, where a fireplace provided a welcome warmth. The drivers shared canvas-sided lean-tos provided with a bonfire in front; but for the lord of Amefel and his captain and his servants, and for the king's officers, there was the guesthouse, which boasted four proper rooms besides the warm common room. But supper was waiting for all of them, and they were able at last to put off the armor they had worn since before dawn, and to set aside their weapons and sit down to a hot meal. "These are countryfolk," Uwen said approvingly of the monks. "These are good countryfolk, no rich city men. They put the soldiers and the muleteers and all right into walls, which with this wind startin' up and the damp and all is a fine thing, a very fine thing.""

The wind had become very bitter at the last, nipping noses and making riders' toes cold as the sun went down, marking a night of small comfort for anyone beyond a safe fireside and in the open.

Master Emuin, on the road (asleep, as seemed, in a wagon, as Tristen felt from moment to moment a slight uneasy balance) would not fare half so well, and despite master Emuin's tenancy in the drafty tower, the unfettered gusts outside were bitter and strong. But there was nothing he could do to lend wings to oxen, and he knew no way he could hurry distant wagons. He only hoped the axles bore the weight of master Emuin's load of baggage and brought him here as soon as might be.

With a waft of cold air from outside, Anwyll came in to join them midway through their supper, reporting everyone under cover and the soldiers exceedingly grateful for grain and water they had not had to carry for themselves—water which had healing virtues for man and beast.

"The shrine is famous for the water," Uwen explained in a low voice. "It heals, so it does, the stomach complaints. His Highness . . ." Uwen cleared his throat quietly. "His Highness'd set great store by it, on account of the holy precinct."

The water tasted of sulfur, to a tongue familiar with the powders of a wizard's workshop; but Uwen's quiet tone and hushed reminder of His Highness advised him it was a matter of gods, which Efanor would revere.

"They sell amulets," Captain Anwyll added, "which have the virtue of the water. And the local blessing."

"This is a safe place," Tristen said, since some acknowledgment of the virtues of it seemed called for. "It feels so." And to the rescue of the moment, the monks brought ale, three pitchers of it. "From Marisyn," the chief monk said, and they finished their supper, with sweet buttered cakes, and talked of safe things like wagon wheels and harness until Anwyll was through with his supper and left them.

The sulfur-tasting water satisfied thirst. Tristen much doubted the amulets, after Emuin's dismissal of Efanor's; but some mark of courtesy seemed due. The monks had done far more for his comfort than ever the great shrine in Guelemara had done.

"What shall we do to repay the monastery?" he asked Uwen at length. "Shall we give them gold?"

"It's the custom to give a gift."

"Then will you do that?" he asked, and gave Uwen the purse Idrys had given him, supposing that that was enough: the rest of their money was not in purses but in that great chest the company quartermaster guarded.

"'At were a good thought," Uwen said. "I'll see to it."

"Do. But," he added, "make sure of the coins as you give them. Idrys cautioned me strongly."

"That I will," Uwen said, "and have the lord abbot bless ever' one of 'em as I deal it out."

"A very good thought," he said. He was here because of a Sihhë coin as well as a lightning bolt, he well understood so, and he no longer trusted everyone he met, even when he made a gesture of friendship and respect to them. It seemed a sad and sorry way to proceed. But he sent Uwen to pay a coin and test the balance of the heavens tonight, in the very unlikely chance that wizardry had truly transmuted his last one.

He sat sipping the remnant of his ale before the fire, aware of monks who tiptoed close among the columns to stare at him, and aware of Anwyll and his men, who in pursuing duties in the cold kept letting the wind in.

He was aware of Emuin, too, on the road and uncomfortable, and that venture into the gray space seemed riskier than in the daytime. Perhaps it *was* the weather, with the wind keening around the eaves of what was a strange lodging, even once visited. He had had his way today in sunlight, but the clouds were moving in again. The shadows which abounded in the cluttered edges of the common room leapt and flowed like the firelight as wind fluttered down the chimney . . . not wicked Shadows, but there were a few more dangerous ones, he suspected, among the natural ones.

He was glad when Uwen came back, after, it seemed to him, too long a time.

"The lord abbot's right pleased, and the captain and all."

"Why should the captain be pleased?"

Uwen ducked his head somewhat and seemed to have said a small word too much.

"On account of the luck. Havin' a lord do things for luck, it makes a soldier happier."

"The soldiers are unhappy?"

"Well, there's some as is anxious about Your Grace, that's the truth, with the lightning and all. But," Uwen added, cheerfully, "they ain't sorry to be here, counting ye a lord that wins his battles, m'lord, which is a long sight better 'n one that don't."

"It seems I hardly won the one against the Quinalt."

"I don't think it were the Quinalt that done ye wrong, m'lord, an' so say others."

He looked straight at Uwen, and Uwen, with something he had gathered himself to say, went on:

"Likeliest Murandys, maybe Ryssand, is what they're sayin' around the fire. Some thinks it was magical, but others says it's again' His Majesty on account of Her Grace, which the barons don't like . . . Murandys is the name some say."

Uwen had a knack for hearing things, in the kitchens, in the stables, with the common men wherever he was, and most particularly with grooms and soldiers. He paid attention when Uwen told him such things, and trusted Uwen's estimations as much as he trusted Idrys' warnings.

"Is Cefwyn in danger?" he asked. That had to be asked first.

"Not so's ye'd say, in danger, m'lord, as folk think. It's that the barons in the north was accustomed to goin' on their own advice in the old king's reign. I'm talking above myself, here, but the old king favored 'em and His Majesty don't, and I pray to the gods His Majesty gets before 'em soon an' checks 'em hard."

Gods were much in his thinking lately, and unresolved. But he was entertaining less and less hope of them. "I wish he may. What more should I wish?"

Uwen looked squarely at him, understanding what he meant, he was well sure. At times he longed for Uwen to know more than he did, and to be able to advise him, as Emuin refused to do.

But Uwen set his own limits. "I couldn't judge, m'lord. Truly, don't ye ask me. I can't tell ye what's right. All the same I trust your heart, m'lord; ye've done naught but good to me. And good to His Majesty. He's on his throne, and I wouldn't say His Grace of Murandys is safe if he crosses the Marhanen, not an hour."

"Yet Cefwyn wouldn't do any man harm. He has no wish to do it."

"That's so, m'lord, but he is a king. And kings ain't common men, as goes wi'out saying."

"Nor am I."

"No, m'lord, ye ain't." Uwen gave a great breath, as that damning statement hung there, and they neither one could mend that, nor mend what had sundered him from the place he had longed to have.

"The whole household come wi' ye, m'lord. Lusin and them has all left the king's service for good an' all, to come wi' ye."

"I am grateful," he said, but had no idea what more to say, when men put themselves and all their substance at risk on the currents that swept him up and carried him here and there in the world. To follow him seemed an unreasonable choice in men who might have had peaceful lives. And at the moment he saw his servants and his guards alike waiting at the side of the room, on benches, some, or squatting down to talk to comrades, none asleep, none appearing impatient of the long day's travel.

He found no gods in this place, no more than in the Quinaltine.

He hoped for the safe rest and peaceful dreams of all the men with him. The Lines were well-ordered here, at the least, a greater comfort and source of strength than the famed water. "The household should go to their beds," he said, "you among the first. I may sit here a while by the fire."

"Yes, m'lord," Uwen said quietly, and went and spoke to Lusin and Tassand. The staff moved quietly off to the hall.

But when Uwen came back alone and settled close by the fire, he was not surprised. Uwen maintained his solitary watch, armed, but not heavily so, wary, but nodding sometimes. "How's Emuin farin'?" Uwen asked at last.

"Master Emuin has had to stop," he said quietly. Emuin was at least warm, if damp, and the cold wind was catching the canvas that sheltered him, an intermittent thumping. "Has Captain Anwyll gone to bed?"

"The captain's turned in, aye. I said I'd watch."

"You might make a pallet."

"Ye might lie down on your own bed, young m'lord."

"I shall. I shall, Uwen. But just now the fire is warm."

"Aye, m'lord."

A question nagged his peace. "Does he fear me, the captain?"

"He's Quinalt, an' ain't never dealt with wizards. Ye do set a body back a little with your seein' master Emuin, m'lord."

"Doubtless so."

Tristen watched the flames, wondering did he dare sleep, and asking himself whether they should simply wait here until tomorrow evening and until master Emuin might overtake them. He had let the captain go to his bed without discussing the notion. But he still might propose it at breakfast, which they did propose to have, before they hitched the wagons. Delaying another day could have risk, once the messenger had reached Amefel and let loose his news in a town known for unrest. If the town expected a thing to happen in a certain number of days and it failed, speculation started, and men did unwise things.

Meanwhile Uwen's head nodded and his chin sank on his breast. And in the gray space, softly, subtly, as Tristen watched the fire, Emuin was with him, a wisp of a presence, a comfort in the shadowy dark.

A wind seemed to blow through the gray, tattering edges. Emuin's presence grew more attenuated still, but whether he was as thin and insubstantial to Emuin he could not say. He resisted all temptation to reach out and hold on to the old man by his own strength. There had been risk in speaking like this in Guelemara, the chance of being spied upon; and he was not sure, resting among so many priests and monks, whether it was entirely safe to make such an approach.

But there was also a decision to make.

—*Shall I bid the company wait?* he asked master Emuin. *We might stay here tomorrow.*

The wind blew stronger. And colder.

—*Master Emuin? Are you well?*

—*Be careful! Emuin said, a mere wisp now. Beware, young lord!*

Something crossed the wind, shadowed it for a moment, uncommon in his venturing here.

—*What is that? he began to ask. And in alarm: Is someone there?*

—*No! Emuin caught at him, but wafted backward as if the wind had blown him, sailed away and down like the leaf from the hilltop. Don't pursue me. Don't look. Don't ask, don't wonder. I fear shadows in that direction, young lord. I do fear them. Perhaps I see them more clearly where I stand. But this is altogether an uneasy night. Go!*

Distances here were not the same. At one moment Emuin had as well have been in Guelemara, in the next as solidly as if he were in the monastery, and yet Emuin had not stirred from his camp nor he from his chair.

And beyond . . . beyond and in some direction he could not equate with the chair or the fireside . . . was an Edge of the sort he had learned was dangerous. It was death . . . or it was at least a loss of some sort. He had seen it appear with Uleman, the lord Regent, Her Grace's father, and lost him very soon after. Of a sudden he was afraid for Emuin, and was amazed how very like Mauryl Emuin had become, with his hair and beard far whiter since summer. It shone, in the light there was. He could easily mistake one for the other.

—*I am not Mauryl, Emuin said fiercely. I have no wish to become him or to set my hand to his workings, no matter your wishes. Don't mistake us, young lord! I cannot amend his Working, never think so! Gods forfend! Don't pull at me so!*

He was duly chastised, and it was a moment before he dared a wider breath.

—*Master Emuin, he said in this waking dream, I meant no such thing. Nor ever mistake you. And I only ask—*

Fear had come in from over that dark Edge. There was no clear direction in the gray place, but it had always more or less corresponded with directions in the world of Men. It seemed to him now that he had been facing north, sitting before the fire. That would put the perilous Edge at the west . . . at the west, where Amefel lay, just across the river, not north, toward Tasmôrden.

But that reckoning set the shadow he had felt in the wind to the east, and the south, which he did not immediately believe. He dared not distract himself with wondering, or trying to find himself in the world of Men. There had been the danger, before. He felt the uncertainty, now, and felt . . .

—Careful!

He bit down on his lip to draw wits and flesh together. But master Emuin retreated from him without stirring a foot, then ceased to be there, just that quickly. Emuin was safe, escaped from the gray space, and he was alone and still in danger, in a place that gusted with winds.

The shadow-haunted stone of the guesthouse was another breath away. He drew that breath large and deep and became aware first of the glowing substance of the wards and the Lines, secondly of the substance under him.

Perhaps he moved in his chair, perhaps jumped with the startlement of solid wood under his fingers. At least Uwen broke off snoring and lifted his head in muzzy startlement.

"Forgive me, m'lord. I didn't mean to drop off like that."

"I must have dreamt," he said. It felt like that, like a bad dream, and he still felt his breath shortened. "To bed, both of us."

"Aye, m'lord," Uwen said, and slowly got up as he did. They went back to the hall and to the fine, snug pair of rooms they had.

But Uwen would not leave him there: Uwen brought his mattress from the other room and settled down on the floor with his sword in his arms, saying he would sleep there or not at all.

Tristen let his sword stand with his shield in the corner, and lay down on a fine goose-feather mattress, but with coarser blankets and with a rougher ceiling above him than he had been accustomed to have since he came to Cefwyn's company—it was bare rafters, which cast shadows from the watch-candle they had left on the table. The sight put him in mind of Ynefel, and his room, and the towering great hall with the stairs winding crazily up the stonework.

That webwork of stairs had creaked in storms. It had been so very fragile. He had known that even when he was living there, and there was nothing more frightening than being on those stairs in the dark, with the whole tower groaning and complaining with the wind. At such times, the stone faces set in its walls seemed to move, and the candle-shadows shifted . . . and sounds issued forth which were not the wind: shrieks as of bending metal, or of iron doors opening, or of souls in pain.

Mauryl's face had seemed to be in that stone. He tried to hold to that thought. Fleeing it gave strength to his enemy, who was dead, but all the same, he would not risk growing uncertain on that point, when so much else was uncertain. Mauryl had gone into the stone, and the timbers had fallen, and Ynefel was not the same, in the autumn in which Cefwyn was king of Ylesuin. He dared not let that memory go.

But the night the candle had gone out, the night he had been on the stairs in the dark . . . strange, he thought from the vantage of a year of Unfoldings, strange in many respects, and after Lewenbrook, that he should still cast back to that night as the most frightening of his life.

The Edge was almost as dreadful. That kind of terror wafted out of it when it appeared. The Shadow at Lewenbrook had been a thunderous, dreadful threat; but one could be angry at it. The Edge, like that moment on the stairs, was a cold, sweating sort of fear, and a venturer in the gray space could observe it in curiosity until quite without warning he felt everything tilt toward it. That it appeared again troubled him . . . and it did not seem to him that the threat of the Edge was situated in the world of Men, not a presentiment of danger, of treacherous guards or accident or weather. He feared it was simply in master Emuin's increasing frailty, the journey, the packing and unpacking and the disturbing of an old man's peace . . . and whether that Edge represented something that only endangered master Emuin when he was in the gray space or whether the danger was always there, he was not sure and did not trust master Emuin to tell him.

Even wondering about it set the gray space in reach again, at a safer remove, true, but perilous, tonight, all the same.

The shadow in the wind whisked past him.

Someone was there.

There. In the confusion of a strange building and strange wards, in the turning-about of stairs and steps . . .

He had last reckoned master Emuin's presence to what he knew by the road was north . . . but where was the fireplace now? And which direction was the head of his bed at the moment?

It was not Emuin. It came furtively, quietly, through the gray, but things could suddenly move very fast, and he was not Tristen of Lewen plain at this instant, he was young Tristen, he was Tristen on the stairs in Mauryl's keep, and knew how a shadow could pounce, and scare, and find access in fear.

Then it seemed less baneful, even anxious to find him. He thought then that it might be Ninévrisë trying in her unschooled way to find him . . . and she left herself open on such a night to unguessed hazards.

No, he said, rebuffed it with a desperate, confused effort, and it left him.

He lay still then, his eyes open on the rafters above him, asking himself where it had been, whether east or west. Ordinarily he knew, but he had confused himself, and he might have harmed it. He was distressed and feared indeed it had been Ninévrisë, and that he might have frightened her.

Be safe, he wished whoever it had been. *Sleep soundly. Be at peace . . .*

Should I wait for you? was what he had reached out to Emuin to ask.

Should I suspect harm? he would have asked at the end of their encounter.

Now he would ask: Have you kept secrets from me, master Emuin?

Or is it only since tonight that the gray place has become dangerous?

CHAPTER 3

The edge of morning brought cold to the monastery. Lanternlight glistened on icy steps as they opened the door to the guesthouse. A guardsman had fallen the three steps to the yard, unhurt, the report was, but only because of the armor.

"You be careful, m'lord," Uwen said when they reached the small porch, and moved gingerly on the steps himself. Tristen rubbed his ungloved fingers across the stonework of the banister, exploring the sting and the depth of the coating. He had seen frost, but never such a heavy coating of it, and he had met no footing quite so treacherous. But he learned in the first, the second step, like the Unfolding of a Word, and walked down the steps in Uwen's wake with increasing sureness.

The men showed themselves undaunted, too, despite a few falls. The younger soldiers played games and pushed and shoved one another like boys; the older men minced about more carefully in the lanternlight across the yard, but the horses and oxen seemed to have no great difficulty, particularly in the churned stiff mud that stood in frosty ridges. Teams moved briskly with their drivers, and grooms brought the saddled horses in quick order of their masters' precedence while the monks scattered sand with brooms.

"M'lord," Aswys came to ask, "will it be Petelly this morning?"

"Yes," he said, watching all the activity of men from the side of the steps, wrapped in a warm cloak Tassand had put about him.

Is it winter, now? he would ask Emuin, who was probably warm in a nest he would not leave until later in the day. Has it begun?

And what will it mean to the wagons, if snow follows the ice?

A slight drover's boy struggled and slid past, scarcely managing to keep upright with his arms full of harness. But Tristen kept quietly to the side of the yard. Ice, in all the colors of white came to him with disquieting force, the deeper Unfolding of a Word, Ice lying in sheets and jagged shards.

The Sihhë-lords had come down from the north, had he not read it?

At some moments he hoped with all his heart that he was the creation of scattered elements, whatever Mauryl had flung together by magic, a new creature, and innocent of past sins. But at other times he had to believe what Idrys had said of him: that he was a revenant, that he was that lord named Barrakkêth . . . and if that was so, should it surprise him that he found ice and winter touched his heart? He had known Barrakkêth's writings by heart before he read them. So ought it to be a wonder that Ice began to unfold to him, and winter began to settle into his knowledge in all its white strength?

He thought of Efanor's little book, which he carried next his shirt, and despaired of gods, despaired of other advice that would replace Emuin's, and Cefwyn's, and Idrys'.

Oh, come, he wished Uwen desperately, speak to me, prevent worse things Unfolding.

"M'lord," Uwen said, an immediate intrusion which frightened him as much as the thoughts inside him. "M'lord, the horses is comin'."

Mundane matter, mundane advisement. Uwen had needed to speak to him. And the sun, the safe and ordinary sun, was a glow in the east, discernible, now. Breath steamed, men and horses enjoying this edge of dawn. His knees felt weak from the fright, and he stood still, watched the drivers move the teams in, and saw the standard-bearers with their horses near the gate. Saw, as Uwen had said, Aswys and his helpers bringing Petelly and Gia.

"A skittish morning, m'lord," Aswys ventured to say.

"So it seems." His knees still lacked strength. He had fallen in fits before this when something so potent came on him. He feared it would happen now, and his heart was beating as if he had been running as he took the reins. Petelly's hide was as cold as the saddle as he mounted up, and he spread his cloak about him and Petelly, to warm them both.

I cannot wait, he thought. I could not have lingered. If Emuin had wished me to wait, I would have heard him.

Do you hear me, master Emuin? There is Ice, there is Ice all around, master Emuin, and I know its nature, master Emuin . . . do you not hear?

The men opened the gates. The sun had just broken above the horizon, and sent out a flood of light on a land rimed and hazed with ice. Rime was on the grass stems along the road, on the stones, on the smallest pebbles, and the rising sun hazed it into delicate morning shades. The puddle near the gate had gained a crinkled coating of ice. Even the ridges of common mud at the edges of yesterday's unsightly puddle had a white coating, and their column of horses and men went out in pale orange clouds of their own breath.

How could he have dreaded such a sight? Everything was touched with dawn, and common things had become wonderful as common things had once been to him. He was on his way. A balance had tipped, around sunrise, and he was on the Road again, where he had business, and urgent business, at that.

For a moment he imagined Ynefel, in such rime-ice and dawn.

Mauryl, he would say. Mauryl, have you seen the stones?

Mauryl, look at the sun above the trees! Look at the light!

And for a moment Mauryl would forget whatever troubled him and his old eyes would gaze at what he found marvelous. And for a moment Mauryl would find wonder in it, too, and tell him the Name of it, and remind him of the thousand things he had forgotten to do, in his distraction of the hour.

He could be distracted, still, by beauty, by the wonder of a stroke of sunlight. Perhaps at such times he made himself open to wizardry—or conversely, was as warded and safe at such moments as Ynefel at its strongest. Perhaps threats simply slid past his attention and he made himself immune. He knew that he wielded magic as well as iron, and yet looked away from it, and made himself fables to explain his own presence in the world, and sought gods who might be more powerful than himself. It would be very comfortable if there were someone more powerful than himself, on this Road, on this particular morning, someone to guide him, even someone to blame: Hasufin Heltain had been a comfort, in that sense, a voice, an answer, where otherwise was only gray and shifting cloud. A few days ago he could not imagine the spring; now he imagined ruling Amefel. Last night he had quit the gray place in fear that there was someone and this morning he thought with regret of his enemy. Last night he had feared an Edge and this morning in a tentative probe of the place he could not find no limit to contain him.

Last night Emuin had been there. This morning Emuin was not, a circumstance which meant nothing more, he told himself, than the very mundane truth of the mortal world, that Emuin was still asleep, and that he would have no thanks for pressing harder and gaining Emuin's attention on a mere whim.

What would he say in this now glorious dawn?

—*Forgive me, master Emuin, but I grew afraid . . .*

—*Comfort me, master Emuin: I miss Cefwyn. I have missed him from before we rode out of Amefel together, and this morning, for no good cause, I doubted . . .*

—*Forgive me, master Emuin, that this morning I sought gods. Now I have no master but my oath to Cefwyn.*

—*On the hilltop where I have arrived, I can see all the things I have ever known. I fly free as a leaf on the wind.*

—*But there are places beyond the hills, and days beyond this one, master Emuin, and there are Shadows where the sun has no power. Do all Men walk as blind as I?*

He dared not press harder with his thoughts. It was so easy to slip deeper and deeper into the gray place, where he feared they were no longer alone. The presence last night ran through his thoughts like an escaping dream. Had he dreamed it, thus at the edge of sleep? Was it a memory, or had it truly happened?

That it fled recollection troubled him.

Might Ninévrisë indeed have reached out?

Might she—or Cefwyn—be in difficulty? Had the barons set about some new mischief, and did Cefwyn need him to come back?

If there was any answer from Emuin, the hills hid it from him, while to his backward glance the column had grown behind him, continuing to form inside the monastery walls like a balled string extending itself, and that unwinding was almost done now. They were well and truly on their way to Amefel.

The magic of the frost grew thinner as the sun climbed, as the frost left the eastern side of hills, then the west, persisted only in the shadows, and at last vanished altogether.

By noon the sun had brought a warmth to their backs, an easy warmth. Even toes in boots grew warm, and Petelly, who had shown an uncommon keenness to frolic this morning had settled down to the general pace.

Master Emuin, Tristen was vaguely aware, was decidedly awake now, had made not quite such an early start, and ached in his joints with the bouncing of the wagon. It was not a good beginning, this trailing along the countryside for miles and days, and he was sorry to leave master Emuin further behind, but what more could he do? he posed the peevish question.

He had no more answer than before, and at their noon rest, weary of worry, fretting in Emuin's protracted and maddening silence, he had Dys brought up in the line and rode him for the rest of the afternoon, a lively contest of wills, since Dys had not worked in a month. Uwen had called up Cassam, his own heavy horse, at the same time, and the two horses being stablemates, and both needing to have a little room around them, they rode at times beside the column, at times ahead.

One could easily drowse on Petelly, rest one's eyes with caution on Gery, but one never forgot the difference of being on Dys. The big hooves went down with a heavier sound, the motion was broader, softer, and more deliberate. Dys' ears were constantly up, then flat, for Dysarys expected enemies. Yet Dys loved attention, too, and since most grooms were afraid of him, he got less of it than he liked . . .

Very like his master, Tristen thought.

But it was a good, level ride, the road presenting no particular difficulty for the wagons and no need to plan alternatives. The bridges on a king's road would bear a loaded cart without worry, or failing that, offered fords with good firm approaches and no great depth. So he had nothing to do but contend with Dys' humors and watch the grass blowing in the breeze. He was aware from time to time of master Emuin, eventually that Emuin had reached the monastery at long last and was safe, but full of aches from being tossed about on the wagonseat and sore from a stint of riding. He was sorry for that. Master Emuin settled in for a belated noon meal, and then took a nap.

But as the hours passed he began to realize master Emuin had no intention of leaving the monastery. And when the sun went down in a bank of cloud and they were pressing into a murky twilight to reach their scheduled camp he was aware of master Emuin sitting by a warm fireside sipping ale.

—*Master Emuin,* he began. But had no answer, only the waft of master Emuin's extreme vexation.

No more had he stood overlong on the tower stairs on those evenings when master Emuin would not open the door. On prior evenings he had simply set the basket down and gone back to his rooms, reckoning the old man had studies and reading to do of some great moment.

But now he was angry, and the end of a long day on the road had not improved his own spirits or set him in a more cheerful mood. More, a wagon broke down, just as they were coming down the last fairly steep hill to the border. It was the farrier's wagon, as it proved.

"All that iron," Uwen said, and there was no way for men to lift it. There would have to be a new axle made, the load all shifted off, then on again. It was within sight of their proposed camp, down where Assurnbrook wended along, intermittent with trees and wild meadow.

"They'll have it by morning," Captain Anwyll came riding up beside them to report. "They'll shape an axle and may have it in good order by daybreak. Otherwise, we can take the rest of the wagons on tomorrow."

"Could be we'd ha' broke 'er in the ford," Uwen said in an attempt to put the best face on matters, "and have all the farrier's iron to save. As well it broke now."

"That's so," he said. "But I wish nothing else breaks before we get there."

"Oh, have a care, m'lord, or we'll all break down in the town gate."

Tristen laughed in spite of his daylong mood. Then he imagined the gates of Henas'amef, as clearly as if he saw them before his eyes. And he recalled the number of camps ahead and saw his company strung out from the monastery at Clusyn to Assurn Ford to Maudbrook in Amefel by tomorrow night, pieces everywhere, and it was not a cheerful prospect.

Meanwhile the surviving wagons squealed and groaned their way down to Assurn's edge, and by last light the men were gathering firewood, while he stood on the side of that dark stream with a view of the brushy hills and old walls on the other side of the brook.

Both sides of Assurnbrook afforded a few moldering stone walls that travelers regularly used for windbreaks and shelter. On the Amefin shore was the greater part of the stonework, the ruin of a shrine, but despite the remaining daylight, they had not chosen to cross to that more extensive shelter, not with a wagon under repair higher up the hill. They chose to stay on the Guelessar side of the water, where travelers over decades had set up several well-maintained hearths out of the wind.

The men stretched out a number of the common tents from the sides of the wagons for shelter; and before Tristen had realized what they intended, they had almost gotten down the pavilion for him, too.

"No," he said to the soldiers, stopping all work, and went to Anwyll to protest any unpacking of the larger tents.

"Your Grace cannot camp in the field."

"Do not the soldiers, sir?" He was vexed, seeing nothing but delays, nothing but encumbrances from hour to hour, and he walked away in impatience when Anwyll tried to argue with him. He found warmth by the nearest of the three common fires, and stood there waiting for his supper, whenever it might appear.

"Did I do wrong?" he asked Uwen, when Uwen came up to stand by him. "Is Anwyll angry with me?"

"No, m'lord," Uwen said, who was likewise bound to sleep without a tent tonight, by his decision. "Fewest of these tents we let catch the morning damp, easier to pack. He ain't that sorry."

He said nothing.

"Ye're glum," Uwen observed after a moment more. "Are ye worrit, m'lord?"

"Anxious to be there," he said, which had become the all-encompassing truth.

They had a modest supper, bread from the monastery, sausages to toast in the fire, cheese, and a moderate amount of ale, after which Anwyll seemed in far better humor and the men were tolerably merry. The farrier's wagon made it down the hill at last, to no little commotion and laughter. Tristen left the fire to see it in, wrapped in his cloak, in a dark outside the fires and the shelters. He sent the weary drivers and the farrier and his crew to a late and anticipated supper, and comforted himself that he had one straggled crew at last accounted for.

He lingered after, cherishing the quiet after the groaning wheels had passed him. It was a place and an hour for shadows, and with no particular dread he realized the presence of one that lurked forlornly near the light, and that feared his impatience. Curiosity had perhaps drawn it. Others prowled the other shore, unhappy shadows that flitted and tricked the eye among the ruins. He had all but heard shadows breathing above the noise of men drinking and telling tales. They might be shadows that belonged to Amefel . . . or to Guelessar. He had no idea. He found no harm in them, only a kind of company.

As for Emuin and the absent rest of their company, Emuin, it seemed, had gone to bed for the night, and attempted a fitful sleep, with no word to him.

—*Are you well, sir?* he attempted to ask at last, mustering his last remnant of charity.

—*Here is no place, no safe place,* was all he had in reply, an impression of an old man's worry . . . but more than that, more than that, he had a sudden clear sense that master Emuin was determined not to be in his company or in converse with him at all.

In the next moment he received a rebuff and felt a departing presence as strongly as if Emuin had slammed a door.

It was maddening.

And it was not like Emuin.

—*Master Emuin!* he called out to no avail, and he paced the shore, seeking to overcome his own angry misgivings that Emuin had not behaved reasonably, that if wagons broke down it was not, perhaps, accident, and that if he had better advice or earlier advice he might not be standing on the side of Assurnbrook blind to the night around him, with his adviser a full day behind and with a king's herald letting loose rumor in Amefel.

—*What am I to do?* he asked the unresponsive night.

The gray place ebbed away utterly, until he heard the running water and the sounds of the horses and the distant voices of men.

—*What am I to do, master Emuin? Answer me!*

Mauryl had used to scare him so. He found himself trembling only partly with the cold, and heard the approach of footsteps in the dark, along the pebbled shore.

"M'lord. M'lord, is ever'thing in order?"

"There's no danger," he said to Uwen's inquiry, and as he said it knew he had just told a great lie, and that he had been telling it to himself all day. "Master Emuin will not be here in anything like good time. He has gone to bed. He will overtake us as he can. Perhaps in Henas'amef."

"Ah, well," Uwen said with a sigh, "gods know what he loaded on them axles."

That was so common a piece of sense he all but laughed despite his temper, and his structure of reasoned disaster tumbled down. It was common, it was maddening, and it was very like the old man: he could well imagine Emuin had found last-moment items that must go onto the wagons, no matter what the advice of the drivers; and here they were, he and Emuin, Emuin's wagons moving far too slowly, the utmost the oxen could pull, and he and Emuin were two fools arguing in the night with the world upheaved and tottering. Emuin had drunk deep of the fine ale, eased his aches, and now he would become oblivious to him and his anxious questions, perhaps to feel a little less foolish and to be in a better humor in the morning.

"I wish we might go faster," he said to Uwen, the two of them standing on the dark shore. "I wish we were on the other side tonight."

"It'd ha' been wet horses and a cold wind for camp tonight."

That was another piece of common sense: with no enemy to deal with, it was folly to press this hard.

"It's a notorious place, besides," Uwen said, "and folk supposes there's haunts."

"There are," he said. "There are, here. But none harmful that I can tell." Last night he had wished to know that all the doors were secure. Tonight, in the open and the face of shadows, he feared none of them. He felt, rather, *safe*. They would not assail any man of his. He was sure that this place was safe.

But he was equally sure that something . . . *something* wanted him on the other side.

"Wind's cold," Uwen said, a polite suggestion, he was sure, that he come in out of the dark and sit by a warm fire where Uwen had far rather be.

Two days on the road had proved a determined sheep could amble faster than the heavy wagons could roll. And within any three days lately, it might rain. Or snow.

It was Amefel on the other side of that brook, and the delay of a night was too long.

He walked back to the fire with Uwen, he sat and drank with Uwen and Captain Anwyll, and listened to Anwyll say they were doing very well, very well indeed, considering the roads and the load on the axles. If they were lucky, none of the wagons would break down coming out of the ford. It was a good gravel bottom. The far bank was the question. So was the overcast sky tonight.

He lay under a canvas roof this night, listening to the water of Assurnbrook flowing nearby, and to the snap and crackle of the fire outside, thinking of the last time he had seen this particular camp, and with what hopes and fears he had ridden into Guelessar with Cefwyn, not knowing what Guelenfolk would think of his presence.

He knew now ... and feared that he should have stayed in Amefel, although he supposed that without his sojourn in Guelessar he would never have seen the court, and without seeing the court and knowing the northern lords he would have found Cefwyn's actions puzzling and unreasonable.

But he was coming back, now, like a stone rolling back to the hole it had shaped around itself, others' intentions not withstanding. He fit, in Amefel, or at least he perceived he might do so, better than anywhere else in his small experience.

And in his strong suspicion, when he moved with that sort of inevitability, that feeling of things settling firmly into a well-shaped place, then it was not chance moving them. He was returning to the place shaped for him. But he had barked his shins on Mauryl's steps too often not to have learned some lesson, and the lesson he had learned from those steps was to look not always at what drew his eye without being aware of the ground on which he stood.

And that ground, in this case, was his nature as Mauryl's Shaping ... or Summoning. There was a dreadful, a perilous difference. ... Whether Mauryl had Shaped him of many elements or Summoned him entire, of one dead soul, at one moment, out of prior moments each with their bonds to a certain shape of things.

So to what small pit was necessity taking him? Was it Mauryl's purpose that was still being satisfied? Or was something else being satisfied?

A wizard's spells could outlive the wizard, in terms that Men understood. But in another and more disturbing sense, in a knowledge he tried to set far from his ordinary thinking, *then* and *now* were not unbreachable walls. It was, in fact, easy to do. It was dangerously easy, for him to do ... and Emuin did not seem to have that power.

But if it were done, by him, by another ... then things were not safe ... were not *safe,* in ways that he felt, but could not define in simple words. Done was not done. Sealed was not sealed. Dead ... was not dead. That was the very least of what Mauryl might have done.

An owl called.

And called again.

Owl, he called back to it, for an unthinking and unguarded moment reaching out into the gray and the surrounding sky. He had never expected Owl in Guelessar, not really. But the crossing at Assurnbrook was another matter altogether, and that sound drew him, welcomed him, though in one part he feared and did not love and yet missed the creature.

Owl?

The sound did not come again. So maybe it was not Owl, only *an* owl, out hunting for its supper.

The morning came with still wind and cold. At the edge of the firelight, a thin shelf of ice showed along the shallow edge of Assurnbrook. Men huddled close at their small fires, having a little breakfast before the orders came to move. But Tristen walked to the edge of the water and stared off into Amefel with an uneasiness that now would not leave him.

"M'lord?" Uwen asked from behind him. "Is aught amiss?"

He was embarrassed, realizing Uwen had asked him at least once before. "We should leave the wagons and cross," he said, and having said it, he found the whole world tumbling into a new order, not a good one, not a bad one, only that when he said it, he was *back* in the reckoning of things, and he had hung outside them, pondering the shapes, all the night.

"M'lord?"

Anwyll had ordered things without him this morning, assumed he was in charge and that the camp would break immediately. That was beginning. Poles were falling. Canvas was being rolled.

"I shall be lord of Amefel over there," he said to Uwen, with a nod toward the far side of the stream, "and over there we shall go on ahead of the wagons. Anwyll may not wish us to do it. But I think half the men and the drivers had as soon keep beside their warm fires and sit here at the ford waiting for master Emuin. So tell the captain if he objects, he will gain nothing but packing up and getting a soaking. If he agrees, all the men might stay warm and dry and comfortable. Over there where I am lord, I will order it."

Uwen looked a good deal set aback, perhaps turning all the conditions of that over in his mind a second time. But then he nodded. "Aye, m'lord, better warm an' dry."

Uwen left to relay the order, and Tristen stood and waited.

He was relieved to have decided. The king's courier would be there today, and he had no doubt at all that the rumors would fly, rumors ranging from an unanticipated royal visit to the garrison being strengthened for a winter campaign—and the province viewed the Guelen Guard with as much suspicion as the Guelen Guard viewed the province.

All these possibilities. But there was only one truth. There was only one act that satisfied the magic that was pulling on him. Only one decision sent the stone rolling back into the place it fit.

Anwyll came walking toward him in some distress, with Uwen trailing behind. "Your Grace," Anwyll began. "I beg Your Grace consider . . . we have wagons and gold in our charge . . ."

"And soldiers to defend them."

"And the need to defend Your Grace. His Majesty gave me orders . . ."

"On the other side of the brook, I command. The men will only get wet and be unhappy. Or have to leave the wagons, which they ought not to do. Or will you prevent me?"

"I have orders to defend Your Grace."

"But none to prevent me."

"No, Your Grace."

"Then there's no good taking down the canvas, sir. The wagons and all the baggage can wait for master Emuin. We shall need men with us, enough here to guard the wagons, and we'll take the best horses with us." Now that he had seized command, the necessities of command took shape in him with perfect certainty. "No wagons, equipage like the Ivanim. One of the sergeants to bring in the column with master Emuin."

A deep breath. A moment's consideration. "Yes, Your Grace."

It was done, then. Anwyll went off; Uwen, too, with increasing enthusiasm for moving quickly. To equip like the Ivanim meant every cavalryman with his remount at lead, and though it was not the Guelen habit, the Guard who had been at Lewenbrook knew what was meant. Anwyll had offered no objections to that aspect of his orders at all, and in a very short time, with a brief commotion in the camp—shouting up and down, personal baggage stowed in wagons and horses traded about until those men to go had no encumbrance but their weapons and the fastest and best horses to carry them—they were ready.

That meant Dys and Cassam and their grooms stayed behind, too; they were not the horses for a race. Uwen chose Liss and Gia. Tristen chose high-spirited Gery for the start of their ride, and Petelly to go at lead.

"Banner-bearers!" Anwyll ordered. "Forward!" And the standard-bearers rode first into the cold, ice-rimmed water. Tristen followed, with Uwen, Anwyll overtaking them to make a third as they crossed. Water came not quite over the stirrups, splashed and chilled where it struck. Horses' breath steamed in the early sunlight as the bottom began to rise, as they rode dripping out of Assurnbrook into Amefel.

"Your Grace," Anwyll said, when they had reached that ground, "you are now in your province."

"And will be in Henas'amef tonight," he said, but it seemed to him Anwyll doubted that part of it.

Time after that, however, seemed to him at last to move at an acceptable rate, not creeping along at the somnolent pace of the wagons. The road led up the brushy shore, past the ruins, to the Amefel he remembered, a gently undulating meadowland, low wooded hills all about.

In another hour the road itself, overgrown with dry weeds and likely little used since summer's end, showed droppings of sheep and goats, occasionally those of cattle, traces of varying ages. At one and another place throughout the morning the sheep-traces they met crossed the road and led off to well-worn trails. Shepherds and farmers used the common land and paid their taxes to Henas'amef, and such tracks went to villages full of peaceful folk, little concerned with the affairs of lords and kings except as it affected their taxes, their sheep, their sons being called to war or left at peace.

Such things mattered, in the accounting he had to give hereafter.

If it meant replacing the lord viceroy without the show and ceremony the viceroy might have preferred, still, everything that protected the villages and the shepherds in these hills was reeling and slipping, and had been since the lightning stroke let the rain into the Quinaltine.

"Ye seem so grim, lad," Uwen said when they were at a momentary rest. "Is summat amiss?"

He considered the question, standing, staring, with his hands on Gery's side. He shook his head then. "No. Less so now. But the messenger will be there by now."

"Aye, m'lord, that he will. Is that a concern?"

He considered that, too, and nodded slightly. "It may be. I feel things out of balance, Uwen, but steadier than they were."

Uwen gazed at him as Uwen would when he was considering a difficult point.

"Lad," Uwen said, "is there wizards afoot?"

It was a third good question. "Always," he said. "Always, for me, there might be wizards."

CHAPTER 4

The banners flew, in the hands of men who had chosen to bear them, in the land they protected. Far away a curl of smoke reported some blacksmith's fire, some sign of work across the land: it was an odd time for cooking fires.

Just after noon they reached Maudbrook, which would have been their stop tonight, had they kept the wagons with them, and where Emuin would camp, likely tomorrow night. The thick planks thundered beneath them as they passed easily over Maudbrook Bridge . . . not a bridge for the wagons: the wagons when they came would use the ford and cross far more slowly.

It was a succession of hills after that, sheep-grazed, tree-crowned, rocky and rough. The streams were a brisk jog across, the brushy sides of the road offered no surprises more than a flight of startled birds and the occasional fox or scuttling hare, invisible but for a whisk of gray. Deer stared from the far distance, alarmed at such haste, but unsure what they ought to do.

They reached the next bridge, a wood-and-stone one, had a cold supper sitting on the margin beside it, with fresh water to drink if they walked down a little. The fires of a village in the distance this time were more numerous, evening fires, chimneys sending up advisement of other folk at supper.

It was Ardenbrook, so they all agreed, and this streamside would have been their second camp in Amefel, with yet another night on the road to spend and another day's travel before them, if not more, asking nothing of the villages. They had in one day's riding made up two days as the oxcarts measured time, even pressing hard; and the men might rightfully look to sit and have their supper, such as it was, with a warm fire for the night. A full two days closer to Henas'amef than anyone in the town could expect, they had gained time on the king's messenger. Tristen saw the weary horses, saw the looks of men who hoped that they might have had the order to make camp.

"We go on," he said, and said it louder, so all the men could hear, not only Anwyll. "We go on. We will camp in sight of the town, if then. It is needful."

There was no muttering, only looks, fearful looks and weary looks, and he had no complaint from Captain Anwyll, either, only a shake of the head as if he thought better, knew better, had intended better, and was dissatisfied.

The horses, too, laid back their ears, puffing against the girths, unwilling, now, to be taken another distance on the road. Petelly was the horse for this last, hard effort; and he sighed and hung his head and stood on three feet, weary and uncooperative.

But back to the road again it was, with the sun lowering in the sky. They struck a steady pace, went on until the sun was a recent memory on the horizon.

Then, in that last wan light, the landmarks were all familiar ones, and the men's spirits began to rise again as a sergeant pointed out a stone outcrop, another saying he knew the lightning-blasted tree at the bottom of the hill, and that there was a sheepfold in the hills yonder, and they were not, after all, that far from the capital.

Petelly suddenly knew where he was, Tristen became sure of it. At a time when the other horses, out of Guelen stables, had become weary, sullen, and inclined to go slower and slower, Petelly suddenly put his ears up and redoubled his pace, nostrils wide, knowing there was a stable, and grain. Gia and Gery, likewise stabled in the citadel this summer, seemed to take the notion from Petelly, and they picked up speed. The other horses, horselike, took their pace from them until the whole company was moving far, far faster than would have been likely after a long day's effort.

There was a twisted tree remembered from the summer's end, the milestones beneath a knob of a hill.

And over a steep roll of the land they first caught sight of another shadowy height, the ancient citadel, under a dim sky, itself under a smudge of evening fires. Purer lights gleamed from the crest of that hill, lights which would be the tall, unshuttered windows above the inner walls of the citadel. The defensive walls obscured the rest, but not the few lights outside the walls, the scattered gleam of some lantern in the stables.

The bare branches of the orchards that stood on this approach screened them from view. They had come from the east, but had swung southerly, the East Gate of the town being all but unused and what men named the East Road passing to the south, joining the South Road before the walls.

"We're just a wee bit behind the gate-closing," Uwen said, which it was, clearly. And after a moment more: "Will ye go ahead in, m'lord? Or camp?"

"Go in," Tristen said, with hardly a thought in it. They were here. They had come closer than he had planned. Now the stone rolled entirely, solidly, fate-guided back to its place.

"I'd take just the banners on, m'lord, and ye hold back with the troop till we have the gates open. Ye might sit and have a sip and stay warm the while an' come in like a lord."

Henas'amef was a more cautious, a more wary town than Guelemara. The gates had used to shut at the first dimming of the light, and still did, as seemed. The king's messenger had delivered word of his arrival, surely; but even so, riding up out of the night, a hundred men were an unsettling sight. Couriers would have to run back and forth between the town gate and the citadel informing the viceroy, who would have to send down to open the gates, and all the while this was going on, the town would be in doubt and their own company would have to stand outside on horses that would see no reason not to go aside to the stables outside the wall, stables which Petelly in particular well knew were at hand. It was in all points, on an ordinary day, more sensible to camp until daylight.

But he burned to be inside the walls, to have uncertainties settled, no matter the inconveniences to all concerned. And he sought a quieter course, one which a slight persuasion might affect.

"You and I and the banners," he said to Uwen.

"Your Grace." Captain Anwyll had maintained a glum silence for the last bitter hour, but now he protested. "In His Majesty's name, I counsel you, no. Never entertain such a notion. Make camp, wait here. His Majesty would never approve Your Grace riding up alone. The town is known for rebellion."

"Uwen, I say. The two of us and the banner-bearers."

Uwen said, soft-voiced: "I'll do what ye wish, m'lord, but the captain's givin' good advice."

"I say we go ask them to open the gates."

"If there ain't no untoward event of His Majesty's message to the viceroy, aye, then maybe us two were enough. But that ain't sayin' what else could go amiss, m'lord, in the dark and wi' rumors loose, as may be. The town's a chancy ride i' the dark. Listen to the captain."

"You and I and the banners," he said, making up his mind. "If they open to us straightway, we'll be inside, and the gates will be open. Then, Captain, or if not, you'll come. I wish no commotion of the town, and I prefer they not see all of us."

"I fear there will be a commotion, at this hour," Anwyll said. "Or worse. Follow Lewen's-son's advice, if not mine: let him go, him and the banners, no more. Or send me. It is not cowardice that urges caution, Your Grace, it is reasonable concern for your safety."

"When you see a light from the open gates, Captain, or if you see us riding back, come in quickly."

"Your Grace, —"

"Come in quickly, I say."

"As Your Grace wishes," Anwyll said glumly.

And, having been reined back, Petelly had it in his head at the moment that he was going to the stables whatever the outcome of the discussion. Tristen spent not another word on argument with the captain or the horse, but climbed down off Petelly's back, put up the coif, put on his helm. "Bring him with you as you can," he said, and entrusted Petelly to a guardsman to bring along. He unslung his shield from his back and stripped off the weather-cover, which was plain black. So was the shield face black, but with the pale Star and Tower of Ynefel, the sign of wizardry, the scandal of the Quinaltine. There had been no time to change it.

Meanwhile all around him, at Anwyll's order, a hundred men quietly settled their equipment in order, changed to their war-trained horses, and armed themselves to follow him in due course.

A last test of Gery's cinch, a judicious tightening, by his own bare hand, trusting not even Uwen's offer to settle his equipment. Then he put on the right-hand gauntlet, set his hand in the shield grip and his foot in the stirrup, still judging the girth as it took his armored weight. Gery had not swelled against the girth, rather took him up in good order, but with a little shiver and a pricking-up of the ears at this breaking-forth of warlike equipment.

There was, however, no nonsense from Gery at this hour, none of Petelly's breaking forward unbidden. None of their horses had called out in the evening quiet. The orchards—a hazard Cefwyn had forborne to cut down despite the threat of war inside the province—screened their approach toward the town gates despite the lack of leaves, and the dark east and clouded south had been constantly at their backs during the last of the sunlight, so they had never for any moment stood out against the sky. Unlike Guelemara, Henas'amef had few outbuildings, only the stables and a few barns and huts where herdsmen dwelt. Now the surrounds of the town were almost entirely dark, the stars brightening overhead.

Banners unfurled, first the white Sihhë Star shining in the gloom of near night, then the Star and Tower. Third and centermost, the Eagle flew, black on deepest red, a banner more ominous and wholly dark in this twilight than the two Sihhë standards. One-handed, managing Gery with his knees and with his shield hand holding the reins, Tristen tightened the last two buckles on his side as they went.

Then three other riders overtook them: Aran, of Tristen's own four guards, came up, and two more guardsmen came with them.

"To guard your backs, m'lord," Aran said, when Tristen glanced at that arrival in displeasure. "By your leave, m'lord."

The well-ditched road ran beside the orchards on one hand and stone-fenced sheep-meadow on the other. Then plowed fields replaced pasture as their road, the East, joined the main South Road. Shortly after that, the West Road swept in beside a sheep wall to make it all one road.

From there, they were on the last long straight approach toward the main gate of the town, the banners flying and snapping in the dark. They crossed the ring road, which went around the town walls and came racing up to the great South Gate, near Cevulirn's camp of this summer, the site now a barren field.

The horses fetched up, stamping and blowing in their impatience. "Ho the gatekeepers!" Lusin shouted out at the lofty town gate, all but obscured by the Tower banner as they confronted the gate and the likely scrutiny of the gate wardens. "Ho there, for His Grace of Amefel! Open the gate! Let His Lordship in!"

"Aye!" came a thin-voiced shout back. "Aye!" But no opening of the gate ensued. Lusin rode by and thumped the wood hard with his shield. That drew an answer.

"Just a moment, just a moment, there!"

No bell had rung yet to advise the higher town, but it might ring at any moment. Tristen expected it, as Gery stamped and blew in impatience. Came a sound of steps from inside, not at the bar of the sally port, which might signal the intent to open, but a heavy, panting thump of a heavy man running up the stairs inside the gatehouse. The thumping ascended all the way up to the stubby right-hand tower of the pair that supported the gate.

"Who's there?" The shout came down from the crest of the wall. Then, faintly: "Begging your pardon, who *is* His Grace of Amefel?"

"Lord Tristen," Uwen shouted up. "By the grace of His Majesty in Guelemara, Duke of Amefel, Lord Warden of Ynefel and Lord Marshal of Althalen! Ye've had the king's messenger, man, have ye not? *Have ye not?*"

"Aye. Aye, we have had a king's messenger. But no word to us!"

"Well, there is now, man! Bear a light, there, bear a light down and unbar the gate, in your own duke's name!"

Another thumping, as the man ran down the stairs.

"The gods' mercy," Tristen heard then distinctly from the other side of the gate, at the very center, with a clatter this time right behind the barred gate, a whisper half-voiced. "Gods' mercy! Do we open?"

"Aye, ye open!" Uwen roared out. "And be quick about it! His Grace has rid clear from Guelessar, he's weary and he's hungry and in his patience wi' good men, he ain't near angry yet, but I wouldn't keep your lord standing out here like some tinker on the road. There ain't anyone but His Grace to give ye yea and nay here and hereafter, man, don't natter about it! Shame on ye! Open this gate!"

"We has to do it," came a faint voice. "We has to do it. Run up to the hill quick and see what's toward! It's himself and the king's men. We has to!"

Something was wrong, Tristen was sure now, and Uwen had wisely laid the matter at the guards' feet: open, open without question or face an angry new lord. He took a firmer purchase on his shield grip, made sure of his reins, not knowing what he might have to do to get the gate open, but open it must: matters otherwise could worsen, step by step.

Nothing so small as the sally port, but the main gate itself began to move, with the thump of pawl and ratchet. The gate swung, and in a moment's confusion Gedd rode into the widening crack, the Eagle banner obscuring all view as he forced it wider still with his horse. Tawwys and Aran rode in with swords in hand, and in the same moment Uwen sent Gia side-passing smartly right against the other wing of the gate, shoving it wide for Lusin and Syllan and a great wall of obscuring black banners. Tristen sent Gery straight through the middle, leading the men behind him in with a rush.

The banner-bearers had no shields, no swords; but the gate wardens, in the lanternlight from the open gatehouse door, scrambled well back, showing no inclination at all to move toward the three pikes leaning in the corner.

"Your Lordship," one of the gate-guards said, looking up at him as he held Gery at a restless halt. "Your Grace," said the other guard, and they both fell to their knees. All battle was over. The gates were wide-open, and the light that splashed across the ground and across that open gate was a clear and ample signal to the guard troops under Anwyll's command, out beyond the orchards.

But the guard who looked up at him in the lanternlight was a face that entrained a memory.

"Is that Ness?" Tristen asked.

The men both looked up at him, wide-eyed.

"Yes, your lordship," Ness said, wide-eyed and openmouthed besides—a good man, a fair man; he had known Ness in the summer.

"Get up. Both of you. And answer me. Is the town willing for me to be here? Or not?"

"Your lordship." Both of them had scrambled up, muddy-kneed, bowing again. "Your Grace," the other said. Both seemed entirely terrified.

"Earl Edwyll has got the citadel," Ness said in a rush. "The viceroy has got the garrison. Earl Edwyll put us back to wardin' the town gates, your lordship, against the king's men come in, and here we are."

"In mortal trouble," the other said, "saving Your Grace remember us."

"Edwyll is holding the Zeide gates?"

"The South Gate. And the lord viceroy is holding the stable-court and its gate. But all the gates up there on the hill is shut, Your Grace. We sent a man up to whichever is in charge, being on the earl's orders, which was to shut the town gate again' any asking, and no regard to king's men."

"But then us not knowing where the right is," the second man said, "and not being properly the earl's men, neither, as might be, here you was, m'lord, with the banners and all, and we flung up the bar soon as we could think on 't. The whole town's awake behind their doors, ain't budged since afternoon except getting water and such, knowing all hell's up on the hill. But they were saying it'd be three days till you'd arrived, m'lord, and there ain't no water in the South Court 'cept the town give it him. And Lord Cuthan weren't coming to anybody's rescue, saying Earl Edwyll ain't any aetheling more than any of the rest of them. But the viceroy ain't asked him to help the Guelenmen."

"Hush," Ness said. "Lord's affairs ain't our affairs and there ain't no more aethelings."

"Well that we came ahead," Uwen remarked in a low voice.

Well that they had come, indeed, Tristen thought. The town gates were breached, and the guards here had surrendered in an instant. By all they could see and hear, too, there had been not a sound to alarm the town, nor any general sympathy shown the rebel earl except the gate wardens sending a messenger up the hill, which accounted for the third pike leaning against the wall. It was still within likelihood that they might apprehend the man Ness had sent if he risked a noisy chase up a cobbled hill, but only by exposing his men to death or capture in doing it, and only at risk of provoking the general commotion they were trying to avoid.

Meanwhile the gate wardens alike looked uncertain as men might be who had opened their town gate on their own advice and now heard the low thunder of a hundred riders on the road coming toward them. The three banners above them, shadowy and transparent across the lanternlight from inside the gatehouse, were there by the king's will, while the Amefin earl the guards had named had clearly chosen a declaration of rebellion against Cefwyn, imprisoning the king's garrison on the hill and declaring his ownership of the place.

And Earl Edwyll was in a defensible position. The north side of the fortress was a blind wall except for the small, high-walled garden, which had no gate and was only accessible from the lower corridor. The other faces of the citadel, east, south, and west, each had a courtyard, each divided from the next by walls, and there was indeed no water on the hill except the one spring in the West Courtyard. The viceroy's men, having seized that area, had secured the only infallible supply of fresh water for themselves . . . and the horses for escape and grain to feed them, as well as the scullery with its stores of food.

"There is the wine and the ale, too," he remarked to Uwen. "The garrison has that, if it has the kitchen storerooms, and the lower hall is between the two for a battlefield."

"Gods 'a-mercy," Uwen said. Uwen knew the lay of the court-yards and the existence of the spring as well as he did. It was on the one hand a ludicrous situation, the battle of the stable-court against an upstart and foolish earl in ill-timed rebellion; and on the other, honest servingfolk and townsmen who had no desire at all to be in the midst of a battle had been put in jeopardy of their lives up there.

"Ye'll set those gates well back, there," Uwen said to the gate wardens, and waved a signal at Gedd and the standards. "We'll be holding the way open. Up standards and smartly so. Guards! Bear a light, there!"

The gate wardens hurried, not without anxious, backward looks as the distant rumble of cavalry on the move echoed off the very walls. Anwyll and the rest were riding for the gate at breakneck speed, not knowing how they had fared. But as the gate-guards brought out the lantern and light spread full over the walls and the banners, the riders checked their full-tilt charge and spread out along the ring road just outside. Out of the dark came the noise of breathless, excited horses coming to a halt, and atop them as they arrived, a darkness glittering with the sheen of armor and weapons. In the faint light from the gate the Marhanen colors on Anwyll's coat shone brighter than the rest.

"Your Grace!" Anwyll called out.

"Captain," Tristen said. "One squad comes up the hill with me for the Stable Gate, one for the Zeide's East Gate by Woolmarket, one by Bell Street for the South Gate, the third to hold here and assure us of this gate. But don't trouble these guards! They're honest men. Captain, take command at the South Gate, do no harm to the town, and be ready to come in when I open the doors!"

"*Yes,* Your Grace." There was no more demur. Anwyll knew the town intimately, and called for the sergeant who knew the streets. "Cossell! Three squads, East Gate! Brys, three squads, follow His Grace!"

"Banners!" Uwen shouted, setting their own men in order, and with no more ado Tristen started Gery moving uphill as his banner-bearers raced to the fore. The man to whom he had given Petelly's lead was in the squad with them, and Petelly created a small stir among the armed men going with them, wanting to get forward . . . Petelly, who knew nothing of king's men or the desperate bid of rebels against the king. He was an Amefin horse, and knew what justice was: his stable and his grain were at the top of the hill.

They rode through the street with a clatter of iron-shod hooves echoing back and forth off the houses and off the high and low walls of the town. As they went, shutters cracked in prudently shut houses, and here and there cautiously opened.

Then, quietly, emboldened, the people alongside them opened doors for a general look, and came out onto their steps, or stared down from the upper windows.

"Lord Sihhë!" someone shouted through the dark streets. It was the name the town had called him before, the name that would have scandalized the Quinalt in Guelemara. "Lord Sihhë!" other voices shouted, and ahead of them shutters cracked open, and doors opened. Light broke faintly onto the street from closely held lamps and firesides, and the white Sihhë Star glowed on the banners. "Lord Sihhë!" people shouted, and poured into the streets, some running dangerously close to the horses. More and more doors opened, a few householders bearing lights sheltered from the wind. The Gate-street Tavern turned out a befuddled, cautiously enthusiastic knot of patrons and servingmen in their aprons.

"Lord Sihhë!" The cry went all along. "Lord Sihhë!" The town cheered him as they had cheered him when he returned from Lewenbrook. "Lord Sihhë!" echoed off the walls and brought commotion and lights to the dark side streets. Now the Sihhë Star and the black Eagle alike showed in fitful gleams from doors and lanterns. "Lord Sihhë!" the people cried.

They were glad to see him, and that was so rare a notion it confounded his warlike expectations and broke quite unexpectedly through the guard he had for two months set about his heart, setting it to beating larger than war or fear could bring on him. He had arrived where he was supposed to be, he had no doubt now. He had come, moreover, where he was needed, and as swordsmanship and the ordering of armies had Unfolded to him, so he knew what he had to do: secure every street by which their enemies might come down the hill and seal all the gates from which new enemies might arrive at their backs. He knew, too, the worth in this people that rushed to the streets . . . *use* their help, gain their goodwill, bring them what they hoped to find, but he had to keep them from breaking into mischief and harm.

And to do that, he had to bring the banners up the hill quickly to make the citadel sure with whom they were dealing, in the darkness of night, and he must *not* rely wholly on the viceroy he was riding to save.

Not rely, for one thing because the king's forces might already be overwhelmed; but most of all because the king's Guelen troops might inflame resentments in the town. He had sent his forces sweeping up like shadow through the streets, on the cries of people that had never loved the Marhanen kings. *Lord Sihhë! Lord Sihhë! Lord Sihhë!* they cried, and he could not mistake the sentiment behind it. It was all too easy to let slip a hatred of Guelen overlords that would not easily be reined in.

Lights broke out now in the side streets as they went, lights spread all along the rows of shops and houses. He saw in an intersection of streets one of the other Dragon squads going up the hill beside them, swift-moving riders silhouetted against the lamplight, there and then gone as they pursued their way uphill in a scattering of accompanying lanterns in the upper town. Their going acquired a voice, a shouting, a roar. Common townsfolk brought sticks and staves to his aid and marched in a growing band behind them as they neared the very gates of the citadel, still shouting, *Lord Sihhë! Lord Sihhë*!

They met a West Gate shut fast, three sets of bars, inner and outer sets swung shut from the side, the portcullis dropped between. A troop of the Guelen Guard was drawn up inside, afoot, in the stablecourt, red coats gleaming faintly in lanternlight, the same as the colors of the Guard with him. An overeager rush of townsmen ran for the bars with staves and kitchen knives.

"Here, here!" Uwen shouted out. "Way for His Grace!" And the people shouted out, "Way for Lord Sihhë!" and they gave back, pushing and shoving one another to clear a space for him.

From Gery's back and above the heads of the mob Tristen could see the viceroy's forces holding in good order. They had fortified themselves behind the triple hedge of iron bars, but it was not an enviable position for the Guelenmen despite the viceroy's command of the stores and the water.

"Ho the guard!" Uwen called through the bars as their horses paced and stamped the cobbled space outside—a knot of Guelenmen themselves, in a ring of Amefin townsfolk on the verge of riot. "His Grace Tristen, Duke of Amefel, the grant of His Majesty Cefwyn by the gods' grace king of Ylesuin! Ho the garrison, in the duke's name and His Majesty's! Where's His Majesty's viceroy?"

An officer on the other side of the gate moved his horse nearer the inmost bars. That man gave an order, imprudently instructing the men in the gatehouse behind the bars to open the inner gate, and to raise the portcullis. At the first clank of the pawl, the mob behind them pressed forward, with only the inward-swinging gates to hold them back. They were strong gates; but the weight of men outside was perilously great.

"Keep back!" Tristen shouted, and rode Gery a half circle about, making a line beyond which the crowd pushed and shoved at each other to clear his path.

"In His Majesty's name!" the viceroy's officer shouted out from inside, near the remaining, inward-tending screen of bars. "Of Your Grace's goodwill, the viceroy bids Your Grace know he has not officially received His Majesty's messenger. The earl has arrested the courier!"

"Ye're relieved!" Uwen shouted against the noise. "His Majesty's made a new duke in Amefel, which is His Grace Tristen of Ynefel and Althalen, who wants to know where is the lord viceroy?"

"His Lordship does not talk to rabble."

"*To the duke of Amefel, I say, and with His Majesty's seal on 't!* Open the damn gate, man, before it falls down."

"His Lordship will not step down until we have seen the king's seal!"

"Good lovin' gods," Uwen began, directing himself to Tristen. A stick flew, and struck the bars. The people shouted to open the gate, and pressed forward. Uwen turned Gia about. "Quiet there! Ware the horses!" He turned and with Gia's shoulder pushed the crowd further back, as a sudden ragged surge of the mob compacted the ranks of the guardsmen with them against the side of the gate. "Back! Back, there, ye fools!"

Uwen was in acute danger. All their company was in danger, from the very forces that came to their support: the hindmost ranks were pushing forward, thinking the gate was open. Tristen turned Gery to come near Uwen, and from him, people still fell back , the front rank pushing at the others to gain him room, pushing with all their force against the tide trying to roll in on them, shouting, "*Lord Sihhë himself!* Give way, give way!"

"Listen to me!" Tristen shouted over their tumult. "Listen to me!" He rode further, forcing a way across the face of the mob. "You!" He pointed at a large man, a strong man. "Go to the South Gate! Bid the earl surrender the king's messenger, and give over command of the citadel to me!"

That man turned and began to force his way back through, cleaving the crowd, gathering up others in a movement that swept like a current back and back as some began to follow the man to the south.

"Listen!" Tristen shouted. "Listen to me!"

Then a curious silence fell . . . a murmurous silence proceeding back through the crowd, until for the mere space of a breath he could make himself heard even to the buildings around the small gate square.

"The king has granted me Amefel!" he cried so all could hear. "He has called his viceroy home!"

A cheer went up which he would not have encouraged, at the news they were to lose the king's representative. "Listen to me!" he cried again, and waited for the little silence he could next obtain. "I wish to go into the fortress tonight and not have any harm done to anyone, and I wish to have nothing broken or taken, only to sleep peacefully in my bed tonight, which is in there!" He pointed to the fortress itself, and waited for the tumult to die. "The lord viceroy will gather what is his and his men's property and depart in good order by daylight! I shall begin to set things in order in Henas'amef and in Amefel as soon as the sun rises. Do harm to none, and no harm will come to you or to your houses tonight, I promise to you all!" He saw his chance, the only safety he might obtain for his men, and waved a signal to the Guelen Guard captain inside. "Open the gate, Captain! Open it now!"

The people broke out in wilder cheering, then, and waved their sticks in the air, and lifted up their lanterns, some of which went out in the bitter wind. He was not sure whether the king's men would regard his mere word, and if he had the power to urge his way as Emuin claimed he did, he willed the few men of sense inside to open that gate and to do so quickly, before a new rumor ran through the crowd or before some random press of bodies from the street below broke the strength of those holding the crowd back from him and from his men. They might, horses and all, be swept against the bars and crushed, if they did not hold that line.

And on the trembling moment, the lord viceroy's men inside desperately and with a deafening rattle ran back the massive chains of the last, the outermost gates that separated them from the mob.

"Stay!" Tristen shouted above the din, and fixed the leaders of the crowd with a sweeping gesture of his arm as he wheeled Gery with the pressure of his leg. The gates behind him gave way and no one in the crowd surged forward. The people only cheered and cheered; and the front line even ceased to strain as people climbed up on the stonework of adjacent buildings to call out news to comrades below.

The people cheered long past the time the viceroy himself, Lord Parsynan, came out the gates to them and tried to speak to him above the commotion. Some in the crowd called uncomplimentary names, and insulted the garrison guard. One rock flew and struck the cobbles, but Uwen and the Dragon Guard with him held firm and kept the space clear. People jammed the approaches to the gate, and lights borne by that crowd went on and on down the hill. From horseback, Tristen could see them as the viceroy, afoot, vainly tried to voice complaints of Amefin rebellion and treachery, but scarcely a word could he hear. People near the gate filled windows, stood on balconies, even climbed up on the stonework of houses as high they could find purchase, all shouting, *"Lord Sihhë! Lord Sihhë!"*

"Your Grace!" The viceroy, Lord Parsynan, was a round, stubborn man, and not easily set off his dignity, but he grew desperate enough to come to the point. "Your Grace! The king's garrison welcomes you on His Majesty's authority, as we hear he has given!" There was to have been far more ado, Tristen was sure, in his setting the lord viceroy out of office, but under the circumstances the lord viceroy was doing the wisest, the safest thing, and the thing he strongly willed the man to do, for what it was worth in the world, even to his appearing before the crowd. It was wicked, Emuin had hinted, and he had no idea whether his will even moved the man, but *give way to me* was the burden of his wish, along with *strike no blows.*

"We have the paper, m'lord!" Uwen said, urging Gia shoulder to shoulder with Gery. "We ha' the clerk to read it, an ye will!"

CHAPTER 5

Among the few encumbrances they had brought with them on their ride from Assurnbrook was that proclamation, and with it, a copy of the letter from Cefwyn to the lord viceroy—or rather such documents were in the hands of the disheveled clerk who had ridden with his company.

But there was far too much shouting and cheering at the moment for anyone to hear the proclamation. Men jostled close, pressing against the horses and pressing them dangerously toward the barred gates of the fortress, and Tristen could not immediately see the clerk among the other riders attempting to maintain order in the lanternlit and riotous dark. In his fear he wished himself *in* the fortress, and he wished the Amefin forces attacking the viceroy to cease their attack . . . he wished so, because he was afraid for the men with him and, afraid, too, for the people of Amefel, who meant him nothing but good.

And, setting aside Emuin's cautions, he knowingly bent great force on that notion: magic, Emuin called it, to secure that quiet, and peace for the sake of lives. Silence, he willed, and, Hear me. *Believe me.*

And in that moment, in a curious, difficult-to-catch way, almost like his sense of the gray place, he felt resistance. Something or someone struggled against his determination.

He had not expected wizardry here, not now. He was off his guard. *This* subtle thing opposed him, and in the next breath he lost his sense of Gery's motion under him and swayed in the saddle, not from weakness, but foolishly, from the horse's unexpected movement.

Begone! he willed it, with all his force.

The opposing force was gone then, was not *in* the gray place, was nowhere that he could detect—like an enemy in full rout, and not unscathed.

An Amefin noble appeared from the crowd . . . he did not know the name, but a man conspicuous in fine dress and rich furs pressed forward to catch his stirrup, all oblivious to the conflict.

"Lord!" that man cried, and before he could take alarm he saw another man, and another, pressing forward to bend the knee as he sat on horseback. "I am Drumman of Baraddan," the first man said. "A loyal man."

"Azant of Dor Elen," said the next, a man with a scarred face. Uwen had meanwhile come close to him with his sword in hand, and another guardsman attempted to push them back, but they cast themselves to their knees in a body, each—and several at the same time—proclaiming his name, his degree, and his unfailing loyalty to the Crown.

"We none of us conspired with Edwyll," one protested. "We never agreed."

He knew them by sight if not by name, the other lords of Amefel, the earls, the thanes he had been accustomed to see in the hall. And now ealdormen of the town of Henas'amef came forward.

The crowd cheered, and pushed back its own borders. "Hush, hush," some urged, and others yelled ruder expressions until they made a sort of astonished silence in the area, apart from the din of voices in the streets.

"We are loyal men!" the earls protested, each and every one, but some scattered voices hooted and called out questions, among them, at one ealdorman's protestation of loyalty: "Tell His Grace about the silver!"

"I am innocent!" the ealdorman in question cried, appalled and staring wildly around at the crowd.

He is lying, Tristen thought, but questions and answers of minor nature mattered very little to him until he might pass the gates and do Cefwyn's bidding.

Then Uwen shouted out, "His Majesty has made His Grace the duke of Amefel! And he's come to do justice and defend the righteous men of this province! The clerk has the proper decree! Shall he read it out?"

"Read it!" someone cried, and "Read it!" all the crowd echoed. "Read it, read it, read it!"

"Quiet for the clerk, then!" Uwen shouted, and the clerk who had ridden with them struggled with his reins and the unrolling of a heavy parchment, while people at the rear of the crowd were still calling for quiet.

The clerk cleared his throat and called for light, and someone brought a torch from a bracket and handed it to a guardsman on horseback, who held it aloft as a murmur began again in the back of the crowd.

"Read it!" Uwen said, with all trembling on the knife's edge of the crowd's patience, so read it the man did, beginning with: "By the grace of the gods and the holy Quinalt . . ." and going on to: "I Cefwyn king do grant . . ." The order was set forth in the high court language, and precious few of the townsfolk understood the words, Tristen feared. But when the clerk came to the part that said, duke of Amefel, the crowd cheered. At each occurrence of the words *duke of Amefel* after that, the townsfolk cheered, and by the end of the reading, in the part that required the lord viceroy to turn over all documents, records, persons, and property of the province to His Grace the duke of Amefel, there was pandemonium in the adjacent streets.

"Fall back, fall back there!" Uwen cried, and rode a line which the people respected, clearing back from him. The banner-bearers followed him, visible to all the crowd, even those far behind, and with the torches and lanterns lighting them if nothing else.

"Guard!" Uwen ordered. "Fall in behind! Form a line!" Uwen gathered a number of the guard in a slow sweep back across the face of the crowd, pressing the crowd back with the presence of the horses, and, moving like a weaver's shuttle, had the gate sealed off from the crowd while the crowd was still cheering and waving at the banners.

"M'lord," Uwen said, and with a sweep of his arm indicated the way inside for all of them in the center of his circle: the lord viceroy, and the earls and thanes and ealdormen who had joined them. Well-done, Tristen thought, proud of Uwen, and with the same deliberate dispatch he led the way beneath the gate arch, under the portcullis, and into the stable-court of the Zeide.

"File in!" he heard Uwen shouting behind him, and in a series of orders none of which ever left the men at standstill, Uwen drew their guard in after them, until only five were left guarding the outside and holding the line. Then Uwen shouted, "Shut the outer gates!" and ordered the portcullis down after them, a great rattling and clamor of iron, as their last five men quickly rode in, and men in the gatehouse winched the gates shut. They had shut the crowd outside, had shepherded the nobles inside . . . and were themselves, with the viceroy, in possession of the stable-court of the Zeide—a crooked court with the stables and the grain sheds and a few pens on the left, the scullery yard, too, and then a broader area with a stairs going up to the torchlit landing and the western doors of the Zeide. These were barricaded and braced with timbers. So was the scullery door barricaded, as Tristen could see at the edge of the lanternlight.

So, to the south, was the wide double gate of the curtain wall that sealed them from the South Court, where they reported the rebels to be.

"Search the stables!" Tristen ordered.

"Yes, m'lord!" Uwen said, and gave those orders.

"The stables are ours, Your Grace," the viceroy said, at his knee . . . Tristen did not look down to see the man, but by now he knew the voice.

"Nonetheless," he said. He trusted nothing Uwen had not passed his eye over, and still scanned the yard for detail. "Does the earl hold the scullery and the lower hall, as well as the South Court?" It would need more men than they had at their disposal to hold off attacks over all the citadel.

"Doubtful, Your Grace, but we have the water, the grain, the horses, and a gate. The kitchen stores as well."

"Well-done in that." He judged it quiet enough to dismount and stepped down from Gery's back, passing the reins to a dismounted guardsman. Immediately all the earls and thanes pressed close to him for reassurance and to urge their views on him. "Secure the scullery from inside," he ordered the sergeant of the guard. "Prepare to enter the halls. No harm to the servants!"

"Yes, Your Grace."

"We have the scullery fortified," Lord Parsynan protested. "If Your Grace will wait till morning . . ."

"I have men arriving at the South Gate," he said, "and the East."

"How many men?"

"Fifty."

"Each?"

"Together."

"They cannot breach the gates."

"Then we must open this one." This with a glance to the South Courtyard.

"They have fortified it from the other side. Your Grace, the town cannot be trusted. You must not commit yourself to a battle here."

"There will be no battle," he said. What he proposed was far under that scale. "We will open the gates. sir."

"These people will cut our throats!"

"Lies!" Earl Drumman cried. "We are *with* Your Grace! Open the gates! Let us bring in Amefin men!"

"Folly!" the viceroy said, with a disparaging wave of his arm. "As good let in armed bandits!"

"We shall open *that* gate with the men we have," Tristen said, with a shrug at the curtain wall that separated them from Earl Edwyll's men. "And we shall open the South Gate." That was the town-entry gate in the court where the earl's men were. "Then Amefin men can come in."

"Your Grace," the viceroy protested.

"Your Grace!" the earls began to shout all together, but he had no interest at the moment in their argument with the viceroy. The scullery was unbarred, the sergeant he had sent was about to take men into the fortress itself, and he strode in that direction and shouted further orders.

"Four men to hold the scullery stairs!"

"Aye, Your Grace!" the sergeant shouted back, and the men went in, quickly.

"Stable's ours, m'lord." Uwen reported. He had come back afoot and out of breath.

"The scullery is open," Tristen said, "and we will have those stairs inside." He envisioned going up that familiar scullery stairway and seeking out the earl in the interior of the Zeide, but for that feeling of opposition he had had a few moments ago. Unease still nagged at him.

And he did not know why he felt uneasy with that western route into the building. But, direct as it was and offering an attack on the enemy's flank, he would not take it.

"Bring axes," Tristen ordered, and nodded toward the curtain wall that divided them from the South Court. "We will have open that gate. *Then* we will talk to the earl."

"You cannot *talk* to the earl!" Lord Parsynan said. "And I beg Your Grace trust only his Guelen troops and not open the South and East Gates to let in even your own men. Twenty-five men on a side is folly! They can never hold the rabble; the entire town will pour in behind them and loot the place if they do nothing worse! Listen to me, Your Grace! If we must move, take the upper floors, the high windows. The courtyard is open from above. Assault from the secure position! Rain archery down from the windows!"

"It would kill very many and ruin the windows, sir."

"Ruin the windows, good lack!"

"I would not ruin the windows. No, if your lordship please."

"Your Grace, listen to me!"

"I do listen, sir. But the South Courtyard also has very many places not in view of the windows, where arrows will not reach. If we had enough men, we might take the fortress halls, but we have not. —Uwen, shout it over at the earl's men to open the gates and come swear loyalty to me. They should have the chance before we open them by force."

"They are traitors!" Parsynan said. "There is no pardon!"

"Uwen," he said, and Uwen left him in haste to follow his orders.

"The man laid hands on a king's herald!" Parsynan cried. "No, Your Grace! Death is the penalty, and Edwyll well knows it. So do all these men! Your Grace *cannot* pardon these men."

"They were not wicked men," he said, fixing Parsynan with a stare, and heard in the distance Uwen's shouting near the gate. He knew in his heart the viceroy had the right of the law in ways he had lately understood in Guelessar . . . but when had old men grown so desperate in Amefel as to make such a useless gesture, taking the citadel of Henas'amef, or half of it, as if the king or the king's men would not come to take it back? He said, defending the earl he had known, however distantly: "They were not rebels, sir, until these few days."

"Yet does he answer you?" Parsynan asked. "Does he open the gate? No, nor will. They are all in collusion. I beg Your Grace trust none of them and by no means open the outer gates!"

"We are loyal men!" Earl Drumman said. "We were always loyal men!"

"Your Grace," Lord Parsynan said sternly, "you cannot pardon treason."

"Your lordships," he heard at his left, and a breathless Guelen guardsman pointed to the building. "Our men is up there, engaged. The earl's trying to come into the west wing by the upstairs and attack our men with axes."

And from his right, Uwen: "M'lord, the earl's men shout through the gate that they'll carry word to the earl. I don't hear 'em rushin' to open up on the other side. And they're still shootin' across the wall. They just ain't hearin' ye."

"Let us bring down the gate," he said. And to Lord Parsynan: "Sir, your men to the fortress hall. Keep it *open,* sir. That is essential."

"Your Grace, prudence would suggest—"

"They are breaking through the fortress halls, sir, at this moment. I suggest you take your men there as you suggested and try to come through the halls. I'll meet you at the south doors, inside." He strode off in some haste toward the curtain wall, sweeping Uwen with him as Parsynan shouted protests at his orders, and then cursed his own men, bidding them rally to the kitchen stairs.

Uwen snagged a man by the arm to give quick orders. The man left running as an arrow hit the pavings and almost clipped his heels.

It was not the only arrow to fall. It was all blind fire coming from the other side of the wall, uncaring what it hit—a hazard primarily to men trying to open the gate. But if he could breach the South Courtyard, he could let in Captain Anwyll to assist him, and the South Courtyard doors to the Zeide itself would give them command of the center stairs, where all halls met inside. That was where he had told Lord Parsynan to meet him . . . and if they did not hold that intersection of stairs and prevent movement between the two wings, they would see bloody battle rage in the three floors of the palace.

More, while the viceroy had possession of all the water, the earl had the smithy and its hammers and bars, as well as the armory. That meant the earl's men in the South Court had no shortage of weapons or arrows, as well as materials with which to bar doors against them, and if he could not press them hard from this side, and soon, they might end by having to besiege the south doors and break door by door into every connected chamber and corridor in that end of the Zeide, including the new great hall, where arrows might again be a fear. It would be folly to seek a battle in that crowded, many-staired interior, and fighting would likely be largely in the dark.

More, he did not *want* to bring harm and death into the place from which he would command the Amefin, and he felt, as strongly as if it were Unfolded to him, that the courtyard was the path they had to take, there, under the safe and open sky, not inside. He led men already on the verge of exhaustion, and if the pace slowed overmuch and their bodies chilled and their spirits began to flag, then the strength would run out of them like water.

"There are hammers and nails in the farrier's shed," he said to Uwen. "The hinges are on their side of the doors. Get ladders, if you can find them—timbers, else. Haste!"

"We'll do our best, m'lord." Uwen sent the nearest men running and Tristen stared in frustration at the wall and gate that separated them from the South Court. Axes had scarred the center of that gate already, clearly to no avail. The town outside the fortress walls might join them in force if he let them in, but they presented a hazard to the citadel and the lives of the king's men, with officerless men joining the fray, and with unskilled, unarmored townsfolk pitted against a lord's armed men. They already risked riot having townsmen behind Guelenfolk at the South and the East Gates, Parsynan was not far from the truth, and he only hoped Anwyll had gotten through unscathed. He did not delude himself the mob would remain peaceful once blood was shed . . . and at this moment all their affairs and the town's safety seemed balanced precariously on a knife's edge, with three of the loyal earls trailing perilously after him, and not so much as a shield among them.

"Protect yourselves!" he shouted at them. "Go back to the stables!" And just then a spent arrow struck Lord Drumman a glancing blow in the shoulder. "Get back!"

He could not delay himself further. An ambitious old man, ill prepared, had launched the rebellion for what might seem foolish reasons, but whoever commanded the rebel forces was no fool, and had no shyness at all to seize the best hold on the Zeide itself he could obtain and to harry them with a constant rain of arrows. That told him the mettle of the man in charge, and if he let that officer have room, he feared a rapidly moving attack chasing through the citadel and into an archer's warfare in the great hall or in the garden and the East Court. Deaths of Guelenfolk or of Amefin could not serve him, a slaughter pressed on him, he suspected, half at least by Lord Parsynan.

But that might happen, it might well happen, the earl having set himself in an impossible position with the king's authority. There had already been disrespect of the king's messenger, at very least.

And he had to ask himself how long the other earls, those now at *his* back, would bear Parsynan's insults. Right now they were supporting a Guelen force in their town, and that was unprecedented. But Amefin pride had bent as far as it could bend.

Meanwhile the thump of unavailing axes alternated with that of hammers attempting the hinges and fittings of the gates—and time they spent at that task gave that rebel officer a chance to lay ambushes, and time wore down his travel-weary men, who had begun to stand about in dazed uncertainty. They had to move.

The stable grain stores, he said to himself, and went running, a lord's dignity to the wind. He seized a number of soldiers from the number watching the axemen and brought them along to the stable.

"Open the door of the shed!" he cried. "Go into the stables! Gather up sacks, barrels, whatever you can lay hands on, and bring them to the wall! Pile them as high as you can!"

They set to, and by the time the shed door was open, Uwen joined him. So did Lusin, Syllan, and his other guards, the banners set by, their hands freed for work as they all, even he, began a rapid conveyance of sacks and planks from the stable yard to the south wall.

"Bring 'em!" Uwen shouted at any man they met, and as exhausted men stared at their piling sacks and barrels below the wall they took the idea and brought anything they could set hand to.

More sacks arrived, a steady stream of stored grain carried to the heap through the hazard of arrows, making a small mountain reinforced by poles from the horse run and the barrow they used for manure. A man went down, an arrow through his arm, his sack spilled, and they carried him away to safety, and carried his sack to the pile. In wild cheerful invention the frustrated Guard began bringing tables and gear from the kitchens, then small barrels from some other place. They heaved a half-constructed ladder up to men atop and near the crest of the wall. The two men who reached the top of the wall shouted for more sacks, more sacks, and as men passed them up, gathering them from scattered elements at the base of the pile, they flung them down on the other side, a steady stream of them, affording a route to the top for more than one man at a time, and a landing on the other side.

Well-done, Tristen thought, seeing his way clear. Encumbered though he was by shield and sword, he climbed up the pile among the Guard passing up the sacks, with the men calling out both first an encouragement and then realizing in dismay that they were being left behind.

He heard Uwen shout that he was coming, as with an elbow atop the narrow wall he had a view of the armory, the smithy, and the earl's men rushing from the South Gate to the defense of the wall in sudden realization that the assault was on them sooner than expected and that the arrows that struck and shattered there were not enough. The lighter-equipped men who had been flinging down sacks jumped with no more than swords in hand as Tristen heaved himself up to the crest with a thump of the hindering shield. He rolled over the jagged masonry rim and plummeted down to the steep hill of the grain sacks below, leaned back and slid down them to the first brace of his foot and the oncoming assault of the earl's men. More of his men were landing behind him, one sliding into his back as he braced himself halfway to his feet, trying to deploy his shield for cover to the men by him. Tristen thrust his shield right against the faces of men coming at him in desperate defense. One he flung back with a shove of the shield alone and the man beside him engaged that one; the other won the edge of his sword. For a moment he and two light-armed men were battling a knot of enemy alone, and then Uwen turned up beside him, shield up, sword advanced. Other men came thumping down among the sacks, arraying themselves to shield new arrivals in greater and greater numbers. They pressed forward from the grain sacks, pushed the enemy that had rushed toward them now into a ragged and increasingly disordered retreat. An officer across the yard tried to rally his forces to oppose what was still a small force, but the earl's men had obstructed their archers, and the hindmost who had rushed up to the attack began immediately not only to give ground, but to run.

"Open the gate!" Tristen shouted at any man who could hear. "Open the gate behind us!"

He thought someone had gone. He led his men forward, across the cobbled South Courtyard into the sporadic fire of archers, at all the speed they could muster. Resistance to their advance collapsed as the last men they pursued ran past the thin ranks of the archers and left them undefended.

Then, officers' shouts notwithstanding, and with a last, sporadic volley of arrows, the shadows of the yard gave up more and more bowmen who otherwise would have remained concealed, archers joining their sword-and-shield men in retreat until nigh on two hundred men were in sporadic, uncertain rout, giving ground across the yard, past the corner of the building and across its face, running until the rebels' right flank was against the broad South Stairs and their left was toward the South Gate, all of it so fast-moving that their archers had found no place to stand.

Tristen forged ahead, giving the rebels no space to breathe. At the rebels' backs was a second curtain wall, the east, its small single gate shut. But the fortress itself offered nearer refuge to men hard-pressed, and the rebel earl's men pushed and shoved one another atop the South Stairs as they opened the doors to the interior, and men poured in, seeking shelter in the Zeide's inner halls and the warren of stairs and corridors inside.

He had far rather the retreat had gone to the east, farthermost small gate of the South Court. He had left them that retreat in hope of their fleeing through the second of the two curtain-wall gates into the East Court. But the rebel officer was drawing his men into a warren of stairs and rooms, where traps might be prepared and where he might have something in mind.

But king's men held the South Court and the West, undisputed.

"Open the all the gates! Open the South *and* the East Gates!" Tristen pointed with his sword for the sake of the Guelenmen, some of whom did not know the East Gate from the one at their backs. "Let Captain Anwyll in by the South! *And open up the East!*"

"Get both the gates, lads! *Go let in Cossell!*" Uwen relayed the order in terms the men knew in a voice that echoed off the walls, as their band engaged the last escaping earl's men on the lower tiers of the South Stairs, the scene of processionals and ceremonies.

"Forward!" Tristen shouted, and kept pressing up the steps as the rebels inside heaved at the great doors to shut them at the backs of their own hindmost men. Resistance collapsed, men went down, and the last few to reach the other side of the doors tried to push them shut in their faces, but Tristen hewed at the defenders with all his might through the narrowing gap, and Uwen pushed, and more of their men pressed forward and added their weight. The doors gave back and back until courage failed the rebels and the doors gave in a sudden lack of force behind them. They forced jammed doors the rest of the way open, shoving bodies before them and treading over dead and wounded as they reached the dark hall, seeking the enemy.

Then men poured in at their flank, out of the dark. "King's men!" Tristen shouted, and "King's men!" the shout went up on either side, Guelenmen narrowly evading each others' mistaken attack as the viceroy's force came in from the west wing to join theirs.

"They've gone east!" he heard Uwen shout. "M'lord, rebels is to the Temple court!"

"Dragons with me!" Tristen shouted, and turned his own men toward the deep dark, past the junction of stairs, chasing the distant noise of retreat in a thunderous advance of their own, all the way past what must be the great hall. The retreat echoed differently then, and his ears told him the rebels had reached the end of the hall and the downward stairs to the East Court. "Shields!" he shouted, as they came rushing up. "Stairs to the right!"

Men met them out of the blind dark, rear guard for the men on the stairs, and for a brief, sharp encounter everything was blind, men striking at men they could not see, pushing resisting men down steps and against the upward push of bodies. Tristen struck few blows himself, pushed with his shield, hit with the flat of his blade, his footing unsteady on unseen steps and fallen men entangling the feet of the living. The halls and stairwell rang with shouts and the clash of arms, and the battle anger was so close, so very close he dared not charge headlong. He pushed as much as fought, used his shield, forced the rebels down the narrow stairs to the door he knew was there. He heard Uwen's voice. He heard the rebels shouting, "Lord Sihhë!" this time in panic, men pressing ahead at the last by sheer weight.

The earl's men tried to stand. There was no room. Then a seam of night sky broke behind the heads of the defenders, and widened, as someone opened the east door. A few escaped outward, and now the battle choked into another panic as men jammed the doors to the outside in utter disorder.

Men with more presence of mind tried to rally once more through and shut that door against Tristen's force, a door which Tristen was equally determined should stand open. He battered them with his shield, pressed back, trampled on the fallen, a moment of extreme peril, and the door, by reason of men fallen in the gap, could not shut again. He reached the open air of the steps, facing the shrines, and a knot of rebels who had run headlong against a fatal wall of Dragon Guard waiting for them, a grim line with shields locked.

Anwyll and Cossell had both come in.

The hammering din of battle and the shouts of armed men spreading out from the doors behind him fell away to a growing, knife-edged silence. A band of maybe sixscore rebels was left standing, half as many more wounded huddled at their feet. He had no doubt that some of the earl's men had disappeared inside, to lose themselves in the halls. The columned shrines and tombs that towered up on either hand of this small courtyard might have sheltered the rebels: the Bryaltine, the Quinaltine, the Teranthine shrines, next the crypts of holy men and Aswyddim were a maze of narrow aisles.

The roofs of the fortress itself might have been to fear, but no attack had come from that direction.

And Cossell had shut the gate again at his back, keeping that way barred from all comers. That wall of Dragon Guard shields was absolute and unyielding.

The silence grew as even smaller movements stopped, throughout, attackers and defenders alike.

CHAPTER 6

"Where is Earl Edwyll?" Tristen asked the earl's men from atop the steps. His voice echoed in the quiet of the yard, and he looked on men who could do nothing other than what their lord bade them. He settled no blame there. He was, among other matters, anxious to see the officer who had managed the defense, who, if he had had battle-hardened men, would have made matters far worse than he had. "Who stands for these men?"

There was some little hesitation, and then swords slanted down disconsolately. But one young man grounded his shield forward of the others, took off his helm one-handed and cast him a defiant look. "Crissand Adiran, thane of Tas Aden, son of Edwyll son of Crissand, son of Edwylls before there ever were Aswyddim in Henas'amef! *I* stand for my father's men, of the house of Meiden!"

A strange feeling went through Tristen's heart then, as if he had heard a spell uttered in the words, in the names, in the Unfolding of a history he might, at some time, in a life before this life, have known, in the titles of a young man who had for a time stood successfully against him.

"And why do you oppose me?" he asked this defiant young man. And that, too, he seemed to remember saying.

There was quiet, in which the flame of torches thumped and a step grated on stone, and men on every hand, fresh from their exertions and in danger still, breathed deep and hard.

"For justice," the young thane said. "For *justice*!"

He said then the third thing it seemed he had once said:

"And do you think I shall not be a just lord?"

Again the silence, in which a man of his own company coughed, a dry, exhausted sound, as of a man who had been running. From the South Court was a distant tumult that sounded as if the townsfolk might be at the gates, no further. Here the young thane faced him in stony silence.

"What would you say justice should be?" Tristen asked in that hush.

"Pardon for them," the young thane said, with a haughty nod toward the men behind him. But an older man moved forward then, with a clatter of metal and a heavy step. "No, m'lord," the man said, "none of that for me. I stand with my lord the earl and with my lord's son."

Tristen thought of Uwen, seeing that man, a soldier, who would not leave the earl's son to save his life. Other men moved then, four of them, the earl's men, standing with the young man, defying him and his offer of justice. In the same moment and with no animosity at all, Uwen moved a little closer to him, and had his shield up and his sword ready for any attack.

Another man joined the five, and then another, all expecting to die, Tristen thought, and every man in the lot surely yearning to join them, and every man else in the courtyard either glad he had no such choice to make or envying the courage they saw.

"I pardon you," Tristen said. "I pardon you all."

"M'lord," Uwen said under his breath, "don't let 'em free, not that easy."

"And I forgive the earl, if he will swear to me." He knew it set him against the viceroy's opinion, and perhaps against the law, but he had no desire to harm such men as the young thane and the men who defended him. "And provided he has not harmed the king's messenger."

"We have the king's herald a prisoner," the young thane said, with this time a small tremor in his voice and a fear in his eyes . . . or it was the uncertain torchlight and the bitter wind. "We have not harmed him. And I will wait to see what this promise is worth."

"This is a dangerous young man." It was Anwyll who stood just behind: Tristen knew the voice. "Lewen's-son's advice is also the law. Do not release these men, Your Grace. You must not."

"I have already given my promise," Tristen said. "And the king will regard it."

Again a silence, and slowly the young man let down his sword, as he had already let down the shield.

"What my father wills," Crissand said. "That I will, with my men, so you keep your word, sir."

"Where is your father?"

Crissand cast a glance up the height of the Zeide itself, and that seemed his answer.

"Have them all lay down their weapons, Your Grace," Anwyll said. "I beg you don't offer any more assurances."

He had no need of Anwyll's advice at the moment. He wished Anwyll silent, but:

"Do as he asks," Crissand said to his men, and slowly the ranks came and cast down their weapons, a clang of iron and a thump of shields cast one onto the other. Crissand added his own, among the last.

"Lusin," Uwen said quietly, "His Grace will have that young man handled wi' due respect, and the seven of them"—Uwen surely meant the men who had joined the thane—"under special guard. — Ye're on m'lord's word, young lord. Ye come up here."

The seven were not willing, but the young man cast a forbidding glance and went of his own accord as far as the steps.

"Your lordship," Crissand said. "I rest on your word, I and the men with me, *and my father,* sir, I ask that."

"And where is the king's messenger?"

"In the Aswydds' apartment. With my father."

To have taken that set of rooms was entirely understandable in a man who claimed the Aswydds' place and titles. It was equally within Tristen's understanding that he could not permit that situation to go on, whether or not it mattered a whit to him: it mattered greatly to Cefwyn and it certainly mattered to the Amefin earls. Edwyll was the nearest kin to the Aswydds Cefwyn had allowed to remain in Henas'amef when he exiled Lady Orien and her sister, and that mercy was now repaid by a gesture every Amefin understood. More, removing the earl with any force would entail damage that itself was significant to the Amefin.

And removing him even by persuasion and the good offices of the man's son would entail going into that place and claiming it for the night, when he had as lief camp in the courtyard tonight, or sleep in the stables, rather than that cursed premises. He wished he had a choice, and he wanted nothing more now than to sit down where he stood.

"Let him come out with no harm and we will settle all the rest by daylight."

"I will go up and try to persuade him, by your leave," the young thane said, much as if it were something he had tried before, even many times, to no avail, and so saying, Crissand looked suddenly overwhelmed, more than he had when faced with weapons. "Or my father's men might, where I cannot. Let them speak to him, sir, on your good word."

The men Crissand proposed were the seven men Uwen had ordered under special guard, he well guessed. And they were not the men he would set free with the earl in reach.

But he had promised, and no good came of breaking his word at the outset.

"*You* will try. Come with me. We shall both try. Bring a torch."

"Your Grace," Anwyll began as he reached the uppermost step, and he found himself very weary of hearing those words in that tone of voice. "Your Grace," Anwyll persisted. "These men *have* no pardon. I must urge your lordship—"

"Am I duke of Amefel?" he asked shortly, "And did not Lord Heryn do as he pleased in his own hall?"

"Far too much," Anwyll said on a breath. "And died for it, Your Grace."

He knew that it was heart-sent advice. Anwyll had done nothing amiss and a great deal right, and faced him with dogged courage and no ill will.

"I hear all you say," he said, the two of them paused, he on the upper step. "And I take it much to heart, sir. But I will pardon them, all the same. Take them and these other men under guard and under my protection and hold them some safe place elsewhere. How does it stand in the South Court?"

"The gates are shut," Anwyll said. "The town has turned out in the street, Your Grace, with knives and staves, all shouting for your lordship, but we dare not let the mob in."

He could hear the uproar past the throbbing in his ears—heard it now beginning beyond the East Gate, in that blind and little-used street that tucked up between storehouses and Zeide defenses. The aid the town offered was dangerous, and he needed none of it now.

But the town also had need of reassurances. He strode down the steps, his personal guard hastening to overtake him, and went past the heap of weapons, into the columned end of the courtyard. At the gatehouse and its first defenses, three of Cossell's men had stayed and gotten the oaken gate shut again.

"Open the inner gate," he said, and they raised the bar and dragged the oak doors back.

Townspeople pressed at the bars beyond the portcullis, a mob with the hazard of torches, and bearing all manner of weapons. But seeing him, they began to shout, "Lord Sihhë!"

He lifted his sword, and gained a silence enough to speak. "The earl's men have surrendered and I have taken them under my protection—do no harm! *Hear me! Do no harm!* Tell it through the town!"

"Lord Sihhë!" the answer came in jubilation—and he walked back through the East Court as he had come, leaving the gates open for the crowd to witness through the bars whatever might befall here.

"Take these men to safekeeping," he ordered Anwyll regarding the prisoners. "Uwen! Bring the thane with us. And bear a light inside. Five men with us, to persuade the earl to surrender and end this."

"Lights," Uwen called out as he climbed the steps and men opened the doors into darkness. "Light, there, on the duke's order!"

Then: "Bring a light here!" he heard soldiers echo inside, up the short stairs and down the hall.

He went in, up dark and bloody steps, past moaning wounded, with men treading cautiously beside him, until he reached the level of the main hall and a crazily spreading firelight along the ceiling. From the far other end of the corridor a man came carrying a torch.

Illumination flared erratically along a hallway littered with wounded and dead, shone on polished floors, on ornate carvings. "Light the hall!" he heard men still shouting to the farthest doors as they trod a crooked course among the dead. The light-bearer reached them, then guided them to the center of the building.

"Come with us," Tristen said to the man with the torch, and started up the left-hand stairs, with Uwen, with his guards, with Crissand. He had his shield, and Uwen carried his own, but his guards, who had had the banners, had their hands unencumbered, and Sergeant Gedd took the idea to snatch a stub of a candle from its holder and borrow fire from the torchbearer. Then Gedd went ahead, enterprisingly setting light to at least one candle in every sconce, all the way to the upper floor, making the steps more visible, bringing a wan, ordinary light to the heart of the Zeide.

But from above another source of light spread along the ceiling, and that proved to be a torch in the hallway, where three men of the viceroy's Guelen Guard besieged the door of the Aswydds' old apartment.

"Your Grace," their sergeant said, recognizing him, "we've sent for axes."

"No, sir. By no means." He was appalled. They were beautiful doors, carved and very heavy. "Not yet. —Have you spoken with the earl? And has he answered at all?"

"His servants answer, your lordship, and won't open for our asking."

That was no surprise. He beckoned the young thane forward, among the viceroy's guard and his own. Crissand rapped uncertainly at the door.

"Father? Father? Do you hear me? Answer." Crissand rapped harder. "Father? I need your advice, sir. Please."

There was no response.

Uwen rapped the door with his sword hilt, no gentle tap. "You mayn't stay there, your lordship. Open. Your son is asking. Soon it may be others wi' less goodwill."

There was no sound at all within.

"This is His Grace Tristen of Ynefel asking!" Uwen shouted this time. "His Grace has brought your son in his safekeepin', and your son is asking ye kindly to open an' surrender the king's messenger, your lordship, which would be very wise to do, before His Grace's patience runs out, an' afore we spoil these fine doors. Ye come out, now!"

There was still no answer, but more, no sound within the apartment.

"Could they have gotten out beforehand?" Uwen asked.

"Not by us," the viceroy's men said.

Tristen knew the place. The same as most rooms of the Zeide, its windows had only a small vent, and if the earl and his men damaged them to get out that way, they were on the second floor above pavings and the courtyards occupied by king's men. It was possible that they had escaped down the stairs into the dark before the fighting, but if that were the case, the earl and his company might be lying among the dead downstairs, or they might be anywhere in the upper floors.

Most urgently, there was the king's messenger to account for.

Uwen thumped the door with his gloved fist, a frown on his face. "Now's certainly a finer time to come out than tomorrow, your lordship, and it won't get better. His Grace is patient, now. And your son is anxious for ye, wi' increasin' good cause."

Still there was no answer.

"Open the door," Tristen said. The question of Lord Edwyll's fate had become more important than the fine doors, and one of the viceroy's men had by now brought up an axe from a martial display down the hall.

"Father!" Crissand shouted out loudly, leaning against the door. "Will you not answer your son?"

There was still no response. Tristen gave the signal and the garrison soldier plied the axe, wonderful dark carving reduced to chips about the lock, and with a widening gap between the latch and the frame.

It was wrong, Tristen was increasingly convinced, remembering Lady Orien, who with her sister had had these rooms after her brother. It was all wrong. They would find nothing friendly in this room. And if not friendly, they had best not have the young thane loose in their midst.

"Sergeant," he said to the viceroy's man in charge, and quietly, as the blows continued and the chips flew, "move the young lord away."

"No," Crissand said, but the sergeant's men laid hands on him, and moved him firmly back.

In that same moment the axe had cleared enough wood from the edge for a sword to lift the bolt, and the soldiers shouldered in an armored rush into a dim, narrow foyer leading to a well-lit room.

Men lay all about that room, dead, down to the man tied with ropes to a chair, near the tall, green-draped windows.

Tristen stood still, surrounded by the green-velvet drapery and the rich bronze-and-gold furnishings of Lady Orien's residence . . . and the ill feeling in the room was stifling. He had not tried the gray space, until now—and it was cold, and ominous. He let down his shield, let it stand against the side of a chair, but he did not let down his defense against the insubstantial hazards he felt.

There began to be an argument outside, passionate and suddenly loud. "No, Your Honor!" someone said, and Crissand reached the foyer in his struggle, stopped as Lusin allowed him no further progress.

"Where is my father?" Crissand cried.

"Dead," Tristen said. "Dead, I fear, every one of them. —Let him go."

Lusin released him, and in a sudden rush Crissand went through the apartment searching. They followed as far as the bedroom that had been Lady Orien's, and there they found Crissand on his knees by the bed, where an old man lay atop the bedclothes, fully clothed, but composed, unlike the others.

"The earl died first," one of the viceroy's Guelens surmised. "An' they followed."

"This ain't a young man to loose in the town tonight," Uwen said, moving close to Tristen's side, speaking to him with his back to the young man and quietly. "I ask ye, m'lord, send the lad wi' these lads down to the guardroom an' put a watch on him, or he'll do someone hurt, hisself an' his own men like as any."

He knew the guardroom and abhorred the thought. But he regarded Uwen's advice when he regarded no other, and the feeling in the air was disquieting, unsettling to reason.

"Take him to the guardroom," Tristen said. "For your own safety, sir. I ask you go with them."

Crissand made no resistance being gathered up in the hands of the guards, but caught Tristen's eye with a white, shocked stare as he passed, as if asking for what reasonable cause all this had happened . . . as Tristen asked himself the same question. He had attempted kindness and charity; and disregarded the advice of knowledgeable men, and all this was the issue of it: the king's messenger, the earl, his servants, all dead, young Crissand stricken with a bitter, unsettling grief, and the harm that he had felt likely in all this journey was real. The earl was dead on the green-velvet coverlet of the bed. The man in the chair in the first room was the king's messenger, bound to that chair, dead by what cause was not evident. The earl's men were all dead, five of them, scattered about the place, three near the heavy sideboard.

"Ain't no mark," Uwen said, pushing a dead man with his foot. "Poison, I'd guess." Uwen's guess was plainly practical, while the gray space roiled with unease.

Then Lusin lifted a cup from among two cups and a pitcher on the table, and turned it sideways.

A red drop spilled out.

"Drunk from," Lusin said.

There were half a dozen cups in all, some on small tables about the room.

"All these, used," Tawwys said, examining another near where he stood. "M'lord, all drunk from."

Servants such as these seemed to be did not drink with their lord on any ordinary occasion. And the king's messenger as well . . . had he drunk wine, bound to a chair, with the fighting raging downstairs?

Folly. Outright folly, and villainy. The other earls had hung back to know the issue of it—then disavowed Edwyll altogether. Perhaps he had committed himself to rebellion even before he had ever intercepted the king's message . . . but coincidence still smelled of wizardry at the least.

And the wine service . . . and the death of a messenger, whose person was sacrosanct, even between warring factions . . .

"Lady Orien's cups," he said aloud, and knew it was not alone Lady Orien's cups . . . but Lady Orien's wards: the Zeide servants had sealed the place after Orien's banishment, after the king returned from Lewenbrook. The rooms had been two months unopened, until the earl moved in.

No few of the men blessed themselves, Uwen halfway so, and then Uwen abandoned the gesture, as Uwen at last renounced such protections in despair.

"Lady Orien's wine," Uwen said. "Well, her ladyship hardly had time to pack, did she?"

Not packed, indeed. All about them was the opulence of the Aswydds, the dark green velvet, the brazen dragons that upheld massive candles, the dragon-legged tables and the eagles that, paired wings almost touching, overshadowed even the velvet-covered bed in the other room, where the earl lay.

The messenger sat bound to his ornately carved chair, alone incapable of drinking.

But there was wine stain on the man's blond beard and on the Marhanen scarlet of his tunic, details apparent, Tristen found, once one walked over to have a closer look. The earl's servants, their lord dead of poison, the citadel falling, had all drunk from the cups and forced the messenger to drink, too, men not bound by the understandings of earls and dukes. Anger was in this room; uncleansed, untenanted, haunted by Aswydd hate, and the earl the remote kin of the Aswydds: he had been drawn in, drawn down, if he had had the smallest portion of the Aswydd gift. Tristen felt the tug of it himself, and dismissed it, with force.

Then he could draw a whole breath.

"Take them wherever they take the dead," he said. "Do whatever you judge fit, Uwen."

"Aye, m'lord," Uwen said. And then a hesitation. "There's some as would say burn the rebels' bodies. Ye want that, m'lord, or buryin' 'em, like honest men?"

"Do what should be done," he said again, at the moment lost as to what that was, or what he had the power to do to mend his arrival here. At the moment he ceded all power of decision to Uwen.

Burials. Burning. Neither destroyed the shadows, and Althalen, where all had burned, was most haunted of all. He only clung to the necessity of moderation in himself. Wide, inconsiderate action, Emuin as well as Mauryl had informed him, led to bruises. And worse.

Worst of all, he cast his own responsibility on Uwen, who could not see into the danger in this place—or know the danger of a strong spirit given Place on the earth.

"Bury them," he decided for himself. "The earl, the servants, all the men who died. Let priests say words, Uwen, whatever they like."

He had heard running steps in the hall, and heard them approaching the door. Men had lately been in haste, and might still be. He took no alarm even as a breathless man of the Dragons pushed his way past objecting guards; but the expression, the pallor, the distress in the man foretold worse yet.

"Your Grace." The man was one of Anwyll's men, but both Uwen and Lusin held him from coming closer in his agitation. "The captain's respects—the lord viceroy is killing the prisoners."

Lightning might have struck. It was like that, throwing into clarity all a dark landscape of Amefin resentments, Guelen angers, potent as the ill that gathered in this room.

"Where?" was his first conscious thought, and the man began to say, "The South Court."

Tristen pushed the man, Lusin, all his guards, aside.

"M'lord!" he heard Uwen call out, heard Uwen shout orders to some men to stay, some to come with them. Tristen gathered up his shield as he went out into the hall, and stayed for nothing else. He began to run, down the hall, down the stairs, and his men chased him with thumping of shields and the rattle of armor and weapons, down to the vacant center hall and the partially restored candlelight.

Beyond the open doors, torchlight shone in the South Court. He ran out onto the landing, saw a confused straggle of guards, Dragons, standing at the bottom, not opposing them as he came down the steps with his men, rather looking for orders, while a dark wall of red-coated men clustered near torchlight in the center of the yard and screams of threat and dying echoed off the walls beyond.

Death, death above, and death here below . . . death proceeding methodically, with the rise and fall of swords against unarmed men, death with outcries of anger and fear, death in a mass of men engaged in killing each other at the last curtain wall.

"Shields!" Tristen called out, and, without mercy: *"Swords!"* as they came up on that dark knot of shadows, Guelen Guard penning Amefin against the corner and cutting them down. A few Amefin had swords. Only a few.

"Dragon Guard!" Uwen roared out in a voice that echoed off the walls. "Guelens! Stand aside! Stand back! Come to order, here! *Way for His Grace, damn ye! Down weapons!"*

Men turned stark-faced from the killing, men drew back at a sergeant's profane voice, except the last handful, gone mad with slaughter, and them Tristen hit with both shield and sword, battering them aside. In the distance Anwyll shouted, "Pull back, pull back for a captain of the Guard!" but Tristen thought only of breaking through the ranks in front of him, overwhelming anyone who resisted him, until the killing stopped.

"Way for His Grace!" Uwen shouted, and at last, again, Anwyll's voice near at hand. "Draw back, draw back!"

Then other voices, many voices, the sergeants: "Stand aside, stand back there, lads!"

Quiet descended, except the drawing of breath, the moans of the wounded.

Tristen found himself with a strewed mass of bodies at his feet, an area fringed by armed guardsmen . . . them, and a small surviving knot of earl's men in the corner of the wall: Crissand, the seven, and a handful more.

Slaughter, plain and thorough, Guelen Guard against unarmed Amefin prisoners.

For a moment he could only think of adding to it anyone who opposed him, and it was perilous, very perilous, for Uwen to come up beside him, but Uwen did, a shadow in a wind that blew out of the Edge of the gray place. He was *there,* on the very brink of death, and he was *here,* his hands clenched on leather and iron, his body insensible to pain, the wind in his nostrils cold and burning his chest.

"M'lord," Uwen said quietly, the only voice in all the world. "M'lord, I'm right by ye. So's Lusin and the lads. We're with ye."

"Why have they done this?" He hardly knew where he had found the words. "Why have they done this?" And the next question stooped and struck, sharp as talons. *"Where is Lord Parsynan?"*

"Lord Parsynan," the call went out and went on and on through

the bloody courtyard. But it found no remedy. Life was ebbing out of the fallen, pooling on the stones, and much as he could deal death, he could not mend it. He saw shadows gathered, some new, and terrified, at the edges of the yard. He saw one hovering just above a body, and he wished it back, and it sank into the body like water into dry earth. He willed others, and was aware of living men around him, and of Uwen holding him by the arm, but what those men did, he had no idea. Wherein he could mend, he mended, but shadows flowed like smoke.

"M'lord," Uwen said. And more sharply, "M'lord. The lord viceroy's captain is asking to withdraw his men. Ye should grant it, m'lord. It was the lord viceroy's orders, which the Guelen Guard did, to their shame, and he ain't to be found, the dastard."

He felt the bite of the cold wind, felt the aches of his body, and turned his face toward his own men, toward Lusin, and toward Gedd and Aran and Tawwys. He saw all around him the desperation and the grief of a night gone wildly amiss.

"Your Grace." Crissand said from close at hand, and for a moment the edges of everything were unnaturally sharp, edged with shadow. "Your Grace, they would have killed us unarmed . . ."

Justice, Crissand had asked him in the East Court, before the shrines and the tombs. And now this.

"You are free," he said sharply. "Go where you choose." He was as sure of both the folly and the rightness of freeing this man as he had not been of all his recent life in Guelessar. He must not countenance a rebel against the Crown. But the viceroy's hate had done this, Guelen hate. He had no doubt at all the earl had had both provocation to rebel and aid in that rebellion. And he *could* do nothing else, on his given and now-violated word and by all that was now between them. "The wounded I shall send to you, each as he can, wherever you choose to lodge or go. I do *justice,* such as I can." He expected to hear *Your Grace* from Anwyll, but there was not a sound from Anwyll about the law. And matters echoed into the gray space, into a roil of disturbance in that place.

"I would go *home,* Your Grace," Crissand said, "and see my mother safe in my father's house."

"Give him escort," Tristen said. And it came to him with a sinking of his heart that the lord viceroy might not have spared even the loyal earls in his slaughter. The torches, few as they were, shed little light on the courtyard, to know who was dead and living. "Help him find his dead. See him home. And find the other earls and their men."

"I'd get the Guelen Guard under its sergeants, m'lord," Uwen said, close by him, "and under its captain, in good order. Let them serve sortin' out the dead. This is a sorry hour—ain't no coverin' it. Let 'em serve here an' stand guard at your orders, and then send 'em to barracks."

"Order it," he said. "And arrest Lord Parsynan."

"M'lord, —"

"*Do so!*"

"*Aye,* m'lord."

He heard Uwen give the orders, heard the captains and the sergeants give orders, and looked straight before him, at the gates, shut again, gates beyond which the people of Henas'amef still wondered about their fate.

It was not a good beginning of his rule here. He had not wished bloodshed. He saw Crissand, weary and bloody, talking to a few of his household, such as remained. He saw dead men scattered across the courtyard, unarmed men, killed by cowardly orders that had slipped past his intentions.

And he looked about him at a courtyard choked with soldiery, at walls on which the torches cast giant shadows of warlike men, at the Zeide itself, the fortress of the citadel, standing with its windows dark as he had never seen them, its doors open and showing the only pure light, the glow of candles.

This was his. *This* was his.

Had they left the camp only this morning? And was it morning again?

And had so much changed?

BOOK THREE

CHAPTER 1

Candles burned in great numbers in the lesser hall, which had no windows, no fireplace. Candles struggled wanly with the pervading cold of a room unopened for two months, since the viceroy had not, for whatever reason, used it in that length of time.

That was the hall Tristen chose in these last hours before the dawn. He still felt the fever-warmth of battle, but in this place the cold of stone and neglect stole under the armor and padding. He chose this lesser hall partly because the great hall was still Cefwyn's, to his scattered wits, and partly because this little, older hall was an easy recourse and easier to light, when his few reliable men had more urgent tasks than scouring up candles.

And he chose it because this little marble chamber was the first place in the Zeide he had ever known, except the guardroom and the hall leading here. He had stood just there, at the foot of the steps. He had been looking up at Cefwyn, who had sat where he sat now; now, Uwen at his back, he looked down at one of Cefwyn's officers, the sort whose obstinacy had made Cefwyn's reign difficult in Guelessar.

Parsynan was stolidly defiant. He had thus far been silent except to say, "Your Grace sent for me?" in those round, precise tones of Guelen nobility that said he was not only unrepentant, but nobler than anyone who accused him, and Tristen looked very long and hard at a man who could do so much harm with so little profit even to himself. He was sure Cefwyn would not have appointed a fool. Yet the man had behaved as one. Cefwyn would not have appointed a Guelen noble so rigidly Quinalt he could not deal with Amefin nobles. Yet this man, in his insistence on the king's law, had all but slaughtered an entire Amefin household, leaving its villages stripped of young men. Even a sometime fool whose life had begun this spring knew the damage Parsynan had done.

And why? Why such useless malice?

The contemplation of Parsynan's actions gave him the same feeling that that apartment upstairs had given him, one of affairs unhinged. Cefwyn would not have appointed a man he knew would do such things. But wizardry could find the weak place in a latch . . . or in a man's character . . . and use it.

Cefwyn's man had assuredly had other failures. The Dragon Guard had found Lord Parsynan not directing his men, not in command of the slaughter he had ordered, but inside the fortress, in his rooms, packing a box of women's jewelry and a small bag of things a man might need when traveling light. He had not involved his servants in preparing to quit Henas'amef and he had not ordered prepared the boxes and bundles that naturally attended a nobleman's movement across the country. The Guard said Parsynan had no lady here. So one had to ask whether he owned the jewels, and why he had not bidden his servants assist him.

"You ordered the prisoners killed," Tristen said now, without preface, "when I ordered them safe."

"According to law, Your Grace, in the king's name, I did so. And they are consequently extremely safe."

"The king sent me here and you are no longer viceroy."

"Still a king's officer, Your Grace."

"Captain Anwyll." With a motion of his hand he requested Anwyll's account, which he had warned Anwyll he must give, and Anwyll came from the door to stand at the side of the steps.

"Your Grace, his lordship took charge of the prisoners. I advised his lordship of Your Grace's orders to have them under guard . . ."

"Dare you say so!" Parsynan cried. "I received no such advisement! I executed *traitors* according to the king's law, and dare any man, noble or commonborn, say they were not traitors? I will *not* be slandered here! I have His Majesty's summons to return to the capital, and that will I, *with* my escort!"

"*Whose* were the jewels?" Tristen asked.

"Given me in gift, Your Grace!"

"You may have a horse and a man to go with you, sir, and when the wagons come I will send your belongings to you."

"You send a king's officer out in the night, as if I were some *servant*?"

"As you were prepared to go, sir, *except* the jewelry, about which I will make inquiry. And you may not slander a king's captain, either."

"I am not under your orders! And I will not be dismissed in this manner or with such implied accusations!"

"Nothing is implied. You *are* in Henas'amef, sir, and the daylight is coming. There were three townsmen swept up in your killing. These were innocent men supporting *me*, sir. I advise you go, and go now, before the sun rises!"

The man hesitated, perhaps the space of two breaths, but it seemed forever. *Leave without a word,* Tristen wished him; and the anger snapped like a bent branch. Parsynan bent his head in scant courtesy, backed, bowed, turned and left, in strictest propriety.

"M'lord," Uwen said faintly at his shoulder, and leaned just a little lower, in the privacy of a hall vacant of all but guardsmen. "M'lord, I beg ye don't wish him ill. There'd be rumors run riot if he slipped on the steps outside, rumors run riot in Amefel, and no end of trouble for us all."

Uwen had never before given him such a caution against malice. Perhaps Uwen saw the anger that had risen in him. But Emuin had said to him . . .

Emuin had said to him . . .

He drew a deep breath and let it go. He had not thought of Emuin. He had not thought of Emuin in hours. Or asked advice.

There was confusion now in the gray place. He felt it on the instant he so much as wondered how things stood there, and he retreated in a heartbeat, resolved not to resort to that place again until he felt things far quieter than they were. The gods' orderly world was sliding, bits and pieces as yet unsettled as to what order they would soon assume, and he stayed the timbers where he could, shored up others in hopes of achieving his own design, all with the sense of limited time in which to do so.

Young Crissand was not dead. Crissand's men had snatched him from the Guelen Guard who had taken him, and they had defended him to the last, but many, many of Crissand's household and the men of his district were dead as a result. And as he had told Lord Parsynan, so were the three brave townsmen who had tried to intervene, though by the viceroy's sole mercy other townsfolk who had rushed in to fight the rebels had been put out of the courtyard before the killing, and the Amefin lords, too, had been shut in the stable-court for their protection.

Parsynan would take his advice and go. That left him with the destruction to deal with, but not the destroyer.

And count among the ruin Parsynan had wrought the damaged reputation of the company of Guelen Guard, the town garrison. They had obeyed orders and carried out the slaughter. Anwyll advised him, and Uwen agreed, that he should send only a token of that regiment with Parsynan, reminding him that he had no direct order to reduce the garrison and that Cefwyn would not take it amiss.

So while some few more of that unit must go back to Guelessar to guard Parsynan's belongings when the wagons came, the rest should remain. Men who had been used in such an act needed to recover themselves and their honor, so said Anwyll and Uwen both, and could do it best here, where they would not have to deal with Parsynan's wrenching the facts of the case aside from the truth or persuading them the orders had ever been honorable. There was nothing the Guelens could take pride in after this, save only if another lord could give them some distinction, one that would wipe out the shame they had now, and Parsynan was not the lord to do it.

Anwyll spoke eloquently for the Guelen Guard; but the shame was not only in the Guelen Guard, who evaded the eyes of men of the Dragon, but in Captain Anwyll, himself, as Tristen saw it. Anwyll had been caught unprepared, had not refused Parsynan's confiscating the prisoners, and now and forever rued the moment he had obeyed a king's officer instead of the duke of Amefel. Once Anwyll had ceded the prisoners to Parsynan, with no idea what Parsynan intended, he could not have prevented the massacre without leading Dragon against Guelen Guard, an action that would have had only blame for the lowly captain and a scant reprimand for the lord who had behaved as Parsynan had. So no one had come off with clean hands, and two regiments of Cefwyn's Guard had had to meet at swords' point.

That was Parsynan's work tonight. No Guelenman had been killed, but the deed was there, and the entire Guelen army might never be the same as if it had never happened . . . while Amefin blood was shed even before the slaughter in the courtyard.

And for all these reasons the day and the new rule in Amefel would dawn less bright than it might have done. Given his private choice of what to do now, Tristen thought, he would go see to his horses, take account of the men he personally knew, find a cup of water that did not come from Lady Orien's cupboard and a bed in which she had not slept . . . or sit anywhere but in this hall letting guilty men go free and dealing with those he had provoked.

But along with the power the new duke of Amefel had to dismiss everything and take those comforts by decree, he found himself obliged. He had watched Cefwyn, in utmost weariness and at any hour, gather himself up and attend what duty wanted attending, and now he knew Cefwyn had given him what neither Mauryl nor Emuin could give him: the model of a lord of men. So he knew what he had to do while he had the strength to hold up his head.

But, but, with that sense of obligation came a temptation in which Mauryl and Emuin *had* taught him, with a strong sense of fear . . . he sorely wished to have done thus, and thus, and so to have prevented all the ill that had happened this night. He wished he could go back to that moment on the East Court steps and not have given the prisoners to Anwyll to escort. He regretted . . . and unlike Uwen and Anwyll, or any man not a wizard, he had a power to reach into the gray space, where moments might be all moments. He saw deaths at his feet, and knew he could seek back into the gray space, revisit that moment—not to change what ultimately had happened, but to gain a vantage much like his clear view from that hilltop in Guelessar, a chance to stand again on that step on the East Court, and to see himself, and Anwyll . . . but more importantly, see the doings in the gray place in that moment as well.

Then he might see what influences had been at work.

He might go back. That was always the temptation. He might walk that Road he had walked from Marna, do what could be done in the gray space, where moments defined themselves differently and where all roads were the same Road.

And would he? Dared he? More to the point, *had* he . . . or would he *ever*?

And had he at any moment on the east steps felt the skin on his arms prickle and the hair rise on his nape? In such a way one felt a visitor from after the event . . . the way he had met a shadow in the woods, once, on his way to the world of Men, a shadow which had been himself, wiser, going back on a Road fraught with peril.

He had come to drive his enemy from that Road, from a Place and a crossroads of events which lent Hasufin's sorcery its power. He had cast Hasufin Heltain away from that foothold on existence. But might Hasufin have others?

—Or might *he*?

He had felt nothing this night, perhaps. But this summer, the first time he had entered the lower hall, he had felt and seen a presence . . . the old mews, they told him, from an age when the modern great hall had been only a space in a far wider East Court. He still felt the terror of it.

And might at least one visitation in that haunted place be his own, involved in some terrible event, perhaps even his decision on the East Court steps? Shadows were certainly abundant there . . . and perhaps they were not all the ghostly kind of shadow, nor the great and violent kind, but the sorrowful kind, the personally frightening kind: shadows of better intentions, better thoughts, regrets traveling down a road that bent back on itself like the year-circle, forever and ever haunting that place, that jointure of might-have-been and might-yet-be.

His hands were cold on the stone. He perceived no ghost of himself here, in this hall, at least, only a scatter of soldiery, doubtless wholly bewildered at his woolgathering.

The battle in the downstairs hall had run past that place of joinings, and blood had fallen on that floor . . .

Blood, which was potent to call the dead, bridge the gaps in time, unify all that was. Emuin would never work such a spell.

But had Mauryl, once? And did it sit in this hall, on this seat, meditating questions of life and death for a province? And did it sit here of its own will? Or of Mauryl's?

"The nobles, m'lord," Uwen prompted him. "They're waitin' for ye, lad."

The soldiers were all staring at him, and did they bless themselves in fear of his lapses, or fear of their own at this haunted hour?

It was the joining point of the night. It was the hour of beginnings and endings.

"Let them in," he said to Uwen.

CHAPTER 2

The Amefin nobles, all released from their confinement in the stable-court, and waiting outside, must have seen Parsynan's angry departure from the hall.

Don't wish Parsynan ill, Uwen said, and no, Tristen said to himself, he would not. But he did not wish Parsynan well, either, and if wishes could lend him wings, he wished the former viceroy out of Amefel before he finished speaking to these men, and wished his influence out of the town before he had begun the pattern of the Amefel he wished to exist.

"I will see the earls," he repeated, and to Uwen, a moment of weariness, and remembering that ducal power in this hall could command little acts as well as life and death and the movement of armies: "Is there a cup of clean water?"

"I'll bring one," Uwen said, and did, from a soldier's water flask. It tasted strongly of sulfur, and Clusyn monastery.

But before he had taken more than two sips of it, the Amefin lords began to come in, exhausted men, indignant men, frightened men.

He gave the flask back to Uwen, and his hand trembled doing it, less to do with the cold stone seat than with utter weariness. He still had blood and soot on his garments, and he faced the tatters of a court, one missing one of its strongest men, one whose alliances bound smaller houses together and made peace between great ones. "Where is thane Crissand?" he asked Uwen, in a low voice. "Has he gone or is he here?"

"'S under close guard outside," Uwen said. "He went to his house an' he come back. His wish is to come into hall an' stand in his father's place, an' there, I've delivered 'is message to ye, an' the rest ain't in my hands, m'lord. Shall we let 'im in?"

The son of a rebel, the son of a decimated house, with grievances the lord viceroy had made real and just, was a weight not only in the world of Men. He foreknew Anwyll's objection. And there *were* consequences. Mauryl had dinned that into his very heart, first principle of wizardry and first in governing.

"Not so easily," Tristen said. "But bring him in."

"Your Grace," Anwyll said, coming up the low steps of the dais also to lean close. "Shall I have the clerk read the document again? Some may not have heard it. Then Your Grace may ask they give the oaths, if it please Your Grace, which you should very soon."

The Guelenfolk guarding him were anxious that there be ceremony, always that there be ceremony and oaths: it was the sort of magic they felt they could work, the setting of wards such as they could do, indeed wards of some potency, if he could judge; and Anwyll, who had his instruction directly from Idrys, was extremely anxious that this at least go smoothly. Otherwise, he pitied Anwyll his return to Guelessar.

"Do so," he said, and at Anwyll's bidding the clerk positioned himself in the spot of best light from the candles in the sconces, canted the parchment for the clearest view and read out the proclamation in good ringing tones, with fewer mistakes than when he had read it before the gates.

This time, in this solemn hall, however, and among these sober men, there were no cheers of *Lord Sihhë!* And this time Tristen paid the reading little heed, instead watching the faces of the earls as he struggled to gather up names he had not used in two months . . . Cuthan, there, foremost of them, had not been in the stable-court when the arrows were flying, but understandably so. He was elderly, a wisp of a man, doddering to look at him, but not so in wits or power: he recalled that from his sojourn here in the summer. Cuthan was a power among the earls, the one man Cefwyn might have made duke of Amefel if Cuthan had been willing; but Cuthan had begged off on account of his age and health. Then Edwyll had put forward his own claims to the honor, and with the man he would choose unwilling and with the man who *was* willing blood-tied to the Aswydds he had just exiled, Cefwyn had installed Lord Parsynan instead.

More agreeable was Murras, a fat, cheerful man, and bravest of the earls was Drumman, lean as a post and one of the youngest, bearing a bloody bandage with evident pride and good humor, his badge of honor from the stable-court. Dusky-skinned Edracht, and gray-streaked Prushan: neither of them loved old Cuthan, which might have made them natural allies for other factions, but neither of them loved his brother lords any better, so far as he had observed.

They were western lords. The Earl Marmaschen, he with the forked beard, a quiet man: whether he was wise was still to learn; and with him Zereshadd, Moridedd, and Brestandin. They were always together, those four, from lands closest about Henas'amef. Their odd names had always been a matter of curiosity: they did not belong in Amefel, and were originally southern, even more than the Ivanim, was his impression, but nothing told him how he was so sure or why nothing else Unfolded.

Of the easterners fronting Guelessar, there was Durell, who drank far too much at festivities, but who was entirely sober this night; there was Civas, a quiet man, a cipher; there was Lund, who looked more like a farmer than an earl, and Azant, who bordered the river.

The clerics had come in, too, having now come out of their hiding places to learn the outcome of the struggle. The Teranthine patriarch, Pachyll, did not look at all displeased: immaculate in his gray, fingering his beard and nodding to himself at almost every line as the clerk read the proclamation. The Bryaltine abbot, Cadell, unadorned and without his symbols on this chancy night, gazed at his new duke with eyes bright and high color suffusing his cheeks. But the Quinalt father stood in the shadows against the opposite wall, near the Guelen soldiers tonight, and had his hands tucked in the safety of his sleeves.

Give the man gifts, Idrys had said. Perhaps that would make him less afraid . . . for this was a frightened man.

And Crissand, dark as Amefin in general were dark, stood in the downward shadow of a candle-sconce, shadowed in weariness and misfortune. There was no restraint on him. But no lord stood near him, nor the priests either. He was the center of the night's misfortune, the heir to an unwanted deed . . . but heir, too, to an Amefin house, standing to claim Meiden, when he might have absented himself until a time of cooler heads and less danger, or begged a friend or a priest to intercede for him. He had come of his own will to state his own case, and thereby risked everything for himself and his people.

Meanwhile the proclamation ran toward its end, with the courtesies and tangles of phrase composed in the Guelen court. The oaths were coming, a second document the clerk had brought, oaths which were unique and entirely unlike those of the rest of Ylesuin. The Aswyddim had been kings in Hen Amas centuries ago, when the five Sihhë-lords came down; so the Bryalt Chronicle said, the Aswyddim, rather than resisting, had flung open their gates, and Barrakkêth had let the Aswydd king of that day continue to call himself aetheling, or royal, as he wished.

So had Barrakkêth's successors permitted it, and so, for expediency, had the Marhanen kings. Thus the Amefin earls swore to a *royal* power of their own, and since the aetheling was an earl among other earls, *that* convolute reasoning let the earls of Amefel all continue in their little holdings, earl being a title which *Guelen* nobility did not acknowledge, but which Amefin folk regarded as each equivalent to duke.

The earls therefore cherished their uniqueness among the provinces of Ylesuin as vital as heart's blood, even if they no longer had towers and no longer ruled with separate small troops of men-at-arms on their own land, not since two kings ago, when Selwyn Marhanen had torn all the earls' towers down, after which most of the earls had taken up residence in houses in Henas'amef, the grand houses all about the square. That was the history of the Red Book. That carefully maintained word *aetheling* let their lord be royal when he was sitting on what the Amefin not too disguisedly called the throne in Henas'amef . . . and the Marhanen had never contested the matter, seeing the Aswydd aetheling owned himself a Marhanen vassal when he was outside his own borders.

There was, remotely, an Aswydd heir standing in this chamber, now. But Crissand was not in contention for his father's claim on that word tonight; so for the first time in the history of Amefel, the earls must either swear to a man neither aetheling nor Aswydd, or they must defy the Marhanen king, precipitating the very crisis Cefwyn had avoided when he deposed and exiled Orien Aswydd and appointed a viceroy over the province.

The earls of Amefel might no longer live in state on their own land, except a few in the east, like Durell; but in their thinking they were a kingdom, and in their thinking they had a right to their own choice of rulers. Why Edwyll had launched so rash a rebellion was still in question, but the causes were everywhere in this assemblage, and wove serpentines in the ancient prerogatives.

The reading was done. The echoes died. The clerk rattled up the second document. "The oaths, the recorded oaths, as last sworn. *His Grace the duke of Amefel summons your lordships each to swear fealty according to the terms written herein . . .*"

What will you do? Tristen wondered. And will you swear, or will you not?

I think you will swear. For the peace and your own welfare, *I wish you to swear.*

Cuthan ducked his head a moment, took a firmer grip with both hands on his gold-headed staff, then looked up as the clerk finished the passage. "Your Grace," Cuthan said, in a voice thready with age and a manner feeble in all but the steadiness of the glance he cast up. "Your Grace, for all my years I would never have guessed His Majesty in Guelessar would have proposed us Mauryl's heir to succeed the Aswyddim."

Proposed. *Proposed*, the man said, and not *decreed*, nor *chosen*. This was a wily old man with a will to find a way to accept the inevitable and still to leave the key principle of Amefin sovereignty alive.

"And will you swear?" Tristen asked.

"Aye," Cuthan said, and nodded decisively. "Aye, to Mauryl's heir, aye, I will."

Fine as dust. Another dicing of loyalties and attachments, a clever, careful, dangerous wording that might itself one day be a matter of contention, and they had no clerk with pen in hand free to record it. "Aye," was the word behind Cuthan, from lords all about the chamber, even Prushan and Edracht, thorns in Cefwyn's side, opposed to Cefwyn's appointment of Parsynan, or any Guelen viceroy; opposed to Edwyll, who wanted to succeed Orien Aswydd. By reason of this old man's cleverness of phrase, obstacles tumbled. There was reason to be grateful to Cuthan. But a man who could settle tempests so cleverly . . . could also raise them, both for his own purposes. The man's aims were yet to discover. Oh, he had seen far more than he wished in Guelessar this autumn.

"I am here both as Mauryl's heir and as His Majesty's friend," Tristen said quietly, doggedly insistent on them, including Cuthan, knowing that from the very beginning. "Lord Edwyll is dead. I did not kill him. As for Lord Parsynan, I have ordered him to leave Amefel, and *I* order the garrison, now."

There was a cold, deep silence in the hall. Not a man moved, not even the random stirring of a large company.

"I wish you all well, and safe." His eye swept the earls, the clerics

. . . and Crissand, standing apart. "The clerk has the oaths exactly as you last swore to Lord Heryn. If you will swear, swear."

"We are all here to swear," Cuthan said with a clearing of his throat, hands clenched whitely on the head of his stick. Other heads nodded. The young clerk whispered something urgent to Uwen, who told him some answer, and the clerk, with the document of oaths in hand, leafed back through it with a crackling of heavy paper.

"The clerk don't know the order of precedence," Uwen said in a low voice, at Tristen's elbow, "except by the book. The earl of Meiden, his heir an' all . . . *'at's the first name.*"

"The earl of Bryn," Tristen said instead, and saw Crissand stand thin-lipped and still as Cuthan, Earl of Bryn, took the precedence.

The Amefin swore standing, and clasped right hands, but did not kneel: only their duke did, when he had to swear to the Marhanen king, in an homage even the Sihhë-lord had never asked of Amefel.

So Tristen stood up to take the old man's hand, looking him in the eye as the clerk began to read, stumbling over the Amefin names. But the old man ran past the prompting at the first pause and set forth his own oath loud and clear by memory:

"I Cuthan, Earl of Bryn, for Taras and Bru Mardan, and all their thanes, swear to defend the rights of him holding Hen Amas, to march to war under his command, to gather levies and revenues, to acknowledge him lord and sovereign over its claims and courts and to abide by his judgments in all disputes."

Sovereign was that surviving word that was the uniqueness of the province. Cefwyn had demanded no changes.

"I Tristen holding Hen Amas," the clerk read out for him, and Tristen repeated . . . Hen Amas, the old name, as before the citadel had become simply *the Zeide* it had been the Kathseide. The name Hen Amas conjured a tower, not a town, to him, conjured a village and orchards against familiar hills; more, the next words Unfolded to him, and he had no need of the clerk to say, at the second swearing,

". . . to defend your rights against all claims and incursions and to judge rightly as your sovereign lord." His part was all the same, while the reciprocal oath was longer for some, shorter for others, ending with, in all cases,

"And so you are true to your oath so I hold to mine before the gods."

But it seemed to him those last few words the clerk had given him were the wrong words, and that it should not be *before the gods*. Despite the book he had against his ribs he could not truthfully swear to Efanor's gods, nor even to Emuin's Nineteen, the wizards' gods. How could he bind himself by that, as Men did?

And why should he think he had ever said differently? he asked himself, and why should he remember orchards where the lowermost streets of the town now stood, and where the outlying stables were?

And why should he remember *this* the lesser hall as the great hall, and choose this for the oath-taking—except that it was the right place? In his earliest days things had Unfolded so rapidly and with such force he had fallen in fits. Now a kind of dizziness came on him. He received other oaths, he said the clerk's words without objection, and hands clasped his hand, hands hard with weapons practice and hands soft with age, hands missing first fingers . . . swordsman's bane . . . and hands so ringed and jeweled they were all but armored in wealth and power. Rustic Amefel did have rich men, and these earls, like Henas'amef, had had wealth unplundered since earliest days.

Love them? No. Not yet. He armored his heart against them as he had learned to do with the lords of Ylesuin. He looked steadily at them as they swore, and some few looked back, but he remembered that Edwyll had not done what he had done in disregard of the rest of the province.

The last of them in the order of precedence was Lund. Crissand still stood, pale and set of countenance, awaiting some word, some acknowledgment, some dismissal or decision. Once the first and the second had sworn, then he had surely known he would not be the third, or the fifth, but that he would swear last, if at all. The order of precedence was not an empty matter. It was like a banner, like the device on a shield, the land rights, the claim on mutual defense, and not a man in the hall could have forgotten that Crissand stood waiting and empty-handed.

Might anger guide this young man to imprudence? He would know it, if that became the case. Ought he to do differently, or show more mercy? He had been generous, until now.

"Crissand, thane of Tas Aden."

He knew trials: Mauryl had set very hard ones; and now he set a severe one, and knew not what way Crissand might turn in the next moment, but now, too, he understood how greatly Mauryl had struggled to restrain himself from wishes and wizardry, not to constrain or create what he would draw out. Cuthan was wise and clever, a great treasure in a hall. But this young man . . . this was the one that touched him. This was the one of all of the earls who would dare his wrath to his face or stand by him to the last.

"May I trust you?" he asked Crissand.

"Your Grace."

"May I trust you?" he said again. He had not heard *my lord* from Crissand Adiran or any man of Meiden. Not yet.

There was a small silence, and the hall was cold, evoking shivers from weary bodies.

"What does Your Grace ask?" Crissand said in the deep silence of all the lords.

"Truth."

"And will Your Grace believe me, whatever I say?"

He reached into the gray space, just a breath of a touch, and Crissand flinched.

"Yes," he said to Crissand, thought, *So,* and saw a glimmering of fear staring back at him.

"My lord," Crissand said, half a whisper, and no more.

"*Now* you say so." He let the silence linger a moment . . . did not draw Crissand deeper into the gray space. But this was a young man with wizard-gift. This was an Aswydd, in a hall where his kin had been kings, dispossessed now, and he, at least tonight, was the agent of that dispossession. The silence went on, and on, and the wind blew through that other place, but softly so. "Will you *tell* me the truth?" Tristen asked.

"My lord," Crissand said, with a lift of his chin, "*what truth* will you? Truth of my father's life? Truth of his death? *Which* truth?"

"*The* truth. No other. Nothing less. Did your father deal with Tasmôrden?"

The earls were thunderstruck, caught on the outskirts of treason, all, all of them but Cuthan, who clenched his staff tightly, and set his jaw like granite. The hands of king's men strayed closer to their swords. And none else in this room were armed.

But Crissand spoke in firm, clear tones. "*Yes,* my lord, he did— Her Grace the Regent being betrothed to the Marhanen, my father dealt with the likeliest rebel in Elwynor."

Treason, treason laid out plain to see. The lord viceroy had advised him of the truth, after all.

But not an irredeemable truth. These lords had sworn. So had he. And all the truth and all the misdeeds that had existed an hour before were in the past, sealed.

"I dismiss your truth. I forgive it," he said to the thane of Tas Aden. "And what say you now?"

"That the Sihhë are back in Hen Amas." The gray space shivered, settled with final force. And Crissand bent the knee and knelt there on the steps of the dais, with the earls and the Dragon Guard for witness. "That you are my lord *and* my king."

Breath might have ceased in the hall.

But it was no more nor less than the Amefin oath, stripped of niggling words like *aetheling*.

"I Crissand, Earl of Meiden, swear so . . ." It had become the oath of fealty, an Amefin lord *kneeling* before him, and what in turn was he to answer? Prudence said he should stop the proceeding, set the self-made earl on his feet by main force, and bind himself to nothing. But he felt the little shiver in the gray space that Ninévrisë could make, or now and again someone passing near him.

The Sihhë are back in Hen Amas.

Dared he say so? Dared Crissand? And dared an aetheling kneel in this hall, as to an overlord?

The clerk frantically searched his pages, a crackle of paper in the stillness, and looked up in consternation. The earl of Meiden finished his brief swearing, with: "So I will be faithful to you, on my oath and my honor," and the hapless clerk searched for his place in an appalled silence.

"I Tristen . . ."

Another flurry of the clerk's pages.

". . . swear you *are* the earl of Meiden, and have the governance of the land of Meiden, and its villages and rights and privileges. I shall defend you and your rights and lands as you defend me and mine. To all this I swear by my life."

The clerk looked up openmouthed, and he realized he had not said the clerk's words. He drew Crissand to his feet. He ignored the stares of the clerk, the earls, the priests, and of his own men, and looked the heir of the Aswydds straight in the eye.

"Tell me true, Meiden: *are* Elwynim forces across the river?"

The rustle of pages had ceased. Everything had ceased.

"The rising would signal them to cross," Crissand said, and he knew he had heard the truth, more, that what Crissand confessed was no surprise to any man in this hall.

"Then I fear you are deceived," Tristen said. "I suspect Tasmôrden would *not* have crossed, not with His Majesty set to plunge into Elwynor from his northern frontier. But he would gladly divert Cefwyn's attention south to Henas'amef over the next fort-night or so while he takes Ilefínian, which he has just moved to do. Once there, he will slaughter Her Grace's men and winter in more comfort, recovering his forces. He would leave *you* to engage Cefwyn this winter, all to his profit, and aid you only sufficient to keep the king fighting here until the spring." He was as sure as he said the words, as if they had Unfolded, but even the guess he made was not as great as the hazard to their lives he felt in the gray space. "Tasmôrden opposes *me*, and he would never have crossed the river until he was sure Cefwyn was here and weakened by the encounter, in a hostile province. Then, yes, he would *fight* in Amefel and spare his own fields. You have provoked the lord viceroy only to Tasmôrden's gain and none of your own."

"My lord Sihhë," Crissand began, and would have sunk back to one knee.

And must not. Tristen seized him by both arms this time and looked him straight in the eye. "*Your Grace* is the title I own. I hold it from His Majesty, his gift, no other."

"My lord, then," Crissand said faintly as Tristen set him back. "At your will."

"What I *will* is a secure border. Heryn Aswydd collected too much tax and spent too much money on dinnerplates. Amefel will muster in the spring and set the Lady Regent on the Regent's throne in Ilefínian. *That* is what I will, sirs."

The latter part was certainly no news to them. Cefwyn had made no secret of his plans, not even from Tasmôrden. He looked out over the assembled earls, saw great sobriety and consternation at his bluntness and at Crissand's, and perhaps a reassessment of Tasmôrden's offers of alliance.

"Some think me foolish," he said to the earls, "and that may be; but I am a fool far less often these days than I was this summer, and I do learn, sirs. I know, for instance, that many Amefin houses have far closer ties across the river than to Ylesuin. If Ylesuin sets Elwynor safely on her throne, then your villagers will walk across the river bridges by broad daylight and trade as you wish. But if Tasmôrden comes, he will make Amefel his battlefield. That is the truth, sirs."

There was not a word of objection.

And he had nothing more to say or do here, and wished nothing more now than to go to his own bed, and to have ease of the belts and weapons he had borne now for a day and a night . . . or was it morning? . . . with no ease of them. Crissand's loyalty would stay or it would go. The gray space was utterly roiled, seething with yea and nay and hazard, and he wished Crissand Adiran out of his vicinity before his unsteady wits did lasting harm and willed something unwise.

"Good night," he said. No one moved for a breath or two, and then one and the other bowed and edged cautiously backward, as if they were each hesitant to be the first to leave. Crissand gazed at him, and in the gray space, winds blew, changing direction on the instant.

Then Crissand bowed his way away from the dais, the guards that had brought him in all standing in uncertainty.

Tristen shook his head at the sergeant, wishing him not to detain the earl of Meiden, or to interfere with him.

And for the rest, he knew no more elaborate ceremony or more ready escape than Cefwyn's habit, which was to walk out by the lord's door, that nearest the dais. He gathered up Uwen, Anwyll, a trail of guards, the clerks, and then Tawwys and Syllan outside in the hall at the same time as the earls and clerics had to sort themselves out by the other door a small distance away.

None of the earls, however, ventured near to trouble him, and shielded what they said with turns of their shoulders and furtive glances as they hurried to be away, either seeking safer nooks of the Zeide in which to gossip, or going home as the court would, by the stable-court stairs and the West Gate.

Tristen walked, instead, aware of the dismay of his own guards, toward the center of the building, where the South Court doors let in and where the confluence of stairways gave a choice of upward directions.

"What shall we do wi' Lord Meiden?" Uwen asked him as he approached that point of choice.

"Let him go," Tristen said. But all his soul said there was profound danger in Crissand Adiran . . . Crissand Aswydd, for Aswydd he surely was. "Let him go where he pleases."

So he ordered. But if Uwen were Idrys, and if he were Cefwyn, then he would know that Meiden would not do anything unwatched, and he would never have to hear of it or trouble his soul unless there was reason.

But Uwen was not Idrys, and he realized only then that he truly had no check on his mercy, and no man to do the dark, the unpleasant things. Uwen asked, perceiving the threat, but Uwen would be grieved to slip furtively about when his lord had made a public show of setting Crissand free on his honor. He had to order it if it would be done, while Idrys would have done it even if his liege had strictly forbidden him.

And he found himself at a pass that Cefwyn with his resources would never have come to. He had given a pledge. Was he now to break it himself? Such things, he being not a Man, had more than ordinary consequence, and he, not being a Man, had more than ordinary need of a Man to do the unpleasant work and examine the dark corners.

They walked by the light of stub candles in sconces up and down the lower hall. The Zeide's servants had appeared out of whatever holes they had hidden in, and candles were not everywhere, as yet, but there were enough lit at enough points to show the servants working end to end of the hall, sweeping and polishing evidence of death from the stones of Hen Amas.

They were the true caretakers of this Place, he thought: lords proposed and disposed and worried about the proprieties and the rights of things, but they mopped the dust and the blood away and made it possible to forget the worst of events.

It was one more change of lords for them, in this year yet unended. There had been four, already, since summer, counting the lord viceroy—who might be the departing rider he heard out in the courtyard, through weapon-scarred doors now closed for the sake of warmth.

The lord viceroy was gone.

He was the fifth lord, in one year.

And in that realization he found himself approaching a scatter-witted weariness. Was it hunger he felt at this hour, or thirst or merely winter chill? His body failed to inform him. Down the corridor ahead, past the great hall, was the ghostly boundary of the mews. There were dead men in the ducal apartment above. There was the lord viceroy's ungathered baggage in the other lordly residence, that which Cefwyn had used up the other stairs. He longed for his own old, modest dwelling on the uppermost floor, but he who had to fear that wizardry supported his wishes had no hope of recovering that apartment save by arranging a calamity to someone else . . . as surely someone else was residing there now. He was equally sure the duke of Amefel had to occupy some other residence: Uwen would never let him choose something so small and modest and entirely adequate, nor would Emuin.

Nor, for that matter, would Cefwyn.

Cefwyn. Cefwyn. Cefwyn. *There* was the question tonight. But it was not a question he could solve by thinking on it, not with wits muddled with a day's riding and a night such as they had just spent. He felt tremors in all his body, a desperate need of sleep.

"Which rooms shall I use?" he asked Uwen, as they reached that choice between the stairway on the left, that led to Cefwyn's former rooms, and that on the right, that led up to the Aswydd bedchambers. "Where shall I sleep?" His own question sounded plaintive in his ears. He was lost as a child, and Uwen shepherded him toward the right-hand stairs.

"They've been preparin' the Aswydd rooms," Uwen said. "The servants ha' been at it for an hour now, a great lot of 'em. It's safest. We ain't searched every hall and nook, nor will have, maybe for days, so's ye should have a care for the dark places an' never go wi'out me, not even wi' Guelen troops: wi' *me,* lad, or maybe Lusin an' the rest, but no others, *no* others, no matter how well ye know 'em."

CHAPTER 3

The apartment smelled of burning cedar and polishing oils. The chair by the tall, green-curtained windows might never have held a dead man—all the dead were gone, to what burial place Tristen had not asked. The servants, working under close guard, had indeed changed the place in very little time, and most significantly there was not a cup, not a bowl, not a vessel or utensil to be seen on any shelf. Guards were in every room, too, standing watch, so that the rooms had not the desolate feeling they might have had after the events of this bloody night: Syllan had taken command of the detachment at the door, while Lusin was off inquiring into things that had to be inquired into regarding the horses and the stables.

Servants passed, with massive copper buckets that foretold a bathtub being filled with hot water.

Clean, hot water. If dead men had been end to end of the floor, Tristen thought, he would have longed for that bath, and he abandoned his last reluctance about the place.

"I want you, and our men, with me," he said to Uwen as they walked through the inner rooms. "I take all your warnings. I want the doors *shut*. Use only the food and drink we brought in." His voice had become a thread. He could not muster more than that. "Let us hope for a quiet rest."

"The captain's had the town watch shut down the taverns," Uwen said, "so the captain says. Can't any man roam the streets carrying his pot of drink with him, and Lord Cuthan's got his household men standin' watch by the tavern, gods save us, so's no crowd gets to barrels of it. Men can be great fools when they're happy."

"And are they happy?" He paused. He was astonished, in the light of the lord viceroy's actions and all else that had gone amiss.

"Oh, indeed they are, m'lord. Folk as feared the town might lie under siege all winter, they're right happy. They don't care if ye're a wizard or ye ain't. By them, ye ain't Guelen, ye ain't any viceroy, and Sihhë ain't any unlucky word hereabouts, either, so to say. Here, if ye call down lightning on the Zeide roof, why, they'll take no offense by 't. *Aye,* they're happy, lad, they're right happy about a peaceful winter. Ye've come *home,* an' may ye have a long and a happy stay here, m'lord, wi' all my heart, dare I wish so?"

A long and a happy stay. And a cheerful, even a bantering and wistful wish from Uwen, who had heard everything in the hall below.

"But may I say, gettin' far above myself, m'lord, ye was right to chide the earls."

"Was I?"

Uwen colored to the roots of his hair. "Sayin' as I'd know," he said with a downcast look. "But ye done well, m'lord. Only—"

"Only?"

"Ye was right, too, about them sayin' *lord Sihhë.* 'At's trouble. The Quinalt father was standin' there with his hands in his sleeves and lookin' to have swallowed a bad bite."

"Idrys says to make a gift to the Quinalt. I think we should for all of the priests, and have them happy."

"If ye went yoursel' an' made it, they'd be happiest of all."

"We have the gold."

"Aye, m'lord." Uwen laughed. "Ye have the whole damn treasury . . . which ye should look into and take account of, at least I would, seein' the lord viceroy was packin' jewels which might have been her ladyship's."

"Orien's?" He had by no means imagined.

"Her ladyship bein' duchess of Amefel, I don't know, but she wore some right fine green 'uns when she were lady here. An' I don't know the color of what the viceroy was packing."

"Twice, then, tonight, Orien."

Uwen's face had gone quite sober. "I'd say so, m'lord, an' right cautious I'd be wi' anything that lady owned."

Tristen passed a glance around them, the draperies, the ornate doors, the penchant for dragons.

"So I am," he said.

They walked back to the entry, and there he stopped and gazed at his domain: heavy chairs, massive tables, tapestries wrought in silk, fanciful globes worked in gold and silver. There were tables covered entirely in gold leaf, and a dining table the legs of which were strange, hostile beasts. With the servants' best efforts he still found the dimly lighted room, with its dark green, gold-tasseled draperies over the windows, stiflingly oppressive, as if air had not moved here, and could not move again.

He walked across the room, surveyed the green fabric that he associated with Heryn and Orien and the Aswydds—rightly associated: it was the Aswydd heraldry. He gave it a tug to draw the drapery back. It slid freely and unexpectedly on its rods, showing diamond-paned glass, and night, and dark—

Stark terror, beyond the window, a shattering of light and dark on glass.

Reflections. Mere reflections. His heart had leapt. And settled.

But it had been real, once. On a certain night this summer he had surprised Lady Orien and her sister in sorcery at the very table as that now in the corner of his eye, with the dragon candlesticks alight, the window vents open and unwarded before her, her sister Tarien, and a small cluster of her ladies. In his imagining at any moment he might hear the rustle of Lady Orien's skirts, smell her heavy perfume.

For an instant he longed to flee this room at least until daylight.

But if he could not master this room, and its shadows, himself being forewarned and wary and far more potent than the earl's thin Aswydd blood, then how could he ever master the Zeide? The threat was negligible, if he met it, dealt with it, banished it.

And what would Emuin say now of this night's doing? Not praise for his foresight, he much feared. He would not compound his discreditable actions by hieing himself and his guards to a dusty, unused bedchamber, all for fear of Aswydd curses, he, who was Mauryl Gestaurien's heir.

"M'lord?" Uwen had come up close to him. "M'lord?"

The window reflected a dark man and an older, worried one, silver-haired, behind him.

Then by a trick of the eyes he was looking out into dark, and night.

Shadows rushed against the window, a solid wall of black. A second trial of him.

He lifted a hand, startled, and a second time saw only the window again, the ordinary night.

Lady Orien had invited shadows into this room repeatedly. She had treated with them, opened this window, compromised the Lines on the earth that Masons had made when they declared the foundations of the Zeide; and it was a dangerous breach to have made. She had sought power to come to herself . . . but being bound inside the Zeide, had either acted in folly or overweening pride. This window had become a gateway to Orien's ambition, her hate, her anger, going out . . . and that had become worse, a highroad to far older spirits entering. *Hasufin Heltain* had almost entered here. That ancient, dispelled spirit had needed only a tiny breach to begin its entry, but fortunately for everyone, it had needed a far, far greater one in order to enter any place as warded as the Zeide had been, and as far from Hasufin's own center of power. Hasufin or whatever passed for Hasufin in this place had not quite succeeded in breaking the wards.

At Ynefel . . . it had done so. And Ynefel, warded by the most potent wizard alive, stood in ruins. Dared anyone think a tiny crack should be disregarded?

The one beneath the horn-paned window . . . had *that* been the entry?

Or had his own young curiosity breached Ynefel's wards?

He touched the side of the window, and drew his finger from that side across the sill, all the way across to the other wall. He touched the metal frame of the little side pane that opened, and ran his fingers across the latch. He repeated the action. Three times, Emuin had said. Once was an accident, twice was divisible, three was neither accident nor divisible. Three was a maze spirits could not bend themselves through with any ease at all.

The reflection showed a dark man and a silver-headed one. Uwen watched his actions, saying not a thing.

"I treasure you above all my household," he said to Uwen's reflection. "I wish you well, Uwen, and I wish you very well. I wish you well."

Three times he said it, and if, as Emuin said, he had an unbreakable hold on magic, he attempted it as consciously as anything he had done in the hall tonight. Uwen was silent a moment. And shadows drifted, no longer potent, on the other side of the glass, fading from the edges of the day.

"I'm glad of that, m'lord," Uwen said finally.

The drapery smelled of incense, unpleasantly so.

"Red," Tristen said, and gathered up a fistful of the green velvet, pulled at it, looked up, where the rod supported it. It would assuredly fall if he pulled it, but it would endanger the wrought panes of the window and the dragon-held tables on either side. No matter his distaste for the place, it was the wealth of Amefel, which he had sworn to increase, and tend, and not to cause harm to it.

But the color meant something among the nobles of Ylesuin, and these, and the draperies downstairs . . . all this green said *Aswydd* at every glance.

"Will Lord Heryn's gold dinnerplates buy new draperies, do you think?"

"They might, m'lord. Might well."

He saw a servant standing then, waiting to be noticed, a reflection across the room. He turned and acknowledged the presence.

"Your Grace, the bath is ready."

"Heat more water. Bring more towels. My men and I all will use the bath."

"'T ain't lordly," Uwen said, "m'lord, and lord ye are, now, lad. The men and me can wash in the scullery."

"Not tonight," he said. "No. Here," he said, and that was an end of it. He went to his bath, and afterward found the servants had stripped the bed in the adjacent chamber, laid on clean bedclothes and strewed herbs over them, crushed, dried petals, as well as set pomanders in silver dishes everywhere, until the place smelled of last summer's flowers . . . or a woman's perfume.

But the air smelled of cooked sausage, too, and when he walked out to the fire to surrender the bath to Uwen, his guards, sitting at the fireplace, offered him hot tea, bread, and toasted sausage. "From our own stores, m'lord," Syllan said. They had toasted it on a knife blade that he was sure had not come from this room.

So Uwen had his bath, and they camped, he and his men, like wayfarers in the splendor of the Aswyddim.

The door opened, and someone came in . . . Lusin, it proved to be, back from the stables, with straw clinging to his cloak. "Bath is waiting," Uwen said.

"Captain," Lusin said, "a word with you, sir."

Uwen got up, and went to hear the report, and no one's attention was quite for the fireside, then. Tristen listened, but heard nothing, only saw Uwen's face grow grim and glum, and saw Uwen shake his head as he answered Lusin, no good news, it was clear. Uwen's shoulders slumped in a second shake of his head.

The cheer had gone out of their gathering. They all watched as Lusin left again and Uwen trudged back to the fire to sit down.

"What news?" Tristen asked.

"His lordship the viceroy is on his way an' out of the town for good an' all," Uwen said. "Didn't stay for a man to go with 'im."

"And are you sad on that account?" Tristen asked.

Uwen heaved a deep sigh. "No, m'lord, not to see his lordship's back, good riddance."

"Then what more? Uwen?"

"His lordship rid out on Liss."

Tristen had been at an ebb of his energies, and now found himself awake and angry.

"We might send a messenger," Syllan said, "m'lord, and ask her back."

"The stablemaster ain't master Haman," Uwen said glumly. "It's some man the viceroy put in charge, and the damn fool let some boy give him Liss, who's been on the road hard going all yesterday, and if he don't run 'er to ruin in the hour, it'll be a wonder."

"He will *not*," Tristen said. He was never so indignant, and never so sure of a thing. He *saw* a roadway, *felt* the shift in the gray space, felt the world shaken and his breath grown thin. The mare shied away from under her heavy burden, her rider flew over her shoulder, and hoofbeats echoed in the hazy gray.

"M'lord?"

The mare slowed, weary as she was, drew the cold air into her nostrils, and smelled grain and warm straw on the wind out of the west. Footsteps and curses approached her. She shied from reaching hands, turned, bolted off to follow that waft through the dark, freed of weight on her back, freed of spur and rein.

"M'lord?" Uwen said, and the mare, Liss, turned north again, across open meadow.

"Find out," he said to Uwen, against all honor, "find out who is in Edwyll's household, and to whom they send messages."

There was a small silence. Uwen had looked tired and distressed. Now the distress grew. But the understanding was there, too, what was required of him, what the exchange was.

"Yes, m'lord."

"I don't trust even Captain Anwyll in this," he said, and included Syllan, Tawwys and Aran in his glance. "You are my guards. You I trust. Find out everything about Crissand. What is shaken is apt to slide loose. Emuin says so, and he knows. Wizardry will always find that unhappy man, that book on the shelf, that cup too near the edge." To no other Men these days would he have spoken so plainly, but with them he had no longer any doubt. "Guard Meiden. Watch him. Name me all his friends, all his enemies. —And find us all the old servants of this hall, so we afford no more chance for such mistakes. Find master Haman, find Cook, the maids in the kitchens. Find those people, and put them back where they were, and restore the Zeide as it was this summer. There was a boy . . ." He had given orders regarding almost all the world within his power. But thinking of all the potential pieces, he cast back to his first day in Henas'amef, and the boy who had guided him into a trap. There, too, was an element that once had moved to some wizardly direction, and he wanted all such pieces within his ken and under his hand. "Paisi is his name. The gate-guards know him. Tell me when you find him."

"M'lord," Uwen said, and Tawwys, and the rest, with bows of heads and solemn attention.

"He will not keep Liss," Tristen said with equal solemnity.

"Yes, m'lord," Uwen said very quietly.

The dismay had quieted. Or had become better hidden. He had brought Uwen to something very different than Uwen would have ever chosen, and offended against Uwen's sensibilities and Uwen's heart. But he saw no other way for all of them to be safe in Amefel.

He sat, in this strange encampment of his men, in front of a fireplace in a place lately full of dead men.

The mare moved at a walk now, weary and aching in her steps. But she smelled apple trees and thistle. She smelled summer, and the wind continually told her lies.

Tristen wished, if he wished for anything more than a province, a palace, and gold dinnerplates, for master Emuin to be here tonight.

And for Cefwyn to be back in his apartment like the sun in the heaven above.

And for them to wake in the morning with everything put right and no war in the offing.

But Cefwyn was no longer a prince in exile, and he was no longer an innocent, spending his wishes on sunbeams and the flight of a leaf.

He thought of the mare, moving from meadow to a nightbound road. He thought of the silly pigeons of the Zeide roofs, and knew the nooks and crannies of high places, like the secrets of the loft at Ynefel. They came. Dawn might find them here. Owl, too, might be out there somewhere, on this chill night: Owl, bane of pigeons and mice.

He had learned when he was still innocent that one creature of his limited world might destroy another. He had known from the first he could not blame Owl, but he still regretted the deaths of the soft-voiced, silly pigeons. Owl had sat on his perch, alone, beyond the barrier in the loft at Ynefel, and the pigeons had lived on the other side. Owl could not have chosen the company of the pigeons. He was a Shadow, at least among the birds, and he lived in the shadows. If he had ever come to the sunny side and joined the pigeons, they would have fled his presence in a great clap and terror of wings, knowing he was a Shadow.

The men around him had let down their watchfulness, and looked as weary as he had ever seen them. And when all the to and fro of bathing and water-carrying was done and the servants were banished to the hall, Tristen found himself wearier and wearier, the wine cup all but falling from a hand that had wielded a sword in the long, shadow-haunted night . . . that lately bloodied silver-wrapped sword which, like some gray, grim bird of prey, had found itself another lurking place, a new fireside to lean by.

Dared he rest? A seam of daylight showed between two dark velvet curtains, but in this room it was still night. He was aware that Uwen went to the door and spoke to someone and came back. He struggled for wakefulness, watching the fire leap and dance, an element the same in every campfire, every fireplace, and never diminishing until one failed to feed it. Master Emuin had sat by such a fire tonight, cold and complaining, almost certainly.

Emuin had finally reached their camp at Assurnbrook, no further.

—*I am here,* he said to master Emuin; and at last, fearfully, had a sense of presence far away. *I am safe, sir.*

But Emuin seemed fast asleep, despite the daylight outside. He found himself no longer angry, no longer desperate. All decisions were made, and it was to Emuin's dreams he spoke, at a time when the gray space seemed small and cramped and cold.

—*I think of Owl. Have I told you of Owl, sir? I think I have become Owl, in a manner of speaking.*

—*The soldiers with us take good care of me, but among the soldiers, I am Owl.*

—*Even to Uwen, I am Owl, now; and he has no idea what I may do. I think he fears me. He never did, and never have I wished him to.*

—*Earl Edwyll attempted to hold the town against us, did you know? And the earl died, in Lady Orien's apartment. I fear they have all conspired against Cefwyn, each for his own advantage, but I have made them a way to say they never did, so now they will try to make it the truth.*

—*The earl's son surrendered to us, with his men, and he has sworn to me. He likely knows all the men the earl dealt with, on this side of the river and the other. I've set Uwen to find that out. Uwen wishes to protect my innocence. But what of his?*

—*The earl's son, Crissand is his name, called me lord Sihhë in everyone's hearing, and swore to me. I accepted the oath.*

There was quiet, profound quiet in the gray space.

—*And you are afraid, master Emuin. You have been afraid since summer's end, since we won at Lewenbrook and drove Hasufin from the field.*

—*Of what are you afraid? Of the Edge? Is it anything so simple?*

—*Why did you not stay in Guelemara, if you will not answer me? Do you oppose me? You said that you still could.*

—*There might be virtue in that. To the best that I have found, Efanor's little book has no secrets for me. I doubt what I should do. I find no advice in it—or in you, sir.*

—*I wonder whether anything I have ever led Uwen to is good.*

CHAPTER 4

They were not astir until broad day, when the servants arrived with a very late breakfast and an escort of Dragon Guard flung the heavy green draperies back on frost-rimmed windows. The Eagle banner on the gatehouse roof opposite flew straight out in the gusts and fell slack by turns, under a chill blue sky. The servants laid the breakfast, stirred up the embers and put on another set of logs before Tristen and Uwen sat down, each other's sole company, and dismissed both Guelenmen and servants.

Today, Tristen supposed, he must begin dealing with his own set of lords, and with Amefel's peculiar problems. He had never yet visited the garden; he had not seen the library and the places he most valued, and he wished he might sit by the fishpond today, feed the fish and the birds and watch the wind blow, an activity which held no life-and-death decision. It was his reward, his personal and particular reward for duty.

But between the frost on the glass and the banner flying wide, the wind must be blowing with a knife edge today: a bitter wind, a heartless wind. It was a morning for beginnings and rooms swept out and records found and proper men set in charge of things. But it was not a comfortable time to visit old and beloved places.

They were no more than buttering the cold bread when Lusin came breathlessly to say that Liss had turned up at the gates early this morning.

"As her reins are broke, from her treading on them," Lusin said cheerily, "so the boy said, but otherwise she looks to be sound. She come up to the stables outside the wall. And ye'll not guess who found 'er."

"Go down if you wish," Tristen said, seeing Uwen first start to rise from table in delight, and then think better of it.

"I'd ha' thought she'd run to Guelessar," Uwen muttered, and rose with a sketch of a bow. "M'lord, by your leave, will I go, and will ye not go about the halls wi'out me?"

"Go. I'll not go anywhere alone." He needed his breakfast, was weary and aching from bruises this morning, and had no need to see Liss to know that she was there and that she was well enough for having run hard and far these last two days.

Nor was he amazed at Liss running to a stable she hardly knew instead of having drifted east toward the Guelen border or the nearest meadow with a village lord's horse in it. He was happy to watch Uwen go with a boyish gladness in his step and a light in his countenance.

As far as the door. Then Uwen stopped with a sober question.

"Where's his lordship the viceroy, m'lord?"

"Walking to Guelessar, I would suppose." He spoke quite seriously, but Uwen laughed delightedly, slapped his leg, and turned and left at a brisk pace.

Tristen finished buttering a slice of bread, and had raspberry jam. But before he had quite finished it, the curtains being open, he saw a flutter of sunlit wings, a noisy, silly congregation on the stone window ledge. He hurried, then, and rose and took the fragments of his breakfast and the end of the loaf for good measure. He opened the window vent by safe daylight, and all his birds, every one arrived, fluttered and crowded one another to reach the bread.

Vain, silly, dear to him . . . before Lewenbrook, he would have doubted they could possibly find the window, when they had never fed here. But as Liss had found the stables down below the walls, here they were at the right window of all the windows of the Zeide, and he let himself believe he could have his own small pleasures as well as arrange them for others. The sun shone on their backs, touched jewel green on the gray-backed greediest one, who looked at him with a wise, round eye, and then with no hint of shame bullied a violet-tinted gray from the ledge to reach a piece of bread.

"Behave," he said to them, and yet bent no will to it. They were what they were. So were the lords of Ylesuin. Could he, he thought, in far better spirits this morning, reasonably expect them to be other than they had been . . . or ask too much of Amefin districts with ancient rivalries?

The little violet-breasted one was back, and found his breakfast, fighting among the others. The difficulty was the pane and the ledge. It let only one or two at a time come at the bread, and much of the bread fell off during the struggles in the flapping of wings.

Was that, too, not like the great lords?

The servants arrived to take away the breakfast; and Uwen came back, breathless and sober, a commotion striding in with straw on his boots and, oddly, a purse and a writing case in his hand.

"She come back safe, m'lord, which ain't all by half. She come wi' a fine purse of gold an' a writin' case which she had from his lordship, besides she found master Haman, too, who brought her up the hill! His lordship had turned him an' his boys out to the lower stables, an' when Liss come trottin' in wi' her fancy gear and a purse o' gold an' a writin' case, Haman . . . bein' an honest man an' a quick 'un . . . brought 'er right up to the stable-court an' told the guards when we waked we should ha' word of it. On your advice I said he should come back to his old place an' I told the Guard stablemaster take all the Guard remounts down the hill to the outside stables. They was so crowded last night they had Guard horses standin' in the pigsty, to the shame of it, an' all lookin' like the sty itself. Meanwhile Haman's gone to fetch his boys an' there'll be an accountin' o' that in short order. —But here's what Liss' brought wi' her, besides master Haman, and I'll guess his lordship ain't pleased."

The purse Uwen gave him felt as heavy as the one Idrys had given him when he set out to Amefel, and he judged it a reasonable sum for the lord of a province to carry by the only standard he had, so perhaps he should not assume theft . . . but in a man found with a bag of women's jewelry the matter was certainly suspect. The writing case was a cylinder of leather with a cap that held a small container of ink and three clipped and rumpled goose quills, but of greater interest, it held a rolled document, and while Uwen talked on excitedly about master Haman and the stableboys and about Liss having come to the other horses in spite of being a Guelen horse, he unrolled it to see what it was.

It had been sealed in the manner of a letter, but the seal was cut, so it was not a message the viceroy had prepared to take on his journey. It was someone else's letter in Lord Parsynan's possession, presumably already read, but not disposed of.

It said:

*The vacancy of Amefel is filled. His Majesty has
seen fit to appoint the Marshal of Althalen to the
post. Pray advantage yourself of my hospitality when
you reach godly lands.*

Godly lands were, in the Quinalt's way of speaking, any place in
Ylesuin but Amefel. And the Marshal of Althalen was himself.

The letter bore the seal and name of Lord Ryssand, Corswyndam,
least beloved and most troublesome of Cefwyn's northern lords. He
had been close enough to the court in Guelemara to have seen Lord
Corswyndam's countenance *and* his work, and to be very sure he
was not Ninévrisë's friend or Cefwyn's, for that matter.

"Lord Ryssand would seem to invite the viceroy to stay with him
when he comes home to Guelemara," he remarked to Uwen. "Or
possibly to lodge in his hold in Ryssand, since he invites the viceroy
to enjoy his hospitality: Ryssand's lodgings in Guelemara are under
Cefwyn's roof. The letter also seems to advise the viceroy of exactly
what we came to say, but it had to come before we did and perhaps
even before the king's messenger."

"Then he must have rid hard," Uwen said, "and left soon's the
word was out. The king's messengers is steady on the road, but they
most times stop a' nights. I'll wager His Majesty wouldn't like that
letter-writin' in the least. Sendin' a message to somebody ahead of a
king's herald, about the king's business? It ain't right, and probably
it ain't lawful."

"So Corswyndam has been dealing directly with the viceroy, not
telling Cefwyn," Tristen said, and was uneasy in that thought. "If
Corswyndam needs to talk to the viceroy so urgently and privately
as that, I think I should send this letter to Cefwyn to read as soon as
possible."

"I think that were a very good thought," Uwen said. "An' I'll
guess his lordship'll be prayin' to the blessed gods Liss ran home or
strayed into thieves. He won't guess she run back to us. —But he
will be meetin' wi' master Emuin an' the wagons on the road, now,
won't he? And he'll be askin' master Emuin for help and tellin' master Emuin all sorts of lies, won't he, then? Master Emuin might
delay the lord viceroy if he knew the man's doin's, m'lord, just, you
know, gi' 'im a touch o' colic."

It was a clever notion. The wagons held potions and powders enough
to give a troop of men indigestion. But Tristen had ceased to think
master Emuin would prevent anything. There was little hope there.

And if he were to send the message straight to Cefwyn, various hands would handle it, or at least attempt to handle it, from the front gate to the Lord Chamberlain, Annas. Annas was very much to trust . . . but the other hands he did not know, and suspected.

Idrys on the other hand was experienced in matters of misdeed, and the path to the Lord Commander through soldiers' hands he estimated as far less contested.

"This case and the message must reach Idrys," he said to Uwen. "Not His Majesty. And it must go as quickly as possible. The man should only say to Idrys that I thought he should see it. Ryssand doesn't know it's in our hands. He won't know until the viceroy arrives in Guelemara, he may not be sure of it even then, as you say, and by then Idrys will have made plans."

"We might prevent the lord viceroy gettin' there at all, which is surer still. We can send men out after 'im, arrest 'im an' hold 'm against His Majesty's sendin' for 'im."

That, too, was worth a thought. But he decided otherwise. "No. Idrys may prefer to do something else." He wished he were more sure of that opinion; Uwen gave sound advice, on what Uwen knew. "Send the message straight to Idrys. It's the best thing."

"Aye, m'lord," Uwen said, and took the case. "I'll send it, fast as these legs can find a likely man."

Uwen left. The door shut.

Treason, that letter said without a doubt. Any baron of Ylesuin might freely quarrel with a Marhanen king's policy . . . and had done so. But they were *not* free to have private dealings with a man who should report first to Cefwyn, an invitation issued in such haste the duke of Ryssand's messenger had outridden a king's herald.

Did dinner invitations come with such desperate measures?

And was forewarning Parsynan only for the sake of the jewels and other pilferage, or what other thing might a forewarning have advised Parsynan to do?

To pack . . . and to arrange things for his absence . . .

To lay traps? To remove certain things? Parsynan had tried to take the jewels, surely for his own benefit; had taken a sizable sum of gold; *and* a message, perhaps to prove to servants and guards his right to access Lord Ryssand without delay and perhaps in secret, or to prove to others Lord Ryssand had written to him. That was the only use he could construe for it; and his own working had surely snarled Lord Parsynan's affairs, top to bottom. He wished he might do the same for Lord Ryssand.

He watched his pigeons, lately combatants on the ledge, green-coat and violet-breast walking separately, having chased off the others, and thought that he never should have left Cefwyn. He thought it so desperately he almost dared attempt to reach Her Grace herself with a message, but Ninévrisë's gift was so small, the distance so great, the danger in the gray space so insistent that he backed away from the attempt in haste. No, that was not wise.

By now the barons Cefwyn detested had compelled Cefwyn to take back Sulriggan. Dared he hope a horse threw the lord of Llymaryn as well as the lord viceroy? Perhaps Lord Corswyndam, too . . . a kingdomwide plague of ill-behaving horses, perhaps . . . was it wicked to imagine it? It was certainly to his liking. To Cefwyn's good he could wish all the barons' horses might be wild and unbiddable. So with all Cefwyn's troublesome lords.

But he checked himself abruptly, asking himself what would Mauryl say? What would Emuin? Yet, yet if men conspired behind their lawful monarch's back . . . did a sworn friend's virtue dictate letting them pursue their harmful work unscathed? If men must take harm, Ryssand and Parsynan were deserving of it, were they not? If Duke Corswyndam slipped on the stairs and no worse than went to his bed for a fortnight, Cefwyn might have a chance to read this letter and deal with Parsynan, and do justice for the house of Meiden.

Had he not sworn to do justice when he swore fealty to Cefwyn? And would that not satisfy it?

But to wish harm on others was wicked even to think of, was it not?

When he thought of it, he had left Mauryl's care and walked into the world with no real knowledge of Wickedness, and Emuin had taught him very little of it. When the dark doings of ordinary Men Unfolded to him, they Unfolded not so much a blazoned banner of Evil as a tattered quilt of Misdeed, all far from the clear understanding he would have wished to gain of Good and Evil. Hasufin might have been evil . . . but did not lords prosper their own folk and strive against rivals quite commonly? He failed to see wherein Hasufin was worse than Cefwyn's grandfather.

And while Wickedness and Evil were abundant in Efanor's little book, and he could read that the gods disliked both, whence came Wickedness in the first place, if the gods created all the world? Did they create something they detested, along with the mountains and the rivers? Efanor's book informed him of nothing on that score, except to say that Men and their works were wholly evil, but some were good . . . very like Emuin's defining the length of autumn to him. So it seemed to come down to Efanor's advice, and Efanor's little book and an amulet of silver and sheep's blood . . . which was to say, nothing.

Perhaps he should have taken Uwen's advice in the absence of wizardly counsel. Perhaps he should yet show Emuin that document, and ask Emuin what to do, before it ever came to Idrys' grim actions.

Yet dared he cast responsibility on Emuin, who spent so much effort avoiding it?

No, that was not fair, or true. Emuin spent his effort avoiding responsibility for *him*, and that was a far, far different thing. Emuin wanted little done. There was a certain wisdom in doing little, when one was obliged to act in ignorance.

His own ignorance, however, was not so wide as it once had been . . . and his will to act, accordingly, was wider than it had been this summer.

He waited, watching the roofs of Henas'amef from the window bordered in frost and green curtains, watching the pigeons. In time Uwen came back from his mission.

"The captain's sendin' Lyn, who's a reliable man, won't be no stoppin' in the High Street tavern wi' Lyn; and Haman's picked a fine pair of horses from the stables for 'im. He'll be dust again' the sky soon as ye can wish, and I give him orders to ride right past th' viceroy like a bird on the wing. But are ye sure about master Emuin? Shouldn't ye warn 'im, lad, at least instruct 'im t' gi' that man the worst horse he can lay hands on?"

Uwen was a clever man, and in part he thought yes. At least enlist Emuin's help whether he saw the message or not.

But to tempt Emuin to act against his judgment . . .

"No," he said. "No. Ride through. The viceroy will lie. If Emuin will not hear *me* in the gray space, he will hardly be happier to have a message other men can see. Lyn should ride past and not stop. That may worry master Emuin," he added on a sober thought; and then said in some lingering vexation, "But if it does, perhaps he'll suspect the viceroy's story entirely and make some haste to reach us."

"Aye, m'lord."

Uwen left again in great haste and in no long space after Uwen had had time to reach the front stairs came the clatter of a rider headed out across the South Courtyard and out the South Gate.

So Liss had brought them a gift the lord viceroy would pay all his gold not to have in Idrys' hands. And master Haman had turned up.

That was good, too, though Tristen found himself not in the least surprised, only a little fearful for the broad scope of his decisions and at the same time expecting more such threads of Amefel-as-it-was to come into his hands.

Petelly had his old stall back, Tristen found as he walked into the stables in a quieter hour of the mid-afternoon. There were no apples in the barrel, there was dirty straw and manure scattered in the aisle, a disgraceful state of affairs, and Haman, newly arrived back in his domain, was shouting about horse brushes and pilfered halters when he and Uwen came in. "Bandits!" Haman cried.

But master Haman hurried over to him as he patted Petelly's offered nose, Gia thrusting her head out of her next-door stall to watch. "Your Grace," Haman said. "Gods bless Your Grace, these stables will be back in order as quick as we can move. We were never so glad in our lives, m'lord, as when we heard ye'd remembered us."

Master Haman was greatly moved, his weathered face showing more tender passion than its habitual lines had graven in it, and meanwhile boys with buckets and manure forks and barrows were in rapid movement up and down the aisle, evidence that with master Haman in charge the horses' welfare would never be a concern. Uwen reported Dys was down in the lower stables with Aswys. So was Cassam. Gia was down, too, for rest, with Gery. But Liss had a red ribbon braided into her forelock, and was curried so she shone.

"Well-done," he said, "very well done." And as he was walking out with Uwen, to the inspection of the rest of the yard, lo! there was Cook marching in by the West Gate bearing a ladle in her fist like a battle mace, and in her train, a number of the scullery maids bearing along pots and kettles. Two of the Dragon Guard, on horse-back, improbably brought up the rear.

"The cook and the three maids was all found at Silver Street, m'lord," a guardsman said with a salute. "The pots were hidden in the gatehouse cistern."

"M'lord!" Cook said with a deep curtsy, and so all the maids bobbed down and up in rapid succession, their faces all consternation.

"Why were the pots hidden?" Tristen could not forbear asking.

"So's they weren't stolen, m'lord," Cook said with another curtsy, "as the viceroy turned us out for puttin' his Guard layabouts out o' the scullery." This with a fierce look. "They turn't me out, an' the lads, too, an' so we hid the good copper pots in the cistern, an' since then they hain't had a kettle but the great one that's hard to shift. Here's all the fine spoons, too." At that a maid tipped the pot she carried, and there were, indeed, spoons. "We come back ourselves like honest folk an' reported to the Guard about the pots."

"You'll take great care," Tristen said. "Earl Edwyll died of poison Lady Orien left. Be very careful of the stores. And I have missed the pies."

"That I will, m'lord! That I will indeed! An' pies you shall have, m'lord!" Cook's broad face splotched when she was distraught, or now when she seemed happy. "Gods bless, gods bless, an' a long life to Your Grace."

He feared she had broken the law by taking the pots and the spoons, but justice required his not seeing it. "Let them free," he instructed the guards. "They'll set the kitchen in order. —I suppose the scullery lads will turn up in due course," he said to Uwen.

"I've no doubt. Word's out that ye want the old staff, an' they're turnin' up by twos and threes an' by troops and regiments. We sent word out, too, that ye want the gate wardens o' th' West back, but Ness says they're fair scairt, on account of layin' violent hands on ye this summer."

"Say they should come. I'm not angry."

"'At's what I said to Ness." Uwen shook his head. "An' I'll say again. We'll find 'em."

"Your Grace." A clerk had been hovering at the edge of his vision for the last several moments, the clerk who had ridden with them, distressed and in the company of a Guelen guardsman. "Your Grace. If Your Grace could spare a moment . . ."

Tristen paused to listen, and the clerk bowed again. But it was the guardsman who spoke:

"There's letters burnt, your lordship, and a dead man in the library."

He had asked himself what such a man as Parsynan would choose to do, given advance warning. He delayed not at all, but strode off, himself, Uwen, Syllan, and Tawwys with him. "What sort of letters?" he asked the clerk. "Are they entirely burned? Can you make anything of them?"

"A book of record, a record of some kind, perhaps of the very letters." The man was all but trembling. "And a man who may be the archivist, dead, beneath a table. No one had been in there with the fighting and all, and I came in to build a fire myself, the servants not answering; I never even saw the dead man, Your Grace, until I saw the scroll ends in the fireplace, and he was right beside me. Right beside me!"

"Stabbed?" Uwen asked.

"No blood," the guardsman said. "An' the book in the fireplace, m'lord, and the scroll ends. It seemed your lordship should know."

"We ain't let anyone into any place we ain't searched," Uwen said, "even yet. Have ye seen the archivists, either one, man?"

"Neither." The clerk hitched a double step keeping up with them as they climbed the stable-court stairs. "Unless this is one. It's an old man."

"It might be," Tristen said, as they passed the doors. The way to the archive took them past the lesser hall, and behind the central stairs, into the back hallway.

There were two guards posted over the archive, which ended that hallway, past the garden windows, guards who came to attention and opened the door without question.

Codices were not shelved, but piled on tables. Scrolls were stacked, not in their columbaria, and when he walked to the far side of the room the fireplace that provided warmth to the library indeed held the ends of scrolls and the burned spine of a codex.

"Here's scoundrels' work for certain," Uwen said, and Tristen surveyed the calamity, and the body of the man recently dead, a tangle of robes and white hair curled up as if for sleep, beside a heavy chair and partially concealed by the adjacent reading table.

"This is the senior archivist. There were two."

"There's just the one, Your Grace," the sergeant said, and pointed into the shadows, to a hole the table shadowed. The plastered masonry had been taken apart, revealing a hiding place.

"Find the other archivist," Tristen said, wanting that very much, but finding it far less readily accessible than Liss . . . and it was not because of his not knowing the man. The two who had worked here were both old men, both quarreled with each other bitterly. Now they were one dead, the other fled; and there was no apparent reason except Amefin business, the sort of which this archive kept account. It was not likely Lord Parsynan's correspondence in the fire: there was no reason for Parsynan to store in the archive any letter he wished kept secret and there was no reason to chisel it out of a wall. It might be a certain portion of Lord Heryn's archive. Cefwyn had ordered that sent to Guelemara, along with unique books of history and record, but there might have been something concealed.

"There's nothing left," the clerk said, stooping to pick up the burned remnant of the book. He opened it to show only the margin and a handful of words, and charred parchment flaked away in his careless handling. Tristen knelt at the fireplace, carefully extracted the browned yet unburned end of a parchment. It was blank, a margin edge. "Your Grace will soot his hands," the clerk said, but Tristen reached in among ashes warm at their heart and another, which had burned up and down its length, but which had the scroll top at its heart—crumbling ash, for the most part, and the wax of the seals had surely fed the fire that consumed it.

The salutation was still legible: *to the aetheling. . . .*

He walked to the window, where there was more light, and pried further, into charred black whereon the ink was gray. He made out the words *Althalen* and *Gestaurien . . .*

And he knew the spidery hand. He had seen it every day in Ynefel. He had watched Mauryl write and cipher, day after day, endlessly at his work.

The charred portion fell away in his fingers. *Gestaurien* vanished in soot and fragments.

He stood shaken, grieved and angry.

"I want the archivist," he said, but even knowing that the Guard had had the town gates shut last night and watched the traffic there carefully today, there was no warning to watch for an elderly, unarmed man. "Find me a box. Now."

"Find his lordship a box!" the sergeant said, but the clerk, hurrying to redeem himself, turned a scroll lectern upside down, and Tristen knelt and carefully laid the fragments in the box it made, piece by treasured piece, as he had never had the chance to collect anything from Ynefel but Mauryl's direct gifts.

And why these now lay with a dead man he could only half guess: that they were potent, yes; that the archivists had always known they were here, likely; that they wanted to come to him now, conceivable; that someone would have wished to prevent that, understandable.

But did humble archivists turn and murder one another and destroy their charge?

It was conceivable these exceeded what a man could conceal about his person, if he had turned thief. Or they might be all. *Find the archivist,* was the burden of his thought, but it went out into the gray and lost itself in a town full of similar men, similar lives, only a few that sparked fire, and those nothing, nothing to do with this act.

One was surely Crissand. About that one he felt a pang of grief, felt the cold of stone. One was in the East Court, likewise within stone, likely a priest. One was about some business he could not define. But more subtle, like a fish slipping through sunlit ripples, invisible, something else flicked past his notice.

And *that* something flickered off toward the east, toward Emuin, toward the monastery, toward Guelessar.

Beware, he wished Emuin, and all at once rued his decision not to warn Emuin regarding either the message from Ryssand or the messenger to Idrys. He knelt with ruin in his hands and willed it mended, but only a flickering presence answered him, undefined, flickering hither and thither through his recollections, difficult to catch, wary, wily, and not without complicity . . . he felt so.

The clerk's face was pale in the sunlight from the windows and utterly sober. "Your Grace," the young man whispered fearfully. "If I could have been here sooner, last night . . ."

But the clerk had been in hall, reading the documents. The archivists were entrusted with the integrity of this place. And guards had been at the door . . . what more could a clerk do, where wizards failed? The deed was done, the second archivist had fled with whatever he had taken away, and Tristen much doubted they would find the man within the town.

Uwen said not a thing. But the sergeant from the detail at the door stood by fretting in silence, as if he, too, were somehow at fault. "Syllan," Tristen said, and gave him the burned fragments in their contrived container. "Take this to my quarters, gently, very gently, and be careful of drafts."

"My lord," Syllan said, and took it away, leaving them the archivist and the cavity in the wall. The industrious sergeant looked into it. But it proved empty.

But was the aetheling to whom Mauryl might have once written Lord Heryn? Mauryl had lived long, very long, and all those years might have been in these scrolls, decades of messages flowing between the Warden of Ynefel and the aetheling of Amefel, or things older still.

This entire place had been ordered only as much as Mauryl's papers, or Emuin's, which was to say, not at all . . . and quite unlike the orderly arrangement in that of Guelemara. He had seen the latter, and knew at a single stroke he looked on a library that, like a wizard's papers, concealed, rather than revealed. The two archivists had detested one another and come to their final disagreement. It was by no means certain that the thief had destroyed all there was of Mauryl's letters: he could not have left unseen with a great many records. If he had taken anything away with him, it would have been the choicest, or at least the one a Man would most value.

He had ordered a search. He had saved the fragments, for what sharp eyes could learn from them. The junior clerk was too heavy-handed; he awaited the senior, with Emuin.

But hope of finding the thief? It was small. If Mauryl's work wanted to be found, he would warrant it might be; or if lost, it would be that. He very much doubted a second archivist appointed by Heryn Aswydd could have contrived such a theft on his own.

Where fled?

Across the river, perhaps. But the gray space gave no clues but eastward, eastward, eastward, not toward the river, but toward Assurnbrook. And he stayed very still, not reaching further against resistance. Neither did Emuin.

The Aswydd's archivist, the thief was, after all.

Uwen came up to stand by him. "Were it wizard-work?" Uwen asked in a low voice. "Is there some danger?"

"None. I think, none. They were old letters, 't was all. I suspect the archivists hid them from the Quinalt, from Cefwyn's clerks. I suspect there were more of them and the clerk took the choicest to whatever place he's fled. —But murder. Murder is far too much for fear. Here was anger, a great anger."

"Wouldn't be the first time two old men had a fallin' out."

He stared at the shadows, at the base of the wall where dark flowed, beneath the tables, around the cabinets, within the wall. There was anger still here, but a muted, sorrowful anger.

"Find a mason," he said, "and repair the wall. Make it sound again. Hear me. Do it today, before the sun sets."

"Aye, m'lord," Uwen said, and went and gave that order to the Guelen sergeant.

Tristen, meanwhile, stared out low windows that overlooked a walk that led to a gate, and through that gate was the other place he treasured, seen dimly, through inside glass no servant had cleaned in years. He saw leafless trees, brown, weed-choked beds on the approach to that gate. And he thought of summer.

"Bury the man," he said, turning about. "Have the windows cleaned." They looked never to have been, in the regular upkeep of the Zeide, as if servants were forbidden here. "You," he said to the Guelen clerk, "stand in charge of the archive. Set all this to rights.

Account of what's here, books of record and books of knowledge, letters, deeds, and whatever else exists here."

"Your lordship," the man said. The clerk stood still and stunned, amidst a library its keepers had set in deliberate disorder. But the clerks yet to come had other things to do, a province and its records, most of which were in this disorder. He had one man, one, to begin the work, and begin it must, before other things vanished.

Tristen walked out the doors then, to the thump of a guard salute at the doors. Uwen and Tawwys trod close at his heels, never asking what he had read, or why he had ordered the ashes taken upstairs. He invited neither converse nor solace. He was distressed—knew he was angry, but not at whom: at the vanished archivist, perhaps; at Parsynan's destruction, assuredly; at Emuin, possibly; even at Mauryl, remotely; knew he was afraid—of the scope of the disorder he perceived, certainly; of the disturbance he felt in the gray space, very much so; and of wizardly desertions, absolutely and helplessly.

It was not a conscious thought that sent him toward the doors midway of the short corridor: it was the desire of his heart; it was a flight for rescue in the place that had always given him shelter. The opening of that door brought a flood of icy outside air; and the few steps set him and his guards under a sky clouded and changed from the dawn.

He had come back to the garden . . . at last, was back in the place that he most enjoyed of all places, a place of winding paths, low evergreen, well-shaped trees, and summer shade.

Indeed, he found in its heart the same neglect he had seen from the library windows, the herbs and flowers brown and dead as everything in the countryside . . . but he was not surprised. The trees were bare. That was only autumn. Understandably the walks were deserted: the wind blew cold across the walls, two of which were the building itself, and one of which was the library walk; and the other, a low one, it shared with the stable-court. It, at least, was not plundered, and held no dead men or vengeful shadows nor scars of yesterday's fighting. He had found one thing unharmed, untouched, undamaged. And it was the most priceless thing of all.

He walked to the edge of the pond. Fragments of leaves studded the gravel rim, but the tame fish that lived in the pond were still there, still safe . . . thinner than their wont, but safe.

"No one's fed them," he said.

"They sleep in th' cold," Uwen said. "But I'll ask, m'lord. There's things to tidy here."

"Will they die if the water freezes?"

"I'll imagine they stay here all the year," Uwen said, looking around him, "but these beds is to dig an' turn two months ago, says this man what was once a farmer, and that says to me there's gardeners gone wi' the rest of the servants and not yet at work here, maybe gone back to kinfolk an' farms 'round about. We'll find 'em, don't ye fret, lad."

He was very glad Uwen called him that. Uwen was as distressed about the library as Uwen could imagine to be, and after a breath or two of watching the water Tristen put aside all anger with the guard, or with the clerk, or anyone remotely involved with the disaster. The brightly clad ladies and lords of the summer would come back like the singing birds, when the days grew warm again. Things that he remembered *would* come again and the year-circle would meet itself in this place of all places.

Here he could believe in his summer of innocence. He could remember the trees of this garden as green and thick-leaved and whispering to the wind . . . and that was an archive as important, as intricately written, and as potent for him as the library. This place, failing all others in the Zeide, gave him a staying place for his heart, his imaginings, his wishing—his outright magic if ever Sihhë magic resided in him . . . he watched a few of his silly pigeons who had lighted on the walk, pursuing their business with their odd gait, feathers ruffling in the wind.

In this place, most of all, he cherished fragile things. And was it a loss, that of Mauryl's letters? It likely was. It likely was a great loss. But in a way it kept things orderly . . . kept lives in their own places, as Mauryl's place and time was Ynefel, where everything was brown and full of dust, cobwebs, and ruin. It had held such a secret place, in the loft . . . but that was gone; and with it went Ynefel, and Mauryl.

Now, standing in this garden brown with autumn, he wished this place to be again the way he had seen it, a green heart in the ancient stones. It came to him that something of the kind had always been here, must be here, from the time the Masons laid down the Lines of the garden wall and built the building.

But, too . . . he had never understood until he had seen the Holy Father misconstruing a Line . . . there had been the gardeners' work, patient over centuries, and the servants' work, and all the people who had laid loving hands on the earth and the walls of the Zeide . . . all of them had gone on establishing those Lines by their simple acts, daily repeated, and strong as any wizard's ward.

Were not Masons common Men? And did not they work magic? And might not gardeners?

He had come here to Rule, and to Defend a land against harm, and within its limits as within this garden, he realized himself defended by all these living hands, all these servants, this people, these guards. And when he wished it safe, strength underlay it as dry, deserted Ynefel had had none of that within it at all but the mice, the pigeons, and Owl. He had not expected to *be* defended, but he was. He breathed it in, he felt it under his feet and around him and he sat down on the stone bench, the Unfolding was that strong. To disguise his confusion he bent and tossed in a pebble from the side of the pond. The fish, chilled as Uwen said, scarcely moved, but the ripples went out. Under the gray-shining surface, even through winter ice, the fish would live and wait, enduring through the death that was around them.

Crissand, he thought. Crissand. *Crissand.*

He will come here, he thought for no reason. Not today, perhaps, but he will come in his own time. He must. He is mine, as no one, even Uwen, even Cefwyn, has ever been . . . as this place is mine, and all who have their lives here.

The wind, meanwhile, was cold, and riffled the surface of the pond, blew at their cloaks and chilled to the bone.

A wisp of something flew on the wind. It was ash from the kitchen fire, he thought at first as he looked up. But he saw another, and another.

"Snow," Syllan remarked, looking up at the gray sky. "Here's snow, m'lord."

He looked up, too, and saw the snow fly across the dark evergreens. He saw one snowflake land on his sleeve, and marveled at it, how delicate it was.

Delicate and beautiful, and many, many of them would turn all the land white. He caught them on his glove, jewels of differing structure, and it Unfolded to him that the shapes were numberless and nameless. They melted to nothing, but more kept falling.

He was aware almost at the same instant of a pitching wagon, and a trace of snow across the backs of oxen, and it was gone like a wisp of a thought, with a surly unpleasantness.

Master Emuin, in great discomfort, and at long last, was making an urgent effort to reach Henas'amef and wished him to know it.

CHAPTER 5

Wisps of white flew on the wind, past windows gone cold and lifeless—two days of spitting snow and bitter wind had done no more than frost the edges of the slates, and the few remaining pigeons walked, disconsolate, on the adjacent roof.

Amazing how a presence never frequent could be so missed in a man's life or how eerie the lack of pigeons could seem. Perhaps the loss and the omen felt more grievous since the weather had set in cold and gray as it had. But with nothing but that loss outside, Cefwyn avoided looking out the windows, while his restless pacing delivered him to their vicinity every time he set himself on his feet.

He will be at Assurnbrook, Cefwyn had thought on one morning, and on this one, *he should be arriving in Henas'amef today, bag and baggage and master Emuin. He'll be safe now and so will Emuin. Gods save us all.*

"Your Majesty." Idrys, black shadow that he was, had been absent with some business at the door—servants came and went—or had gone out for a time; Cefwyn had no idea which. Now the Lord Commander intruded, grim and businesslike. "His Grace of Murandys with a petition."

"Outside?" He almost welcomed distraction.

"In the hall downstairs, whence he hopes to be summoned to your presence, he, with Ryssand's son, bearing a petition."

He had rather most men in the kingdom than Murandys, and

Murandys before Brugan, Ryssand's arrant ox of a son. But today even that distraction tempted him. "Regarding?"

Idrys' eyes darted to a stray page who had ventured into this, the gold room, which had the map tables, and in which the pages were never permitted.

"Out!" Cefwyn said, and the page darted for the door, turned, bowed.

"But Her Grace sent a message," the page blurted out, and bowed again, and ducked about, ready to flee.

"Stay! Give it me!"

"Your Majesty!" the page said, white-faced, and offered the rolled, sealed paper to his hand. Relieved of it, the boy fled, and sped left and right around a priceless orrery.

"Damned boys," Cefwyn said then. "*That* is a new one. From Panys. They rattle about in this great place and bounce off the walls and furnishings."

"The consequences of majesty," Idrys muttered. "Likewise this petition in the downstairs hall."

"Regarding?" It occurred to him they had just been at that point, before Ninévrisë's messenger had come to him (a messenger, because neither the consort-to-be nor the lord of Murandys could approach the king uninvited, but a towheaded child could.) He felt constrained, trapped, surrounded. "Sulriggan can't be here yet. So, pray, what have we? Murandys and his damned salt fish? A petition from young Brugan to be first across the bridges come spring?"

"Murandys on behalf of others, and would it were so pleasant as that." Idrys' face was glum. "I have not gotten a copy of this document, which was composed in close secret, I suspect, in the Quinaltine, by elements aside from the Holy Father, notably Ryssand's priest, and Romynd of Murandys. I pray you, my lord king, not to sign that document nor invite Murandys himself today. Ask only for the document. What little I do know suggests traps in it. Numerous ones. And priests are behind it."

When Idrys said so in that tone of voice, it was time to break out the battle gear. "Aiming at what?"

"Ultimately? Your Majesty's endorsement of the Quinalt over all religious orders."

"They dare."

"Not yet, but will dare. One clause, if you please, regards revenues. The *regularization* of the Crown's annual gift to a set sum."

"Two pence if they press me!"

"More. They wish a Quinalt presence assured *in Her Grace's* provinces."

"Kingdom!"

"This is the wording, as best I know. It has a clause . . ." Idrys hesitated. And that meant it was very objectionable. ". . . accepting Her Grace as a prince within the Quinalt domain."

"Sovereign ruler." They had battled out that phrase in treaty. And now did this petition deny it? "Damn them!"

"The Holy Father, lately trembling in disfavor, has stayed behind in the Quinaltine and let only a cat's-paw bring this infamous document. I'm sure His Holiness would wish Your Majesty at least to notice his brave act of loyalty."

"Oh, aye! Whose lunacy is this?"

"The blunt fact is, His Holiness cannot rein in his priests and I think if he dared write Your Majesty a plea for help, he would. His acceptance of Your Majesty's terms has weakened his voice where it regards certain elements. That is serious for peace within the Quinaltine."

"Six days," Cefwyn said. "Six days, and I am wed and then heads will be in jeopardy, gods blast Murandys and Ryssand!"

"I fear the Holy Father has the orthodoxy sniffing round his money chests, his private library, and his closets. The danger to him is real, Your Majesty. Ryssand has suborned his private priests, and joined those who do not favor the Patriarch. This petition has perched at your door with an importune, pious lord, aching for his sins, concerned for the realm's descent into wizardous influences, suspicious of the victory at Lewenbrook, and above all Her Grace's Bryalt priest, if Your Highness wishes to know what's set the fox into the henyard in the Quinalt. The orthodoxy inside the Quinalt is counting the days, knows your disposition toward them, and they will grasp at any straw. I have not been able to secure a copy of this document; all I have is rumor. But it may even be a petition for a Convocation of the Council. I believe a threat is mounting against the Holy Father, aided by Ryssand and Murandys. In this, gods attend, *Sulriggan* may be Your Majesty's ally, if weather doesn't preclude his getting here; he may be a defense to the Patriarch. In the meanwhile I wish to have a look at this petition before Your Majesty contemplates an audience for its bearers and certainly before Your Majesty formally receives it."

In former days, in his dissolute princehood, he would call for wine and women of the enemy's ambitious kinship . . . or their hire. He would sink himself in an unavailability trembling toward an absolute incapacity to do what his besiegers wished, while abed with their precious, perfumed influences . . . leading them on with such hope, and never performance.

"Sober modesty has many disadvantages," he remarked to Idrys, who alone of all men but Annas would know precisely what he meant. "So does negotiating with celibate *priests.*"

"Call Luriel to court. That news will discommode her uncle, and distract him. Her presence, even more so. And her acceptance by Your Majesty would certainly distract him."

Imply a liaison or feign one, on the very eve of his wedding? Torment Murandys between the hope of influence and the fear of disgrace? Redeem the slight to Luriel, restore her value to her uncle?

He drew a long breath and asked himself whether Ninévrisë would possibly, remotely condone it.

But no, his bride was wise and she was tolerant and she was even canny enough she might agree in complete understanding and for the welfare of her kingdom; but he could not subject her to Guelen scorn, he could not have her pride assaulted by whispers and he could not enter Elwynor in the spring with her people resenting the slight thus done their Lady Regent. Every hint of scandal would come back in bloodshed, Guelen and Elwynim alike. Luriel's ability to place her uncle in untenable positions had been her delight and his in times past; he was very sure Murandys had not brought that hellion to halter, disgraced as she had made herself. But she and he had had their falling-out, and he could not use her in the old way.

Tempting, though, the very thought of Murandys' agonized hope . . . and consternation.

"I cannot be the wastrel prince any longer." A deep sigh, and a scowl. "I cannot be Efanor and sink myself in holiness, either."

"Then you must be the king," Idrys said with brutal truth.

"That I must."

"Then make them love you or make them fear you. If you are king, you cannot go by halves of it."

"Love!"

"Unlikely as it might be."

"They *love* their own advantage, master crow."

"And love their wives and sons and daughters, love their comforts, their—"

"Their horses, their hounds and hawks and mistresses, but I can hardly be a horse or a hound, can I, master crow?"

"Nor hawk, nor mistress to Ryssand or these zealots. No more can His Holiness. To have these zealots in the ascendant would be as much a calamity for His Holiness as for you. But point it out to him and you may have his assistance with Corswyndam now that the ledge above his steps is less trafficked. You have accommodated him. Now charge him the fee."

He laughed, not a pleasant laugh, but pained and boding ill for Ryssand. And thanked the gods Idrys still confronted him when he needed a contrary, disagreeable voice.

"Tristen having left," Cefwyn said. "Who would have thought it would make such a silence in the town?"

"Why, no gossip, no rumors, no whisper," Idrys said, hands tucked comfortably behind him as the gray sunlight fell coldly on them both. "The town is still amazed to silence, considering his departure."

"Would it had been Murandys."

"The old dog's whelp hunts no better than the sire, my lord king, or I might suggest a horse might startle this very afternoon with fatal result."

A fortunate accident. But young Brugan would then succeed Corswyndam to the duchy of Ryssand, and Brugan was a greedy fool.

Maybe, again, and on the other hand, a fool was better, to rule troublesome Ryssand.

He pondered all its advantages, and pondered, too, the folly of a weak king.

"I am not yet my grandfather," he said with some resolve. And added, in brutal honesty. "And the son being worse than Corswyndam, a young and intemperate fool as well as ambitious, he saves my virtue. I wouldn't stick at removing the father, if it weren't for needing Corswyndam's experience at the river next spring. Brugan would have his contingent slaughtered to a man in the first hour. Gods, *gods!* I fear fools!"

"So will you send for Luriel?"

Idrys' jokes were frequently grim. And provoked him to short, brittle laughter. "Oh, aye. With trumpets."

"My lord king has a vast population of fools to draw on."

"She is less a fool than her uncle. She was young, she was too confident, too ambitious by half. She will not be queen. But she will not lack for suitors, or for power. *Yes,* send for her. By royal command. I *warned* Murandys, and now he has the result of it."

"Shall I go down and ask him for the petition, saying I will send it to the clerks to read? That might take a number of days."

"No! Say I am taken with headache and will retire. I have given no orders, nor permitted my chamberlain nor any officer to accept anything in my name."

"That will serve for today. There is tomorrow. And I am curious about the content."

"Tomorrow I see my tailor. I must see my tailor. I find the coat too snug. It's a calamity. And the day after . . . I'll think of it tomorrow. Damn them!" He found his spirits entirely fallen. He imagined all manner of ills before the wedding, and longed to take to his bed and claim headache for all the six days intervening.

But then the gossips would be taking omens by that, declaring the king was ill, joyfully arranging the succession.

It was one more round, one more attempt to delay the wedding, this time with priests and subclauses.

"Go bid Murandys and the young fool wait for the audience day. I have a headache and a meeting with my tailor. Can a bridegroom be expected to think of revenues? Suggest so, at least. —Suggest to Panys I may seek a match for his eligible son. A royal whim."

"Your Majesty," Idrys said, and left with satisfaction evident.

It was done. They were besieged, but the walls held firm. And with Sulriggan doubtless to arrive and with Idrys bound to send letters to Murandys' niece, one might trust intervention might precede the snows . . . trifling snows, Cefwyn judged, looking out the window he avoided, not enough to prevent Sulriggan reaching the trough of money and power, not enough to prevent Lady Luriel from reaching court . . . oh, the quandary the lady would be in: an invitation, and last year's wardrobe.

Was it only last year that he had danced with Luriel?

The wax had poured thickly onto the little scroll and it was bound about with enough ribbon for a state document. He took his dagger to it, and scattered the rim of the map table with shattered sealing wax and bits of ribbon. It was wrapped about with a vengeance, no simple slitting of strings, Ninévrisë's intent to necessitate destruction no spy could repair.

I love you, it began, as all her messages began. Then:

"His Highness," a page said, a high, childish voice. "And the duke of Ivanor."

Efanor, with *Cevulirn*?

There was consternation in the hall. Even the prince did not burst through into the king's map room uninvited, and Efanor and Cevulirn trailed an outcry of pages.

Cefwyn waved a hand, permitted the intrusion, and the pages stopped.

Efanor shut the door in their faces, faced him, with Cevulirn, grim-faced.

"They have a petition against Her Grace."

"Quinalt rights in Elwynor. Idrys informed me so."

Efanor paused for two breaths, and his shoulders fell. "But did Idrys say what's *not* in the petition?"

"What is *not* in the petition?"

Efanor caught a breath and failed to say.

"Infidelity," Cevulirn said quietly.

"Cleisynde," Efanor said. "Cevulirn had a message from Prichwarrin's niece. They have a witness, and they will make the charge public."

Efanor might have said more. He failed to hear it for the moment, turned away and remembered the letter in his hands.

> *Artisane does not scruple to lie. Henceforth she is my enemy. I am beset and alone, and trust not even the page who brings you this message, except Dame Margolis says he is an honest boy. I fear what may reach you. Be assured of my love.*

"Damn them all!" He thrust the message into his belt and strode for the door.

"Brother!" Efanor said, attempting to block the door, to no avail. He ripped it open.

"Annas! Fetch Idrys!"

Pages ran.

"Your Majesty," Cevulirn said, a low voice he regarded of past experience. "The proof rests with Ryssand's daughter Artisane, who is prepared to swear."

Idrys failed to appear. Annas, however, was as quick as aged legs could carry him.

"The page."

"Her Grace's page?"

"The very."

"Has left, my lord king, frightened out of his wits, to look at him. Was there a reply to be sent, after all? Shall a boy carry it?"

"No! Is Murandys still in the lower hall?"

"I've no idea, Your Majesty, but I'll inquire."

"If he's left, find him! If he's not left, *I'll* find him! This will *not* stand! Gods blast that fox-faced girl!"

"Cefwyn!" Efanor said. "Temper will not serve, here!"

"It served our grandfather, and it will serve me!" He was out the door, and they followed, both. He walked through a startled scatter of pages and servants, past the tall windows, gathered on his coat and swept up the full complement of guards as he left, his, Efanor's, and Cevulirn's two men.

No furtive, ill-reported visitation, this, but a thumping, rattling collection of men and weapons as the king went downstairs. Guards at the stairs came to attention. The hall showed vacant.

"I'll have the lord of Murandys!" he shouted to the hall in general, waking echoes. "And his damned petition! And Ryssand! *Find him!*"

Men ran. He stood on the steps, and Idrys arrived, saw the tenor of things and asked no questions of him, nor did a thing but stand to the side.

And in not many moments came the tread of Murandys and a ducal entourage from the east end of the hall, servants scattering like mice along their route, finding niches that took them aside from the course of confrontation.

Murandys had the petition, a parchment trailing ribbons. He had Brugan beside him.

"Your Majesty," Murandys began, proffering the document. "Herein—"

Cefwyn struck it from Prichwarrin's hand. It rattled some distance, and Prichwarrin stared at him in shock.

"Your Majesty surely is misled," Prichwarrin said, tucking his hand against him. His face was white . . . he was not a young man. "This petition for the welfare of the realm and the Holy Quinalt . . ."

". . . is a sham. And a treasonous sham to boot."

"Never so, Your Majesty."

"You press me much too far, Murandys. Have a care to your neck. A lord is not immune."

"These things must be settled before the wedding. They are essential—"

"No. They are not. The pigs may enjoy your petition, and beware lest I send you to feed it to them."

"Your Majesty *is* misled," Brugan said, looming over most of the guards in attendance, and full of confidence. "And if there's misleading, my sister witnessed it. Midnight visitations. Her Grace calling out at night after the lord of Ynefel . . . the . . ."

"Liar," Cevulirn said. And death—someone's death—became inevitable.

Please the gods, Cefwyn thought, realizing to his dismay a fool, twice Cevulirn's size and strength and half his age, had maneuvered himself into a direct challenge.

Brugan grinned.

The Elwynim marriage, the entire southern alliance stood in jeopardy. Cevulirn *had* no heir.

"Your Majesty can sign the petition," Murandys said, wheyfaced, "and things might be hushed, for the good of the realm."

A hiss of steel accompanied that into silence. *Cevulirn* had drawn, against all law and custom, under the king's roof. Brugan backed, drew, and Idrys came away from his posture near the wall, hand near his sword. Cefwyn inhaled deeply and lifted a hand, forbidding Idrys, and his guards, and the duke and his guards, as Cevulirn stepped down from the last step.

"Brother," Efanor said faintly.

"Hush," he said.

There was a tentative posturing on Brugan's side, an attempt to draw Cevulirn after him. Cevulirn grounded his sword against his off-hand boot, and waited, an older man not attempting the young man's game.

Brugan shouted and rushed with a sweep of his blade.

Blade grated off blade, Brugan went past toward the very steps and guards flung themselves in his path, an iron and determined wall. Cefwyn seized a sword from the nearest, and settled it in his own grip as Brugan reestimated the lord of the Ivanim, a slow circling, this time, a slower advance attended by the rattle and thump of other guards running to the scene, held at bay by a wall of onlookers.

"Stop this!" Prichwarrin cried. "Your Majesty!"

"Bid them stop, Prichwarrin! You incited this! *You* stop them!"

"Ivanor!" was Prichwarrin's next appeal, but Cevulirn paid him no heed, and Brugan, from a crouching, cautious stalking, sprang with a wild sweep of his blade.

A second time blades rang and grated past one another, and Cevulirn was not in the path.

Brugan spun around, straight into Cevulirn's edge. Blood fountained, followed the weapon in its sweep, and described a delicate spatter on a carved white column across the hall. Brugan went down like the ox he resembled, and Cefwyn observed it in a sense of satisfaction unrelated to the catastrophe the act represented.

"Ivanor has drawn weapons in the king's presence!" Prichwarrin cried. "Arrest him!"

Cefwyn raised the sword as the first of Prichwarrin's guards imprudently moved. The men stopped.

"The king," Cefwyn said in measured tones, "may forgive the lord of Ivanor. Any man else that draws I will cut down like a dog."

"Your Majesty!"

"I weary of you, Murandys. I have made one duchess over a province. I may make another."

"This is the son of a loyal baron, murdered in your presence, his heir, his sole son!"

"A loyal baron!" He pointed at the discarded parchment with his borrowed sword. "Gather that up!" he said, and one of his guards complied. "Every man who signed that is party to this, and will be questioned. Any man who impugns the honor of myself or my household or Her Grace or her household will be accounted a traitor. You have bedeviled me, you have insinuated, insulted, inveigled, and imposed on my goodwill too long! I am not my father, sir. I am *not* my father, and you have been fatally mistaken to think so!"

He had the satisfaction of seeing stark fear seep through the self-importance of Lord Murandys, before the cold reckoning crept into him that while he was rid of Ryssand's heir, he had declared a war on the northern barons, and could not continue it, not now.

Men gathered up Brugan and bore him away down the hall, a trail of blood which Prichwarrin was obliged to follow. Servants had not yet stirred forth.

Cefwyn ventured a look at Cevulirn, who had calmly cleared the blood from his blade and stood, despite the spatter, composed and awaiting some word from him . . . as something had now to be done between Ryssand and Ivanor, and the king had to mediate it. Idrys stood silent, giving away nothing of what he thought, but he was not frowning. Efanor stood near him, pale and shaken, but having his dagger in his hand—Marhanen at last.

Cefwyn gave the sword back to its owner.

"Ivanor," he said then to Cevulirn, and indicated the way up the stairs. At the top, where the stairs went up to Ninévrisë's apartment, he cast a glance up, wishing he could go in person, lay eyes on her, hold her and assure her.

As it was he might send a page, and a brief message:

> *The accusation was raised in my presence, answered by His Grace of Ivanor, and will be bitterly repented by Ryssand. Dismiss Artisane at your pleasure. I no longer suffer fools, nor should my bride suffer them any longer.*

But it was not all a victory. Ryssand would take this exceedingly hard, and become not less, but more set on challenges, very likely directly so, if Ryssand could find men who would face Cevulirn. And a man might take on one challenge, but not challenge after challenge, all hired by Ryssand's gold . . . if they were at all willing to contest on the field, and not in some dark stairway. He put nothing past Ryssand.

And before he had quite reached the crest of the stairs he knew he had to protect his southern alliance against just such an attempt, and he had to send away one more of his friends, to save all the rest. Snowy evening that it was beginning to be, Cevulirn himself should ride, not delaying for men or servants . . . most lords could not move with such dispatch, but the lord of the Ivanim might, with a handful of men, and before Ryssand knew that he had gone.

CHAPTER 6

Snow came down in this sinking
of the persistent wind just enough to powder the roofs of the Zeide.
An iron-hued canopy of cloud dulled the late-afternoon light so the
white stones looked gray and the gray steps turned to pewter. And
there had been no word, the Guard scouring the town, of the missing documents. No one had seen the archivist, and the Guard had
blocked the gates from the start of the fighting until midday of that
first day; but after that, they had opened, first when master Haman
came in bringing Liss and after that to known individuals, until with
the discovery of missing documents and murder, the order came to
shut them. Anwyll reported some stablelads and pigkeepers had
come and gone, various of the Guard, and their stablehands, the
quartermaster and his staff, a freeholder or two, and woodcutters,
charcoalers, and the considerable number of chief men over
orchards and outlying establishments of all sorts belonging to the
ducal lands and to various of the town-dwelling lords, besides a
miller with a load of flour and a tanner and various others taking
out refuse and coming back.

In short a flood of people had gone in and out the gates that second day, and now more found need to go in and out, the weather
holding passable and people growing anxious about last-moment
winter supplies, so Uwen said. To Tristen's notice the gray space
stayed but slightly troubled, master Emuin was camped in utter discomfort and utter lack of news at Maudbrook—the farrier's wagon
had broken down utterly, and blocked the ford. Yes, Emuin had

heard a rider pass in the night; and yes, had seen the lord viceroy and had provided the stranded man a horse and several of his guards, how not? And what had set the man in such a plight and in such haste?

There Tristen found himself reticent. The gray space still felt uneasy, and the servants whispered of cold spots in the library and on the East Court stairs, for which the Quinalt father provided charms and against which the Bryalt father performed a rite and ordered candles lit. It pleased the servants, and might have done some good; but justice still went begging, and satisfaction, Tristen thought, would come more slowly.

The ashes of Mauryl's letters yielded very little to his study . . . nothing thus far but requests for flour and candles, and a warning of flood in some long-ago spring. He could hear Mauryl's voice in the writing; he ran fingers over the charred paper and remembered Mauryl at his writing, while the wind of a different year pried and wailed at the windows.

The snow still no more than outlined the stonework and the roof tiles, and made a white haze between the town and the orchards. The banner, not that far away on the gate, was at times dim and pale.

Snow did not prevent the town dignitaries and the lords, however, coming to the Zeide, wrapped up in furs still with snow clinging to them. The business of the town was simple, the matter of markets and taxes. Meanwhile he sought an accounting from the armory, which was well prepared; and wished he had the Amefin records which were returning with Emuin.

More, he wished to send men into districts, particularly those bordering Elwynor, in case any villages should be harboring Elwynim, either fugitives or Tasmôrden's men. But sending Dragon or Guelen Guard into districts as uneasy as Henas'amef had become under Parsynan's rule begged trouble; and that left him only the resource of his lords and *their* messengers, the lord of Amefel having otherwise been stripped of personal forces at Heryn's fall.

So the Amefin lords came, and immediately presented their several matters regarding lands and winter court. Tristen held informal audience with several of them in the evening.

"Join me at supper," he said, with thoughts of the gatherings Cefwyn had held in that hall, memories of a hall noisy and sometimes argumentative, but a time, too, at which men might prove more easily swayed in judgment. The great hall was larger than their gathering needed by far; but the servants had lit a fire and arranged a blaze of candles; and Cook provided her famous pies and sausages and good cheese from the market, acquired at the last moment and when the numbers to feed suddenly increased. (I had the lasses taste everything, Cook had assured Lusin, and they hain't a one come to grief yet.)

Cuthan was one of the three who came to supper, and Drumman and Azant, each foremost in the several factions that existed among the earls. Drumman and Azant spoke for their country interests, and begged understanding on the taxes, which they feared would be heavy on account of the war; and which the recent counting had given them to fear would be the case. "His Majesty's men have been going about looking at every haystack," as Azant said, "and the land's taxed poor already, Your Grace."

"Arm your young men for the spring," Tristen said to them. "By any means you can, see them ready. I've not had the accountings yet, but I know what His Majesty intends, which is the defense of the southern bridges. And I must count on you to send out to the villages and advise them."

"Your Grace says we will not see war in Amefel," Azant objected.

"Not by His Majesty's intent, or mine. But to be under arms and at the bridgeheads will assure we see less. If his plans for Amefel go awry, Tasmôrden may find his men having less heart for war against us *or* the northern provinces. But we cannot have Elwynim camping in the hills as they did this summer without our knowledge, sirs. And the villages must report any strangers as quickly as feet can run here."

"My district will do so," the earl said. "But we are suffering already in His Majesty's wars."

Crissand had not come to their small festivity and it had not seemed right to ask him. The house of Meiden was mourning its dead, so Uwen said; and there were many to bury, not alone in the town, but out in the villages. Those sad carts had gained permission to pass the gates, too, and there would be mourning out across the sweep of Meiden land, once the terrible news reached villages that had lost half their young men.

"We also have Meiden's burden to carry through the winter," he said, for he had had Uwen's report, and Anwyll's, regarding the extent of Meiden's plight and how the muster in the spring would affect them and other villages. "Earl Crissand is sending supplies for the villages that have suffered, to see them through the winter, but we should all stand ready to send supplies. And oxen."

("Which where a village has lost so many men, ain't so bad at the first o' winter, wi' the harvest all in," Uwen had said in reporting it, "but there's chores all winter wi' livestock, that's hard, an' spring wi' the mud an' th' plowin' . . . there's brutal work. Oxen is the best help, oxen an' a good plow, an' all the oxen an' carts goin' for the war, that's hard on them villages, where th' widows an' orphans is settin' in a crop.")

"On that account I've determined we'll move supplies this winter, then," he said. "Fortify the river margin and give Tasmôrden reason for concern. We shall own the bridges, and have supplies we need not move in the spring on muddy roads, if we move now."

"A hard winter for men under canvas, hard for men and beast." So Azant objected.

"But the oxen will have done their work, and be home for plowing," Tristen said. "Will they not, sirs? And our supplies will be there waiting for us, and a camp already made. That means our army will move with far greater speed; and our mounted troops can be there in far shorter time to answer any massing of Elwynim forces."

"Supplies that will lure Tasmôrden, if nothing else, my lord," Cuthan said. "We may draw war to us, and lose everything."

"The bridges are undecked, are they not? And by us. We have the timbers. They cannot cross else, in any force, without bringing timbers to the bridges, which occasion oxen, with all that entails. Once we have supplies in place, our garrison is supplied for the winter and we need only maintain a watchfire ready."

"We have never mustered in the winter," Azant said.

He searched his recollection, whether that was true, and thought it was not, but that such a muster of Amefel might have been very long ago. "Nevertheless," he said, not thinking of the vast movement of armies, and snow, and dark shapes confronting them. There were sober faces at the table with him.

"To have the supply made," Azant said. "There's much relief to the villages in that, but bitter cold, and hard duty . . ."

"What would we have all winter?" Tristen said. "Who will guard those bridges, else? Do we plan to sit in Henas'amef and trust Tasmôrden's men are not more hardy and more brave? What shall we deserve, sirs, if we leave the bridges unguarded, and if you were in Tasmôrden's place, what would you do?"

There was silence. Azant shifted a glance to Anwyll, conspicuous now in Marhanen scarlet: the Dragon Guard had assumed its own colors and emblem, and taken off the black Amefin Eagle. The Eagle banner hung full-spread on the wall, green Aswydd draperies on either hand, the heraldry of this, the great hall.

And did they say by that glance they expected the king's garrison to defend the border, and themselves to sit in their homes all winter?

"If Amefel will be defended," Tristen said, "*we* will defend it. The Guelens and the Dragons will go home with the spring; or possibly before. If we fail, the border may fall, sirs, and your lands and your houses and the houses and fields of your villagers are at risk. If Tasmôrden laid plans to come this direction to support Edwyll, he may not know the situation here, or he may find it out and still continue with his plan if only to try to draw the war to these fields, where he has, sirs, *better maps*. We dare not trust otherwise. And yes, we shall do exactly that: winter camp, return the ox teams to the villages, and arm ourselves against whatever comes. We may have help from Lanfarnesse, from Ivanor and Olmern, and even Imor; or we may not, if His Majesty calls them north to open an attack there. The king bade me defend Amefel, and Amefin men will take up arms this winter, and exercise in the snow. When Amefel does move, it will be at the pace of horses, not oxen. So Amefel used to do. So it will do again."

There was a silence lately obdurate, then the slow nodding of Drumman's head, and then Azant's.

"Does Your Grace have sure word of the king's intent?" Azant asked. "And how does Her Grace fare in Guelessar?"

It was more than a question regarding Ninévrisë's happiness or Cefwyn's: it was a wary, canny question under the eyes of Guelenmen.

"Direct word, sir, and his promise. There's no question. He will marry Her Grace and the treaty has not changed from what they swore here in Amefel." Azant had asked a question he had held back; he himself had reserved one. "Does anyone have current knowledge of dealings inside Elwynor?"

Glances did not quite meet his. Only Cuthan looked at him directly in that instant.

"I think Your Grace is quite correct: there were messages. Meiden might know; but I would never assert that to be so."

Drumman's sister was Edwyll's wife, and Crissand's mother. Uwen had reported it to him, and yet no one had mentioned that fact, not even Drumman. The lady had taken refuge in Drumman's house when the fighting began, and had not come back when Crissand had gone home, though Crissand had called on Lord Drumman's residence and spoken to her there in the morning . . . understandable, certainly.

Crissand had buried his father. His mother had not attended the ceremony. And Lord Drumman sat silent at the table when the matter of messages to Elwynor was raised, silent whether held by honorable restraint, or by guilty consciousness of his folly with Edwyll. Drumman had not yet mentioned his sister, or her whereabouts. Now, perhaps, he found himself with an unwelcome secret and nowhere to deliver it.

"Lord Drumman?"

Drumman flushed red and looked at him. But his stare, no, had nothing of fear, only estimation. "I will be your firm ally, my lord, and will fight your enemies. There are rash men in this court, made rash by outrageous tax and the promise of more of it. There is your truth, my lord. Will we be taxed again?"

"His Majesty said nothing to me of more taxes. I have clerks who will inform me what may be needed; my wants are few, save I feed and house and horse the staff I have and see the bridges defended. If you know particular things that were done amiss, advise me. I will not have the spring planting forgotten, I will not remove both men and oxen from the villages, and I will not see hunger in the villages." The last was Uwen's advice, direct and simple. "The men who will stand behind the lords of Amefel will be well-fed, well-armed, and trained with their weapons; and they will know their villages are in good order."

"Your Grace." Drumman's flush had not abated. He looked like a man screwing up his courage for a desperate statement. "Our several clerks can inform you what may not be in Your Grace's accounts from the lord viceroy's tenure *and* from Lord Heryn's. And they will be true accounts."

"If the tax harms the villages, I'll inform His Majesty, who knows the state of affairs here as well as I: he has no wish to impoverish the province."

"That Your Grace will look into the matter of the accounts is more justice than Amefel has seen in a hundred years," Cuthan said. "And Bryn will arm in good order."

"Aye," said Azant, and, "Aye," from Drumman, and there seemed a great relief among the lords, down to Cook's fine apple tarts. There was laughter, now, and good humor, but not quite free good humor: he marked that; and the conversation was on the snow and how the winter would go, in their estimation, which was that the snow might deepen early, or it might not. In the one case they might be held from establishing supply at the bridges; in the other they would not. It informed him, it was interesting, what condition the roads might be in, for his plans for the spring; yet the lords were easing their way carefully through harmless subjects, and the looks that flew from Drumman to Cuthan and from Cuthan to Drumman when the other was holding forth were not happy looks.

They were men divided by the rebellion, he thought, and men still divided by their opinions, not all of which he had heard.

And more than that had risen up to trouble him. He had judged the temper of the town itself as one thing—but he judged the temper of the earls as another. It was far more complex a weave, and shot through with betrayals and old jealousies; and it did not give him comfort at all in what he had heard.

Guards and even Guard captains did not drink or eat at table with their lord. But Uwen, Lusin, and Anwyll were amenable to a cup of ale in the privacy of their lord's apartment, to lean back and talk in informality. So Cefwyn was wont to speak to Idrys in private; and so he and Uwen were accustomed to do. Tonight he invited Lusin and Anwyll. Lusin was not surprised; his fellows were on duty at the door, as guards always were, and he settled down with a cup and sighed with relief not to be standing. Anwyll was the most ill at ease, but accepted a cup, too.

So they all sat by the fire with sleet rattling against the tall, velvet-shrouded windows.

"Cuthan deserves his reputation," Tristen said to begin with. "I think if Edwyll had ruled for a time before being besieged by the Marhanen, Drumman and Azant might have joined him, but Cuthan wouldn't. And he'd have been safe. If Tasmôrden had come in, Drumman and Azant would have ruled with Edwyll; but I think Cuthan would still have survived. And if His Majesty had come and taken the town, Cuthan would have been quick to come forward as a loyal man, and Cuthan would still have survived, and become very close to whatever duke Cefwyn appointed. If Cuthan doesn't lead, others do; but if he leads, others follow him. Am I right?"

"If his lordship o' Bryn had joined wi' Edwyll," Uwen observed, pouring himself and Anwyll a cup of ale, "we'd ha' had a hellish ride up them streets. But thank the gods not all on 'em joined. They might ha' hailed arrows down on us off ever' rooftop in the town."

That thought had certainly been with them during the ride up from the gates. The thought that had occurred to him during dinner was no more comfortable. "Might Bryn have been forewarned?

Might he have seen Ryssand's letter, and known we were coming? And if he, then did Edwyll, all along, know whom he was fighting? Or why, outside of prudence or loyalty to the king, did the *rest* of the lords hold back from supporting Edwyll? Why were they not on those rooftops?"

He had sharp looks from all three captains, and he doubted it was the first question they had had inside themselves.

"I'd look careful at Drumman," Uwen said, "who I think was closest to goin' wi' the rebels. Drumman knew what was toward, didn't he, or the lady wouldn't be shelterin' there from the time Edwyll done what he done? I think the viceroy spilled what he knew to somebody like Lord Cuthan. Maybe Edwyll didn't believe anything the viceroy said, and took the courtyard wi' the notion to hold it and see what terms might be, but the others was again' it. 'At's my humble guess."

Drumman had sheltered Crissand's mother. But at the last Drumman had come to the stable-court to support the king's forces, leaving only Crissand to stand by his father once the rumor of Mauryl's heir had run the streets. *Lord Sihhë!* the people had shouted—and had the whole town foreknown and awaited his coming, while Edwyll attempted to bar him from the citadel?

Tristen listened, and asked himself had Edwyll possibly done what he had done knowingly? Had Edwyll opposed him, or had Edwyll intended to hand over the citadel if the rumors of his appointment were true? Crissand had commanded that the defense in the South Court go on, having had no such instruction, quite clearly; and held and held while he waited for his father to send word down from the apartment where he had gone . . . had continued the defense while even Drumman had joined the other side and while they had shouted through the gate, clearly naming who offered a cessation of hostilities and a way out without more deaths.

But no word came from the earl his father. So Crissand held, and held, not knowing Edwyll was dead, a tragic waste of lives almost equal to what the viceroy had done.

Tristen turned a somber look toward Uwen. "If there was an ill-working," he said to Uwen, "it did its worst that night."

But the thought that Edwyll might have fought against him knowingly, when the son professed loyalty more strongly, more extravagantly than Cuthan, whom he strongly suspected. Had Crissand, the brave, the loyal man—had Crissand lied to him so deeply, so callously?

There was one ground where truth shone through—and in pain

he reached out on the instant, seeking truth, caring nothing for caution, and had an impression exactly where Crissand was. More, he suddenly had Crissand's attention. A cup had shattered, there, not here. Crissand had leapt up, caught his balance.

—*Have you lied to me? he asked Crissand directly, while the gray space roiled with cloud as bitter cold as what spat sleet at the windows. Have you lied?*

—*My lord! the thought came back, and Crissand reached wildly for substance and direction, lost, and afraid, not accustomed to this place, and snatched into it without warning. My lord, wherein should you say I lied? Where have I sinned against you?*

He found not guile, no guilt. He saw Crissand, a shadowy form in the mist and the roiling cloud. He willed himself closer and was there, and saw Crissand's distress face-to-face.

—*Your father told you nothing of his dealings. He sent your mother to Drumman and prepared to stand me off . . . did he not? Did he not, sir? And how many others stood with him?*

Fear washed back at him, a tide through the gray space. Crissand attempted flight, but had no skill at all . . . had never ventured here, clearly so. To have found otherwise would have raised other questions, of wizardry, and theft and knowledge. And he meant to know the answers.

—*Mauryl's letters are gone from the archive and the master archivist is dead, the other fled. Do you know aught of that, sir, or did your father?*

"M'lord?" Uwen asked.

—*Do you know, sir?*

Fear crashed around him, palpable as the winds. —*My lord, Crissand said, and tried to leave his presence, but he did not let Crissand go.*

—*Why did your father act? Why did he move when he did? Dare you call it chance?*

—*To join Elwynor, Crissand said, to join us with Elwynor was all his aim. Nothing of the archive, nothing of the archivist or of murder, or of rebellion against you, my lord, as I live!*

—*For all of a day you held the citadel, dispatched guards to the gate and knew the content of the king's message. Did you then not know?*

—*I had no orders else! Crissand protested. I was to hold the courtyard, I was to hold, and nothing more, my lord. My father had a message . . .*

"M'lord?"

Tears shattered the firelight insofar as he was aware of his own body. He would not look at Uwen.

—Whence a message?

—Out of Elwynor. I think it was out of Elwynor, my lord.

—Run, he said to Crissand, *and the clouds of the gray space were leaden as storm. Run, Meiden, if you are guilty. Run where you choose and as far from me as you can.*

Crissand was gone on the instant, fled away of his own volition, but not in fear, now.

Was it anger? Was it a sense of betrayal matching his own?

Captain Anwyll had leaned forward in his chair. Uwen had cautioned him with a hand.

"I think," Tristen said, catching a large breath, and trying to pretend that nothing untoward had just passed, "I think that Cuthan is a wise man where it comes to his own safety. But if he saw that message, I think Edwyll had no word of it at all until he read the king's message and knew what Cuthan had done to him." Anger was growing and growing in him, that a man had sat at his table and been so pleasant, and so false. "Ness and his friend, down at the gate, had *no* forewarning. And Edwyll posted them. The town knew nothing. *Cuthan* knew and warned the rest of the earls, if he warned them at all, only *after* Edwyll had committed treason. I said, did I not . . . if Cuthan doesn't lead, someone does. But Cuthan did not lead. And he made the others afraid."

"'At's possible," Uwen said. "'At's well possible. Cuthan never come to the stable yard. Bein' an old man makes it hard for 'im, but it is to ask why there was only Edwyll sittin' up here wi' armed men. If Edwyll was expectin' Elwynim to his relief, they're late."

"Tasmôrden is laying siege to the capital of Elwynor. It was Cefwyn's attention he wanted southerly at this moment, and long after. But it took more than Edwyll. And Amefel has long dealt with both sides. Tell Syllan take two men of the Dragons, go after Drumman and Azant. Bring them back." He had a clear notion, now, where Crissand was . . . coatless, in the street, in the snow, striding straight for the stable-court gate. "Lusin."

"M'lord."

"Go yourself, with Tawwys. Hold the lord of Meiden at the stable-court gate. And bring him a warm cloak."

CHAPTER 7

H ave great care," Cefwyn said
to Cevulirn.

"Have great care yourself, Your Majesty." It was night. The lord
of the Ivanim had his guards outside the royal apartment and his
horse and weapons were in the hands of loyal men. "Your Majesty's
welfare is my concern."

"I am wary." He offered an embrace, and unaccustomed as it was,
Cevulirn accepted it, a body stiff with mail and leather and years in the
saddle. "I shall miss you. I shall miss you this winter. *Thank* you for my
lady's sake. We will remember this. And we will see you in the spring."

"My lord king." Cevulirn took his cloak from the man who had
brought it from his rooms, that and no more. Royal guards stood at
Cevulirn's door, upstairs, protecting it against any other intrusion.
Efanor had been closeted with the Holy Father for hours, seeking to
secure his support.

"Fare well," Cefwyn said, and stood watching as Cevulirn gathered up his guard and walked out the door, leaving a vacancy in the
court, a bitterly regretted one.

Ninévrisë might have wished to come downstairs to this parting.
He had set guards there, too, and advised her against it, at a time
when news was rushing through late gatherings and convoking
councils and speeding by quiet messengers wherever the king's enemies and friends might gather. Artisane's whereabouts was a question, with her brother lying dead, but he had ascertained it was not
near Ninévrisë, and that was sufficient.

Now he parted with another friend, and went back to his desk to write a longer missive to his bride, and a request to attend in court tomorrow. There would be questions, quieter ones, he trusted.

He heard horses come and go on the cobbles outside, heard sleet against the window. It was a hard night to be on the road, and he counted nothing safe until he knew Cevulirn and his well-armed veterans were outside the gates.

"My lord king." Annas interrupted his message-writing. The pen had dried in mid-thought. *Public acceptance,* he had been about to write, before he forgot his phrase. But the ink failed and made only a sketchy line. "My lord king, Lord Corswyndam is on his way, and requests audience."

He could deny the lord of Ryssand. He could always arrest Ryssand on no more than his displeasure. But he had to ask himself whether he would have a kingdom the following day, and how many of the northern lords he was prepared to arrest. He had executed Heryn Aswydd, deposed and banished his sister Orien, but as duchess of Amefel she had inherited from her brother a dearth of sworn men. Corswyndam, on the other hand, had an army and a bitter grievance, which for cold policy he would almost undoubtedly choose to direct at Ivanor.

But neither could the king of Ylesuin have two of his provinces at war with one another.

"I will see him in hall," he said, and capped the ink. "Advise Idrys."

Put on at least a better coat? The Marhanen red, embroidered with gold, perhaps.

No. He sent a page for the bezainted leather, and his sword, and had put both on by the time Annas reported Corswyndam downstairs, and Prichwarrin and several other of the lords, with more possible.

"Where is Idrys?" he asked Annas.

"We've not reached him. I beg Your Majesty wait."

It was too delicate a balance. "Damn him," he said, though he suspected Idrys' absence meant Idrys was at work somewhere urgently and on his business. "This can't wait."

He gathered up his guards, a sufficient number of them. A page ran up, bearing the circlet crown in anxious hands . . . Annas' orders, he was certain; and he put it on, then led on down the hall, thump and clatter of guards and weapons in halls used to bloody scenes, down a stairs reputed haunted by his grandfather's deeds and under candle-sconces his grandfather had ordered filled day and night, to allow no dark for ghosts.

He went down to the throne room, where a gathering of pale-faced minor courtiers bowed like grass in a wind, and into a hall where murmuring knots of Ylesuin's nobility cleared his unexpected path from the main doors down to the dais. There his guards clattered into order on either side of the steps and behind him, grounded their weapons with a thump, and settled the angry Majesty of Ylesuin to face his barons.

Corswyndam centered himself in front of the dais and stared up at him. "My son, my heir, is *dead*, my lord king, and the foreign—"

"*Do* not say it! *Do* not say it, Ryssand! You are ill informed, and your son was fatally ill-informed. If you think I will not have another lord of Ryssand, you are mistaken, and if you have thought me soft, *you are mistaken*! Pigs will bed on parchment, do you understand? Ribbons and seals and all, *pigs* will bed on it! Do not press me further."

"Your Majesty!" Ryssand said, white-faced, tear-streaked. "My lord king, you are advised by traitors and practiced on by sorcery!"

"Dare you say!"

Murandys came to stand beside Ryssand. So did Nelefreíssan.

"Here is the north, lord king! Here is the north of Ylesuin. And what says Your Majesty now?"

One of the great doors cracked and closed. Efanor had come in, but no one saw. Idrys followed. *There* were the wandered and the strayed. And Idrys came around the periphery of the room, silently, as his wont. Efanor, who just came from the Quinaltine, gave him a confident nod, a triumph over doubt, and Cefwyn drew a whole breath.

"I say you are perilously close to treason, and a member of your house has drawn weapons in my presence."

"How could my son prevail against Your Majesty? Your presence disarmed him! Ivanor no less than *murdered* my son, and the petition for the Holy Quinalt is cast to the pigs, Your Majesty? Your Majesty has listened to the malign influences, to influences that despise the gods, that practice black sorcery, until loyal men are butchered in the halls in the royal presence and *sorcery* insinuates itself into the highest councils in the land!"

Idrys had reached his side, and proffered a small message-scroll, a remark from Idrys or his brother the Prince, he was sure, until he opened it and read it.

And looked out on Corswyndam's angry presence with perfect equanimity.

He held up the scroll, which bore Corswyndam's seal, a small document. The gesture and his smile brought the shouting to an end. The whole court was still.

"Come forward, Ryssand. Come."

There was a long, long moment Ryssand trembled on the verge of defiance; but prudence and a long acquaintance with the Marhanen surely warred with righteous outrage. Ryssand came closer, came up the steps, Idrys and all the guards quite, quite wary, Cefwyn was sure, and the bezaint shirt was for once a comfort.

"Do you know this document?" Cefwyn waggled it, rolled, in two fingers. "Would you wish it read?"

"May I see it, sire?"

Cefwyn ceded it, watched Ryssand unfurl it, and Ryssand's face go pale.

"From the duke of Amefel," Idrys said smoothly. "His messenger, who said the duke found it on Lord Parsynan's horse, and found it curious that a lord of Ylesuin should send a message ahead of a royal courier."

"Very curious," Cefwyn said, and held out his hand for the message, a steady, demanding hand, as Corswyndam's, ceding it back to him, was neither steady nor demanding. "My deep sorrow for your loss, sir. Go mourn it in private. It would be untimely to read this to the court, considering your grief."

"My lord king," Corswyndam said in a small, choked voice, and, quite pale, he backed away, bowed, retreated, not just to the bottom of the steps, but beyond, and in a rising mutter of the crowd, out the door.

"Lord Corswyndam is overwhelmed," Cefwyn said without mercy, "and needs retreat to Ryssand for a space of appropriate mourning. Good evening, sirs, gods rest you. Gods send him comfort, and all of you good grace."

He rose, looked at his brother, smiled at the court, turned on Idrys a questioning look, to which Idrys only looked pleased.

The recall, this time to the lesser hall, brought two pale and bewildered earls to the foot of the dais, in a chill, less-lit chamber, but it echoed less, and was familiar ground. Tristen preferred it. He took his seat, his guards at every door, and looked out at Drumman and Azant, who were, after Edwyll, chiefest of the rebels, he was quite sure.

There were bows, courtesy due him. He was little interested in those.

"I have one question," he said to them. "Did Lord Cuthan show you a letter? Or tell you of it?"

"A letter, my lord?" This from Azant. But Drumman failed to speak.

"Did you know of a letter? It's the same question. Or tell me this, and tell me the truth: why did Edwyll occupy the citadel alone, and where are the Elwynim forces, and what have you done you wished to conceal from me? I wish you to tell me the truth, by your oaths given in this room, on these steps, sirs. I *wish* it, and you will tell me, will you not, sirs?"

"My lord," said Drumman, and fell to his knees on the second step. "My lord."

"The truth, sir. I will have an answer before you cause me to harm an innocent man."

"Earl Tasmôrden sent messages to Edwyll, my lord, and we all knew. The king's census drew us all to talking, the king's wedding would give his claims on Elwynor a legitimacy they have never had . . ."

It was an assumption the treaty with Her Grace was valueless, but he let that pass in silence while Drumman poured out the rest.

"Tasmôrden would signal the time; and we would overthrow the viceroy. And when it came, the hour it came . . . that word . . . Cuthan said he had seen a letter, in the viceroy's possession, that replaced the viceroy and sent troops."

"And did Cuthan say that I was coming, sir?"

"No, my lord. I swear he did not." Drumman shook his head, and so did Azant.

"And did he advise Edwyll?"

"No one knows what he advised Edwyll. The hour was on us. And Cuthan warned us. But Edwyll had already seized the king's messenger the hour he rode into town. And we were all in fear then."

Tasmôrden had moved his forces on Ilefínian, sent a message across the river to create as much confusion as possible . . . it needed no wizardry to effect a message, none to poison a party of men by accident. But wizards thrived on chance and accident, and worked best through vengeful men. The deeds of kind ones were more self-determined.

"So Cuthan is not your friend," Tristen said.

"Nor yours, Your Grace," Drumman said.

"Nor anyone's," Azant said.

"Whose man is he, do you suppose? And why did he hate Edwyll so?"

"Heryn Aswydd," Drumman said. "He is Lord Heryn's man."

Tristen drew in a breath. "Edwyll was Aswydd."

"And *not* Lord Heryn's man, nor ever was. Hence His Majesty never exiled him. He never supported Lord Heryn's policies, Your Grace, but opposed them in council, opposed them to the edge of loyalty to the Marhanen, which Edwyll would not grant."

"Cuthan was offered the duchy."

Azant shook his head. "Cuthan would never swear to the Marhanen. He cultivated Lord Parsynan because it served his needs. And Parsynan warned *him* of all of us, thinking him a loyal man, the hour the rebellion broke." Azant likewise fell to his knees. "My lord, we have been desperate men. We held back, we joined you, my lord, intending to save Lord Edwyll, and we had done it, until Parsynan took it in his hands to settle grudges . . . we were never rebels against you, my lord."

"And do you speak for Cuthan?"

"He is still," Drumman murmured, "still Lord Heryn's man."

Tristen considered the two lords, kneeling, as Amefin did not customarily kneel . . . turned his hand, where it rested on the throne, and signaled them both to rise.

"Go home," he said quietly, "in peace."

"Lord Sihhë," Drumman whispered, and bowed, and with Azant, went away.

The room was still after. His guards did not move from their places. Nor did Uwen.

"Lord Cuthan may come to me as these lords came, tonight," Tristen said in a moment more, "or he may have a horse and all his household, tonight, and cross the river by whatever means he can find. There are boats, I think, at Maldy village. Because he is an old man, he wants help getting there."

"M'lord," Uwen said.

"I am *not* Owl," he said, doubtless to Uwen's bewilderment. He had gazed at the far end of the room, where he saw not the vision that troubled his dreams these last nights, that of the old mews with light shining through broken planks, a place astir with wings and dusty years. "I will see Earl Crissand, now, if you will, Uwen. I have questions for him, but none so strict as those I have for Lord Cuthan."

CHAPTER 8

$\mathbf{E}$muin arrived a week late, in a gust of snow, toward the mid-afternoon. The bell rang, advising of an important visitor, and Ness, from the gate, arrived to say so; and soon the train of ox-drawn carts and wagons and pack-bearing mules began to make a commotion in the stable yard. Master Emuin would not leave it despite the falling snow, which did not surprise Tristen in the least. Every bird's nest and bottle would find its way to master Emuin's tower, which was vacant, and swept: Tristen had foreseen that necessity, and that master Emuin would simply begin sending baggage upstairs, or go himself, expecting it.

"Good day, sir," Tristen said from the west outside stairs, looking down, and finding master Emuin in the midst of chaos. All of the cobbles except the patch where master Emuin stood were trampled snow obscured with offset baggage. Some, off-loaded, were going out the open ironwork gate; more were coming in, including a wagon, which was having difficulty.

"There you are!" Emuin said sharply. "Do we find the town burned down? The cellars plundered?"

Tristen came down the steps, with Lusin and the guards behind him. "Did the lord viceroy say so?"

"He gave me dire reports of disorder. I expect ashes, at least active conflagration."

"The town is quiet," he said. "The Bryaltine abbot came this afternoon. The Quinaltine father here is far friendlier than the Patriarch in Guelessar. He sent a basket of apples."

"A relief, a decided relief."

"Earl Edwyll is dead. His son has the earldom. Earl Cuthan fled to Elwynor, by boat; we found Mauryl's papers in his possession, little use he could make of them. I think he only meant me not to have them."

Emuin gave him a sharp look, and looked longer.

"I had to make decisions," Tristen said, "and made them, sir." It was no place to discuss details of policy, this swirling, bawling yard, but it was common knowledge now through all the town.

"Well," Emuin said, seeming only moderately surprised. "Well," he said again, and said no more about it, choosing instead to shout at a servant to be careful with the boxes.

"You would not advise me, sir," Tristen said, not without asperity.

"So I did not," Emuin said. "Stand in the path of Mauryl's working? I? I have come to provide counsel—not direction, young lord, as lord you are."

"*Mauryl's* working? Dare you say so, sir?"

"That is all I dare. You have made your path, young lord. *Now* I am here. Not before."

The wagon finally gained the courtyard, with Tassand and the others of his servants, whom he was glad to see, and to whom he only needed say, "Orien's apartment," to have Tassand completely informed, and immediately busy, and his baggage and belongings destined for upstairs.

He went inside, then, into the noise and confusion of arriving baggage, of a hundred more Guelen troops to be housed, and clerks finding their accommodations. Boxes and bundles passed him. He retreated to the safety of the upper floors, leaving master Emuin to call on him when he pleased, since he knew he could never persuade master Emuin to leave his precious boxes—only two months removed from the tower, and now coming back again—in the hands of servants.

His household was complete, wizard, wardrobe, and all.

He settled again to the table on which the appeals and petitions waited, and took up those he hoped to accept. Master Rosyn, the tailor, was one who had served Cefwyn, and who now begged to deliver "werk of most excellent qualitie." Master Rosyn had written the letter in his own hand. And he was a good and diligent man. Tristen put that down as something he might simply give to Tassand to arrange. Red and black was the banner under which the commons of Amefel had marched to Lewen field, and red was, in one of those small definite notions of his mind, the color of Amefel, the Aswydds only holders of it by conquest.

And whence that knowledge? For a moment he saw the hill on which the fortress of the Zeide sat as girded by winter wilderness, only the smallest hint of the town, and the sense of direction said that that town, almost a village, had stood where now the more remote stables were, exactly there. It was a night, and lights showed at the Zeide gate; and where the long, sprawling streets of the town went down now to the outer walls of a populous town, now there were only a few trees, a road that wended up to a wall little different from that which stood today, but gates of iron and oak.

"My lord duke," Tassand said, arriving with another load of baggage, snow in his disheveled hair. "Will ye mind the comin' an' goin'?"

"Not in the least," he said. The stir of servants dispelled the vision, wrought its own magic. Tassand went to the window, drew the green draperies wide, let in both sun and chill. The light outside was white, white the adjacent roof, and blinding white the sky.

He had warded the window. But Tassand and the servants warded him. Uwen came up with a load of his own baggage, refusing the servants who offered to carry it. All the men were seeking out baggage that had arrived, belongings parted with, simple things they had done without.

He went back to his writing, sat down at Lady Orien's desk, and took up his pen.

> *I have taken Henas'amef and dislodged the lord viceroy, who killed unarmed men against my orders. Tasmôrden promised the earl of Meiden assistance against your army if the earl would seize and hold Amefel, which he had begun to do. Cuthan, warned by the letter from Ryssand which I sent Your Majesty, dissuaded the others at the last moment. Tasmôrden is occupied with Ilefínian, I am well sure, and would never have provided the help he promised: his aim was for Edwyll's action here to distract you from the eastern approach you might make against his forces and to discourage Ylesuin from any relief that you might send to Ilefínian. So Tasmôrden would have time to take firmer hold of the town before the spring, and meanwhile Edwyll would wear down your forces and engage you to the south. His attempt has failed. I have exiled Lord Cuthan.*

The town has been quiet for four days. I have taken the oaths from all the earls, and I have confirmed Meiden's heir, Crissand, who will fill his father's place. I regret the deaths of the earl's men, as well as your honest messenger.

Meanwhile I have secured the archives, and I am learning what I need to know.

I wish Your Majesty very well and Her Grace also, and do not forget His Highness's kindness.

A dragon sat on the desk beside it, a dragon that held the inkpot, and spread wings wide on either hand. On all sides were the green draperies, the Aswydd colors, and he did not know when, in the need for more important things, they might contrive to change them.

He set the quill back into the dragon's claw, rolled the message and tied it with cord. Then he tipped red wax, red for Amefel, onto the cord and stamped it with the ring Cefwyn knew, no ducal seal. It was enough.

The apartment was very quiet, very still, in a lull of the servants' traffic, the bronze-and-gilt dragons looming dark against the light of the window.

It was foolish, perhaps, to be afraid of them. They were metal. But he thought of the oak and the carving, and the constraint of the wood to be what it was not.

He thought of wings, and of his silly pigeons, and of Owl abroad in a snowy, winter world. At least he found his household in some order today, if he might say as much of master Emuin, of whom he could detect cold feet, cold hands, a cold nose, and the taste of tea.

EPILOGUE

Pearls shone in candlelight, and the bride looked up, a hint of violets. Cefwyn closed warm fingers in his own, half heard the droning of the Holy Father, the promised blessing. It was Ninévrisë that filled his eyes and shortly filled his arms. It was the custom to kiss a Guelen bride.

And Cefwyn soundly did.